THE SMOKE KING

Maurice Leitch was born in County Antrim and educated in Belfast. His first novel, *The Liberty Lad*, was published in 1965, followed by *Poor Lazarus*, winner of the 1969 Guardian Fiction Prize. *Silver's City* won the Whitbread Prize for Fiction in 1981. He has also written radio plays, short stories, television screenplays and documentaries. He lives in North London with his family.

MAURICE LEITCH

THE SMOKE KING

Secker & Warburg
London

Published by Secker & Warburg 1998

2 4 6 8 10 9 7 5 3 1

Copyright © Maurice Leitch 1998

Maurice Leitch has asserted his right under the
Copyright, Designs and Patents Act 1988 to be identified
as the author of this work

First published in Great Britain in 1998 by Secker & Warburg
Random House, 20 Vauxhall Bridge Road, London SW1V 2SA

Random House Australia (Pty) Limited
20 Alfred Street, Milsons Point, Sydney,
New South Wales 2061, Australia

Random House New Zealand Limited
18 Poland Road, Glenfield,
Auckland 10, New Zealand

Random House South Africa (Pty) Limited
Endulini, 5A Jubilee Road, Parktown 2193, South Africa

Random House UK Limited Reg. No. 954009

A CIP catalogue record for this book
is available from the British Library

ISBN 0 436 20506 8

Papers used by Random House UK Limited are natural,
recyclable products made from wood grown in sustainable forests.
The manufacturing processes conform to the environmental
regulations of the country of origin.

Every effort has been made to obtain necessary permissions
with reference to copyright material. The publishers apologise
if inadvertently any sources remain unacknowledged.

Typeset by Deltatype Ltd, Birkenhead, Merseyside

Printed and bound in Great Britain by
Mackays of Chatham PLC

ACKNOWLEDGEMENTS

My gratitude to Ned Chaillet for his American ear, Keith Darvill for his musical one and, in memoriam, John Blackwell for his editorial genius. Last, but most important of all, Geoff Mulligan, who knows how much I appreciate his continuing support and friendship.

I am daubing God in night,
I am swabbing Hell in white:
I am the Smoke King
I am black.

– W.E.B. Du Bois

ONE

This is what the boy remembers, but didn't tell the sergeant of police, the night Mrs Jelley was shot dead across the counter of her own bar. He was nowhere near where it happened, none of them were, but that didn't matter because in the end everybody got drawn into it. Even someone like himself.

He's dancing with his mother in their tiny kitchen, one of her hands holding his, the other an open book, while she concentrates on the pattern the steps make on the spread page. Footprints in snow are what they remind him of, except hers are white, the man's black. *Like Willie's*, he thinks, as he breathes in her gardenia scent, absorbs the damp, unsettling heat through the thin Celanese of her frock.

"Why is it called foxtrot?"

"Sure as heck beats me, kiddo," she tells him, going into some shimmy of her own devising, and the younger children ranged along their old broken sofa howl with glee, loving it as they always do when she talks like someone out of some

Hollywood film. Or Willie Washington. All this is for his benefit.

"You're the man of the house, after all," she keeps on telling him, but he knows he isn't. Not since Willie entered their lives with his Spearmint gum, peanut butter, Ritz crackers, ice-cream and angel cake. Once a whole roast leg of lamb that dwindled in the meat-safe outside until only a polished white nub remained.

"Hold me close," she commands. "It says here we must move as one. That's how it's done. Your mammy's a poet. And don't even know it."

And once more his brothers and sisters erupt in simple-minded delight. The record scratches to a conclusion, some bunch called The Savoy Sultans. She tells him to turn it over while she dabs on yet another charge of perfume.

It's early September, heavy, heat-filled days and nights that make their tiny gate-lodge throb like an oven, the doll's-house windows, pointed at the top, painted permanently shut, only breath of air entering as if by chance whenever the front door swings ajar.

Handling the heavy record like precious china he feels sweat on his hands and quickly, surreptitiously, sniffs, for he loves her smell, seeking traces where it lingers in the indentations of pillows or in drawers where he has no right to pry, something lost and lamented from a time when once he shared her bed.

"Get a move on, dolly daydream," she calls to him as if reading his guilty desires and he starts, elbow catching the edge of the kitchen table and that old record slides from his grasp, slippery suddenly, shattering in a thousand pieces on the tiled floor.

Everyone holds their breath and stares at the glittering debris as if by will-power they can make it whole again. She,

2

however, reaches across, slapping him, something she has never ever done before. Never. He stares back at her, hand cupped to his blazing cheek. Wilma the youngest starts to cry. "Willie bought me that. Is that why you broke it? *Is it? Is it?*"

She's shaking him now. Her scent, the scent he tells himself he relishes so inordinately, comes in waves. Perfumed rage.

He clings to the table. The gramophone dances, lamplight glancing off its silver arm and claw. The remaining records, pouched in the lid, rattle. Then it stops as suddenly as it has begun and she falls into a chair sobbing, fat scalding tears staining the scrubbed white wood of their table. The boy stands looking down at them, at her, his foolish, weeping mother in the spotted dress she has saved her precious coupons for, a whole ration book just for this one night, and now it's ruined. He has ruined it for her.

"Can I have the bits?" Tom asks in a tiny, wondering voice. And, indeed, there is still something precious about those fragments scattered there, even the boy can see that, each retaining who knows what, a sudden snatch of voice, a trumpet call, a drumbeat imprinted on the whorled surface.

Then, "Somebody get the shovel. I don't want blood on my good sheets," for all are barefoot, and Wilma fetches brush and pan and his mother sweeps up the remains of the Sultans and, morsel by morsel, feeds them to the flames. The segments blaze blue then green, melting rapidly into the embers, and their faces, like the walls of the room, are washed by a sudden chemical glare.

The children shriek. It's a night for them to remember. The boy certainly will, long after those other events of that sultry Autumn evening are to dim despite the terrible consequences for all of them.

"Come here," his mother commands, taking his face between two hot palms.

"Did I hurt you?" she whispers so the others won't hear. "Tell me I didn't. Who cares about some silly bit of old wax, anyway?"

And she slides a replacement on to the spindle, releasing the catch, and his favourite begins to spin. "My Very Good Friend The Milkman."

"Well, girls and boys, boys and girls, what's it to be? Foxtrot? Quickstep? Jitterbug?" And all burst out laughing at the very idea of their own mother being swung around a dance floor like a slingshot, then up and over some man's head, clothes flying.

This is the mother they love, mad, unpredictable, for she dances alone in the centre of the floor now for their private diversion, *Learn To Dance With Arthur Murray* cast aside, an invisible partner held at arm's length, a look of high-bred disdain on her face.

"Do you know my husband by any chance? Major Cyril Kincaid? Most distinguished military career in three theatres of war. Retired from active service now, of course. To his deep and lasting regret. Absolutely itching to return to the fray against the foul Boche a second time, but he does have a very large piece of shrapnel wedged tightly up his bum. Wounded in the Dardanelles. You must have noticed the way he walks, surely."

And it is the Major to the life, not his shrill lady-wife any more, pained expression, stiff-legged gait and all, stamping about their kitchen floor to Fats Waller. The children hug one another in ecstasy, then as quickly cover their mouths as if the dread couple from the great white house at the end of their avenue might be outside, listening in the shadows.

Stinging cheek forgotten, the boy watches his mother perform for them. Something new or, better still, some old routine, like when the paraffin runs out and she lights a candle and tells stories, projecting animal heads on the wall with her clenched fist. Then the younger ones are too terrified to climb the ladder to the loft where fieldmice winter and once a bat flapped about while they shrieked in a huddle under the quilt.

That is that other side of her, never knowing when to quit, going on beyond the point where any normal person would desist. When they occur the boy does what he can to contain such excesses but there are other times when he feels far too young and frail for the task. He weeps then, bitter tears of frustration out in the privy, staring at the news-papered walls and hopefully getting distracted by the stories to be read there.

Tonight she is in one of those same excited states, the slap administered earlier something she has no control over, in the same way the record had leapt from his hand. An accident. Blame is pointless in either case and so, swelling in his sudden maturity, he volunteers, "I'll go and look for him," for he can see her getting more and more anxious. Nine o'clock then half-past has come and gone and still no sign of that grinning dark face or his soft whistle preceding him up the long white road from the army base on the shores of the Lough.

"Oh, will you?" she breathes, embracing him in a sudden damp rush. "Will you, pet? My own wee man, my own wee man of the house." And his brothers and sisters add their own clamour, hearts set on booty from the PX.

Outside the night air wraps the boy in a clammy embrace and he finds himself questioning the sense of keeping such a blaze going indoors in weather such as this. But then his mother has a mania about heaping on wood winter and summer. She grows noticeably depressed if the fire in the grate shows signs of going out.

The gravel of the driveway spurts underfoot but in the dark the detonation sounds doubly obtrusive so he switches to the silence of the grass verge instead, heading for the pillared entrance gates and the road along which their visitor must come.

He can hear the Major's pheasants clicking dreamily in their coverts on either side of him. Somewhere, too, but far off, a farm dog, or maybe it is a fox, barks briefly, while over all Ussher Greer's hydraulic ram gulps rhythmically on a deep bass note pumping water into an old sunken claw-footed bath in the top pasture.

Counting silently to himself the boy wonders whether his own heartbeat matches the sound. It seems logical somehow, yet he doesn't know why, all hearts, clocks and machines in the world magically geared as one.

Part of him is apprehensive at being out alone like this with so much invisibly going on in the darkness, but another part revels in the certainty it is all for him, all this, his own personal domain.

He thinks of how snug and settled they had been in their cosy gate-lodge needing no one but themselves before the stranger came on the scene with his hot, glistening skin and yeasty smell that made the small kitchen even more like a baker's oven. He told them he worked as a cook, so perhaps it was the smell of his trade he carried about with him like a second scent.

Sitting in their cramped kitchen he stretched out his pink palms to the heat – it appears he delights in open fires just as much as his own mother – and the younger children touched the crease of his trousers in awe, and all the other splendours of that miraculously pressed uniform with its corporal's stripes sewn on upside-down for some unexplained reason.

Unimpressed, the boy watched from the shadows, even when the big man in khaki went out of his way to draw him into the charmed circle. His mother tried to woo him as well, he saw that, and it was hard not to relent, seeing her anxiety to please and be pleased by the easygoing GI and his ways.

Now as the boy crouches in his lair of dark grass waiting for a sign of their visitor and his wobbly approach – he still hasn't mastered riding a bicycle, and him a grown man, too – he thinks of that same old roadster, his mother shrieking astride its bar, legs outstretched like a girl, while Willie navigated Greer's field in big swooping circles. He had never seen her so carefree, so youthful as on that day, and although a corner of him resented that a stranger could work such a change in her another part rejoiced for her. It is that side which surfaces now, anticipating the look on her face when she sees the two of them arriving together wheeling the old rusted pushbike between them up the avenue.

As he huddles there, shivering a little, for it's getting cool, he imagines he can hear the gramophone, Fats Waller winging a personal message down the lonely length of the avenue to keep him company on his vigil. And it comes to him suddenly that Fats Waller is black also, like Willie. No one has told him so, he just knows it to be a fact for some reason.

Willie Washington had been the first black person he had ever seen outside films and travelogues. But then you couldn't touch, smell or have them touch you back in the Macushla, as it is called, for Mr Costello the owner is a Catholic, but well-liked by everyone, everyone. And they looked different on celluloid too, never as well turned-out or as good-looking as their very own "tan yank" in his beautifully pressed gaberdine set off by gold buttons – *gold* – and his cap like a flattened boat which they all take it in turns

7

to wear for the fun of it, even his mother. Inside it smells of coconut, which comes from the stuff Willie puts on his hair. And another thing, nothing on a cinema screen could ever prepare you for the *feel* of that hair.

In many ways they are privileged to have their own real live GI, as the man reading the news on the wireless keeps calling them. Not many people in these parts can say that. On reflection, he isn't such a bad egg after all, their new friend, with his bunches of flowers and boxes of candy. Better still, the bundles of funny papers which they spread about the house in an orgy of extravagance, including the privy, to be enjoyed at leisure.

Dreaming already of Dick Tracy and Steve Canyon, Prince Valiant, too, with his girlish bob, he sees a light appear on the far reaches of the avenue moving towards him. At first he thinks it might be the Major out stalking poachers, a recurring bugbear of his, and so he burrows deeper into the dock and dandelion.

But then he hears his mother calling out, "Raymond, Raymond, where are you?" in a soft and frightened voice.

She holds the old carbide lamp in her hand and it is a measure of her anxiety that she has managed to get it to light.

"Here. I'm here," he answers rising from his nest and in a moment she is close and clasping him in another of those damp embraces of hers.

"I've been worried sick," she tells him, mouth in his hair. "Where have you been? What have you been doing? It's too late now, can't you see that? He's not coming, he's not coming."

And he can tell tears aren't very far off and to stem that flow he tells her, "Maybe he couldn't get away. Maybe he's on night-duty or something. Wait another ten minutes."

He hears her sigh then and he knows she wants to be

8

persuaded and together they sink into the hollow he has made in the grass.

"Do you think. . . ?" she murmurs, the question unravelling in the air.

Close to where they lie the gently hissing bicycle-lamp with its little emerald eye illuminates a forest of bleached stalks. The boy studies the bright tangle for a sign of miniature life, a comic-book world, deepest black on dazzling white, as if Miss America herself might appear at any moment leading a band of her followers to safety out of the jungle.

An owl hoots somewhere in the trees and his mother grabs him in sudden terror. He bears it without flinching.

Then he hears her say, "We'll get our death in this damp grass. He's not coming, I tell you. He must have . . ." And again the sentence hangs in the air for them to complete in their own way.

But the boy is thinking of his brothers and sisters clutching each other on their ancient lumpy sofa. They would never go to bed on their own while the kitchen remains unoccupied below. It comes to him how special this man has become for her to leave them alone in that way, for into his head there sidles now in spite of himself a cruel memory, perhaps the cruellest there will ever be in his life, of poor wee dead Brian sitting oblivious and alone in that tightening circle of flame, the brother none of them ever got to know or love properly.

His mother told them he was in heaven, happy and smiling as always, dressed, too, just as he was on the day he had slipped away from them drawn by the shouts of the Montgomery boys setting fire to the whins by the railway line. Was there something wrong with him, when what he saw were blackened mummy's wrappings, something horrible and faceless inside, instead of baby clothes several sizes

9

too small for him? Could he be punished for thinking such things?

His mother says, "We'll go home now," rising to her feet, and as she does so they both hear the sound of a car approaching.

For a moment she hangs there and he can tell she is wondering if this can be him arriving by some different mode of transport but then she drops back beside him in the grass, kicking over the lamp as she does so.

"Keep down," she whispers and he feels her hot presence envelop him. He knows he is too old for her to keep on still holding him in this way but he lies there, unmoving, willing his senses to stay uninvolved.

The roar of the engine grows louder. It comes labouring up over Thompson's brae and they can see it is not a car but a motor-bike and sidecar without lights and there is a man in the sidecar part sitting bolt upright as if in a pew in church. He passes slowly by mere feet away and through the tangle of grass stems they can see him clearly, straight-backed, bare-headed, staring directly in front of him. He has on a heavy, dark overcoat buttoned to the collar and his hair is silvery white.

The boy hears his mother draw a sharp intake of breath and her grip tightens, drawing him even deeper into the grass. The combination drives slowly over the brow of the hill, one tiny tail-light fixed on them like an unblinking red eye before disappearing for good. All they have been able to see of the man in the saddle is a leather helmet and goggles. The boy can feel his mother shivering.

"Have they gone?" she whispers, holding her head at an angle as if listening for a returning sound.

"Who was it?"

"How should *I* know?" she tells him, but the boy can tell she is lying.

10

"Come on," she says, rising to her feet, "it's way past your bedtime," and he feels his head swim as he comes upright.

For the first time he notices stars have come out, a great pulsing swirl in the night sky, dense as milk.

"What was that?" his mother says as though miracles might still occur but it is only an old gate creaking.

He takes her hand, it seems correct somehow, for he can tell she is crying in the darkness, and together they go back up the long pale straight drive.

TWO

Raleigh, he kept pondering all the way into town, *Why should they go and name a bicycle after the capital of his home state?* Made in Nottingham. Wherever the hell that might be. It made no sense to him.

But then if he were to tell the truth he was a little ginned up. Back of the cookhouse that same day Stovepipe Davis had brewed a fresh run of jungle-juice and he had sampled some of it, more to please old Stovepipe than anything, but also because he was feeling in such a heavenly mood. Money to burn and a pretty little lady friend titivating herself up just for him. He did a soft-shoe shuffle in the gravel just thinking of it.

A mile or two back by the side of the road lay an old ruined cottage and it was here he had stashed the bicycle deep in a nettle bed. Leaving it to lean outside a pub somewhere was just asking for some other drunk doughboy to come along and ride off on it. Anyway, he had grown attached to that old boneshaker never having owned a pushbike of his own before. It made him feel young and foolish and Pearl's kids loved seeing him arrive weighted down with packages like the US mailman.

After he'd laid her carefully to rest among the weeds and long, coarse grass he'd lowered himself on to an old mossy stone, first having spread a clean khaki handkerchief to protect his pressed pants. Time to kill, he told himself.

But then he preferred it that way, the evening, followed by the long night itself, stretching ahead like an unbroken, shiny chain, link upon link of anticipation in the company of someone he cared for and who cared for him. Maybe even a little more on her side of the arrangement, if ever he decided to think about it.

He was barely twenty-three years of age, in the prime of his life, and never had he felt so confident, so pleased with himself. Lighting up a Camel from the pack in his breast pocket he watched the smoke rings change colour. His woman's eyes were that same shade, he told himself. Like her name. Pearly. With little greeny-yellow flecks sprinkled in for good measure. Details of that sort had never struck him before but then he hadn't been with a white woman either until now. Sitting there just thinking of her in that way raised a bump in his pants.

His gaze took in the vigorous growth of weed spreading out like a rough sea beyond his buried feet. A hundred years back this must all have once been cultivated land. People's lives going on unchanged that way he found hard to take on board. Then other times he felt as if they must be just like he was, same old poverty shit and all.

For instance, what difference between outhouses back home and the ones here? And the kids going around barefoot, bare-assed, too, a lot of the time? And didn't they use plough-horses in the fields same as mules? And how about Pearl not having proper electricity, just plain old kerosene that stunk the place up same as in Peabody County.

Tell me that, he demanded fiercely, as if having a heated argument with somebody, *tell me that, boy. Shit.*

And far as that subject went, didn't most people here just take a dump in the open as and when the notion took them, same as back home? Staring at him from the weeds right now was a real prize specimen, a great tan torpedo like something squeezed out by a mule, only he could tell it was human.

Idly he gazed at it, taking in the accompanying garland of pulled grass whoever it was had used to wipe himself clean, for it was difficult to imagine a woman pulling her skivvies down in that fashion out here. The image excited him, trousers bunching a second time.

Flies buzzed above the glistening mound and as he studied their lazy rise and fall it hit him this one was recent and suddenly he feared for the safety of his hiding-place. Next thing he spotted a used rubber, stretched and limp, dangling from a nearby bush like a Christmas decoration.

"*Son of a bitch!*" he swore. And as he did so he heard the unmistakable grind and roar of an army truck approaching, for a brief and crazy moment associating it with those two souvenirs, one brown, the other pale pink, staring back at him from the weeds.

The truck started slowing down. By this time he was crouched back of the stump of wall he had been sitting on so contentedly moments earlier.

Someone called out, "*This is as far as you go — assholes!*" and he heard brakes slam, followed by the retch and shudder of the engine.

"Jest keep walkin' till you hit those bright lights! Big hotels, movie-theatres, fancy steak restaurants. Just like the ones you boys're used to back home, I guess." And whoever it was drove away laughing.

Hunkered down in his hidey-hole the corporal strained to listen. It was like being a little kid again, lying low smelling the damp, earthy heat, only now something threatening was unfolding out there beyond his ramparts of grass. And for that reason he decided against showing himself, hoping these strangers, these interlopers on his private domain, would move on.

Then he heard one of them growl, "Where does that piece a white shit get off talkin' to us that way? I'd as soon cut that red-headed son of a bitch as look at him, leavin' us out here in the back of beyond this way. I bet he done it deliberate." "Hold your water," came number two voice. "Ain't none of us wants no trouble. Few beers to celebrate Clyde's birthday here, that's all we had in mind. Ain't it so, Clyde, old buddy?"

"Y-you got it. N-no t-trouble." Clyde sounded half-cut already.

All were colored and GIs like himself, but what was their outfit? Certainly not the 5th Quartermaster Company. The urge to find out was tempered by the stronger instinct of keeping his hiding-place to himself.

Then the middle one, the sensible one, said, "Can't be all that far off, this burg. What's it called again?"

"Bally-go-Backwards, Bally somethin' or other. Ain't they all, for fuck's sake?"

Clyde began to laugh, a high, neighing, annoying kind of laugh.

"You find that funny, jackass?"

"Hey, hey, now, come on, soldier, put the blade back where it belongs. All good compadres here, remember?"

"No share-croppin' tongue-tied sonofabitch is gonna laugh at me."

"But he ain't a-laughin' at you, he's jest happy, that's all. Look at him. How about it, Clyde, baby? Somethin' to send us on our merry little way?"

And after a short pause the crouching man heard someone

15

trickle through the scale on a harmonica, then slide into a fancy rendition of "Paper Doll", for Clyde was pretty nifty with all those little shakes and sobs, and although he couldn't see anything he imagined the cupped, brown hand going a-flutter, that faraway look in the eyes too that harmonica players affect. Something told him Clyde would be a real good man to have around the stove on a cold winter's night, those old evergreens tumbling out, maybe even a few requests thrown in. As for the other two – well, one in particular – he wasn't all that certain he cared for any further acquaintance there.

As he was beginning to wonder if they were going to roost here indefinitely the tune melted off into march time and then the three of them, soft-soled and silent as ghosts, took off just as he'd been praying they would.

So his spirits climbed way, way up again and he lit another cigarette while listening to that old Höhner fade off and away into the distance.

When the Camel had been smoked right down to the brand on the paper he got to his feet, dusting himself off. Tiny green burrs hard as ball-bearings were clinging to his pants' legs, stubborn little mothers. He didn't move until he had removed every last one.

He looked over to where the bicycle lay buried in the grass up to the dark snout of its saddle. Knowing what he now knew about this place he would just have to risk leaving it here, for the day was running out fast and he had things to do before the stores closed.

A good half hour of brisk walking brought him to the outskirts of town. Well, more a largeish village, to be accurate. He passed a battered tin hoarding, two cute little black and white heifers, heads buried in a bucket, advertising Invicta Animal Feed – all cows were brown and cream where he came from — then another with "The Wages Of Sin Is Death" written across it. Both were severely pockmarked as if used for target practice. It reminded him of home.

People appeared on bicycles or walking like himself and all jerked their heads at him in that wacky, sideways, Irish way. He grinned back, then some schoolkids waylaid him and from the cache in his breast tunic pocket he dished out Spearmint. It gave him a warm feeling to unload his largesse in this way.

If you could only see me now, Bubba, he thought to himself, Bubba Moultrie being the boss of that old gin he used to slave in until Uncle Sam crooked a long and bony finger at him from the recruiting posters.

He passed a Rexall sign same as the ones at home, except here the window was full of strange preparations, remedies he'd never heard of, or could put a use to, Sloan's Liniment, Friar's Balsam, Carrageen Moss. Chemists, too, they called them, instead of drugstores.

Some vague recall of make-up and perfume in a display case came to mind so he pushed on the glass door — a sign saying Bile Beans, something he was familiar with — and a bell went *ping*. An oldish guy in a white coat stood facing him behind the prescription counter.

"Can I help you, young man?" He was smiling at him and suddenly the corporal felt ill at ease, some not-so-ancient memory stirring of men like this back home who used politeness as a weapon to make you feel inferior.

"Somethin' for a friend," he grunted.

The druggist continued smiling at him over gold-rimmed eye-glasses. "Then it's Sharon and young Myrtle you need for to take care of you." Something old-maidish about him, hands white and boneless, that sweetish smell, peppermint and disinfectant in equal proportions.

17

"Maybe some lip rouge," he heard himself say.

"Sharon, show the gentleman some lipsticks. The reserved stock."

One of the girls standing stricken with shyness behind the counter to his right dropped from sight and he found himself facing her companion, a heavy-set girl with a wall-eye and bangs. Her name suited her, for he recalled just such a girl who stacked shelves in the Piggly Wiggly back in Ducktown. Myrtle Kells, her name was. A lot of the names here were similar to the ones he was used to. People looked much the same too, but then some of the guys back at the base argued all white people looked alike no matter where you went.

The girl delving behind the counter came up finally with a cardboard carton and began pulling out lipstick cases. She started to unscrew them for his benefit, lining them up one by one on the polished wood for all the world like a little regiment of dogs' dicks. Her face had gone roughly the same shade. He wondered if she was struck by the resemblance too.

This had been a mistake on his part and he knew it. Even *he* could tell this was pre-war junk, maybe even earlier, stashed away like most things in this part of the world, not the top-of-the-range merchandise he could so easily have gotten for himself at the PX. But then he'd remembered too late about getting Pearl something for the dance. Blame it on Stovepipe Davis and his jungle-juice. In the movies they always handed their girl one of those little bitty bunches of flowers covered in cellophane – corsage, they called it – but where was a guy going to find something like that in this one-horse burg? Funny how he had gotten so fussy since joining this man's army.

Still he went ahead with it anyway, picking out the brightest, reddest one from that selection of pink little pricks spread before him. Chinese Poppy. Tangee brand. For his sake he just hoped Pearl wouldn't be too disappointed.

As it was being wrapped for him in tissue paper the proprietor spoke up from the drugs section.

"Not as many of you boys in town as usual, I notice. Doesn't seem like Friday night, somehow."

The corporal kept his eyes fastened on the girl's fingers, white girls' fingers, plump and pink like candied sweet potatoes.

What the old guy was getting at, of course, was Friday nights was for coloreds like himself, Saturdays, white only. All day Saturday, in their case. Some of the guys in the 5th Quartermaster Service Company weren't too happy about that state of affairs but mainly those were just uppity niggers from up North and the big cities. As far as he was concerned Jim Crow was something you grew up with, learned to live with, even if he did follow you halfway across the goddam globe.

The only time he thought about it much was when Pearl brought it up. When it came to "injustice", as she put it, she could be a real firecracker, but then she just happened to be white. He pictured her now drawing the new lipstick across the bow of her mouth, pouting into the glass in that sweet babyish way of hers. It was something he loved to watch when he got the chance, although usually the war-paint was well and truly in place by the time he got there.

What he really wanted more than anything was to see her start from the bare skin out, each layer of mystery put on slowly for his benefit, but he knew she'd never let him see her like that. Even when they made love in the fields or down by the foreshore, or that time on the island with nobody but some old billy-goat eyeballing the two of them under his army issue greatcoat, she wouldn't let him look at her all over. Just patches and pockets of flesh, pale parts of a

19

puzzle with his imagination supplying all the most interesting places. Like now, for instance, for he was conscious of that old familiar swelling in the lower pants region again.

"Still, it's early yet. All the evening ahead to have yourself a good time, eh?"

He could have sworn he was staring directly at his crotch as he spoke.

Some of the guys were always on about whitey's obsession with the size of his pecker, a fact of life they said. As far as he was concerned he had no opinions either way, never having seen one of a different colour. Just like this old guy, he felt certain, with his little round eyeglasses and row of pens peeking out from his breast coat pocket.

For one crazy moment he felt like satisfying his natural curiosity, dropping his pants and displaying John Thomas for his inspection, the girls', too, which would be a helluva lot more pleasurable. At least he wouldn't be a dishonour to his race and the boys in 5th Company, for already he had what could only be described as a half-way hard-on.

"Three of your friends did pass by a little earlier. Didn't come in, though. Not as well turned out as yourself, mind, corporal." The stripes had finally registered. "Isn't that so, young Sharon?"

Young Sharon – she was a good ten years his own senior – finished tying a neat bow on his dinky package. His heart went out to her, for she had done her utmost with the little she had at her disposal. But then all these folk were like that, he told himself, fighting their own little war against rationing and shortages, even damn near hunger at times, while he and his buddies lived high on the hog behind their perimeter fence.

When he had handed over his money for the lipstick and touched his cap to her he backed out of the store.

20

"Do call again!" the druggist cried, getting the last word in, that being the sort of old buzzard he was.

Outside in the street the hot afternoon glare had subsided. Shadows were lengthening, turning blue, swallows swooping and swerving at roof-top level like tiny feathered Mustangs. He saw a man in a tan shop-coat lazily unhook zinc buckets with a long pole in front of a hardware store. There was something calming in the way the man went about his task, like someone who had done this every single night at this time for a lifetime and who would go on doing so in the same unhurried way. The thought should have depressed him, the boredom of it. Instead he felt envious, wishing he was the man, in his place, here and now, even if it was only a one-horse town. Even he could see that, coming as he did from the bottoms himself. It made no sense but one thing he did know: he wanted to sit here dopily gazing until every last item of stock had been taken inside and stowed away and the door closed on the night for good.

He looked at his wristwatch. Three more hours to kill. But his mood had changed now, for time dragged out its weary length like some sluggish old snake in the dust until he could be with his date. He longed suddenly to hear the voices of his own kind, swap a few jokes, down some beers, all the things an enlisted man is supposed to do on a one-day pass. In his best uniform and polished facings he felt conspicuous on this deserted and foreign street.

He began walking as if he had a purpose and wasn't at a loose end. The phrase swam into his head with considerable force as if making sense for the first time. Drifting, unattached, like a stray dog. That shifty look as well.

Taking a side turning he proceeded past a row of poor-looking dwellings, their low roofs covered with thatch where birds nested. The doors were cut off at waist-level and he felt eyes on him as he passed their dark, smoky interiors. He

21

could smell that stuff they burned. Pearl told him they dug it out of the ground then dried it, the poorer classes, Catholics.

This was where they lived, Pearl said, near their chapel so they didn't have far to travel to Mass. He could tell she didn't like them by the way she said the word. Like her he had been brought up Baptist – he supposed – but religion was a much more serious item here than back in Peabody County, one of the things they had spelled out to them on the transport coming over.

A plump young lieutenant from Intelligence had given a pep talk on the subject in front of a blackboard up on deck, all the things to watch out for and not just VD either.

"Most of the time the two communities they get along just fine, but other times, anniversaries mostly, religion and politics can combine to cause deep division, two topics it's advisable never to discuss in any company, mixed or otherwise. Never take sides even if you are tempted. It's not your concern. We are only temporary guests. Remember that. Historically and economically speaking, the Catholics have had a raw deal. But don't forget the Protestants who feel passionately British are our natural allies in this war, not the Irish, who have stayed neutral. So you have a situation where all of the Protestants hate the Germans and what they stand for, but only some of the Catholics, and so then you get a further complication where . . ."

At this point most of those joes like himself switched off and took a nap while the freckle-faced young lieutenant began to sweat, turning his eyes heavenward for divine inspiration.

What not to do if you didn't want a dose sounded a much simpler notion to take on board, although no one hunkered there on the cold wet plates of the ship had the courage to enquire about the infamous "umbrella therapy" everyone talked about all the time. Just thinking of it brought tears to the eyes as well as a burning sensation lower down. That stainless steel thing going up, then coming down again, *open, for Christ's sake*! To ram home the point the lieutenant earlier had chalked up in big letters a school-kid could read, Flies Spread Diseases, Keep Yours Buttoned.

Beyond the houses again was some sort of football field, a mule grazing dead-centre of the pitch, one hind leg tethered to a stake in the ground. It had a cross on its back. Conceivably there might be some religious connection here, he decided, for beside the field was the chapel Pearl had told him about, only bigger and a lot more impressive than he'd been led to expect. Its black stone walls and slated roof looked built to last, not like the matchboard churches he was used to. A marble statue straddled the entrance, some saint or other, Comgall, Cathal, Cormac . . . A name like that had been mentioned, he recalled. As he mooched past, organ music was playing softly inside.

Further on was a cemetery full of old stone crosses and beyond that again a schoolhouse and yard as lifeless as its neighbours.

By this time he was feeling decidedly low, like the last man alive, homesick, even, for remembered sights and sounds half a world away, even that old cotton gin with its murderous dust and racket, even old Bubba himself, all two hundred fifty pounds of him, sitting watching him from his rocker in the office doorway. Even that great old tub of lard would be a welcome sight, he reckoned, just about now, so when he turned a corner and saw the three servicemen swinging their legs on a low wall his heart soared. They were wearing field jackets, boots and gaiters, and he knew they just had to be the ones he had overheard earlier back there in the ruins.

As he drew alongside the middle one called out, "Lordy, lordy, thanks be praised for a friendly dark face!"

23

His own was much paler than his two companions'. With his little Mex moustache and processed hair he looked like a dance-band crooner.

"Say, sport, when does the first house around here open its doors?"

Behind the wall where the trio had parked themselves the corporal could see a long low building roofed with galvanised tin and a sign across its double doors which read Macushla. He recognised it as the town's one and only movie-house, not by the name, which sounded foreign, as well as unpronounceable, but by the showcase on the wall alongside advertising *Weekend In Havana*, starring Alice Faye, Carmen Miranda and Caesar Romero.

Before he could manage a reply one of the other GIs wise-cracked, "How about next fall?" and his buddies practically fell off the wall laughing, especially the young skinny one who looked like a popsicle in khaki.

"'Bout eight-thirty, I guess," he said, trying to be polite. "Ain't it somewheres on the poster?" But none of the three seemed all that interested any longer.

"What are the chances of a thirsty guy getting a drink around these parts? We been on the road since six a.m., no word of a lie."

"Hey, what about the movie?" asked Popsicle.

"I seen it," said the unsmiling one. The corporal was thinking of the knife he carried in his pocket.

"Well, I ain't. I like musicals. They're my favourite type movie."

"Look, Clyde, why don't this nice soldier in his nice clean uniform here tell us exactly where to get ourselves a brew and maybe later we can *all* take in the movie. That is, if the corporal don't already have himself a heavy date." He was looking at the little wrapped package in his hand as he spoke.

24

Clyde giggled and slapped his skinny thigh. "Shit!" he said. "Women!"

"I am sure they do exist in these remote parts. Right, soldier?"

The corporal was feeling confused suddenly, as if the potato jack he'd been drinking earlier had returned to disable him. His brain refused to function as fast as he would like it to – as fast as his questioner, say, smiling at him from where he perched on the wall. One front tooth was pure gold, making him look even more like a jazz musician. Cab Calloway, say. Same grin, too. One of those Harlem niggers who could pass for white.

The corporal felt his neck go all hot and tight under his collar and tie. "What's your outfit, soldier?" he demanded.

"What's yours?"

He told him.

"Now, ain't that a coincidence. We been drafted in this very day to help out in stores. Ain't hardly had time to settle in, mind. Maybe you can fill us in on some essential information. Like where's the nearest pub?"

At that moment a church bell pealed loudly. It seemed to arrive directly out of the air, and the corporal jumped. His audience burst out laughing, even the evil one with the knife in his pants pocket.

"You sure are nervous, corp," said Pencil Moustache.

"Maybe it's us that's making him act that way," said Switch Blade.

"No, no, he just got himself a heavy date, is all."

The corporal was thinking all he had to do to find a way out of this was look at his watch and say, sure, he had someone to see, which happened to be the truth, although not for a couple more hours yet.

Instead he murmured lamely, "There's got to be one somewhere hereabouts, wouldn't you reckon?" Then, hating

25

himself even more, he continued, "I don't come into town all that often, you understand."

The one with the solid gold tooth, the smartass who had been doing most of the talking, figuring, too, jumped off of the wall and said, "What we all waitin' for, then, men?"

As he landed soft in the dirt in his rubber soles he gave off a smell of stale sweat. He needed a shower badly, shave, too. They all did. What were they doing in town this way, dressed in field uniforms? Surely they must know they were off-limits, even if they were part of a new intake. The corporal decided it wasn't his concern and the idea cheered him up in a sneaky, I-told-you-so, sort of a way.

"Sure," he said briskly. "Why not?"

Then the other two came sliding down to join their buddy at the base of the wall.

All of them, they began heading back the way they had come, past the chapel and the school-house and the sports field with the mule still tethered to its stake, a lot cheaper than any old mowing-machine.

He and Gold Tooth moved into the lead while the other two slouched along in the rear. He could hear them laughing to each other and felt certain it was him they were pointing at behind his back, so he carried himself even more stiffly in his walking-out uniform, all knife-edge creases and pressed pleats. Although he couldn't be said to be known in this town he felt conscious of the contrast between himself and his companions. Once more he questioned just how it was they had been allowed out of the base on a pass in this state in the first place. Did they have a pass? *Don't even ask, soldier,* he told himself, *if you know what's good for you.*

What would be good for him and Pearl right now would be to be sitting laughing in the dark together at Carmen Miranda's antics in one of those double seats they had built here especially for lovebirds like themselves.

26

He wondered how many performances the movie would run. Two, three, at the most, he decided, which meant he would have to miss it and although it made no sense, in some crazy way he held this bunch responsible. He walked a shade faster, determined to be shot of all three as soon as the first pub presented itself.

Up a side-street leading off the main drag where the shops were and the respectable business of the town was carried on, he caught sight of one and headed straight for it just as if he drank inside on a regular basis. When he got close, however, it looked abandoned and his spirits fell. The name above the door said Thos. J. Farrell. A dusty Guinness sign dangled in the shuttered window.

"Welcome to the Ritz," murmured the one he disliked most.

They stood there looking for a sign in the glass in the upper part of the door, not a painted one, just some movement, a face, any damn thing. Then Pencil Moustache put his thumb on the brass door-latch, pressing down hard, and the door swung open.

"Hallelujah!" he cried. "If any man thirst let him come unto me!"

He turned round to grin at them. "Did I ever tell you about my dear ole daddy bein' a preacher-man? You don't believe me?"

"Shit, no!" And elbowing one another aside the pair of them pushed inside laughing like a couple of jackasses.

The corporal stood there. He was thinking this was the ideal opportunity to make his exit, but something about that dead street stretching ahead of him like that made him reluctant to face up to its loneliness. His own, too, it suddenly came to him.

The one they called Clyde said, "Ain't you gonna buy a

guy just one lil' ole drink? It's what's 'spected on somebody's birthday, ain't it?"

He looked serious, melancholy, almost, and the corporal thought, sure, some people do tend to get that way at such times, even country gawks like this one with a head and a body somehow not made for each other. Maybe he'd never had a birthday before, a proper one, coming from some Godforsaken hole not unlike his very own Ducktown, so in a fit of misplaced camaraderie he said, "Okay, soldier, the first beer's on me."

Inside it was like a cave, but then these places generally were, the locals seeming to prefer them that way, all musty and evil-smelling. Then again maybe it was just to keep women out, for never once had he spotted a female form except behind the bar, and then it was someone roughly the same age as his grandmother.

This place was deserted save for an old brown and white cat as big as a small dog sleeping on the counter. He could smell it from where he stood, tom-cat's piss bringing tears to the eye. A clock on the wall like the ones he remembered from schoolrooms back home measured out the slow minutes.

"Looks as if someone's passed away in here," observed Pencil Moustache.

"Certainly does smell that way," said number two soldier.

"Christ, you're right," cut in Clyde, wrinkling his nose.

The one with the knife in his pocket, only now he'd taken out a lighter instead, moved over to the sleeping cat, soft and sneaky on the balls of his feet.

"Hey, man, what you got in mind?" asked Pencil Moustache, but in soft tones as if he didn't want to wake that old tom up either.

The other raised a finger to his lips and as they watched still uncertain of his intentions he softly snapped open the lid of his Zippo and spun its wheel. The flame lit up his face and the corporal felt excited by what he saw there.

All his life it had been drummed into him to avoid situations and people like these and up to now he'd managed to do just that, the uniform on his back and the stripes on his sleeve testifying to his success. Yet there were times when he longed to be one of the bad guys for a change and for that split second, seeing that evil grin, he felt those old urges return. Suddenly he yearned to get drunk and cause a little mayhem on his own account and so he stood there watching and waiting, half-involved already, yet poised to back out into the safety of the street.

The cat's tail hung down over the edge of the bar counter like a limp length of ginger-coloured tow and as they continued to watch the evil one with the lighter slowly brought its flame up close to the fluffy tip. A smell of singed fur filled the air yet that old cat continued to lie there like something stuffed. Even when tiny sparks ignited among its fine dry hairs it still didn't move.

Above the bar was a mirror advertising some brand of liquor and the corporal caught sight of his face in the glass alongside that of his three companions. All had that same excited hot look.

Just when they thought they could bear it no longer that old tom finally exploded up off the counter and streaked yowling along the polished surface, then down and out through a door at the back of the bar. They listened to its screeches dying into the distance for what seemed like a long time.

"Leastways the smell's gone," remarked Pencil Moustache and they were still laughing when an old guy in a greasy cap appeared in the doorway through which the cat had disappeared.

"That Ginger," he said, shaking his head. "Beats me what's got into him these days."

"Hot flushes would be my diagnosis," said Pencil Moustache. "Eh, guys?"

Granpa looked at them as if seeing them for the first time. "I suppose you boys will be looking for a drink of some description," he asked with a watery grin.

"This *is* a pub I take it, pops," said the one with the lighter, but stowed in his pocket once more along with the switch blade. The corporal kept thinking of it, couldn't help himself. How long, how thin, handle, horn or hickory, spring-loaded or clasp.

"I've nothing but bottled stout at the moment."

"The way I feel right now, sir, I'd gladly sup sump-oil."

They stood watching as he brought out the four black bottles from under the bar-counter to line them up exactly, reverently, almost, on the wet wood as though they were of rare vintage. The label said Red Heart. On a string leading from his lower vest pocket swung an opener, and he proceeded to press off the serrated metal caps one by one with tiny hisses until a creamy trickle crept down the neck of each bottle.

Everything stood still. Even the tick of the clock appeared to have slowed down. For the first time the corporal saw its place of manufacture was identical to the one painted in a crescent across the dial of his old school-room counterpart. Merrimack, Massachusetts, he read, becoming conscious that his lips might be moving.

"Would you boys care for some glasses?"

Declining the offer, they took up the bottles and putting the narrow cool mouths to their lips allowed the bitter dark liquid to slide down inside.

Clyde, the young one, made a face. "I swear I'll never get used to this stuff. What's it made from anyways? Licorish?"

30

"There'll be a whiskey delivery in three weeks," the old guy told them, apologising for the lack of stock. Indeed there seemed little on the shelves behind him save a few bottles of murky-looking lemonade and some old tins of Prince Edward.

"Set 'em up a second time, pops," ordered Pencil Moustache putting down his empty. He had drained it in one, Adam's apple bobbing like a cork.

The corporal pulled out a handful of change, spreading it across the counter at random, for he still hadn't got used to this money, simply allowing shopkeepers to pick out whatever they required. Pearl had warned him about it but all the guys felt much the same about pounds, shillings and pence, this strange heavy stuff which seriously damaged the lining of the pockets and which bought nothing you ever wanted or really needed.

Pencil Moustache looked down at the drift of coins on the wet wood and said, "Hey, just what you think you're doin', soldier boy?"

He was smiling pleasantly but his voice said something different entirely and the corporal realised suddenly this was the mean one and not the son of a bitch fondling the blade in his pant's pocket.

"This round's on me," he heard himself declare strongly. "I gotta go."

"Sure you gotta go, we all know that, but your moolah ain't no good here. Ain't that so, now, boys?"

Clyde tittered while the other one lit a cigarette with his Zippo which moments earlier had singed the cat.

The old guy gazed longingly at the pack in his hand. As the corporal waited, grateful for this tiny respite, the smoker shook out a couple and the old guy extracted them eagerly.

Pencil Moustache said, "Here, pops, treat yourself to a

proper smoke," handing over a full pack. "What's that brand of shit you people smoke anyway? Woodbine, ain't it?"

"What's a woodbine, for fuck's sake?" asked Clyde.

"Come to think of it, Camel ain't too smart a name for a cigarette either," said Pencil Moustache.

There was silence for a moment as they all pondered on it, the old guy too.

"Some people who don't know no better might just believe it's because they taste like dung. Sun-dried, of course."

"Ain't no camels nor no deserts in Virginia," said Zippo. "Far as I recall."

"Well, one thing's for certain, sure as hell we'll be seein' a lot more of them both before too long. North Africa, here we come. Ain't that the ole war-plan, corporal?"

The corporal slowly sipped his stout. He was feeling confused again, his judgement of who was the bad guy here seriously impaired, the trouble being they all seemed to be switching roles with each fresh turn of the conversation. Clyde, for instance, had turned moody now for some reason while the other two were grinning like a couple of kids on a Sunday-school outing. He looked at the cool, dark bottle in his fist. Could that be the culprit?

"Did I hear you say you'd be working alongside us all in the stores then?" He hadn't, for it was untrue.

"In the mess-hall," he told him without elaborating, although he wanted to add "master cook" for it was something he was proud of.

His questioner's gold tooth gleamed even more intensely. It seemed to do so each time he delivered a wisecrack, but he reached forward suddenly and prodded him in the gut.

"Yeah, you certainly could lose a few pounds, big guy." The corporal drew back at the unexpectedness of it.

His shock must have showed for the other said hurriedly,

32

"No offence meant, only kidding, only kidding," raising his hand as if to defend himself.

For a brief second the corporal took comfort from his own bulk hearing it referred to in that way. Why, if hardy came to hardy, he could whup all three of them, no sweat, he told himself, even if a stick-knife did come into play.

He took another gulp of that old black beer, feeling his spirits revive along with it, and when he looked at the bar he could see another line of bottles materialise there as if by magic.

Looking back on it this had to be the moment when he started to get seriously drunk. He felt relaxed, seeing himself expand, even smile a little, in the mirror facing him. The old guy leaned forward, wiping the wood with a damp rag every so often, but only so he could hear better what they were talking about.

The topic was home news and the corporal was surprised to learn just how much these three seemed to know about what was happening state-side. Like George Civak, for instance, the New York Aspirin Bandit, who always asked his victims for one as a prelude to rape then strangulation. He'd just been sent to the gas-chamber to meet his Maker, if he had one. Nobody had told him about the Detroit race riots either. Zippo – he referred to him in that way now for no introductions had been made, and wouldn't neither – got himself all fired up about events in his home city. He told them it was only the beginning, niggers like them, he said, were not going to take that old white massa shit any longer, even if it meant burning every last kike-owned factory to the ground and their stinking, rotten jobs along with it.

Surprising himself he added his own contribution, for something had been sparked off by the other's anger. Blame it on the beer, but he found himself recounting the episode of the black soldier castrated on Weymouth Pier, England, just because he'd danced all evening with a white girl.

"Shit, who d-done it?" asked Clyde, a look of horror on his pitted young face.

"Bunch of other GIs. Georgia crackers, mostly. It was all hushed up. Leastways they thought it was."

There was a moment's intense silence in the bar except for the measured detonations from the schoolroom type clock. Even the old guy had ceased mopping up. Seeing him poised all ears like that it came to the corporal he shouldn't be talking out of turn this way in front of a "civilian", so pointing to the old yellowed dial he enquired, "May I enquire if that clock is correct, sir?"

"About seven minutes fast," the old guy replied setting up a fresh round at the speed of light.

"No more for me please, guys. I really gotta go."

"White g-girl, is she?" asked Clyde and they all laughed at the idiocy of the question.

"Lucky guy," said Pencil Moustache, lifting his bottle to his lips, which the corporal now noted had a little dark rim from all that black beer they were drinking. They all did. With the back of his hand he wiped his own mouth, but covertly, for he still had this urge not to give offence by setting himself apart, wanting to be like they were, just another GI boozing it up, horsing around.

"Your friend, she got sisters?"

They were all grinning at him now and buckling under that wave of good-will he said, "What the hell, she can wait," reaching for a full bottle on the counter in front of him.

At some point – by now there was confusion regarding the time-scale, the clock face becoming blurred for some reason – he asked for the john. The old guy looked at him.

"Can," he repeated.

34

Pencil Moustache took up the refrain. "Head? Crapper?"

Zippo said, "Shit-house," with unnecessary emphasis, he felt, and, nodding, the old guy led him out to a yard piled waist-high with crates of empties. Winding their way through the maze they came to a door-less privy and the old man left him swaying there looking up at the night sky which, unaccountably, had darkened for some reason.

Deep in the recesses was a bucket in a wooden surround and fearful for his uniform the corporal concertinaed his pants about his ankles then lowered himself on to the seat.

When he'd finished he looked about him for the customary wad of newspaper threaded on a string, but drew a blank. Crouched there, elbows on bare knees, he thought longingly of all that grass within easy reach back where he'd buried the bicycle.

As he sat there he could make out the shape of the old ginger tom on top of the crates. It appeared to be studying him. "Puss, puss," he whispered, as though it might help him out of his dilemma. Its eyes shone like twin car-lamps in the light coming from the open back door. It carried on regarding him, pityingly, it seemed to him.

Conscious of the smell leaking from between his clenched thighs, he gave in and took out the little wrapped package he had inside his tunic pocket. He was reluctant to do it, for it seemed to add further weight to his betrayal, but he stripped off the tissue paper then used it on himself.

Out in the yard his head swam for a minute as he came upright. He could see stars, real ones, in the blue blackness overhead. A pang of homesickness overtook him for warm nights back in the cottonfields and brakes of his home state. There was a river bank where he would often lie and study the constellations, sometimes with a jug, sometimes not. Right now he had that same sensation, like floating downstream on his back. Whether it came from the liquor or the movement of the planets, even a combination of both, he couldn't be certain. Just another of those great imponderables, he reckoned.

Straightening himself up, he headed back towards the lighted doorway, but halfway across the littered expanse he heard raised voices. One of them belonged to a stranger and he halted on the spot, sobering instantly. The tones were unmistakably American like his own, but harder, Northern. White, at a guess. He felt a surge of panic, moving smartly out of the oblong of light thrown across the yard. Edging along the back wall he put his face close to an open window and listened.

He heard a second strange voice growl, "Just get the fuck back to your units and don't mess with me. See this?"

There was the sound of a carbine bolt being slammed in and out.

"Any more fuckin' lip and I'll put a round all the way up each of your fuckin' black asses."

"I'd do as the man says," came the first voice, only calmer, more reasonable in tone. "We don't give a monkey's tit if you have been travellin' all day. None of you has a pass, and even if you had, you're still improperly dressed. That's a grade two offence."

Silence followed and the man listening at the open window had a distinct image of the stand-off taking place in the bar he had just left between the two Snowdrops in their spotless white helmets and the three unshaven dogfaces holding up the bar. He felt fear as if he was implicated, starting to shake, then something brushed against his leg and looking down he saw it was that old cat again. It stared up at him, eyes like yellow headlights. He had always hated cats, even now, a grown man. It was as if they knew too damn much for their own good and he kicked out. It hissed at him arching its back. Then he got scared again thinking it might draw attention to his being out here in the yard. What he was feeling was irrational, he knew, for he had a stamped twenty-four pass right here in his top pocket, yet the sense of having done something he could be punished for was impossible to shake off.

Lord, he prayed silently, *please don't let that crazy son of a bitch pull a knife in there. Make him go, make all of them go.*

He was on the point of adding all sorts of promises just to sweeten the plea when he heard the front door slam followed by silence then a laugh from one of the MPs.

"Did you see those coons' faces? I just love this job, don't you?"

"One of these days, Earl, somebody's gonna introduce that gut of yourn to six inches of sharpened steel."

"Over my dead body they will."

Both of them found that funny.

Then the man listening heard them start in to question the old guy about how long the GIs had been drinking there and whether they had caused him any sort of trouble.

"None, officer. Perfect gentlemen, all three of them."
Thank you, Lord, I won't forget this.

"That's what we like to hear. Ain't that so, good buddy?"

"Affirmative, sarge, affirmative."

The man with his face pressed to the window experienced a sudden tremor seeing three stripes in his mind's eye for the first time, something he hadn't counted on, like one of them turning out to have a moustache or a scar running down his face. Whenever he got a picture inside his head this way he always found it hard to dislodge.

"Any of our colored boys give you a problem, sir, you know where to find us. We're on foot patrol way past midnight. They can get a shade excitable at times, specially if there's a white woman involved. Matter of temperament, you understand?" The old man made no reply but the

37

corporal could imagine him nodding energetically, anxious to please, faced with a couple of uniforms with so much white all over them. Up to now he himself had always managed to avoid dealings with men who showed up in the dark that way and determined to keep it so. He waited a longer time than was strictly necessary out in the cold after he heard the front door close behind them.

He still felt nervous, though, as if he'd had a narrow escape from something, and when he came back into the bar and the old man poured him a whiskey from a hidden bottle under the counter he drank it straight down in one. They didn't speak, avoiding each other's eyes as if sharing something to be ashamed of.

The corporal, standing with his elbows resting on the bar, started getting drunk again. He needed to obliterate the memory of the past half hour and, succeeding only too well, woke up some time later on a sagging settee in a room he had never been in before.

The colour scheme was dark brown and a sink, a stove and a pine dresser stood against different walls and he realised he was in somebody's kitchen. Someone had covered him with a ratty old afghan rug. It smelt of cat's piss.

For a moment he lay there despite the reek of ammonia in his nostrils. The only light entered dimly from the glassed-in panel of a door which he suspected might lead to the bar beyond. It was the scent of that old feline which told him where he was.

He started feeling himself all over then to see if he was still in one piece and after that he did the same with each of his pockets to check he hadn't been robbed. He hadn't. But in one of them he discovered an extra item, a brand new lipstick case. Rolling its coolness in the palm of his hand he couldn't for the life of him recall how it had got there. His brain refused to help out in the matter so, groaning softly, he crossed to the sink and poured some water from a jug into an enamel basin resting there. Splashing it over his face he dried himself on his army issue handkerchief. It smelt of beer and the smoke of countless cigarettes.

Moments later, re-entering the bar, he was startled to find three locals silently facing him on a bench along one wall. All wore those flat-type cloth caps, but then everyone did. Even more curious, rarely had he seen anyone bare-headed, even on fine days, so it couldn't all be down to climate, could it? Seeing them staring at him in that manner he pulled out his own folded army cap from under his epaulet and stuck it in place.

They were eyeing him as if they'd known he'd been lying in there all along, discussing him, too, in soft, wondering tones so as not to disturb or upset him. It made him feel like some kind of dangerous wild animal, for he was remembering what the Snowdrop sergeant had said earlier. Maybe that guy Zippo had a point acting mad all the time. Maybe he should take a leaf out of his book. Mister Nice Guy. Mister Jim Crow, more like, face aching from all that water-melon grinning all the time.

In the mirror advertising liquor his eyes looked red. His uniform was missing much of that earlier band-box appeal also, probably stunk of cat, but then nobody else took a bath around here neither. Even Pearl made her ablutions piecemeal, he suspected, one strip at a time. On the instalment plan. Just the way she allowed him, or didn't, to see her with no clothes on.

Standing there squinting into a clear place in that old glass – it had a real busy pattern of harps and shamrocks – he saw his face change as realisation hit home, her name like that putting everything into place, even that mysterious lipstick in his trouser pocket.

He glanced at the clock. Ten-thirty. Two hours of his life

gone missing, not accounted for, or able to be explained away, least of all to a certain someone in a little doll-house, glad rags on, and smelling like a posy just for him.

Groaning loudly he tore out of that bar and into the dead and darkened street. Not a glimmer of light could be seen. The blackout was in force, some sort of unofficial curfew, too, judging by the eerie absence of life. The place looked different, another street, town, maybe, and he fetched up against an iron gate set in an archway to get his bearings back.

He felt dizzy, trying to work out just how much, and more important, what he'd drunk that day. It was his way of getting to grips with his condition, maybe take some of the edge off it if he was lucky, for he still had a stubborn belief in such theories. It was as if sometimes he had to build up a set of rules for himself from scratch just because of everyone telling him how stupid and worthless he was all the time, mainly, but not entirely, because of his color.

He began hunting through his pockets for a cigarette but the nearly full pack he'd had earlier was missing, probably handed over to the old pub guy before he passed out. He could imagine himself doing it, the gratitude welling up in him for not giving him away to the MPs. A kind of dull anger at his own slavishness started burning him up, followed by the need for confrontation of some sort.

Screwing up his eyes he looked about him, trying to decide which route to take. Left, he chose, and hugging the darkened house-fronts, began to move along the street. It came to him just how crazy this was, a coloured guy feeling his way through a blacked-out town in the middle of Ireland some place. The thought softened his mood a little but not enough to distract him from his determination to have it out with somebody for once, whatever *it* might be.

Another drink wouldn't go amiss, he told himself, just to

keep the motor primed and running until that moment arrived.

Accordingly, like the fool he was, he went searching for another pub, found it, too, and with it something else entirely which he did not need or wish for any part of. Like some great load of cow crap, there it was waiting for him all along, and whoever was in charge would have himself a real good laugh unloading it all over him.

Right now what he saw ahead was a square of some kind, new to him and somehow larger, more prosperous than the town could properly afford. Even in the dark like this it reminded him of one of those little county seats at home harking back to a better, bygone age. A building with steps leading up to it like a courthouse took up nearly half of one side and there was something that looked very like a statue bang in the middle behind a collar of railings.

The corporal hung back, merging into the shadows. Already his eyes were growing accustomed to the variations of blackness. Now he could make out a church, Protestant, and next door the usual crop of headstones. Some were of the palest marble. Like teeth, he thought, instinctively covering his mouth with his hand.

Beyond the boneyard proper was a run of what looked like store-fronts, dead and dark until daylight, but the middle one seemed to have a fine streak of light running down the side of its window frame not much thicker than a knife-edge. He had the strongest possible feeling there had to be life of the kind he was seeking in back of that blind and so, after a moment's hesitation, he began crossing the deserted square.

His feet made no sound — Lord be praised for good old US army rubber — the invisibility of face and hands an additional bonus. The sensation of being abroad undetected in a strange and foreign place came as a warm surprise. He almost felt like laughing aloud, for it reminded him of that yarn some GIs were supposed to be putting about being really white and having been selected as night-fighters by the government before shipping out. An injection, they said, had been given to turn their skins black, another would reverse the process on their return. Some clever nigger son of a gun had thought that one up all by himself.

Soft as a wraith he continued padding across the square. Yeah, he had been right. That certainly was an old statue standing there behind its railings on a little stepped platform, some ancient general-type figure in a billycock hat, sword outstretched, staring off towards the courthouse.

Breaking stride he halted beside the sculpted figure. There was a date and below that the name of a battle but he couldn't make out anything precise. The railings had sharpened ends. He held on to the nearest one looking heavenwards. A dusting of stars had appeared without his knowledge. They looked familiar. Old friends.

He shivered, but only because he felt cold. Whiskey, he promised himself, just one. And after? He had no idea. He wasn't accountable any longer, responsibility dropping from him like water off a roof. For once he felt like being brutish, bad-assed, just the way people said niggers like him were supposed to behave when the shackles were off. He shook his wrists as though testing the theory. They felt loose, pleasantly rubbery. Legs, too.

The thin streak of light beckoned. Already he was in there slamming down his riches on the bar, calling for service, throwing his weight around, all one hundred eighty pounds of it, all of those things he'd always been too afraid, too nervous to do. Mister Jim Crow. *Fuck it, and fuck you too, Stonewall Jackson*, he told that old general on his plinth, heading for the distant sliver of yellow lamplight. He reached the church – First Unitarian, on a painted board.

Then just as he was gliding past the graveyard a voice

came from the shadows throwing him more than all those spooky old headstones put together.

"Wear something white at night. Ain't no one ever told you that yet, soldier boy?"

He froze staring into the blackness.

"People can meet up with all sorts of real nasty accidents otherwise."

"Who's there?" he croaked. "Who is it?" although already he knew the answer.

"Why, it's your ole buddies, that's who. Don't you remember? The ones you ran out on 'bout a coupla hours back."

"Show yourself," he heard himself say.

Someone else laughed. "Sounds jest like one of them MPs, don't he now?"

It was the one he'd christened Zippo. He sounded drunk, dangerous, too. Much more so than earlier, which was saying a lot.

"Listen," he said, "I was just takin' a crap, that's all."

"Mighty big crap."

"Mighty big asshole."

"Fuck you," he said, getting his courage back.

"No, fuck you, corporal." And for the second time that evening he heard the snick of an M1 bolt going back.

Sweet Jesus, he prayed, *why me?* He came forward as if to confront his fate for he was so scared by this time that anything was possible.

They were standing close together under some sort of rustic shelter affair with a little shingle roof on top to keep the rain off, the minister, most probably, as he met the mourners. All were wearing helmets and carrying carbines.

"That's right, soldier," said Pencil Moustache. "Approach and be recognised."

"Listen, you guys," he said trying to keep the tremble out

of his voice, "I don't know what you're aimin' to do here, but whatever it is it ain't exactly smart, believe me."

"Well, ain't that *real* nice. I do believe the corporal here is concerned."

"For his own sweet ass, he is."

Thus far the one they called Clyde hadn't uttered a word. He leaned up against the side of the arch, his face buried in the cavern of his helmet. His neck looked hardly thicker than a stick of celery. *Snap*, thought the corporal for no apparent reason, other than if things were to get really rough a single shove should do the trick as far as he was concerned. Buddies One and Two were a different proposition. Yet he had no clear intent of how to react either way beyond continuing to peer in at them in their bower.

Pencil Moustache enquired, "Tell us something. Are your pals them two MPs drinking in that pub over there?"

"They ain't no friends of mine."

"Jest answer the man's question, fat boy," chimed in Zippo, unpleasant as ever.

The corporal stood his ground, confronting his enemies, for that was how he saw them now. Somewhere along the line he had done something bad, he told himself, and now he was paying for it. He could almost smell that great redemptive pile of shit waiting to descend upon his head.

"I don't know," he said. "I ain't been in there yet."

Then Clyde the skinny one spoke out for the first time. "Mebbe he's right. Mebbe we should jest hightail it outa here like he says."

"Did I hear you say *hightail it*?" snarled Zippo. "Tell me, do I look like some kinda jack rabbit to you, shit-kicker? Do I, boy?" And he had the business end of his carbine pressed hard against the other's chin-strap in a trice.

The corporal moved quickly forward to prevent any

44

further madness. "Listen," he pleaded, "if I go in and check it out will you guys promise to go back to the base?"

There was silence.

"Have we got a deal?"

Zippo lowered his weapon and seconds later Pencil Moustache emerged from the shadows, smiling his greaseball smile. "Hey, man, it's jest a friendly argument, is all. Personally, I say them two Snowdrops are long gone, but then I'm in a minority. All we want to do is settle this thing. A bet's involved. You understand what I'm sayin'?"

They faced one another, both lying and both knowing it.

"Okay," the corporal told him, going along with this game whatever it was, whatever the consequences, for he had no other option any longer as he saw it. "You all stay where you are till I come back out again. You hear me now?"

"Sure thing," said Pencil Moustache, Clyde nervously joining in from the recesses. Zippo remained silent.

Half way across no-man's land heading for the crack of light and, hopefully, less hazardous company, the corporal detected what he thought was the sound of someone softly cocking a carbine. The shaved fuzz on the back of his neck bristled, then he heard a second oiled bolt being eased back and he reached the pub door awash with sweat.

His hand searched for then found the doorhandle in the dark – it felt icy cold to the touch – he pushed and almost fell into the lamp-lit interior.

Back of the bar a big heavyset woman in a print apron was filling a jug from a barrel resting on the counter. Watching her were two MPs, one white, the other coloured like himself. That came as a surprise and for a second, shocked, he stared at the dark features.

Further along the bar a Tilley lamp hissed, bouncing a painful glare off both helmets. Apart from that the place was empty. The landlady finished what she was doing then hoisted herself back up on to a stool behind the bar. It made her look like she was in control of things, way above everybody. Still she didn't say anything, just looked straight ahead as if waiting for the MPs to do the talking. The corporal felt much the same way only a lot more nervous as the silence stretched like a string of gum.

Then the white MP spat on the floor and said, "What you doin' here, soldier? Ain't nobody told you all leave's been cancelled as from eighteen hundred hours?"

The corporal looked down at the gob of spit feeling like a fourteen year old again, an awkward, overweight teenager in the wrong place at the wrong time.

"Where you been hidin' yourself, anyways? Every pub in town we been in puttin' the word about. Ain't that the truth, now, Perce?"

The colored MP nodded. Somehow he didn't fit the way the corporal had pictured him back there in the crapper, that slow, reasonable voice countering the raw tones of his partner. He had a long horse-like face pushing his chin-strap to the furthermost limits, also a real bad case of boils on his neck, enough to make anybody mean.

"I know you from somewheres, don't I?" he said turning his eyes on him. "Ain't you some kinda mess-monkey?"

The corporal shook his head. Lie number two came out when the other MP asked if he had come across any other GIs on his travels. Again he signalled, no.

He stood there under their gaze not having said a word so far wondering if he could get away with acting dumb indefinitely. The woman behind the bar was watching him too. She had hairs growing out of her chin and nostrils like little stiff wires and he wondered if she knew they were there. Some people never really looked closely in a mirror at themselves, had no real call to, even certain women he suspected.

"Looks as if Rip Van Winkle here is our last one, Perce. This is your lucky night, dogface. You can get yourself a ride back in the jeep with us."

"I gotta go," he blurted breaking his vow of silence, for a terrible panic had suddenly overtaken him.

"Hold your horses, we ain't ready yet. Pour the poor sap a beer, Mrs J. One for the road."

With a deep and breathy sigh she slipped down off her high stool, for she carried a heap of weight.

"No, you don't understand, I gotta take a leak," he lied, backtracking for the door.

"Not out there, soldier," called out the MP. "The can's this way."

"Thinks he's back in the bottoms," said the colored Snowdrop. "Thinks the street's a toilet."

In the midst of his misery the corporal wondered why this one should be so mean, and to one of his own race too, but then he had seen it so many times before, hadn't he, in this man's army. This man being white and calling all the shots.

By now his hand was on the door-knob. *Left or right*, he agonised, for he was confused about almost everything by this stage, except getting out of here. All were staring at him as if his intentions were written on his face. The woman held a bottle with a red label on it ready to pour. All of a sudden his mouth felt very dry.

"You don't understand," he said a second time, turning the brass knob behind his back as he did so, successfully, for next moment the door was wide open and spilling out light in a yellow flood into the street.

"Hold it right there, soldier!" cried the first MP but he didn't obey the order, instead moving fast and crouched slightly away from the oblong glare and the vision of both sets of watchers. His outstretched palms scraped along the wall for guidance, for it was hard to see just where he was heading after the brightness inside.

"Don't go out there, Earl!" he heard the colored MP yell as if he could predict future events, but his companion ignored the warning, appearing full in the frame of the doorway.

"Where are you, you dumb-ass son of a bitch? Show your black ass or by Jesus H. Christ I'll —"

He didn't get any further for out of the darkness from the graveyard side of the square there issued a volley, six shots at least, like crackers going off, maybe even overlapping a little, who could tell, certainly not the corporal who was on his face in the dirt by the base of the wall. He heard the MP in the doorway cry out then fall backwards, unblocking the light.

"You crazy bastard," he appeared to say, and the man lying a dozen feet away in the dust felt the first intimation that he might be blamed for this.

The lamp went over and out with a crash of brittle glass, followed by the sound of someone dragging somebody along a floor.

As he was being hauled back inside the shot man kept on groaning, "Jesus, Jesus, oh, Christ." Then, clear as a bell, he said, "That crazy nigger has done for me, Percy."

All this time the woman had been moaning, the sound gradually getting louder like an approaching steam train. Now she started screaming full tilt and as though she'd set some sort of signal off the firing started up again, but really blasting this time. He could hear the rounds smashing bottles in the bar and see the flashes, too, coming from the far side of the square. Close to his cheek he smelt dog crud, or it may have been his own, for his pants felt wet between the legs.

48

The scent was a strong one, even stronger than the cordite in the air.

The firing stopped then and all went quiet except for the woman groaning softly inside. A light came on in one of the houses followed by another and another as curtains were drawn and the restrictions of war-time and blackout were forgotten. Raised voices could be heard, shouts, questions.

The crouching man heard someone, an old man, call out, "Mind the gas! Mind the gas!" as if the Boche himself had struck directly into the sleeping heart of this part of Ireland. Finally a siren started its slow, screeching climb in another section of town.

The man hugging the bottom of the wall began to regain control of his limbs. Bent over and weaving, like somebody drunk or blind or both, one hand outstretched, his fingertips traced the stones lovingly as if they would lead him from that place and its terrible consequences.

Only when he reached quieter, darker parts where the events and sounds of the night's disturbance hadn't yet penetrated did he straighten up and move forward in a steady lope which increased in energy and speed once he made out the first faint outlines of hedges and fields.

THREE

On the crest of what was known as the Rushy Hill, Francey McKeever choked back on the mixture and the labouring two-stroke coughed then died swiftly, both men, rider and passenger, stiffening in anticipation of the fierce, unpowered descent ahead. Lawlor gripped the handles of the sidecar. Although closer to the road he was now on a level with his driver, who had fallen forward, goggles into the wind, like a child willing his mount to even greater speeds. He was also humming to himself in imitation of the now throttled engine.

Francey was regarded as simple, but on nights like these the sergeant was in his hands, content to allow himself be driven home, the night air gradually clearing the whiskey fumes from his brain. Theirs was a ritual based on trust, Lawlor drinking solitary and undisturbed in the pub's darkened kitchen and then at midnight, later sometimes, the widow's son wheeling out the combination and the two of them setting off along the most remote, unused back roads towards the distant town and barracks. The pushbike, the old police-issue roadster, would then be discreetly delivered the following day with one flat tyre, another key element in the conspiracy which in reality fooled nobody.

The wind beating on his face grew to gale force, road grit rattling on the underbelly of the sidecar like pellets off a toy drum. Lawlor's hands went numb as he bore the blast, leaning into it like a figurehead. His eyes streamed but still they registered how the trees and hedges on either side stood upright against all the logic of this hurricane on his face and in his ears. Often at this point he had the urge to stand up, daring the elements to do their damnedest, howling into the rushing blackness.

Drink was at the root of it, of course, he recognised that, but he still felt there had to be something else, not just the booze, about acting in such a way, defying the rules for once, instead of always being the way he was when sober, Sergeant Denis Francis Lawlor, old enough to know better, holding on to get his pension, *just*, knuckles whitened, as now.

Ahead of him the facing slope of the great dip reared up in the half-dark, heading straight and true for the horizon. *Like a Roman road*, he thought, except those marching squadrons had never crossed the Irish Sea. On his honeymoon twenty-two years earlier he had seen such highways slicing through the English downs. He and Nuala had stood together hand in hand listening to the larks under an immensity of blue. It frightened her, she'd told him, all that space, that awful endless road more than anything, without respite, like something in an American desert. He had laughed at her foolishness – she'd never been outside Ireland except in imagination fed by the films – but secretly he felt it too, couldn't wait to get back home to their own scaled-down, nursery landscape. They remounted their bicycles then, taking a side road more human in scale in the direction of Stonehenge.

Lawlor felt his eyes water, but whether it was the memory

of that day so far away, so very long ago, or the rushing of the air, he couldn't be certain.

By now the three-wheeler had passed the half-way mark and was racing up the steep incline. Their speed began to wane and with it the roar, too, of the wind. Feeling began returning to Lawlor's face and hands. He could hear Francey's frenzied humming growing louder the more they slowed. He had also begun a curious bobbing action as if urging the combination with their joint weight to make it to the top of the hill.

Lawlor sat stupefied by his side. He had no real interest in the outcome of the contest, merely squatted there, living ballast. Slower and slower turned the wheels. It seemed they might start rolling backwards at any moment, gravity exerting its due. Francey's whole face was in motion. He had also started beating on the handlebars with his gloved hands. Gauntlets. Encased almost entirely in leather, he creaked like a piece of human harness, even more so now as he jerked and twisted in the saddle.

Lawlor let his mind go blank, closing his eyes, relaxing his grip on the curving rail in front of him. He could smell petrol, grease, leather, hot oil, metal, nothing else, even though he was surrounded by Nature and all of those troubling night scents. He was in a cocoon, a man-made bubble, in the charge of a half-wit and he didn't give a damn as to what might or might not happen to him next. Didn't care. Running backwards to oblivion might just have the edge, however, if it came to a choice.

Then he felt their pace quicken slightly, not back, but forwards. Opening his eyes he saw that by some miracle of mind over matter they had managed to breast the hill. Francey jerked his thumb at him in triumph. It looked enormous in its covering of pigskin.

They were rolling freely now, another rushing descent

52

ahead, but he must have tired of the game for Francey let the clutch in, and after a jerk and cough or two the engine sparked then roared back to life.

The sleeping countryside unrolled past on either side, not a light nor suspicion of one, yet Lawlor knew there were farmhouses and cottages out there buried in darkness, some sleeping, some not. He knew every inch of this terrain after all, *his* territory, which he would yield to no man, even though he'd only come to these parts twenty years earlier from his native Cavan when the old Royal Irish Constabulary disbanded and he had transferred to the new Northern force.

They drove through a blinding swathe of mist lying like damp cotton wool in a hollow where a stream purred under a bridge. He pictured the black water as it manoeuvred the rounded stones, sleeping trout, motionless, in, yet out of the current, and felt moved again, some half-remembered fragment from childhood refusing to surface and reveal itself.

Three miles further on Francey choked the engine yet again, but this time carefully coasted the old Velocette to a standstill. This was also part of the fortnightly ritual and Lawlor visualised their resting place on this lonely stretch of by-road as being darkened by oil-stains because of the number of nights they had pulled over here and, knowing Francey, always in that exact, same spot. With his helmet and goggles in place he sat erect like an idol staring straight ahead, oblivious, while Lawlor climbed up out of the cockpit.

His legs felt decidedly wobbly, head still light, but then they usually did at this point. What he planned on doing next would get him back to some semblance of sobriety before he arrived home to brave those two grinning bastards waiting up for him in the barracks. The Two Bs, he called them, Boal and Burnside, shovelling the coal on like a couple of stevedores the minute they got his back turned. A wave of

53

heat would hit him like a *sirocco* the instant he opened that Day Room door. He suspected they did it deliberately just to see him flinch and his colour flare up whenever he met the full force of it.

There was a gap in the hedge and he made his way through, staggering a little. Underfoot the ground was churned to mud, a thick, clinging soup, as though from frequent traffic. Human tracks with occasional animal ones. He had no need to look down to know which predominated.

Staying on the path – his boots would be a disgrace, but let that be seen to later – soon he could hear the flow of water, the clear liquid babble of a spring being fed through a pipe and falling into a basin below.

For a moment he stood listening. The sound seemed to carry far beyond its immediate surroundings. People had told him it could, indeed, be heard for great distances, adding to the potency already it enjoyed in the local imagination. Known as a "healing well" it attracted sufferers with their ailments from far and near and now, as he came closer, he saw the telltale scraps hanging from the thorn bush growing out of the hillside above the spout.

He bent and drank from the flow. The water numbed the inside of his mouth and chilled his stomach as it went down, but he persisted until he felt bloated and a little sick. The taste was like metal on the tongue. He pictured that underground journey to the light through seam and fault, absorbing minerals as it went. He took a breather, one hand resting on the cold galvanised pipe.

A breeze stirred the votive offerings impaled on the thorns. The sick bottled the water, leaving relics of their maladies to rot in the open, mass-cards, ribbons, items of cheap religious jewellery, photographs, sometimes, the images bleached away by the effects of sun and weather.

Lawlor shuddered, thinking of what might have been left to pollute the site instead of such sterile mementoes – bloodied pads and bandages, perhaps, artificial limbs, trusses, grinning dentures.

Turning aside he put two fingers down his throat, retching silently. His mouth filled with bile. He drank once more to wash the taste away. Stooping lower he held out his hands to cup the flow, splashing face and neck more and more violently until his tunic collar was soaked.

In the midst of his ablutions, if they could be called that, he heard the wail of a distant siren and froze, his wet cheeks going chill. At first he thought, *aircraft*, then in the singular, a stray, for who would want to drop a bomb – bombs – on their insignificant little hole. Clugston's saw-mill could hardly be said to contribute to the war effort. Straining, he listened for the throb of engines overhead but the skies were silent. The eerie cry continued, drifting without break or variation across the fields four, maybe, five miles in a straight line from its source.

He thought of whoever was cranking it up there in the cupola of the courthouse. Once a month there was a drill just to see if the mechanics were working properly, but this was no dummy run. He could tell, something purposeful about the tempo and the impression, too, it could go on for a very long time if necessary.

By now several farm dogs had chimed in from various points of the compass. He noticed, too, a light across the valley in breach of the blackout. For an instant the policeman in him made a mental note pinpointing the location. Then the reality of what was happening, not to him, personally, a drunk immersed in his own private rituals, but to the people of the town beyond, the town whose care and protection was still in his charge, managed to sober him up more than all the wind and water he had anointed himself with this long night. He started to run back along the track then, boot soles sucking at the mire.

Francey hadn't moved, his profile stiff as that on a medal, as Lawlor burst through the gap, half-falling into the sidecar.

"As fast as you can go!" he cried out to him. "Give her the gun!"

The siren was still screeching at the top of its pitch, yet it was doubtful whether Francey had even noticed, so intent did he become on his own preoccupations. Only when Lawlor thumped the flank of the sidecar with his fist did he rise up in the stirrups. Thrusting down once, a second time, he got the plugs to fire and, trailing a plume of bluish smoke, they shot off in the direction of that high, keening alarm.

Their journey seemed to take an eternity, yet couldn't have, for they were travelling so fast the sound of the racing engine obliterated that of the siren. Lawlor could sense their whole travelling contraption straining to its limits. Occasionally airborne, he felt his stomach turn over and, giving in to the sensation, hung over the side on one of the flatter stretches and brought up more of that evening's intake of whiskey.

On the outskirts of town beside Gilbert Clugston's weighbridge Francey steered the combination to a halt – it was where they normally parted company – but Lawlor waved him on.

"The barracks," he commanded, "Market Street," as if he didn't know where it was.

They passed rows of darkened houses. He could sense people in doorways in their night-clothes peering out. Some were conferring, it seemed to him, the rumour-mills already grinding away.

A voice called out, "There goes the big peeler!" in recognition of his profile as he rattled past. He couldn't be certain whether antagonism informed the remark or not and instinctively glared back in the direction of whoever had spoken. This was Irish Street where his co-religionists lived. Quite a few looked on him as a traitor, he knew for a fact, because of the uniform with its badge of crown supplanting the harp.

The barracks was situated between the Ulster Bank and Masonic Hall. It had a double arrangement of gates to forestall attack, an outer arched set like something fronting a mediaeval fortress, and a smaller, more modest pair giving access to the building proper. First thing Lawlor noticed as he staggered from his chariot was that these gates were now wide apart. This alarmed him even more than the screech of the siren earlier, for he had a deep-seated personal dread of ever being at the mercy of a mob again after what had happened to him on his last posting. Recalling that terrible night and half-hearing already the crackle of gunfire and the cries of the besieging Shinners, without word or gesture he left Francey and ran in under the outer archway.

The window of the Day Room was blazing like a beacon. The door of the barracks with its surmounting royal crest was also wide to the world. For the briefest of moments he found himself glancing up to see if the union jack on its pole hadn't already been usurped by the tricolour. As soon as his feet touched the stone steps he began shouting, revolver already outstretched the length of its lanyard.

"Boal! Burnside!" he called out. Their caps and greatcoats were missing from the hooks behind the door.

He stood for an instant listening to the echo of his own roar up the flagged hallway, then he stormed into the Day Room. Someone had placed the lamp up as close to the glass of the windows as it could go and that someone was on his feet with a rifle levelled at him.

"Sergeant Lawlor," said the man and grounded his Lee Enfield. It was one of the B Specials, Bertie McMeekin.

Lawlor looked up at the clock as if already preparing his report. Five minutes after midnight.

"What's happened? Was there an attack?"

The man stared at him as if the word was in a foreign tongue. His uniform had been thrown on. He was wearing brown shoes.

"There's been a shooting," he said.

"Here? At the barracks?"

"No. In the town."

Lawlor slid the revolver back in its holster but left the flap undone. "Put some more coal on," he told the man. "The fire's nearly out." He had no idea why he'd said it, relief, perhaps, or something unconscious to do with the two missing constables and their funny-ha-ha business with the fire. "And do up your tunic, for God's sake, man. You never know who might walk in." His own appearance wasn't much of an example. He didn't dare look down at his boots.

"DI Quigg's already been here. He came directly Crawford phoned him."

"Burnside did what?"

"Nobody knew where you were. You couldn't be contacted."

Lawlor felt sick. He sat down at the table with the day-book on it open at Saturday the tenth of October 1942. The date mocked him, as did the blank foolscap page awaiting his concoction of events over the past five hours.

Patrol commenced 7.00 pm. I took the Edenturk Road heading towards that area known as the Fews. No sign of lights or any infringement of the blackout despite an anonymous tip-off that someone was signalling to enemy aircraft from the Rushy Hill. Making my way homeward I sustained a puncture in the rear tyre and was forced to proceed on foot. Luckily I was able to flag down a passing motorcyclist who provided much welcome transport back to base. Patrol concluded 12.04 hours. Sunday, he was thinking, we're already into Sunday.

The idiot in the brown shoes – colour-blind, possibly – was hurling coal at the back of the grate. The sound reverberated in his head. Turf would have been a blessing.

"This shooting," he enquired as if urgency was furthest from his mind. "Where exactly did it take place?"

The B Special lowered the coal scuttle. "At Jelley's bar. In Scotch Street."

"I know where it is. Anyone hurt?"

"Mrs Jelley and one, maybe two American soldiers. That's all I know. I was told to stay here."

Lawlor stood up. He needed to go to his quarters, straighten himself out, he could still smell vomit, but he knew he must act now in a decisive manner as if still in charge.

"Make sure all is secure" – *whatever that might mean* – he told the poor ape in the badly fitting, badly dyed, blue-black uniform. He drew himself upright for the first time. For a moment it looked as if a salute might even be forthcoming, but Lawlor turned away, embarrassed enough already.

At the door he said, "And take that lamp out of the window. We're not a huer-house touting for custom, you know." *You bastard*, he thought to himself, *they have you nearly as bad as themselves in this place.*

He strode down the short stretch of path almost sober now, then under the archway to the street outside. The siren high in the bell-tower of the courthouse continued to make a faint bleating noise like something refusing to die. Then he saw the motor-cycle combination and Francey astride it, straight-backed and alert, and felt a guilty pang, for he had forgotten all about him. He crossed to the still-warm machine.

"Francey," he said quietly, hand resting on the rim of the sidecar, "you can go home now. It's all right. I can manage."

He didn't thank him for his services, that wasn't part of their arrangement, and even if he had, probably it would have confused the other, setting off some sort of emotional response neither of them could understand or handle decently.

Lawlor had a powerful urge to break the rules this once. After all he had involved this innocent in his dirty schemes, used him shamelessly for his own ends, and on a regular basis too. For a moment he stood there, an awkward block of a man in his weighty greatcoat, dwarfing his companion.

"Francey . . ." he began, but couldn't continue. Certain things become the habits of a lifetime, like holding back, holding in, the uniform acting like a suit of armour. At night after he took it off he felt a sense of release, swelling almost, in his vest and drawers, lying looking up at the rippled ceiling of what was still referred to as "the married quarters". The bed, brass and laughably overwrought for such a spartan establishment, was made for twin giants.

Francey rose up on the footrests, kick-starting the engine into life. The sound filled the empty street like the roar of a bomber then idled to a throaty purr.

Lawlor stood aside but the man in leather leaned across suddenly reaching into the well of the sidecar. He pulled something out of the recesses, presenting it almost proudly to Lawlor. It was his sergeant's cap. Lawlor took it from him, hesitating, holding it for a moment until he realised Francey was waiting for him to put it on. So he did so while the other sat and watched from his vibrating perch, the newest and latest addition to their Saturday-night ritual. Only then did he let out the clutch and glide off, the narrow letter-box mask on the headlamp throwing a wavering yellow projection on to the road ahead.

Lawlor watched and waited until the feeble red tail-light disappeared from view, then began making his way towards the scene of the crime.

It wasn't long before he came upon knots of people huddled outside their houses, all with the air of refugees, even though they were close to home. Dressed in an assortment of ancient overcoats and blankets, nervously they scanned the night sky. The sergeant's stride became much more purposeful and commanding. It didn't take long for the old instincts to reassert themselves. He found himself taking pleasure in the way they seemed to shrink from his passage, allowing him sole mastery of the street. The metal tips on his boots echoed on the cobbles. His greatcoat swung free, exposing revolver and baton strapped to the Sam Brown belt.

Then a woman, braver than the rest, called out to him, "Have they caught the parachutist yet, Sergeant?"

Breaking his stride, Lawlor peered at her. He felt sure he knew this woman.

"Parachutist?" The word sounded foreign, hopelessly exotic on his lips.

"What parachutist?"

The woman came towards him from the shadows. She had a gas-mask case slung about her neck hanging down like an oversized papoose over her army surplus overcoat. The district was awash with khaki clothing, sometimes the petrol blue of the Royal Air Force, although that was harder to come by. There was a flourishing trade in war department property, much of it stolen. The first thing they did was strip away the insignia, then the labels in the lining. The buttons were standard. Couldn't be traced.

Lawlor scrutinised his questioner. She looked decent enough, but this war was doing strange things to people, things which often led to his involvement.

"The German pilot," she continued. "The one who baled out over the Market Square. Is he still at large?"

Lawlor looked at her. "Missus dear," he said gently, for she seemed respectable despite the get-up, not like some of the other riff-raff eyeing him from the shelter of their doorways, "go back to your warm bed." His gaze took in the watchers. Raising his voice, he told her, "This is purely a civil matter. The enemy is not involved. Some shots were fired, certainly, but the emergency is now over and the situation well in hand. Please return to your homes and may I remind you again that the blackout regulations are still in force."

One or two people directing pocket torches at their feet promptly switched them off. A candle flame behind a window pane wavered then went out. The woman in the army greatcoat continued to stand her ground but Lawlor made no attempt to convince her further. Gradually the others began melting off indoors.

Straddling the crown of the roadway, he continued raking them with that policeman's stare of his, the one perfected over the years. What it said was, I know certain facts about all of you, facts which may or may not bring down my displeasure, even chastisement, so have a care. God help him, he had more than a streak of the little tin god in him. Should have been a priest, God help him even more. The stare, of course, was all bluff, pure pretence. The older he became the less he seemed to know about any of these people here, beyond the usual items on the crime sheet, theft, assault or sexual misdemeanour involving under-age girls or, in some remoter parts of his beat, the occasional complaisant farm animal.

He began to walk away, but at the foot of the street someone shouted, "Up the IRA! Heil Hitler!" after him in what he took to be an assumed voice. He didn't even bother turning his head, just carried on towards Jelley's public house and what he expected would be humiliation on a grand scale.

Drawn up in the square outside the Unitarian Church was a US army truck and beside it two jeeps. At least a dozen military policemen in their white helmets, belts and arm-bands, moved about in the glare of undimmed headlamps. For a moment Lawlor felt his disapproval take hold, then he calmed down, knowing how the Yanks rarely bothered with anything they regarded as a purely civilian restriction like a blackout. Theirs was a private war fought from behind the confines of their perimeter base fence. He often suspected they believed no one would dare bomb a little piece of America, even if it was on foreign soil.

He came closer. The MPs ignored him. Some were smoking and, as always, chewing, chewing. Then he saw Quigg's Wolseley with another car which he didn't recog-nise, parked in the shadows.

At that moment Boal came out of the churchyard carrying something white. He approached almost jauntily and grinned at him, his normal greeting.

"What's going on here?" demanded Lawlor. "And what's that you've got in your hand, for Christ's sake?"

"Evidence." He shook the pale sack. It swung slightly as if weighted. "Spent bullet cases. Nine, so far. Want to have a look?"

"Where's Burnside?"

"Inside the pub, I think, with the DI. He wants to see you right away." He meant Quigg. "We told him you were out on night patrol."

"Which I was." As he said it the other eyed him, bold as brass, and too late Lawlor realised he had over-reacted. What he should have done, of course, was not react at all but these two between them somehow always managed to make him feel shifty, even when he had nothing to feel guilty about. Right now, of course, he had plenty on his conscience.

Buttoning up his greatcoat, as casually as he could he enquired, "Has anyone been arrested yet?"

"Not as far as I know. But you'd better ask the DI that. I'm sure he'll want to put you in the picture himself, sergeant."

Lawlor left him at that point still clutching one of Mrs Neeson's best starched Irish linen pillow-cases.

A military policeman was leaning up against the door-jamb of Jelley's pub, a short rifle cradled in his arms. He brought the weapon up and forward, then relaxed his stance when he saw Lawlor's uniform. Lawlor went past him, stooping slightly, for he was well above regulation height like all the men who had come North from the old RIC, farmers' sons, heads as hard as the hickory batons they carried.

Someone had set a Tilley lamp on the bar-counter, its glare reflecting harshly off the whiskey mirrors and bottles lining the back wall. Quigg stood, pipe in mouth, in the centre of the room. Also present was a US army officer and that little gobshite Major Kincaid from Glebe House. There was no sign of Burnside. Lawlor took his cap off and stood stiffly, not quite at attention, but near enough.

"Ah, the wanderer returns," said the DI and Kincaid smiled his foxy smile. He was wearing a rubberised rainproof and a deerstalker sprigged with fishing flies.

"I was out on night patrol," said Lawlor. His face felt hot.

"To be sure. What would the country people do without you, sergeant, making certain farming folk sleep safe in their beds."

Some day, some day, he and the DI were going to have a reckoning. He had dreams about the two of them battling it out, stripped to the waist, man to man, in a quiet spot somewhere with no onlookers. Nothing to be heard in that

64

remote upland place but the sound of blows landing and their grunts as they circled one another. There was a film he had seen once with Victor McLaglen . . .

"The precise sequence of events has still to be determined but what we do know is one person has been killed and another is at death's door in the Cottage Hospital. We have a witness who was inside the bar at the time of the affray." Quigg looked over at the American officer as he spoke.

The officer, a lanky fair-haired man with rimless glasses, said, "Private Percy Laird is still too badly shocked to make a full and detailed statement, but he has informed me the shots came from outside and, almost certainly, from one of our own army-issue carbines. There may well have been other weapons involved because of the number of rounds fired."

For the first time Lawlor saw that the mirrors were badly starred and that there were gaps in the rows of bottles. There was also a strong smell of spilt liquor, rum predominating, for some reason. On the floor lay a heap of bloodstained bedding someone had used to staunch the flow from the wounds of the victims. He imagined the scene, the shooting, the terror and panic, above all, the fresh gore, letter-box red, and felt guilty and sick at being so far away when he should have been the first to arrive.

Kincaid cleared his throat. "Captain Harper," he began in that high, irritating English voice of his, "I'm sure you'll agree with me it would be irresponsible in the extreme to release anything other than the sketchiest of details regarding tonight's dreadful occurrence until we know all the facts. These are trying times and peoples' nerves are at full stretch. Rumours spread like wildfire in a small community like ours and no one wants to fan the blaze any further by letting it be known the bullet or bullets which struck poor Mrs Jelley came from the rifle of a *coloured* soldier."

There was silence in the room except for the hiss of the

Tilley lamp. Lawlor studied his caked boots. The other two stared into space. What they'd just heard seemed to fizz softly like a fuse and, eyes downcast, Lawlor waited for the inevitable detonation. It didn't arrive.

Instead, the American captain mildly replied, "As I've already stated I'd really prefer to interview Private Laird in greater depth and in the proper surroundings, which is back at the base. As regards the other matter you mention, please believe me I'm fully aware of the delicacy of the situation. My own home state happens to be Kentucky, gentlemen." Here he smiled at Kincaid, which Lawlor interpreted as a sign of weakness and which he also knew would be marked down as such.

Kincaid drew a silver flask from his overcoat pocket. "Snort, captain?" he offered, unscrewing the cap. "Not as sweet as your own native bourbon, but good ten-year-old Tullamore, nevertheless."

The captain declined, as did Quigg. Lawlor stood there, barred from the magic circle. The snub was deliberate, he realised, but then, perhaps not, for the Kincaids of this world rarely concerned themselves with such niceties. Still, he did derive a certain amused satisfaction from the fact that the place was coming down with broached bottles. He continued standing clutching his peaked cap, invisible, despite being the biggest person there by far.

Then the Yank officer, captain – the room was bursting with rank and insignia, suddenly it occurred to Lawlor, including Kincaid's own, for he insisted on using that of major despite being non-serving – addressed him directly. "Forgive us, sergeant, for seeming to talk above your head in this awful fashion. Would you care for some one of us to fill you in before we proceed?"

He smiled as said it, his accent soft and courteous, straight out of some film where darkie servants mixed mint juleps and an open carriage containing Vivien Leigh stirred up the gravel in front of one particular white colonial mansion.

But then Quigg butted in, and the rosy picture faded at the sound of those grating North Antrim tones of his. "I'll provide the sergeant here with everything he needs to know on our return to the barracks. Gentlemen, there's nothing more any of us can do here tonight. I'll have the place sealed off for the CID people when they arrive first thing in the morning. Thank you both for getting here so promptly."

Lawlor kept his eyes lowered to the floorboards. There was a ragged stain the size of a smallish hearth rug which looked recent. He realised he had been standing on it ever since he'd arrived.

As he followed Quigg out into the night he heard Kincaid say, "You really must come up to Glebe House and have a spot of supper with us one of these evenings, captain. Which part of the Deep South did you say you hailed from again?"

Across the square in front of Chestnutt's shoe-shop a small crowd had gathered. Some of them looked like the same people he had spoken to in Irish Street earlier. Burnside was talking to them but as soon as he saw the DI he came scooting across, face bright and eager as a juvenile's. "I've told them nothing as you ordered, DI Quigg. Do you want them dispersed? It's the usual riff-raff."

"No, no, they'll soon get sick of catching their death in this chill. Anyway, there's nothing for them to see. However, I would like you and the other constable to stand guard over the premises, front and rear, until CID get here."

Burnside saluted extravagantly, finding time to slide a quick gloating glance in Lawlor's direction. "Anything you say, DI. Only too pleased to be of assistance."

Unable to bear it any longer, Lawlor butted in. "I'd be more than happy to relieve the two constables."

Quigg stared up at the carved star let into the stonework of the Masonic Hall, drawing deeply on his briar. It had one of those little pierced metal lids.

"No," he said, "I don't think that's altogether necessary. Not now. After the horse has bolted why lock the stable door, eh?"

He walked off then towards his motor car parked in the shadow of the church wall. Lawlor was thinking what sport the two Bs were going to have with that tart little morsel. He could just see them, better still, hear them, batting it back and forth across the Day Room once he was out of earshot. Horse, stable, door. Ho, ho, ho . . .

Quigg was already behind the wheel of his Wolseley drawing on a pair of chamois-leather driving gloves by the time he caught up with him. Lawlor slid into the cool, upholstery-scented interior by his side wondering if the smell of drink still lingered on his breath. A button was pressed and their faces were illumined suddenly by a spectrum of coloured bulbs coming alive on the walnut-veneered dashboard.

As they pulled out Lawlor saw that the other car, long, low, with leather straps securing its bonnet, was Kincaid's Alvis. *No worries regarding petrol rationing there*, he thought, unlike poor Francey McKeever forever freewheeling to conserve the precious little juice he had.

Their headlights froze the lounging MPs. One or two saluted but without any real interest or dedication and Quigg muttered something under his breath about "Uncle Sam's gallant fighting men."

The sergeant sat staring straight ahead as the deserted streets of the town, *his town*, he reflected bitterly, *not Quigg's*, were raked by the racing beam of the headlamps. Yet the place looked unreal somehow, much bigger, too, than he had ever imagined it to be. He felt like a stranger arriving at dead of night in a foreign capital. They drove by houses, shops, public buildings he passed almost every day of his life, yet all had that same air of unfamiliarity as though peopled by ghosts who, on waking, would speak a language he couldn't understand. A cat, yellow-eyed and oddly skeletal, crouched, fixed in their glare. It too looked alien, not an Irish cat. For an instant Lawlor thought they were going to run it over but then at the last moment it streaked to the side and vanished.

Quigg held the steering-wheel as though it were alive, a thin, brown, laminated snake, for he was a nervous driver, which seemed uncharacteristic. Lawlor could smell his scent, Sobranie and that shiny stuff he used to to keep his hair in place, moulded to his scalp like a damp bathing-cap. He was wearing a tweed topcoat over his uniform, an ulster, appropriately enough.

This was the closest they had ever been together, travelling, touching like this, and Lawlor could sense disquiet leak through the heavy herringbone against his sleeve. For the first time that evening he felt some semblance of confidence return. His fingers explored the cool complexity of the door-pocket low on his left side. Pleated leather, an elasticated throat, the finest English craftsmanship. A car to be proud of, and Quigg certainly loved his car. He began scratching the polished leather with his thumbnail, furtively, systematically, the way a child might smear nose-pickings on the best furniture out of spite.

In front of the barracks Quigg pulled up carefully as though protecting the tread of his tyres. He switched off the ignition and the Christmas-tree lights on the dash, vivid greens, blues, reds, dimmed, then died with the engine.

Lawlor made a gesture to push open his door, but the other said, "Just a minute," and like that same child of a

69

moment ago he half-believed his secret crime had been discovered.

He sat there feeling intimacy grow. The pale headcloth seemed to glow as though lit from a hidden source. He noted that the lamp in the Day Room window had been moved giving a more diffused, even domestic glow. He felt eager to be back inside, the heavy door barred and bolted against all that had happened out here this long night. And so when the man by his side started raking over those same terrible events yet again, in much more exacting detail for his benefit this time, he only half-listened, resenting every word. Every so often Quigg would suspend his summary, as though waiting for some professional response. After all, both had long trained themselves to appear serious seekers after the truth on the outside, even if now, as in Lawlor's case, they had long since switched off the receiving apparatus within.

Finally Quigg came to the end of his recital. "A truly awful, awful business," he sighed. "A respectable woman gunned down on her own premises by some drunk or deranged darkie."

"More than one," Lawlor corrected mildly.

"Who knows? Anyhow, none of that is our concern, thank God."

"What do you mean?" Suddenly he was involved for the first time and passionately at that.

"What I say. We have no jurisdiction, the regulations are specific." Quigg struck a match, holding the flame to the bowl of his pipe. It gave his face the look of a celluloid villain. He sucked and the flame flattened.

"Sergeant," he said, when the briar was drawing, "I realise you've never been over-concerned with paperwork, but even you must be aware of something called the Visiting Forces Act. You certainly were sent a copy six months ago. All criminal cases involving US forces are to be prosecuted and tried by their own military tribunals according to US law. A reasonably accurate quotation, I believe."

"But Mrs Jelley is one of *our* people. I know her. I've been in her pub."

Quigg looked at him. "I can well imagine you have."

There was silence for a moment broken only by the sound made by the pipe, a soft, liquid, bubbling rush after every fresh draw. Lawlor suddenly saw the stout widow lying there in her life-blood, that same noise coming from her, filling her lungs and throat. This time he managed to open the door properly and a light came on over their bared heads.

"Sergeant," said Quigg, not bothering to detain him this time, "you're not a religious man, are you?"

Lawlor had one foot on the ground, the other in the well of the car. The question coming as it did like that, half of him in, half out, struck him as unfair. Only it wasn't, was it, a question. More a statement of fact. He grunted, hoping that would be sufficient response, and to his relief Quigg thumbed the starter.

Lawlor closed the door on the man and his damn proselytising for he had a half suspicion some sort of conversion attempt might have been intended. Everyone knew the DI was something of a Holy Roller in his off-duty moments.

"Lawlor," he heard his name called out before the car drove off. "Lawlor, leave the Americans to clear up this business in their own way. Make your report by all means, but let that be the end of it. Goodnight."

There was a gospel ribbon pasted across the inside of the back window, just two words, Jesus Saves. Lawlor wondered if it was right and proper to have such a thing on an official car, but then only a lost soul like himself would ever dream of harbouring such a query.

★

The Church of Ireland clock was striking as he entered through the first gate, two clear, frosty-sounding detonations.

The report could wait until morning. Three-quarters of official foolscap should just about do it, the GR embossed in green at its head. But if Quigg imagined that was to be the end of it as far as he was concerned, then he was mistaken, for something had begun to quicken in the sergeant, something unusual for him, something he could only describe as excited anticipation.

FOUR

In the middle of the night the boy awoke in the grip of a bad
dream. Heart thumping, he lay there staring up into
blackness. It was the one about the dead babies again.

Afterwards he could never remember what it was that
frightened him, but he did know it still lurked out there,
ready to sneak back in again like their cat, no matter how
long it took. He tried closing his eyes to tempt it, then
opened them wildly in a fresh spasm of terror in case it
obliged. Bad dreams and cats. Both were like twin nightmares, equally troubling to him.

Either side his sleeping brothers lay under a pile of ancient
overcoats. Once someone told him other people had blankets
heaped on their beds, something called eiderdowns, proper
sheets, too, not hand-made itchy squares with Early Riser
and a fading blackbird still on them from the original flour-
bags.

Above his head a skylight pierced the painted expanse of
sloping boards. He fixed his attention on it knowing exactly
where it was despite the dark, until slowly it surrendered its
outlines. Travelling in his head he moved out through the

single slanted pane to where the Major's woods thrashed and moaned softly. They made an *oh, oh, oh*-ing sound reminding him of a poem he'd had to memorise. "The wind was a torrent of darkness among the gusty trees, the moon was a ghostly galleon tossed among cloudy seas."

Miss Winifred Buick was the teacher who taught him that. She only stayed a short time though, because she'd had a dead baby, the trouble being she wasn't married at the time.

His mother wasn't married. Once a man had called him a wee by-blow after he had caught him trespassing in his garden. He knew what the word meant, wanted to tell his mother, but daren't in case she went marching up to the man. His mother was afraid of no living soul, she liked telling them. The boy wondered if he would ever manage to grow up to be like her instead of dreaming about still-born corpses all the time.

According to the stories she told before bed, whilst making toast on the end of a long fork, they were everywhere, some buried at dead of night, secretly, others just disposed of any old place. That was what he had the nightmares about, tiny bundles turning up unexpectedly, like the time Greer's lint-hole was drained and there they were lying in the *glaur* like so many expired fish.

Yet another time, one had been washed up against the teeth of the floodgates down at the weir. And one was even supposed to have been thrown from the Derry express at Springvale Halt. The thought of it happening when he might easily have been standing there with the Sunday School excursion made him more sleepless than ever. He didn't care to go near the seaside after that, not if something soft and unspeakable in a brown paper parcel was to come whizzing out at him from a carriage window.

Lying in the darkness, hemmed in by the soft, sleeping shapes of young Tom and Eric, he sensed himself stiffen, for

74

he felt certain he had heard something outside, something different from the normal sounds of the demesne on a blowy night. He rose up off the pillow on the points of his elbows. There it came again, some *thing*, some *one*, moving about, circling their house.

He strained to hear better and Tom ground his teeth and muttered something in his sleep. He had nightmares, too, pissing the bed every so often, which felt warm at the time and not so bad, then cold and wet a little later on, which was.

All sorts of terrible things started passing now through the boy's head connected with his dream. He imagined someone with a sack and a spade, someone returning to the scene of the crime, for it was a crime, although his mother never said as much. His mother never judged other people, she said, in case they judged her. His mother was afraid of no man, she also insisted, but right now she was fast asleep downstairs, baby Wilma by her side, and he was up here awake, all that stood in the way of the prowler and his intentions. *Man of the house*, he thought bitterly.

Praying whoever it was might still go away, might even be a product of his imagination, he put his head beneath the overcoats. At least four layers, their combined weight was enough to hold one a prisoner until morning. The baby scent of his brothers filled his nostrils. He could feel their heat, slightly dampish, although he didn't think Tom had wet the bed, at least not yet.

Unable to bear it – that soft trusting innocence was painful as a wound – he surfaced into the cold attic air. Neck craning, he listened until numbness set in. The square of night sky framed by the skylight looked far paler now. Not long before daylight, he calculated, but only half-heartedly, for time was an almost unknown factor in their house, the only clock always either going fast or slow or not at all.

The noise came again. This time there was no mistaking it,

for someone used a swear-word after what sounded like a small collision. The boy pictured whoever it was out there rubbing his head or an ankle and felt a bit better.

He began easing himself away from the clammy embrace of his two brothers.

Tom in his sleep said, "Don't, Spot, don't!" Spot was their cat and Tom was as nervous of him as he was.

Then he felt his leg start to go wet and warm at the same time and he rose up out of the nest of old overcoats faster and more roughly than he had intended. For a moment he was afraid he might have disturbed the two sleepers, but, no, they breathed on regardless, deep in baby dreams.

He began to crawl across the chill oilcloth towards the square let into the floor where the stairs began. Shivering now, for he was wearing an old vest and nothing else, he put his head out over the edge of the opening. The smell of the kitchen came rising up. Burnt toast. For she always seemed to manage it, carried away by her own bedtime stories. He could just make out the faint glow of the fire and and that last log charring slowly away. It must be nice to sleep in the kitchen, he thought, in the warmth.

He pushed his head further out into the void. By craning he could see a dark heap on the floor by the dresser which was Wilma and his mother. He wondered if they would be entwined, and for a moment envied that closeness. Once he was the one to share that narrow old settle-bed. He tried remembering what it must have been like but couldn't any more, a bit like the pictures in dreams that vanished as soon as you woke up, no matter how hard you tried to recapture them, slippery as fish.

The noise came again. The prowler had already circled the house, it occurred to him, was coming around a second time. The thought of blind hands sliding over those outer walls brought his terror to a high pitch. Head foremost, he began slithering down the open stairs into the kitchen as if the prowler might already have found a way in, might just reach up and seize him by his bare legs from below.

There were no banisters to hold on to, just a shallow, stepped descent to the bare chequered tiles below, all of them, Wilma included, adept at swarming up and down, sometimes through, the open treads, agile as monkeys.

When he was halfway he heard someone, the *one*, scratching on the glass of one of the little window-panes either side of the door.

The boy heard a voice whisper his mother's name, "Pearl."

Then, "Pearly," it came a second time, as if he knew her. With his vest up under his arms and his bare bum in the cold he hung there holding on to the worn wood.

When he was younger there had been other men who came calling around the house at night, their voices hoarse, yet soft at the same time. It was after Bob, one of their fathers, went back to Portsmouth with his kitbag on his shoulder that it started. His mother had gone to the police about it and it ceased. Until now, that is.

Propped by the side of the door was an old, battered club and the boy eyed it longingly from where he hung on the stairs, even though he knew he would never be able to bring himself to use it. One of the absent fathers had brought it back from leave. It might even have been cheery Bob with his suntan. For a long time they had all played with it, imagining themselves to be cannibals until they tired of the game. Now it was used to mash the hens' meat. He imagined the rough knobbly feel of it and its sour smell from the Indian corn, that is, if by some miracle, he ever found the courage to wield it.

"Pearl, it's me! Honey, wake up!"

His mother moaned. Then he heard her say, "Who is it?" even though she recognised the voice. They both did.

Reversing himself, on hands and knees he climbed back up the stairs as softly and silently as he had come, as if he had never left his brothers and their bed in the first place.

Something held him back though from creeping straight into that warm nest and it wasn't the thought of dampness leaking from Tom, either. He felt he had to listen unseen, even though it was grown-ups' business he wouldn't understand. It was like storing up information to be sifted at a later date, a lot later, perhaps, even when he was old enough to do things his way and not other peoples' – his mother, he was thinking of – when he really would be the man of the house. One thing for certain he did know, there would be no callers tom-catting about their place in the dead of night, not while he ran things.

Stretched on his stomach, as close to the open trap as he dared, he heard her whisper, "Willie, is that you?" and felt irritated a second time at the stupidity of the question. From the direction of her voice he realised she was now on her feet.

"Wait a minute," she told their unseen visitor and by her tone and the sounds that went with it he knew she was trying to make herself as presentable as possible.

Biting his knuckles at the indignity of it, the betrayal, for where was her consideration for *them*, he closed his eyes to blot out the image of his mother behaving like some hussy half her age. *Hussy*, he whispered in his head, branding her, for it was a terrible word, according to what he'd heard in the school-yard.

He listened to the key turn, then the bolt slide across, and the prowler was in their kitchen. The boy could hear his breathing, hard, catching him as if he'd been running.

"What's happened to you? The state of you. Look at

you," his mother said, seeing something he couldn't. Her voice sounded frightened.

Then she said, "Let's go outside. We don't want to wake the children," and there was a pause followed by the door being closed softly behind them. *We*, he was thinking. The word burned like an iron.

He lay there straining but could hear nothing save silence. Their old Westclox had stopped again. The cold had brought his skin out in bumps but he knew he would have to bear it for as long as it took, whatever it might be.

Then their door creaked a second time and he heard his mother whisper, "I'll wake the boy."

On bare feet he crossed swiftly to the bed, sliding back into the warmth. Briefly Tom murmured something, releasing a hot little trickle against his thigh. He almost welcomed it now. Feigning sleep under the weight of overcoats, he listened until he sensed she was near, her head and shoulders rising up through the opening in the floor.

"Raymond?" came her soft tones. "Are you asleep, pet?"

In his nest of old army clothing the boy decided to punish her. He wondered how long he could hold his breath. Long enough to give her a scare, make her feel guilty.

"Raymond, are you awake?" The voice was in the bedroom now.

It came nearer. "Raymond?" his name sounding close to his buried head. Then he felt a touch on his shoulder through the layers and unable to bear it any longer he came upright to confront her with her treachery. Her face looked white, even in the shadows of the room.

"I need you downstairs," she whispered. "Put on your clothes, there's a good boy." She was holding his jersey and trousers bundled up in her hand.

He didn't say a word, just took them from her, for he was tired of pretending. It seemed to him she wouldn't even have noticed anyway. Then she went to the trap and lowered herself from view.

As he dressed in the semi-darkness he heard them whispering together but the instant he came down they stopped. Willie was crouched by the almost dead fire hugging his knees. He had his head bowed as if in prayer.

"Willie's here," said his mother and he looked at her. There seemed to be no limit to her stupidity this night.

"What's the matter with him?" As he said it the man by the fireplace moaned softly and the boy had a moment of dread that he had brought some deadly disease into their midst. He moved back, distancing himself from possible infection.

Grey dawn was beginning to seep through their narrow pointed windows. Four in all, they looked more like something built to withstand arrows than let in light. There was a date cut into the stone over the door. 1808, it said. But guns were in use then, weren't they?

His mother said, "I want you to stay here till I get back. Look after the house for me," and for the first time he saw she was already dressed for the outdoors, coat and a scarf covering her head, the one with those stupid parrots all over it.

"You're not going to that old dance, are you? Not now." She came close, fingering his cheek, and he smelt that stuff she rubbed into her skin every night. Snowfire.

"No, I'll be back in a wee while. I've got to look after Willie. You like Willie, don't you?"

He glanced at the crouching stranger beside their hearth, and he was a stranger now. He didn't answer.

"Come along, Willie," she said as if to someone his own age and he rose awkwardly.

His uniform was marked, even torn in places, and his cap, he noticed, was gone from its usual resting-place under one shoulder flap. A wet patch spread down the opening of his trousers as if he suffered from Tom's trouble. There was also a strong smell of drink. Something else too, like number two. For a moment Willie looked as if he might fall back down again, but his mother took him by one arm and steadying him began leading him over to the door.

"I'll be straight back. I promise," she said. Then, crossing to the bed in the corner where Wilma still slept, she stripped off the top overcoat and, carrying it, led Willie outside.

After they'd gone the boy stood listening to the silence. The light was growing stronger all the time but had a pale, milky quality he couldn't recognise. It came to him he'd never been up this late, or this early, before. It gave him an eerie feeling to be the only one awake except for those wild creatures whose movements were the opposite of his. For the first time he could make out faint birdsong, but muted, not really into the swing of things yet.

What did she want the old coat for? He tried not to think about it for it was too painful, yet couldn't keep his mind away from those other couples stretched like clinging corpses the length of Paradise Walk, as it was known. Once they'd made their way back in the dark that way and young Tom, trust him, had wanted to know what were they all doing there like that.

"Waiting for the mushrooms to grow," his mother had whispered, hurrying them past.

At the time the boy was as curious as Tom was, as innocent, too, until one day after school it had been explained to him by Wesley McQuillan who was a farmer's son and knew about such things.

They had walked home together taking that same route. Bruised channels marked the grassy ditches from the night before. Like two detectives they poked and sniffed, collecting the silver paper from the cigarette packets and Wrigley's wrappers for school, then Wesley blew up one of the pink balloon things that littered the lane. Back and forth they patted it high in the air between them until it burst on a thistle.

Wesley had told him what the couples were doing together was called *dolling*. The man put his thing into the woman's, he said, the same way their bull did with a cow, only from the front. There was an open invitation to come up to Home Farm to see for himself if he didn't believe him, any time.

Horses were the most interesting by far, said Wesley, a thing on them the size of a man's arm. You had to put it in for them, did he know that? And a boar's peezle revolved like a screw. Round and round and round, white stuff flying. It only took a couple of minutes. On the other hand men and women could keep at it the whole night long. Old Paddy their labouring man had told him that. That's why they lay out here on the man's coat.

The boy's mouth felt very dry suddenly. Padding on bare feet, he crossed to the enamel bucket and drank a mugful of cool well water. It tasted different somehow, not being able to see it in the dark. Then he climbed the stairs and stared down at his sleeping brothers for a good half minute or so. After that he put his boots on, not bothering with the laces. He hurried now, having come to a decision.

In the kitchen he bent over Wilma's flushed face. Little angel-face. Her baby breath had a faint milky smell to it.

At the door he looked back for some missing element, something not right. The silence hummed like somebody holding their breath, waiting for something to happen. He didn't want anything to happen so he went to the clock on the dresser and set it in motion, turning the tiny toy key until it jammed, so its slow, familiar tick would keep the sleepers company until he returned.

Outside the sky showed tatters of pink in the direction of Ussher Greer's place. In between, all around, lay the Major's woods, still now as if their night of abandon had ended. As he stood there Dan their rooster in his wired-in run at the back of the house gave his first proper crow of the day.

The sound jerked him into motion, sending him down the path beyond the old ruined gateposts. Some instinct drove him that way. It was as if he were inside those heads, one dark, one pale, as they travelled deeper into the trees to be alone together and out of sight.

Hurrying along the narrow track padded with pine-needles he prayed he would be mistaken about what he might find when he caught up with them. It was wrong, of course, to spy on people, but it was out of his hands now. He liked the sound of that, *out of his hands*, repeating it silently to himself like a Sunday School text. For the first time it came to him Jesus was watching him up there high above the feathery tops of the trees.

At this point the path started veering off in a gentle curve. The boy knew it well having come this way before. He also knew it broke in two quite soon like a wishbone and he would have to decide which fork to take.

All the trees were identical now, planted in regular formation by the Major for pit-props, starting off as Christmas trees, ending up full-grown firs. Their foliage cut out the sky. It was a part of the plantation he didn't care for much because of its green gloom. Above all, the silence. Birds rarely sang here, nothing else much moved, either, it occurred to him.

Sinking down on the soft piney drifts you could see a long way. He did so now but could discern nothing save an army of tree-trunks marching off to where the Major's land ended and Ussher Greer's began. Somewhere in between, the couple he trailed must have branched off. His instinct told him, *left*, even though it would bring them all close to the big house and the Major's dogs. In places the trodden path was no wider than a rabbit's run. His feet made no sound and he felt safer because of it, with the thought in his head of those liver-and-white hounds making no distinction between a fox and someone the size of himself.

He kept on going until he could see the outline of a mound in the distance, in a place where the trees thinned away to nothing, grass-covered, but much too like a green egg to be natural. It was the old Ice-House, still connected, people said, by a tunnel to the Major's own kitchen.

Something made him proceed more cautiously, slipping from tree to tree as if it had turned into a game of Red Indians. His palms grew sticky from touching the bark.

Then he saw them, his mother and Willie. They were standing in front of the Ice-House. Instantly he dropped flat, then started snaking closer. The smell of pine-needles and resin on his hands made his head swim. About a tree-length away he knew he could go no nearer, even though he wanted to, desperately. Cheek pressed up against the thickest conifer, he lay taking everything in as if the rest of his life depended on it.

Willie and his mother were talking, arguing, it seemed. Face to face they confronted one another. Then a terrible thing happened without warning, more shocking to him in that moment than if he had discovered them lying together on a coat on the bare ground. Willie dropped to his knees in front of his mother, clasping her to him. He was weeping, it seemed to the boy, face upturned, glistening, and in that instant his feelings changed towards the kneeling man, everything previously he had respected or liked vanishing as mist.

His mother stood there letting him hold her in that way.

84

Surely she must pull away, sharing that same contempt. But she didn't. Instead she placed her hand on the top of the soldier's round dark head the way you would with a child, someone like him, her own flesh and blood, and as she did so, seeing it, a feeling of betrayal went through him like a knife.

They stayed in that position, it seemed, for a long time. The boy felt he had seen enough, wanting to creep back the way he'd come but he knew he had to endure this to the end – whatever it was. He saw his mother struggle to raise the kneeling man to his feet. She held him to her, as if supporting someone drunk or sick. Maybe he was, the boy thought, but could feel no sympathy. They took a few steps together then she bent to pick up something from the ground. It was the overcoat. They went towards the mound. Then they disappeared.

Once upon a time a rusty iron gate barred the entrance to the Ice-House but it had fallen off its hinges to lie flat, invisible now, part of the earth itself. The boy felt fearful and protective at the thought of his mother entering that dark, cave-like opening.

On the few occasions he had been drawn this way, from a safe distance he had pitched in a stone or two to test the echoes, spirits, too, maybe, even tease them a little, for people did say the place was haunted. The splash of water could be heard, but there was no way of telling how deep.

Lying there with his bare knees digging into the pine-needles – *like sand, why were they always damp underneath?* – he wondered what to do. He knew he couldn't leave, not yet, even though the children were beginning to bother him.

What if they woke to find themselves abandoned? It was the biggest most secret dread in his entire life, his mother going off leaving them to fend for themselves. How could

85

they? Sometimes she said it, too, when she was angry or joking. Often he couldn't tell which was which.

"If you're not careful I'll just pack my attaché case and go one of these days, you wait and see if I don't," she'd say and then one of them would cry out, "But you haven't got an attaché case!"

"How do *you* know?" she'd say. "*You* don't know everything."

That was what frightened him the most, not knowing things. Like now.

He concentrated on the black hole in the side of the Ice-House trying to imagine what was going on inside that flooded cave. *Bats*, he thought. She must care for Willie Washington an awful lot to get her to go into a place where they hung down like hairy fruit in the dark.

He really hated him now for making his mother do things she didn't want to do. Then a new and greater panic took over. What if they were running away together? What if it was *her* idea, not Willie's?

He pulled himself upright, holding on to the thick oozing trunk. It must have been planted long before the others. Probably about the same time as they built the Ice-House. The Kincaids, that was. He thought of his mother mimicking the Major, performing for them in their kitchen. She was a real turn, his mother. It was up to him to save her from herself, save her from Willie Washington.

Black men had big things, too, Wesley McQuillan had said, that's why the women were mad to go with them. He couldn't imagine it, yet could, in a horrible way, that dark thing putting itself into his mother, that space, that place, between her legs, hairy.

He felt he was about to spew up, then as his mouth filled with spit, she came stooping out of the Ice-House. She stood

86

there blinking, looking about her as if she were in some strange place. No sign of the overcoat.

The boy edged back out of sight, for the tree was twice as thick as he was. He watched as she continued standing there in her maroon coat and scarf that Willie had bought for her. Parrots. Green and blue and yellow. The sight of it, them, made him hate him all the more.

Finally she began to move towards him, back the way they had come and, crouching low like a brave, once more, he sped through the trees, the path showing far lighter now.

He knew she was returning to them, not running away with Willie after all, but there was enough doubt in his mind to tell him that something had changed and for the worse for all of them in their house. He wasn't certain he would be able to control it the way he had managed to do with other things up to now.

Their rooster was crowing for the whole county to hear. He could also hear Ussher Greer's collie Rex rounding up the cows in the big meadow for milking. He wondered if his mother would send them off to Sunday School that day or not.

FIVE

They were sitting around the table, a mound of boiled potatoes bursting out of their skins at its centre, when Tom spotted the face grinning in at them through their single pointed window. "Mammy!" he cried. "Duffy!" and Wilma ran away to hide for she was terrified of the gamekeeper for some reason. Raymond started to rise too, but Pearl stopped him. "Eat your dinner," she commanded.

She was in an anxious, overly protective mood, had been since first rising, the house still and neglected-looking, the children sleeping with that defenceless, just-washed look that always made her insides melt to water. When finally they stirred and gazed around, knuckling their eyes in wonder, it was a joy to behold, for she had been scrubbing, dusting and re-arranging since well before six but, silently, determined not to wake them.

Eric, innocent baby-face, had asked, "Is it Christmas already?" for that was when Auntie McBriar came visiting, she who was house-proud and censorious, inspecting everything. It was because of her spring-cleaning came when it did at a different time from everyone else. But then they weren't like everyone else. This day of all days she wanted to savour that apartness, that feeling of isolation to the full, for it seemed to her it might be the last time they would enjoy it. And because of it she felt angry at the man peering in at them.

"*Stupid horse-faced big glipe*," silently she swore to herself, trying to ignore him, for he might go away if they continued to eat, leaving them in peace. But it was not to be, for he tapped on the diamond-shaped pane, something new and unexpected, and at the sound the three boys raised their heads like startled animals.

"Shite!" she said out loud and went to the door.

He was standing waiting for her as if expecting her to heed his summons all along.

"Well?" she asked. "What is it?" not giving him the satisfaction of addressing him properly. *What sort of a name was Pascal, anyway?* She knew only too well, of course, one of those Fenian saints' names they ransack the calendar for. The idea of it and the sound of it inside her head only inflamed her the more.

He slouched there twisting his cap in his raw red hands, hair plastered down over his scalp like strands of damp hay. It was rare to see a man, any man, with head bare. Willie, it was, who had first pointed that out to her as if it was some form of exotic native custom, like nose-piercing or tattooing, she had always taken for granted.

Willie, she thought, with terror, interpreting the grin on the face in front of her as retribution. *He's come to tell me they've found him.* Worse, they knew of her own part in it. Instinctively she blocked the open door at her back as if protecting the innocents inside from any involvement.

"The Major wants you up at the house. The missus told me to tell you. That's why I'm here. Like this."

The cap was revolving in his grasp like a whirligig. She

could smell him from here, that sour gamey reek she associated with dead vermin, for he liked to decorate the woods and byways with his trophies, magpies, squirrels, crows, weasels – the odd fox and badger, too – which upset the children when they came across one of those little flattened corpses nailed to a tree or the cross-bar of a gate. She suspected he enjoyed the distress it caused.

"Now?" she asked. She was trembling.

"Aye, now," he answered, avoiding her eyes. "As soon as ever you can." Then he said, "They'll be havin' a big soiree this evenin'. The world and his wife. They want you to lend a hand. Help out," and suddenly she was overcome with gratitude, for she heard her tone soften.

"I'll be right there. Tell Mrs Kincaid that."

Then she went inside closing the door on him, for he had delivered his message.

"Raymond," she said, "I'm needed up at Glebe House. Can I trust you to look after things? No fighting or mischief now?"

He looked up at her from his plate, that face of his, old before his time, her little man of the house.

"I'll bring you all back something nice. They're having a great big party." Wilma, who had crept back from her refuge under the stairs, piped up, "When's Willie coming? He promised us he'd bring us more candy."

And, unable to control her tongue, she heard herself say, "The candyman's dead," and they looked at her. It was in jest, of course, a family saying, but it hadn't come out that way, she knew it, they knew it, too. She laughed quickly then, tousling their heads to take the sting away, and then she stripped to her slip to have a quick scrub in the basin on the old marble-topped washstand under the window.

She caught Raymond glancing across at the view but she didn't care, so relieved was she at not being found out.

Anyway, she suspected Duffy had seen her half-clothed on more than a few occasions lately. Certainly she knew he spied on them, skulking out there among the trees like those same creatures he trapped and hung up to rot as a warning to their fellows. It never made any sense to her that. Her belief was Duffy did it because he liked doing it, no other reason. It would be nice to see him flattened out himself, pinned up by the paws on a tree somewhere. As an example to others who might be tempted to come prowling where they weren't wanted.

The thought, the image of it, made her choke as she was drying her face and the children turned to look at her. *Mad mammy*. She could see it in their faces. And not wanting to disappoint her loyal audience she sprinkled them with soapy water until they shrieked, even Raymond, then blessed them with mock religiosity. "In the name of the father, son and holy ghost . . ."

*My poor wee wean*s, she thought, *your own mammy might as well christen you, for no one else ever will, that's for sure.*

To her surprise Duffy was still hanging about outside when she had dressed herself in preparation for her day's labour in the kitchens of the big white house. Glass and silverware, most likely, for Mrs K trusted her with her precious heirlooms. There were crests on the backs of the spoons and the wine and water glasses *pinged* if you snapped them with a fingernail. Old Waterford.

Ignoring the creature who was pretending a close interest in her hen-run, she strode away, dislodging gouts of gravel, but in a matter of moments he was by her side.

Cap in hand and still with that foolish grin on his dial, he panted, "The world and his wife, I hear tell. Even a cabinet minister. And all the big-bug Americans."

She kept her gaze fixed firmly in front of her as if he was invisible, only the smell betraying a presence.

91

"Did youse hear about that poor woman and the niggers?" Her heart beat faster. "Slaughtered in cold blood. In her own pub, too. Just because she refused them drink after hours." He hesitated. "As well as *the other*." There was a smirk in his voice. She could hear it distinctly.

For the first time she looked sideways at him. "Who told you all this?"

"You mean you haven't heard? Sure, it's the talk of the country by now, so it is." His accent seemed to be getting more pronounced. Usually he mumbled, not wishing to draw attention to his origins. This sudden confidence, as if they were familiars, made her despise him the more.

Slowing down, she asked, "Are they caught yet — the ones who done it?"

"So they say. The Major has the full gen. Do youse want me to find out for you? I can ask him if you like."

Heart thudding — could he hear it? — she said, "What would you go and do that for? Why would I be interested? It's the poor woman I'm sorry for."

They were walking along now like a couple out for a stroll together. She hated herself for it.

"Aye, you're right there," he said. "A man can always take care of hisself, but no woman is safe once them darkies get a feed of drink into them. Only the one thing on their minds."

She felt like saying, *and what makes you so different*, for she could sense the lust rising off him like steam off a turd, God forgive her for her foul tongue. The Lord pardon her a second time, maybe she had tortured him on past occasions by behaving brazenly at the window, knowing full well he was out there in heat in some thicket or other.

And then the notion struck home — all that stuff about darkies and what they got up to — *did he know about Willie and herself?* Surely he must have seen them together, for she made no secret of her feelings, had never tried to hide them, him either, for that matter. Until last night. For the first time she thought of that damp, dark underground prison she'd consigned him to, for she had managed somehow to bury the events of the small hours by concentrating on her housework in that crazy driven fashion while the children slept, oblivious of what their mother had done to them. The worst part was she had involved them. It was true. If anything happened to her because of her actions they would suffer too, maybe even more so. Orphans as well as by-blows.

Duffy said, "Mind you, they can't all be bad, can they, now? Any time I've run across one of them they couldn't be nicer."

He left the way open for her to comment further, but feeling she had given away too much as it was she kept her counsel the rest of the way. He wanted desperately to talk and she let him, this strange creature in his boiler-suit glazed with dirt. She tried not to think of what awful things had left their imprint there. Instead she allowed herself to speculate about him and his life, something she had never really ever done before, existing out there all by himself in that terrible old dump of a place at the far end of the estate. It was supposed to be the match of her own cottage, but had been allowed to slide into rack and ruin long before he appeared on the scene. Raymond had told her he slept on the floor surrounded by a million empty bully-beef tins. It merely confirmed her belief that when it came to tidiness Catholics were all the same no matter what part of the country they hailed from.

Not really listening to his babble, she decided it might be wise to encourage him just a little from now on, not to be so hard, so unapproachable. She was thinking of Willie and herself. The fewer enemies on home ground they had the better.

As if in tune with her change of heart he asked, "Could

93

youse be doin' with the odd oul' rabbit or hare now and again? For the pot?"

She smiled her assent. It made her sick, but she did it. There were a lot of unpleasant things she might have to train herself to do from now on in. She told herself that.

They parted by the edge of the semi-circular sweep of white gravel in front of the house. She went left past the two big ornamental urns in the direction of the kitchens at the rear. He should have gone the other way into the woods back to his precious traps, but he didn't, just remained standing there looking after her. She could feel his gaze on her, hot and concentrated, and, God forgive her, didn't she pull her coat forward tight across her backside just to give him a better view of its mechanics in action.

The underground regions of the house where the kitchens, sculleries and pantries had their domain were already bustling with activity. Threading her way through the white-aproned cooks and helpers she went directly to a small room off to the side where the upended glasses were already laid out on a trestle table in readiness for her to wash and polish. There was a sink in the corner with one tap, cold. Hot water came in a kettle from the Aga.

She hung up her cloth coat feeling less self-conscious the moment she saw it hanging there on a hook, for she was ashamed of how cheap and frayed it had become. Willie had promised to buy her a new one for her birthday. Already she had picked out the model she had in mind from McConnell's. Wrap-over. Plum velour. The coupons were a problem but she would just about make the quota in time for the big day. Only three weeks away.

She stood there holding a tumbler, wet and weighty in her grasp, and almost dropped it on the tiled floor at the thought of what she had let herself in for. What would become of them? Would she ever see a birthday with her own children again?

In the far scullery wall was set a heavy, paint-encrusted door, blackened with age. It had never been opened, at least not in her presence, and if there was a key no one in the kitchens seemed to know of its whereabouts. She knew where it led, however, that door, for someone had once told her.

Setting the glass down on its spread cloth she steadied herself against the edge of the table. Behind her she could hear the clatter of cooking, someone whistling, coal being funnelled into the red roaring maw of the Aga and felt removed from that world where no one had any secrets. Taking up the next tumbler from the ranks of glassware – she always left the best pieces to the last – she concentrated on her work, terrified in case her attention might slide off towards that ancient door and what separated her from her secret, lying crouched and shivering there in the darkness at the distant end of its underground passage.

At noon she ate some bread and broth with the others at the great white, furrowed table as big as her own kitchen. There were dumplings in her bowl and she found it hard to swallow those firm bobbing doughy balls. She did her best though, keeping her head down as though intent on nothing save the food in front of her.

The talk, of course, was all about the events of the previous night. Pearl allowed it to pass over, through her, like so much breath-driven air. No matter what she heard, she told herself, she must continue to believe in Willie's version. Luckily the others gathered about the table weren't interested in her or her opinions. She'd always managed to stay clear of local concerns or gossip, at least she thought she had. Having four children with no father hadn't made it easy, but living in that wee salt-box at the end of the avenue away from peoples' prying gaze did help. The discussion around her was now entering a more heated phase. Terrible tales about niggers and darkies and what they would and wouldn't do when drunk, aroused, or both, were being swapped like cigarette cards. She burned inwardly but it was anger tempered by fear, the fear of being found out, past as well as present, for, she marvelled, had they been so secretive in their courtship then? It hardly seemed possible, especially in a community like theirs. For a brief and heady moment there, at that table surrounded by chatterers and the noise of their eating, she actually believed they might have led a charmed life, she and her chocolate soldier-boy flitting through the woods and fields at dusk under a cloak of invisibility.

But it passed quickly, replaced by that old cold dread again. God forgive her, but for another awful moment there she debated whether it mightn't be for the best for everybody concerned, but especially for herself and her little family, if Corporal Willie Washington stayed where he was locked up behind that door in the dark for good.

Later, back in the scullery, she committed the unforgivable, she broke a glass. She watched in horror as it toppled off the edge of the table, so slowly, it seemed to her, oh, so slowly, to shatter on the flagged floor. It was a little liqueur glass, fragile and delicately fluted. At least it had been, for now it lay in a hundred diamond pieces winking up at her. Luckily the clatter in the kitchen behind her was too great for any of the others to notice and quickly she swept up the shards into a dish-cloth then stowed the damp bundle in her coat pocket. There was blood on her finger. It was her punishment, she told herself, that and the breaking of the glass, for thinking all those terrible things about Willie.

★

At two she had finished. Mrs Cupples the cook wanted her to stay on to help lay the table, enough knives, spoons, forks for a coronation, she complained. But she lied, saying wee Wilma was sick, and the fat old woman cluck-clucked, pressing some madeira cake in a paper napkin into her pocket. Thank God it wasn't the one with the broken glass in it. All the way home she felt that other hard, smothered lump nudging her thigh through its layers of cloth.

Halfway down the long, straight avenue she spotted movement, then a scattering of dark-uniformed figures among the trees that lined the route. At least half a dozen, she reckoned, B Specials, and went cold at the thought they might be lying in wait for her.

As she came closer she saw one of them making his water up against one of the Major's precious beeches. He had his back to her but it was obvious what he was doing. He turned his head, grinning at her as she drew level. It was that young Trevor Rolston from Darragh Cross. She kept on walking at the same unhurried pace but inside her heart was thumping. A much older man with three stripes on his arm saluted and said, "Afternoon, miss," and she felt confused at the friendliness of his tone. Still in mid-flow, for she could see the dark, spreading stain of his piss against the bark, Rolston called out, "How're you doin', Pearly?" and the sergeant rebuked him, saying, "Behave yourself. Go behind a tree."

For some reason she faltered at that point for she felt flustered and found herself stupidly staring at the man with his back to her as if the sight was of interest to her. Young Rolston met her gaze and, still grinning, shook himself. At the last possible moment she turned away, sparing herself a glimpse of what he held in his hand, for she felt certain he was quite up to exposing himself.

The lot of them put together, she thought angrily, walking on, as she heard their laughter, loud and concerted now, breaking out at her back. This time the old sergeant made no attempt at a reprimand.

That evening sitting by the fire listening to the wireless, its oblong orange dial shining in the dimness, they made out the sound of an approaching car above "Henry Hall's Guest Night". Before she could stop them the children had rushed outside to stand in a row gaping, as the first in a procession of shiny motors swept past bearing the Major's guests up to the house. She herself stayed over by the window well out of view.

At one point a military staff-car drew level on fat, bursting tyres, an American flag about the size of Raymond's exercise book flying from its bonnet. For some odd reason she expected something larger, grander, somehow, like every-thing else coming out of that wonderful country. In the back seat a silver-haired, red-faced man in uniform rode alone. He had a kindly face, she registered that before his camouflaged car disappeared in a small storm of gravel chips.

The traffic continued for a good half hour at least. It was an exciting event for her little family and she hadn't the heart to order them inside, even though she hated to think of them lined up open-mouthed out there like some gipsy band. But then they *were* badly off, weren't they, why pretend otherwise? Yet often she had done just that, whenever they asked her, "Are we really poor, mammy?"

"Not as poor as some people," she told them.

"*Who? Who?*" they would cry then, even though they'd heard the answer countless times before. Thank heavens for those big-eyed, swollen-bellied waifs far away in Africa, she consoled herself, and those missionary pictures of them in *Daybreak* she could always cite as proof.

Once Raymond had asked, "Are we poorer than Catholics?" and she had lied.

"No, we're not, and never will be. Always you remember that."

He had looked at her as though the evidence of his own two eyes was already beginning to lead him to question her and her judgements.

Standing there with the music from the wireless singing softly in the background, she suddenly hated those rich people speeding past behind rolled-up car windows. She could smell them in her imagination, too, their perfumed fur coats and the cigar reek of the men driving or, being driven, in a lot of cases. None of them gave a thought for her, ever would, she told herself, or her children standing out there in the chill goggling at their exalted progress. But were their own children better-mannered or smarter? They were not, she told herself, with a proud flaring of defiance. Just better dressed, better fed, that's all.

And then she thought of the man who had tried in his own sweet way to remedy that unfair state of affairs with his bounty, the man she had earlier wished had never entered their lives. It was only a tiny lapse, she told herself, but she wept, nevertheless, at her own treachery, seeing him once more lying there curled up in the damp and dirt of a pit, no other description would fit, while at the far end of a passage, the other side of an old door, a bunch of toffs drank and gorged themselves, danced, too, she wouldn't be a bit surprised, under chandeliers like searchlights that made a mockery of any blackout. Willie's blackout was permanent, she told herself, and would remain so unless she did something about it.

It was the first real time she had thought of him by actual name all that long day, as if by not doing so she might somehow make him disappear in some way, lose shape, face, too, but, now, picturing him lying listening to a distant gramophone in the dark and not knowing how or from whence it came, she wept some more.

She made her own blackout arrangements after that, an old army blanket, dyed the appropriate hue, she hung from two nails hammered into the wood at the top of the casement frame. When they saw the sudden blinding of the lamplight from outside, the three of them, they came galloping back in, blowing on their hands and stamping their feet hard on the tiles as though it was mid-winter and not mild October.

"What would happen, mammy, if we didn't put the curtains up?" asked Tom.

But for the life of her she couldn't play her part in that running fantasy of being divebombed by the Luftwaffe just lurking up there above the cloud-cover night after night, in the off-chance that their guard as well as curtain might slip just that one time. An Iron Cross waiting back in Berlin for the first man to spot the glow from their Valor oil-lamp.

Raymond said, "Nobody's interested in our old light anyway. Why would they be? Sure we're out in the back of beyond."

They all looked at him, she, too, for this was a stranger talking, someone who had outgrown their cosy little world of make-believe.

"What's back of beyond?" asked Wilma and she told her, "A quiet, peaceful wee spot where no one ever comes near you or bothers you," and as she said it she had a sudden powerful yearning for just such a paradise, like one of those pictures in Sunday School lit by bright primary colours, populated by carefree young people and their contented elders resting in the shade of palm trees.

Then she said, "Raymond's right, the Germans have more important places to drop their bombs on than old Glebe House." It was her way of keeping in with him for she

100

would need the full extent of his goodwill and co-operation later that night.

Some little while after that she allowed him the privilege of making toast, holding out the pale cut slices to the embers, speared on the prongs of their old bent fork, until they went golden, then black. The smell of charred loaf bread quickly filled the tiny room but she said nothing, just scraped away the sooty crust before spreading on the butter.

When the nine o'clock news was over – Alamein, Alamein, and more Alamein – they settled down to listen to "Saturday Night Theatre", another treat normally denied them. Fortunately it wasn't one of those old plays guaranteed to produce nightmares, but something silly to do with a will and a prize pig set in an English country house. As those cut-glass accents came chiming through the stretched fabric of the speaker from a London none of them in that kitchen could ever visualise except in imagination or from *Picture Post*, she wondered if bombs were presently falling above the actors' heads. She could feel nothing for them, however, not even the population at large beyond the BBC, for they, all of them, spoke in that same way as the Kincaids and their guests did.

They were different from the likes of her and hers, she reminded herself. More important, uncaring, so why should they deserve sympathy from the sort of people who lived in a shoe-box? And what if a stray bomb did happen to whistle down a quarter of a mile away up at the fancy end of that old avenue, what loss would it be to her? A handful of purple-faced old farts in evening dress, a big-shot American, even if he had a nice face, the Minister of Agriculture, no less, or so they said in the kitchens. Why should she care?

God, she thought, *wouldn't those B Specials on guard duty have a collective fit?* All pissing themselves, and not up against some tree either like that young Rolston fellow.

101

At school the teacher told her she had too much imagination for her own good as if it was some sort of disease, probably infectious, by the way that old bitch always kept her in a desk well away from the others. Like nits, she thought, but then everybody had nits then, or ringworm. Maybe she was right, Miss McComb, for even now her head continued to explode with images of falling chandeliers, spilled wine and blood, smoke, flames, screaming pandemonium. And as the radio play she had barely heard a word of rolled towards its pointless conclusion she saw clearer than anything so far Willie's face, even though it was in pitch darkness. He had his hands clapped over his ears as if to blot out the noises in her imagination at the end of that tunnel, and the terror and incomprehension she recognised there purged her brain instantly like a furious jet of icy water.

Long before the closing announcements came the three younger children were in the land of Nod. She rolled Wilma into her bed in the far corner of the kitchen, then she and Raymond hoisted Tom's and Eric's dead weight up the stairs between them to their own sleeping-quarters. Raymond looked at her, then down at the two dark heads lying on the striped ticking. She knew he didn't want to join them, not yet, and she was happy to indulge him for she also knew she depended on him for what she must do.

Downstairs they sat by the fire and she pampered him some more, allowing him to prod and tease the coals with the poker. His eyes shone as he created caverns and palaces of his own devising in the red and white embers. Too much imagination, like his mother.

Reaching out she said softly, "Put a record on. You know. That one Willie got you."

She watched his concentration as he set the turntable spinning, then lowered the ebony disc on to the silver prong.

102

Finally and, most delicately, the needle in its first groove, the scratching terrifying as always, foretaste of something potentially disastrous. He stared down willing it to work and, of course, it did, a miracle each time that couldn't be explained, music arriving out of thin air via a sharpened point of steel. Frank Crumit sang "Abdul, Abulbul Amir", and when he had finished Raymond turned the record over. "The Song Of The Prune."

Across in the bed in the darkened corner of the kitchen Wilma stirred in her sleep, murmuring, "Mammy?" not because of the sound of the gramophone, but because of their laughter. She went over to her then, cradling her, breathing in that sweet milky scent she remembered they all had at that early age.

When the child was fast asleep again she returned to the fire, and he was staring into its heart, deep in thought, the thoughts of someone soon to be mannish and embarrassed by all their present sillinesses together.

"Raymond," she said quickly as though he might grow away from her that very instant like some creature shedding its baby skin and herself along with it. "Raymond, will you do something for me?"

He looked at her. "For Willie, you mean."

"There's nobody else he can turn to. He needs us."

"Are we his only friends?"

"It looks that way."

There was silence for a moment as he took the poker up again, probing a lump of fused slack until it crumpled, then flared anew.

"What did he do?"

"Nothing. That's it. They're blaming him for something he didn't do."

"Where is he?"

"I can't tell you that."

As they sat there, the glow of the fire staining the walls, the low, boarded ceiling, for she had blown out the Valor by this time to save lamp-oil, the first car drove past outside and she wondered if it might be the one carrying the American officer. *Willie's boss,* she thought. The idea of that and his proximity to her, to Willie, caused her to tremble.

"Will you do it?"

"Do what?" There it was, that touch of masculine impatience.

"I've got to go to him. You understand that, you do, don't you?"

"Like the last time?"

"It's only till he gets settled. Till he's safe. You understand?"

He nodded. Then he said, "Mammy . . ." and she felt relieved, hearing the old childish dependency back in his voice once more.

"What is it, pet?"

"You're not going to leave us, are you? Run away with Willie."

She squeezed him to her. "Of course I'm not. I'd never, ever do such a thing. Never, ever, ever," and after each fresh expression of the word her grip tightened until she felt she might crush him, so overwhelming were her feelings for this child crouched at the hearth like someone unfairly aged beyond his years.

After that they sat staring into the grate in silence for a long while watching the fire decay in upon itself.

Another car went past, then another. She wished she'd counted them the first time around for she knew she wouldn't be able to act, not properly, until the last one had left. Raymond seemed to know it too. His head began to droop with sleep, but he would shake himself each time it occurred. She pretended she hadn't noticed. She knew he was staying awake for her sake.

At a quarter to twelve when there had been no sound of an engine for a long while she rose and went into the scullery. She lit a candle and by its glimmer began filling an old flour bag she'd been saving for a pillow case with as much food as they could spare, a loaf of baker's bread, two tins of Spam from the army base, half a dozen eggs she wrapped individually like china in newspaper, and, as an afterthought, an apple and a Paris bun. Then she put in a knife, a spoon and a tin-opener, even though the Spam had its own little key pressed flat against the lid.

Holding up the candle she looked about her to see if there was some other essential she might have missed but her brain refused to co-operate. The feel of the weighted bag in her grasp had finally brought it home to her just how perilous a course she had committed herself to.

Standing there with the chill of the linoleum biting through her slippers suddenly she thought, *I'm depriving my own children*, even though she knew they would never have to do without, never, she would always see to that, but she thought it anyway and the idea wouldn't go away, as if there was some other much deeper betrayal involved in what she was doing. At the last minute, for she must act quickly before any fresh guilt attached itself, she grabbed up an old saucepan and thrust that too deep into the flour bag.

When she came back into the kitchen again Raymond's head had finally fallen low on his breast. His eyes were closed. She halted a moment to study him as though it might be the last chance she would get.

Then, "Raymond, Raymond, honey, I'm ready to go," and he awoke suddenly, startlingly, glaring at her and the bulging sack in her hand. *Father Christmas*, she thought. If only it were.

"You can go up to bed now, pet. I'll put the fire-guard on," for she had a horror of unattended fires, they all did, ever since poor Brian perished in that terrible way. He watched as she fitted the meshed cover over the open mouth of the grate.

"I won't be long," she told him. "I'll be back before you know it."

She took her coat down from the row of pegs on the inside of the door and then, with her back turned quickly, she bundled up another old rag of a thing hanging there and thrust it too into the flour bag. It was the one she fed the hens in when it was raining but for some reason she didn't want him to see her take it out of the house to give to Willie.

"Off to bed now," she commanded and he began the ascent of what they grandly called the stairs. Glorified ladder, more like. For a good minute and a half she waited after he disappeared into the dark mouth of the upper loft, listening to the sounds of the sleeping house and not wanting to leave its cosy familiarity or those who remained inside defenceless and alone. But she knew she must go through with it, must, so, with the bulging sack gripped by its neck, silently she raised the latch and stepped out into the night.

At first the shock of the blackness paralysed her. She thought of their old carbide bicycle lamp on its shelf in the scullery but told herself it must remain there. The last thing needed was a bobbing light among the Major's trees. The squad of Bs she'd encountered earlier might still be deployed where she'd left them. Target practice, with her as bulls-eye, for that lot would be like a dream come true.

The demesne at dead of night was a new and terrifying experience. Suddenly she was in alien territory where invisible creatures lay listening to her clumsy passage, or studied her with eyes that could see what she could not. High overhead a low wind sighed among branches outlined against a sky peppered with stars, but not enough of them to light her way. At first she moved like a blind person holding the flour bag out ahead of her like a buffer. Its whiteness worried her but after a time, as the remembered path started opening up before her, she let it fall by her side, relying on her strengthening sight to make her way towards the Ice-House.

Her spirits rose once she glimpsed its swelling presence. Conveniently the woodland thinned out at that point and she halted for a moment, lowering the sack to the ground. Here it was, first stage of her mission completed. If she took things one step at a time, she told herself, without panic, neither looking back nor forward in fear, she had a fair chance of success.

She moved forward. Her old plimsolls, Raymond's cast-offs, made no sound on the compacted earth. The closer she got to that opening ahead of her, like a solitary closed eye in a great head, the more carefully she picked her steps. She laid the flour bag by the base of a tree-trunk so her approach might be even more deliberate, for that terror-stricken face had started forming in her head again, turning from side to side as if to catch each sound, imagined or otherwise. She was determined not to add her own, not until she was near enough to call his name.

Finally she was at the low arched entrance. It looked even more forbidding at midnight, not fit for the shelter of an animal, let alone a human. Leaning forward, she caught a whiff of the damp rotting smell that came from the interior.

"Willie," she whispered into the blackness, "are you there?" as if there could be any doubt. And then, "It's me, Pearl." Another stupid statement.

She listened and her heart smote her. What if something terrible had happened during the time she'd left him there? Gassed? Drowned? Perished from the chill? Worse, what if he had engineered it himself, for never had she seen anyone as desperate as he was when she'd turned her back on him the previous night.

"Willie." This time her voice was stronger, carrying, and her courage was rewarded for suddenly she caught a glimpse of light back in the depths of that awful place and she saw it was his lighter, the one he was so proud of. Nippo, Hippo, some such funny name.

He held it close to his face so she could see him, but it didn't look like him, for his skin glistened oddly, like wet slate. Both of them were crouching low like cripples as though they might lose sight of one another, then he reached the entrance and in that same moment they straightened up and embraced in the open. She was crying, she couldn't help it, and his cheeks were wet with something other than sweat as well.

"We must go, we must hurry," she told him after they'd stopped hugging and shaking, carrying on like long-lost lovers. But she could still smell that terrible place on him, rank, rotten like Duffy, it struck her, and even so she made him go back in again to fetch the old coat she'd given him to cover himself the night before. He looked at her.

"You must," she told him, "you have to. Somebody might find it."

Her coat, she was thinking, and again she was overcome with fear, fear of what she was letting herself in for, her and those four sleeping babes in the house where the trees ended.

Then he ducked and went back inside again and she waited for him with the filled flour bag ready in her hand.

He emerged pawing at his face. *Cobwebs*, she thought. The place must be thick with them, hanging like gauze, filthy things. Her old overcoat was bundled up in his other hand as if he hated it, never wanted to see it, touch it again, soiled forever in his mind because of where it had been.

"Come," she said, "follow me. I know a place where no one will find you. Where no one ever goes. Where you'll be safe," and she set off, taking a different route from the one that led her there.

He kept stumbling and bumping into things as if his eyesight had been impaired by being in the dark so long, but she kept on closing her ears to the sounds of his distress. She felt a fierce pride in herself and her ability to traverse the dark woods like this. God forgive her, it made her harden her heart against the clumsy creature blundering along like some weary, accident-prone bear in her shadow.

They came to a place where the trees ended. Ahead she could make out an expanse of open fields and beyond that the gleam of running water. Slowing down, for she was nervous about taking this particular short cut, she held up her hand and he almost bumped into her, his breathing laboured like an old man's.

"We must cross the river," she told him. "It'll save us a lot of time," and then, as an afterthought, "Don't worry, it's not deep," as if to a child. They moved forward together, two insects creeping across a plate, and just as vulnerable, too, she decided, her eyes darting from side to side, hearing painfully attuned for a shout at any moment, but they reached the near bank safely and she bent to pull off her shoes. He stood watching her as she did so, and then as she rolled her skirts to the thigh, tucking them into the elastic of her knickers. When she straightened up, presenting him with her new appearance, he still hadn't moved, just continued to stare dumbly at her as if waiting for her to do the same for him.

"Come," she said, stepping into the stream. His shoes and trousers were his own concern, she told herself. Anyway,

109

they looked ruined beyond redemption. Strange, but she could barely remember him as that spruce, sweetly smelling soldier-boy before those awful events of the previous night had turned him into a scarecrow in stained khaki.

The icy current striking her bare ankles made her gasp, the pebbles in the bed of the stream shifting under her. Quickly the level rose to her knees and beyond, despite what she thought she remembered. She could hear him splashing in her wake, lifting and lowering his great planks of shoes as if it wasn't water in them but molten lead. His teeth were chattering now as well, but she couldn't look back, couldn't bring herself to do it.

At the farther bank she continued wading downstream close to the overhang until she found a place where it was easy for them to climb out. She waited on the grassy bank until he joined her, scrambling ashore like someone from a shipwreck. *Will he make it*, she considered, marvelling at her own detachment. Then, most worrying of all, *did she care any longer?*

"Not far now," she told him and began heading across the far field towards a fringe of alders before he could catch breath or, what she dreaded most, ask questions of her. Once she got into those trees, she convinced herself, explanations wouldn't be necessary, for then he would remember and realise where it was she was taking him and a burden would fall away from her.

They entered the ragged little plantation. The soil here was poor, for it was strewn with drift and stones washed up over the ages by the waters of the great Lough. She could see it clearly now, flat and vast like a tin shield, spreading out from the shore, a sea, an inland sea, their very own Caspian, landlocked, too, and at night like this every bit as mysterious in her mind as that Russian version.

Once she had taken him out on its broad expanse, this

man grunting unhappily at her heels, an excursion, just the two of them, rowing all the way to the island and back on a lovely calm summer's day. He had tried his hand at the oars but couldn't get the hang of it no matter how hard he tried. She'd found that incredible, that he couldn't seem to synchronise the pulling power of his own two arms, such brawny arms, too, for he had stripped to his olive-green singlet the better to play the man's role.

Finally he'd given up, sitting in the stern, a cigar between his teeth, watching her pull and lift, pull and lift. It was her father who had taught her how to handle a boat when he was fishing for pollan on summer evenings.

Willie had laughed as if it was all one enormous joke and she loved him for that for any other man would have been badly put out, his day ruined. But that was another time and he wasn't her laughing joking Willie any more. No cigars for him. She wondered suddenly how long his cigarettes would last him where he was going. An image of him eking out his dwindling supply one by one, counting them over and over again as if they might have increased by some magic power in the darkness of the packet, brought home to her the realities of just what lay ahead.

He said, "Pearly, honey," first words he had spoken so far and she jumped.

"What are we doin' here, honey?"

He was looking around him as if he'd landed up on the moon. He ran his dark hands over his ruined clothes as if they didn't belong to him, but to someone else, someone who had taken over his life.

She came up close, pressing her palms to both his cheeks, to hold his attention, get her message through once and for all.

"Willie," she said, "I'm taking you to the island, *our* island. Remember the day we had the picnic? The goats? The row-

111

boat?" But his eyes looked past her, hurt and uncompre-
hending.

She tried again as if with a backward pupil. "No one ever
goes there. You'll be safe. Until we know what to do with
you. Do you understand?"

Then he said, "What you got in the sack?" and it came to
her she would have to go on doing everything by herself,
expecting little in the way of help from this quarter, for the
question made no sense. From the way he said it he might
just as well have asked, *what's my name*, or even, *what's yours?*

Making no reply she went forward to where a low hut lay
in the shelter of the alder bushes like a beached wreck. Inside
its rotten frame was the boat they had taken out that day. No
one else ever came near it, or the place either, for when her
father died his old craft stayed neglected and forgotten,
locked away in the darkness of its corrugated-tin and timber
shed. But she had a key, the only key, and now it went into
the padlock, turning easily, and after that she dragged open
the door, letting in the night air. It sagged low on its hinges
digging a semi-circle deep in the dirt. Soil mixed with sand.

And she stopped dead at that point, for what came next
couldn't be achieved by one person on their own. Willie was
standing where she'd left him, staring down at the flour sack
on the ground at his feet as if intent on getting to the heart of
its secrets. She called him by name once and slowly he
brought his great dark head up and around.

"Willie," she called out, and then a second time. "I need
you, Willie," and at that he seemed to emerge from a deep
sleep and came towards her.

"Help me," she said.

The floor of the shed was ankle-deep in sand. It continued
in that fashion all the way to the lapping water's edge, a
connecting pale ribbon of grey shingle along which the boat
could be made to slide prow first.

They began hauling it out together, all Willie's strength miraculously reasserting itself. He grunted and strained and she stood aside to give him room, his backside pushing hard against the tight covering of his khaki trousers. He was ample in that department, something she had always admired, though never in other men. His was firm, twin mounds of muscle, smooth and hairless, too, and as she studied him, to her surprise and shame, she kept remembering their love-making that day on the island, lying together under the sky wrapped in his greatcoat. Desire momentarily caused a little warm knot to unclench in the pit of her stomach before she went back into the shed again.

When she returned, dragging both oars, all lustful thoughts of Willie's thrusting bare buttocks had flown, for back there in the musty-smelling dark she'd been terrified of putting her hand on a rat. They were there, she could sense it, although what they lived on in such an uninhabited hole of a place was a mystery. She wondered if there might be rats on the island. She knew they could swim, for she had seen them often enough, their matted pelts forging along the underhang of the river bank like sleek torpedoes.

By now Willie had the boat in the water, stern directly facing her. A name used to be painted there, *Eliza*, in blue, her grandmother's name. Time and weather had erased it totally, or maybe the old Victorian pigments weren't of the durable variety.

Willie held the boat steady while she clambered in. She settled herself on the thwarts and fitted the oars down snugly on their iron pins. The grips felt solid, smooth and reassuring under her palms as if she'd never been away.

"Get in," she ordered, then remembering the flour sack lying on the shore, called out, "The bag. Bring the bag," and he let go the stern and she floated away a foot or so, bobbing gently on the calm silver-grey waters.

113

She smelt the odour of lake water, earthy and blood-warm, somehow, comforting, in her case, for she'd never felt relaxed with the sea or its renowned bracing qualities. Buoyed up there by the gentle rise and fall she felt content for the very first time, at ease, in her element, for she considered the Lough to be her ally and friend.

Then Willie arrived, spoiling the spell, tossing the bag in ahead of himself. His great weight sank the stern of the boat to within half a foot of the surface and then she dug in the oars heading out into deep water. Willie sat facing her as she pulled on the smooth wooden handles. They had been oiled by her father's sweat, now hers. She thought of Raymond coming next in line, and then she thought of all of them asleep together back there beyond Ussher Greer's fields, his river, and then the woods on the far side of that.

Crouched four feet away Willie seemed to be staring right through her as if already he could see their destination and what lay in store for him, lonely as a leper in that empty place.

She remembered what she'd said earlier that day in her fit of tiredness. "The candyman is dead." It had come out of her like a puff of air, unthinking as a breath, unkind, too, but now as she looked into those lifeless eyes in front of her she wondered whether she might have been right the first time.

Pull, she commanded herself, *pull*, and the water hissed past either side of her, silver, snakelike, in the light of a hunter's moon.

SIX

The widow Jelley's funeral took place the following Wednesday, early closing day, but the town's business-folk would have shut up shop anyway not just as a mark of respect, though many disapproved of the deceased woman's trade, but because of the nature and circumstances of her death. Lawlor had rarely seen a bigger turn-out.

A light rain was falling as he stood alone outside the barracks waiting for the glittering snout of the cortège to creep his way. His greatcoat shone with its freight of fine mist. His chinstrap chafed his freshly shaved jowls. At some point he knew he would have to insert himself into the slowly moving stream of mourners but found himself more than a trifle anxious about it for some reason, as though timing might be crucial.

Although he hadn't had a proper drink, not since the night of the shooting, anyway, his nerves still weren't all that reliable. Razor nicks stung like the very devil and a tic kept jumping in his left eyelid like some tiny invisible worm.

He could see the coffin plainly now, floating towards him behind the hearse, borne by four men clasping the damp shoulders of one another's overcoats under the polished wood of its base. Then, at intervals, another quartet of bearers would take their place. Marching behind came a solid phalanx of relatives and neighbours ready to come forward. Dickey the undertaker, in his top-hat and shin-length crombie, marshalled them into position, selecting men of similar height and build.

He accomplished it faultlessly with little pats and whispers as though imparting something personal to each man singled out. Watching him oil the proceedings Lawlor experienced a fresh dart of anxiety, wondering if he would be expected to take a "lift" himself, and, if so, who would Dickey find to pair him with. He saw one man, a red-faced rural type, near the tail of the procession, reasonably close in stature and weight. Fixing his gaze on him as if they might have an affinity already, he could feel the damp penetrate his woollen pelt.

Why did it always rain at funerals in this benighted part of the world, he asked himself. Men and headstones soaking in the wet. Not all that easy telling them apart in some of these country graveyards he had attended. Enduring everything a harsh Maker cared to throw at them. Stiff-backed. Stiff-necked. Protestant. He wondered if Father Driscoll would turn out or not, then spotted his mottled dome bobbing in the stream of uncovered heads.

Other faces and figures swam into recognition now, townspeople he encountered on an almost daily basis, yet he had to concentrate hard, for their dark clothing wrapped them in a uniform of conformity. Faces, too, shared that same stern solidarity. The word *mob* came to mind for some unaccountable reason.

Only three motor cars in the entire procession because of the petrol shortage, Dickey's long, six-cylinder hearse, and behind that, Kincaid's Alvis, followed by DI Quigg's

Wolseley. Exhaust pipes fuming in the cold, they purred along on plumped-out tyres, punctuating the stream of mourners.

Kincaid had a single passenger, some representative of the American brass, while Quigg carried two city CID men, both wearing bowler hats as if they knew no better. Separating the cars slow-marched a squad of B Specials, Kincaid being Area Commandant, while trailing the police car came six American MPs, all white, for obvious reasons.

The procession curved around the Courthouse then past the Scout Hall, Carnegie Library, Church of Ireland, Masonic Hall. A flag flew at half mast from its upper storey.

Lawlor held himself upright, constrained by his uniform. The Sam Brown belt needed letting out another notch. Every year a fresh perforation, sometimes more. Bicycling merely kept the lower half in shape, if that was the right expression. Legs of a twenty-year-old. He caught himself smiling at the absurdity of it, that secret safely hidden under the trouser serge and wool of the combinations. For a brief irreverent moment on the wet pavement there he thought of sex, but couldn't fasten on a single woman in the town, townland even, to imagine having it with.

Finally the hearse came purring past. Idly he wondered if Dickey poured all that privileged petrol allocation of his into its thirsty tank and nowhere else. His driver stared straight ahead as though carved, Bobby Fawcett, a taciturn individual to the point of almost being as mute as his cargoes. His wife, they said, was a sure thing. *Open all hours*, as he once overheard Burnside so elegantly phrase it.

The coffin followed, french-polished, brass-handled and railed, certainly not Utility. People stinted themselves the best part of a lifetime so they could have a proper send-off when the time came. He wondered if he should make an appearance at the house later. All that boiled ham and

117

fruitcake. Drink, too. The two Bs would certainly be there. Try and stop them.

Kincaid's tourer slid up, that pillar-of-the-establishment face of his, stern profile of the county's next Unionist MP – he hoped. Beside him the stout, crop-haired American from the base, Colonel something-or-other, one of those foreign-sounding names ending in *stein* or *eyer*. He really should know it by now, but it stayed buried like so many of the other signatures piled up in triplicate on his desk. He wondered how much longer he could get away with things. *Things*.

Then Quigg, nemesis, drew abreast. He looked out at him as if measuring him up for a suit of civvies already. As soon as the car had passed, two round hard hats like cannon balls filling the rear window, Lawlor fell into step with the remaining mourners, staying on the pavement, though. He felt the compromise was the proper one, apart, yet seen to be paying his respects. The strolling men on his left kept their eyes fixed straight ahead of them. He might as well have been invisible.

They proceeded along Irish Street, women and children gaping like natives from doorways. The few males to be seen stood frozen, the older ones with doffed caps, and Lawlor felt his neck hair bristle passing those closed faces.

Last time a procession had taken this route it had been stoned for being an Orange one. He'd had to draw his baton, charging clumsily and ineffectually alongside the others in the small squad of reinforcements Quigg had supplied. A woman had spat full in his face, a surprising salvo of spittle from such an old bitch. It had stung like acid, he recalled, but only because of the state he was in. The urge to crack skulls on a random basis had been a hard one to restrain.

Back in the barracks he'd produced a bottle of Redbreast, sharing it with Boal and Burnside. They were as elated as he was, longing to repeat the performance, only this time dishing out some proper medicine to those Fenian bastards with the benefits of hindsight. For the first time in an age they were united, toasting themselves before the blaze of the Day Room fire, Lawlor remembering an earlier period in his life and similar bravado, while putting out of mind that other horror of being trapped and outnumbered by certain of the same breed, only equipped on that occasion with weapons stolen from his own armoury.

Now as he marched past he stared them out, at least the ones who had the temerity to stare back. *Prevail or be prevailed upon*, he thought. Sometimes it was hard being on the qui vive all the time, the exception being, of course, those nights spent in McKeever's pub back-kitchen. He looked ahead towards the pale canvas hood of Kincaid's car. He wondered if he had that little silver flask in the glove compartment to keep the cold out.

They walked behind the coffin all the way to the graveyard, a good two miles from the place where the dead woman had lived and breathed her last. Normally the hearse would have been pressed into service for part of the route but Lawlor suspected Dickey had decided, or been given orders, to make this funeral as impressive as possible. People would continue to talk about it and the big turn-out long after the worms got down to the more serious side of their business.

The old Dissenters' burial-ground was where the Jelleys had their family plot, some of the headstones with dates going back into the early seventeen hundreds. Many were embedded in the earth like oblong paving slabs. Between overgrown banks the cortège wound its way uphill, the pallbearers slipping in the mire, Dickey frantically jigging around

119

the tilted prow of the coffin. You could tell he wasn't too pleased about this part of the final journey.

Lawlor broke away from the slithering mob, scaling a grassy incline to where a solitary yew bulged on the skyline. As he went toiling up the slope glances were flung in his direction but he didn't care, his uniform affording him the privilege of an outsider. Sometimes it worked that way. For, instead of against.

Catching his breath he stood with his back to the spreading bulk of the poison tree, moisture beading its dense foliage. He studied the ritual taking place below as if it were as outlandish as something in a cinema travelogue, despite having witnessed it a hundred times before, the minister's white bands fluttering in the breeze as he droned on soundlessly, Dickey at his side, protective of the purple-draped coffin on its folding stand, the grave-diggers, bare-headed for the moment, leaning on shovels. The crowd fanned out from the open grave as if drawn, yet repelled, at the same time, by the gaping hole.

High on his knoll Lawlor observed and made notes, as detached from the scene as the tree at his back. He almost fancied himself invisible, his greatcoat blending into the almost identical shading of its leaves. Despite the mass of black below he was able to identify individuals, faces. Quigg and his two city detectives – a comic double-act, he decided – Kincaid on a shooting-stick, people usually to be found behind shop and bank counters, the various worthies of the town's golf and Rotary clubs, and then the rest, keeping their place and distance. His dealings were with them and he wondered if they recognised that fact even if they were camouflaged in their Sunday best and at a funeral. His presence would be a reminder, he told himself. Sometimes he permitted himself mean little pleasures of that order. It was one of the few satisfactions of the job.

But his gaze kept circling back to Kincaid propped on his single sharpened steel peg. A space had been cleared for him among all those standing men – even the American officer had moved apart to be with his white-helmeted squad of MPs – as if some unseen force emanated from that slight figure. He was wearing his usual, raincoat rubberised against the weather, soft brown paddy hat, riding-boots, a black tie the only concession to the occasion.

Lawlor stared at him willing him to look up and meet his gaze. It was a childish desire for some sort of recognition on his part, perhaps retribution, and had a lot to do with something that had taken place two days earlier.

This was the way it had come about.

Sunday, he had the barracks to himself, for it was the unspoken agreement that Boal and Burnside should spend the day with relatives, or wherever it was they took themselves off to. He never enquired, and neither did they proffer any information on the subject, which suited all three.

Roaming the emptied quarters, restless, but pleasantly so – at first – he regained possession, the only sound that of the wind-up clock on the Day Room wall, or the scratch of pen on paper when he added his final comments to the week's reports. It gave him the feeling of what it must be like being in a foreign embassy somewhere while outside the natives went about their religious rituals. Bells would peal at intervals, but not for him.

All that day he moved about from echoing room to room with an agitation much greater than usual. The fatal shooting and its consequences kept creeping back like a nagging but unplaceable ache. In spite of what Quigg had told him – ordered him – about not getting involved, he continued to take it personally. He tried re-enacting the crime in his head but details of a visual nature refused to surface. Something strange seemed to be happening, for he found even the victim's face remained a blur despite having seen it in life, oh, countless times. Widow, childless, overweight. He repeated the words to himself as if they might release some corresponding image.

He slid out the electoral roll from its dusty recess – Mrs Neeson the housekeeper wasn't worth the money they paid her – and opened up the heavy olive-green covers. With his thumbnail he ran down the list of voters who had business properties in the town. Many also had the privilege of marking their ballot papers at least three times just so the poor, who happened mainly to be Catholics, stayed in their place where they belonged at the foot of the voting ladder. No one he'd ever come across seemed to question the practice, at least not openly, himself included.

But, then, why should he? The "other sort", as they were usually referred to, would burn him out as soon as look at him. In the past it had already happened to him once, in another place, because of the uniform on his back. Everything stripped away, job, home, pension, a marriage, too, in his case, because of a terror campaign directed against the so-called forces of the crown.

Facing him as he pored over the thick ruled pages, as though reminding him who was responsible, was a tinted portrait of the new king, standard issue on a thousand walls the length and breadth of the country. That shy face, a shade too boyish for its own good, smiled down on him as oblivious and uncaring of his existence as Lawlor was of his.

He found her name. Jelley. Abigail. Publican. 23 Scotch Street. How often had she taken advantage of her voting rights, he wondered. Not a lot, he suspected, not after her old man passed away, knowing her place. And she didn't appear in public, being awkward in her girth. Wore tennis

122

shoes winter and summer. Yet still he couldn't fit a face to her. Not for the life of him. He opened up the day-book at the most recent entry.

"Proceeded to Jelley's licensed premises on DI Quigg's orders," he read in Boal's backward sloping hand. The hand of a sexual deviant yet to be caught, he had often concluded. Liked to spy on courting couples. Could barely contain his ardour these nights when the ditches were alive with locals groaning under their own personal army of occupation. How did it go – Utility knickers, one yank and they're off?

"Inside the premises where the shooting occurred, one casualty, male, American personnel, already deceased, and lying nearby one civilian, female, also shot. Doctor Delargy of the Cottage Hospital attending to her. Also present was a Captain Harper of the US army, DI Quigg and Major Cyril Kincaid. Constable Burnside was ordered to remain at the rear of the premises while I was instructed to go to the First Unitarian graveyard opposite to collect evidence, namely a number of spent bullet cases. This I proceeded to do. Shortly after, at 11.45 p.m., a US staff car arrived and conveyed Mrs Jelley to the Cottage Hospital. The body of the dead soldier was then taken away to the army base a few minutes later. At 12.10 approximately Sergeant Lawlor arrived at the scene from night patrol."

Flushed, flootered and flustered, as per usual. Had obviously been drinking at that wee pub he goes to out in the back of beyond he thinks nobody knows about. A right rebel kip, if ever there was one. McKeever's. Some of these fine nights somebody's going to put a bullet in him, sure as fate. Too drunk to even notice, by all accounts. Only a matter of time before he gets his walking papers back to wherever he came from. Good riddance, too. DI Quigg has his eye on him . . . He stared down at the ruled blank page wondering how it would be if reports were really like that and not the usual evasive guff. Taking up the pen he dipped it into the green glass inkwell.

"Premises were sealed at 12.57 a.m." he wrote, "and Constables Boal and Burnside placed on guard pending the arrival of CID in the morning. Proceeded back to barracks. Informed by DI Quigg that US Military Intelligence would be handling all aspects of the incident from this point on. Case therefore closed." He initialled it DL, adding the time and date.

The rest of the afternoon he listened to Radio Eireann keeping it murmuring dreamily in the background, the lighted valves in the old Cossor Monarch glowing dimly through the taut fabric of its speaker. A play about the death of Wolfe Tone, then Hospitals Requests. He switched it off when a hurling commentary came on. Carlow versus Offaly.

Music was what he liked best, operetta, Lehar, Strauss, a bit of Puccini, that sort of thing. Late at night often he would tune in upstairs on the other set but, softly, so only he could hear those high Italian tenors, reedy thin, yet all fleshy, big-girthed men according to their photographs. As a treat sometimes the voice of John McCormack would arrive pure as a mountain stream warbling over the airwaves from Athlone, the sleeping heart of Ireland. What used to be *his* Ireland.

Now he found himself tuning in surreptitiously like some fifth columnist, even though everyone else listened openly, even to Lord Haw Haw when he made his evening broadcasts. "*Jairmany calling . . . Jairmany calling . . .*" He could well imagine what certain people would say if ever they overheard those snooty, sneering tones coming from behind his bedroom door.

Then, sometimes, he thought, *why not give them something to talk about if that was what they wanted to believe.* Most of them had tried and sentenced him already as some sort of a quisling in their midst long ago. He cheered up then, quite liking the idea of being a spy, even though he was in the pay of no power other than that of His Brittanic Majesty as represented by the man in the naval uniform watching him from the Day Room wall.

Love. He would do it for love. Better still. Revenge. Retribution for all those mean little small-town slights directed at him over the years.

Humming the chorus from *The White Horse Inn* he sat himself down in the Windsor chair and, with the old tartan rug he used for the purpose spread across his knees, he settled into polishing the buttons of his uniform, buffing them until they shone bright as cats' eyes in the lamplight.

Some time after that he must have dozed off for the next thing he heard was the sound of the two Bs' returning boots on the flagged hallway. They caught him like that there in his semmit with the Silvo tin overturned and trailing a snail's track on the floor at his feet. Burnside had a tiny blue flower tucked into the band of his cap and looked a little tipsy, if he didn't know after all this time he was firmly teetotal. Boal was grinning as if he, too, had made a day of it. "Will I put the kettle on, sarge?" he enquired cheerily. Lawlor hated being called that but told him, yes, tea would be most welcome, pulling on his jacket as he spoke.

"Cut us a slice of Mrs Neeson's fruit-cake there, will you," Burnside called out lazily, planking himself down in a facing chair. "I see you've let the fire go nearly out as usual, sergeant," he said, prodding the embers with the poker. "There could well be that wee touch of frost afore morning."

"Have sense, man," Lawlor told him. "Sure, it's still only early October."

"Ah, but you haven't been out the way we have."

125

Boal brought his head back around the scullery door. "A nip in the air, as the man said about the Japanese parachutist."

"How do you know I wasn't out?"

Both looked at him, then Boal laid a finger sagely against his nose before retreating into the scullery again.

"Will I put the pan on?" they heard him call out amid the din of cupboard doors and drawers being abused. He was the noisiest cook in Christendom. At weekends they took it in turns to dish up when Mrs Neeson was away. "My bachelor boys," she referred to them.

"Your man laid his hands on a nice bit of back bacon out on his rounds," confided Burnside. "With the hair still on it. Just the way you like it, eh, Victor?" he called out.

Boal hooted with glee and Lawlor looked away trying not to betray too much fastidiousness, for both knew how uncomfortable he felt about coarseness.

"Winnie's on in five minutes. That's why we came back," said Burnside rising and going over to the battery set sitting on the window ledge. He twiddled the knob and as the light came on Lawlor realised he had left the arrow on the dial pointing to Athlone.

Piano music tinkled eerily for a moment, then a voice announced, "That was Dame Myra Hess playing a Chopin étude in C sharp minor on a gramophone record." The sound of Big Ben followed, then the same man's voice continued, "And now the Prime Minister, the Right Honourable Winston Churchill will speak to the nation."

Boal reappeared to lean up against the door jamb. He had a checked drying-cloth about his middle and an egg-slice in his hand. They could hear the burgeoning crackle of the frying-pan in the background.

The great man's tones, slow and ponderous, began rolling into the room like a whisky-and-tobacco-inflected fog. As always he spoke of sacrifice and bravery, of ordinary people like themselves heroically defending the home front, expending their blood, sweat and tears.

At one point he lightened the mood with a jocular reference to Herr Schicklgruber and Burnside slapped his thigh and howled but it was the briefest of outbursts, so anxious was he not to miss a solitary word or cadence. It was as if each syllable was a jewel of infinite worth to be memorised, hoarded, then repeated in company whenever the subject of the conflict arose. "As Winnie said himself," was a favourite opening of his.

On the wall facing the royal portrait was pinned a map of the various theatres of war. It had been cut from the *Daily Express* and was already a mass of curving arrows and dotted lines charting the various fronts and offensives. North Africa looked as though it had been singled out for more than its fair share of manic additions and deletions. Lawlor had learnt never to mention Tobruk or Rommel in his presence. Not that he was overly tempted. As far as he was concerned what was happening in the world beyond his own little backwater was as remote as something taking place on another planet. He carried it about with him, an empty space within, where the subject of the war that raged should have been, but wasn't.

Right now he felt more concerned about the bacon he could hear spitting on top of the range in the scullery. He thought about rising to check but daren't in case of offending Burnside while the great British Bulldog was in full cry.

Still, something must have done, for later when the broadcast was at an end and another piano recital was softly playing, his mood seemed to sour.

They were sitting silently at the big scrubbed table, a mountain of provender, enough rations for a family for a month, bacon, eggs and fried bread in front of them, when

Burnside announced, as though out of nowhere, "The enemy in our midst is the one to watch out for."

At first Lawlor thought he must be quoting his siren-suited hero, now snug in his underground bunker tearing into the Johnny Walker most presumably, and fair play to him, then he thought it might be a dig at himself, the foreigner, the outsider, the quisling.

To his shock he then heard the other say, "Your man the Major is as smart a one as ever walked. What he says makes sense. The enemy within. That's the boyo we have to look out for. The boyo in our own backyard. The nigger in the woodshed."

Lawlor looked at him. "He said all that, did he?"

"That he did."

"And when did he say it?"

There was a pause as Boal filled Burnside's mug for him from the white enamel teapot. They glanced across at one another.

"This very afternoon." It was Burnside who spoke.

Lawlor stopped eating, the food turning to swill in his mouth.

"And what were you two doing up at Glebe House, might I ask?"

"It's our day off, remember. We can go where we please."

"Can you now? That can easily be altered, so it can."

They sat there while the distant piano tinkled in faraway London. There was something mocking about the piece and its delivery, at least it seemed that way to Lawlor. He knew he was in the wrong but the rage within wouldn't be appeased. What he felt could not be put into words without making him sound a greater fool than he already seemed. He chewed on his bacon rind as the silence grew.

Then Boal, always the softer of the two, said, "Where's the harm in keeping our eyes and ears open?"

128

"The Major says one of them niggers that shot Mrs Jelley still hasn't been accounted for," Burnside cut in. "He could be anywhere."

"Has he looked in the woodshed?"

Boal choked on a mouthful of food.

"It's no joke, I tell you. People won't be safe in their beds 'till that buck is caught."

Lawlor leaned back in his chair, taking a sharpened match to the spaces between his teeth.

"Crawford," he said, calmer now, "how did Major Kincaid come by all his information?"

"He made it his business to find out."

"Business?"

Burnside leaned forward. His face was beginning to go red. "It's just as well somebody has the town's interests at heart. A madman on the loose and here we are sittin' on our fat arses."

Lawlor rose and went across to the wireless, switching off the unknown pianist in mid-flow.

"Now, listen to me, the pair of you," he said, as the sound of the clock expanded to fill the sudden silence. "As far as we're concerned, we've been relieved of all involvement. That's official. From now on the American authorities take over. Apprehension, detention and conviction of all those involved in the shooting. Is that clear? It's in their hands. Out of ours. Full stop. Case closed."

"Not for the Major, it isn't," said Burnside.

Lawlor felt his face flame and begin to swell. "I don't give a continental fuck what Kincaid thinks or does not think. Do you hear me? Do you? Is that clear?"

The two of them kept their heads cannily lowered to their plates. The obscenity exploding out of him in that manner, and so untypical too, left ripples the way a heavy stone might do after plummeting into a pond. He waited until the reverberations seemed to have ebbed away but it was Burnside, not himself, who came back in first.

"He's organised a search-party for tomorrow. First thing."

"That's right, sergeant. He told us all about it. Dogs, everything." Boal's eyes beseeched, brown, a shade canine, as well, he noticed for the first time.

After counting to ten internally, Lawlor asked, "May I enquire, whereabouts?" His voice had returned to normal.

"Oh, his own place. He said someone like that would head for somewhere heavily wooded. It's in his nature."

"So we're looking for some class of a Red Indian now, is it? Forgive me, but I thought our man was just an ordinary GI, heavily sun-tanned, mark you, but hardly fresh off a reservation."

Boal tittered while Burnside continued munching. He had a spreading bald spot crowned by a bony bare protusion. It moved in rhythm with his jaws. Lawlor watched fascinated as though witnessing a genuine marvel of anatomical science.

He said, "I think I'd better have a wee word with Major John Wayne Kincaid before he hits the trail." He glanced at the clock. Six-fifteen.

"You could catch him now," offered Boal. "Do you want us to come with you?"

"No, tomorrow will do fine. First thing, you say?"

Boal nodded.

"And dogs, is it?"

"Aye, he has that draghound he uses for hunting out of season."

"The one that Ussher Greer threatened to shoot?"

"The very boy. Slipper."

Lawlor sat down again replenishing his mug from the huge chipped pot, its tea-stained insides black as the ace of spades. Or the skin of a certain individual on the run from justice. Frightened eye-whites in a dusky face. He remembered

130

sitting in the Macushla on Friday nights and seeing all those eyes and teeth shining in the darkness. Three rows of spruced-up coloureds smelling like one great perfumery store and all laughing uproariously at Curly, Larry and Moe. People kept turning in wonderment as if surprised that they found the same things funny as they did.

Shortly after Boal switched the wireless on once more as though nothing of consequence had occurred since last it sounded, and the three of them relaxed with loosened collars, sprawled and listening to Tommy Handley and his band of merry lunatics in "ITMA". Lawlor joined in the laughter at Mrs Mopp, Colonel Chinstrap and Funf the Spy, and all the other eccentrics gathered in Foaming-in-the-Mouth. The actors' voices populated the Day Room as the evening outside rapidly closed in. Burnside lit a pipe. Boal put on a pair of spectacles mended at the bridge with Elastoplast and studied his boxing paper. Everything and everyone looked calm and contented just like any other Sunday night, the lamplight gilding them with its own special honeyed glow.

Inside, though, Lawlor fretted still. He bore it as long as he could but a little after nine he rose, stretching and yawning extravagantly, a not very persuasive piece of acting on his part, pleading tiredness. Boal looked up from his pictures of posed prize-fighters – he was pigeon-chested and the least athletic of men, a mystery recruit if ever there was one.

"Early start then, is it, sarge?" he murmured, that sly old cockiness back in strength once more.

Lawlor glanced down at the full-page pull-out of some unknown pug the other was admiring, limbs gleaming, monogrammed silk trunks hoisted half way up his torso.

"Brown Bomber?" he enquired, Joe Louis being the only boxer he knew of.

Boal laughed scornfully. "Sugar Ray Robinson. He's

fighting tonight on the wireless. Don't worry, we'll keep it turned down low, sarge."

We, thought Lawlor, recognising the old team back in business once again.

He went upstairs then to the room with the ceiling that looked as though it might buckle at any minute under the weight of some invisible and gradually growing pressure. The bed, bigger than a billiard table, was heaped with the bedclothes he hadn't bothered to tidy that morning. Looking at it he knew he wouldn't sleep, not like last night.

He began the wearisome business of undressing, starting with the laces of his boots and working his way upwards in the routine he knew was eccentric but had pursued for so long he didn't question it any longer. Sometimes when he was drunk he would catch a glimpse of himself in the tilted cheval glass in the corner, a big man, a stranger, staring back at him, naked except for a policeman's peaked cap and a tiny St Christopher's on a thin chain about his neck, the only relic left of his religion, if a cheap tin-plate medal could be described as such.

Predictably that night he dreamed of Nuala. It was the medal, of course, for she had given it to him when they first went out courting together. Those dreamy days spent along the country verges around Cootehill before things went sour on them.

In the dream she was in a boxing ring, standing there looking about her in surprise as though dropped from another planet, as people often are who appear in other people's dreams, stranded with no say in the matter. The baying of an invisible crowd was deafening, a glare beating down on her unprotected head from an overhead floodlamp. She was wearing her going-away outfit, that pale grey houndstooth two-piece which only served to make her look even more lost and vulnerable.

He kept shouting to her to get out of there but she couldn't hear him because of the din. She seemed oblivious to the danger she was in, of the presence, in particular, in the far corner of a giant negro straining forward towards her on his stool, all teeth, eyeballs and preposterous muscle. Yet she made no move, just kept turning her head in that helpless way that squeezed Lawlor's chest with the unbearable pathos of it.

He tried climbing through the ropes to her but instead of the expected triple strand came up against an almost solid wall of hemp which rebuffed and mocked his efforts. Pulling two of the ropes apart with hands that were already raw, he fought to keep her in view. What he now saw through that narrow space threatened to finish him off. The black boxer had come out of his corner, gloves dangling by his sides, as though the contest was already a foregone conclusion. He was grinning in the direction of his prey, gumshield deforming his mouth and lips.

The perspective changed. Now that great sweating back blocked Lawlor's view. Bobbing desperately, he tried to see around him, but couldn't. The roar of the crowd grew in volume and at its urging the muscle-bound giant shuffled forward to take centre-stage. Head to one side, he appeared to be listening to what they demanded of him. Almost coquettishly, it seemed to the watcher, he toyed with them and for some reason that made him even more frightening, that sick daintiness coming across like that.

Finally there came a lull in things, the noise subsiding as though in anticipation. The heavyweight in his dark trunks placed two great swollen thumbs in their waistband and, as Lawlor watched in horror, slowly he slid them down almost to his knees. Standing there he exposed himself for the crowd's baying approval. But it came to Lawlor that his wife was also directly in the line of that shocking display. It was for *her* benefit, not the fans.

He began tearing at the ropes, then calling out, *"Don't look! Don't look!"* but all the time knowing how could she do otherwise? How could she?

He could see her now through an opening in the ropes, her face, just her sweet face. It might be the last glimpse he would ever catch of her, he told himself. But before that happened he wanted her to look at him, not that other thing, but she seemed incapable as though mesmerised. She kept on staring at whatever it was the black man dangled before her.

"Don't look! Don't look! Turn away!" he yelled.

But she didn't, didn't want to, it seemed, for, unbelievably, she was advancing, not retreating, advancing, not taking her eyes off that animal's unseen manhood with an expression on her face he had never seen before, a look of such avidity that Lawlor felt like screaming on a higher note than any fan in the hall could ever manage, no matter how dedicated or excitable.

And at that point, mercifully, the dream ended for Lawlor. Rather, he awoke, for he knew it still went on as nightmares always do, unreeling silently in the subconscious like a film that has to run its course even if everyone has gone from the cinema. He used to feel like that sometimes when he was younger, staying on in the deserted Roxy in Cootehill long after the screen had reverted to its normal lifeless grey. Out in the alleyway the drama carried on in his head, a coda no one else experienced save him.

He felt like that now in the big bed, damp with his sweat. Had he called out? He lay there listening. There was no sound from the Day Room below, the wireless commentary must have run its course. Perhaps an early round knock-out?

Sugar Ray Robinson looked as though he could well deliver the goods.

He glanced at his watch lying on its curved back on the bedside cabinet. Four thirty-five. The light outside was just beginning to seep through a crack in the curtains. He heard the clop of hooves as old Johnny Malone went by with his two jingling churns, one sweet milk, the other buttermilk. There was something reassuring in the sound, another day, another ordinary day like any other, and gradually Lawlor found he had stopped shaking. After a while the only thing to remind him of his dream was a wet patch on his inner thigh that refused stubbornly to dry.

Setting out for Kincaid's place a couple of hours later he rode past houses with their windows still veiled against the blackout. It gave the place an eerie quality, a united show of mourning which he knew had nothing to do with the dead woman, yet somehow reinforced his commitment to her memory, even though he still found it difficult to picture her as she had been before the fatal bullet changed her appearance for ever.

His tyres hissed softly on the dry road. The risen sun, quivering slightly, hung fat and bulbous between the telegraph poles. It promised to be a fine, calm day ahead. *Perfect day for a hunt*, he caught himself thinking wryly.

Outside of town he took the first fork to the left and was in open country straightaway. Chewing cattle charted his progress from their grassy beds. They made him nervous as though scenting his intentions, some sort of bush telegraph preceding him even as he cycled past.

He came to Ussher Greer's neat two-storeyed farmhouse, a whitewashed cube set against the copper of its sheltering beech plantation. A serious, reclusive man, as transparently honest as his nearest neighbour was not. The two detested each other, the farmer refusing to show the respect his well-to-do neighbour insisted was his God-given right by virtue of a military title and a la-di-da accent.

Lawlor felt he might well have an ally there at the end of that tidy driveway. Perhaps because of it he dismounted at the lane mouth and cupped his hands, drinking directly from the spout that carried water from a distant source. The flow cascaded over a milk-churn, keeping the contents cool until the creamery lorry arrived at mid-morning to collect it.

Ussher Greer was something of a water fanatic. His acres rang with the sounds of diverted streams, ingenious channels that turned wheels and worked paddles. He ran his own generator, ground his own corn. The holding seemed to float on a bed of moisture, veined by a liquid network lovingly tended by the big stooping man with the shock of white hair. He had never married, never socialised. Lawlor envied that self-sufficiency, whilst knowing he would never be able to produce the resolve to carry it off himself.

For a moment he stood there with dripping hands half-hoping to catch a glimpse of the legendary recluse. Once or twice in the past their paths might well have crossed, nothing more than a jerk of the head passing between them. A man might spend a lifetime here with no greater acknowledgement than that. The country was all about loneliness, it had often struck Lawlor. He dried his hands, then passed on.

Presently he arrived at the borders of Ussher Greer's land, a well-maintained wire fence separating the two properties. The road continued between fields on one side and a high curving stone wall along the other. It got its name from that, Sweet Wall Road, built as Outdoor Relief in Famine times by some Kincaid ancestor.

Lawlor began easing off on the pedals. He was thinking. It would make no sense to go bowling boldly up to Kincaid's front door, neither should he arrive all red-faced and sweating after skulking through the woods surrounding the house. For the first time he questioned what he was doing here, what he would say in explanation. Then he thought, why explain, his rank and uniform needed no excuse. Nevertheless, he decided on a middle course.

He had passed an opening in the wall, closed off by a barrier of freshly felled poles, and beyond it a track disappearing into the trees. He wheeled his bicycle back to the gap and after looking both ways lifted the machine to shoulder height then lowered it on the far side. His head pounded with blood and when it had returned to normal he climbed up and over the makeshift barrier of skinned saplings.

Kincaid employed a forester, someone from the South come North to find work in the war-effort. This was his handiwork. No one had ever seen him or spoken to him. Certainly not the latter, given peoples' feelings about the neutral Free State and its citizenry.

The pathway bore the marks of a cart, two deep ruts filled with stagnant water. Lawlor followed them into the woods. Insects hummed and he kept slapping his cheeks when they became too free with his red, perspiring flesh. After about a quarter of an hour the trees began thinning out and he crossed over from the crown of the path to its verge. He walked in the shade, in the grass, slow and cautious now.

Presently he heard a dog yelp as if someone had struck it, and it continued to howl, but on a lower, more cowed note. His heart was beating rapidly now and he could feel sweat running down his back under his vest. He stopped to mop his face and as he did so someone shouted something as if the sight of the handkerchief had given him away. He knew he could only advance now, would have to brazen it out so, putting the handkerchief away – it seemed too much like a

137

flag of truce – he made his way forward to where something overgrown and moundlike rose up between the young firs.

A minute later, emerging from the trees, the idea of something white fluttering in his hand seemed not such a bad idea after all, for he distinctly heard the sound of a rifle bolt – more than one – go snapping back.

There was at least a dozen of them with weapons in their hands, some in uniform, some not, and he recognised most of them a fraction before they identified him. One man, a stranger in a boiler-suit and wellingtons, held a tan-and-white dog on a rope. There was no sign of Kincaid.

Face hot, but with kindling anger now, Lawlor halted a moment to allow his official presence to assert itself. All grounded their Lee Enfields – all except Bertie McMeekin, that is, but he was never the brightest of the bunch at the best of times.

"What in hell's name's going on here? Who's in charge?" He meant Kincaid, of course, but couldn't bring himself to name him.

One of the B Specials, Norman Magee, pointed to a cave-like opening in the mound.

Lawlor came closer, crouching a little as if to inspect the domed structure. It looked man-made despite the covering of vegetation, some kind of tumulus.

The dog began to whimper, straining forward on its leash, and the man in the boiler-suit hauled back brutally so that its tongue lolled out. Lawlor glared at him but he stared back as though outside his jurisdiction. He had to be the Free Stater, it came to him. He felt like saying, "I hope you have a licence for that animal," then put it from his mind for the childish irrelevancy it was.

Then the real owner of the hound emerged stooping from the dark mouth of the mound with a torch in his hand. Blinking in the light, he began brushing down his clothing,

138

methodically, unhurriedly, even though Lawlor knew he had seen him standing there, an unwelcome presence among his little squad of part-timers. When he had completed his grooming to his satisfaction he said, "Good to see you, sergeant. Everyone's welcome."

"Just what in hell's name is going on here?" The profanity was uncalled for he knew but he had caught the dog-handler grinning.

"On second thoughts, I get the impression you haven't come all this way just to offer your services after all. Is there some other matter I can help you with? I'd hate to break the law."

One of the Specials choked and Lawlor glared at him. He had the grace at least to turn away.

"That depends on what you have in mind."

"What we have in mind, sergeant, is a little sport on private property."

"And these men – what are they doing here?" Lawlor indicated the B Specials leaning on their rifles.

Kincaid took a cigarette case from his coat pocket and tapped both ends of one of his tipped fags on the polished metal. Du Maurier. It was just another of those superior little mannerisms of his that made Lawlor feel clumsy and socially inadequate.

"In case you've forgotten, sergeant, may I remind you I happen to be their area commandant."

It was certainly true, but whether that extended to him using the force as unpaid beaters was another matter. Lawlor decided it was time to cut the cackle.

"I have to tell you, Major, I'm none too happy about what's going on here," he began. "According to information received it's no fox you'll be after setting your dogs on."

"They told you that, did they, our two bold gendarmes?"

"It's what they're paid for."

139

"And what are *you* paid for, sergeant?"

They faced one another across the expanse of trampled earth. It came to Lawlor, any scent, if it ever existed, must be tainted by now by all these heavy army-issue boots milling about. He looked over at the dog. A sorry-looking creature, it lay on its belly panting, with sad running eyes as though in agreement with him.

"And just what makes you think the quarry would head in this direction anyhow, instead of somewhere else?" The squad of Specials were watching intently. All of this would be relayed back to the barracks later.

Kincaid was smiling. "Are you a betting man, sergeant, by any chance?" he enquired.

Lawlor looked at him, unsure suddenly of the direction their contest had taken them.

"For if you are, I'm prepared to make a small wager with you that our 'quarry', as you so delicately put it, headed straight here. Like the proverbial arrow."

At that moment a wood pigeon burst from its roost in a nearby tree and one of the younger Specials – Dessie McFarland – threw up his rifle in sudden alarm. His mates laughed at him. The dog throughout lay unmoving as if nothing of interest had occurred.

"Well?" said Kincaid after the hilarity died away. "Are we on?" But, then, after a pause, "No?" as he read Lawlor's expression. He took something from a deep side pocket. It looked like a scrap of khaki-coloured cloth to Lawlor. "Evidence. And fresh, at that."

"You can tell?" queried Lawlor, examining the soiled handkerchief. Bloodstains.

"Came across it back there just now." He pointed to the mound. "Inside my own Ice-House. Along with a stool, human, most definitely recent in origin. Care to check?"

Lawlor shook his head. "None of this proves anything.

He —" hesitating over the word as though reluctant to throw his hand in this early "— he may well have gone back to the base by now. In his bunk, for all we know."

"Not so, sergeant, not so. I've checked myself. I must say I'm a little surprised you haven't done so yourself."

Lawlor was about to say, *it's no longer my responsibility*, but stopped himself in time. Just what in God's name was he doing here anyway? He still couldn't explain it. Not only to other people, but himself as well. Stubbornly he returned to his own mess like an old dog returning to its vomit.

"You seem to know a hell of a lot about somebody you haven't ever met before."

Kincaid puffed carefully on his cigarette, bluish-grey smoke wreathing upwards, keeping the midges at bay. Sadly for Lawlor his freshly shaved cheeks seemed to draw them like raw meat. He slapped at one now and the dog studied him with interest for the first time. So this was the famous Slipper, was it? Didn't look all that legendary.

"Unlike your good self, sergeant, I just happen to have spent a good few years of my life dealing with such people in their native habitat. Know one, know them all, has been my experience. They tend to behave to a certain pattern. Simple-minded, but devious at the same time. That deviousness nevertheless doesn't stop them from soiling their own nest." He wrinkled his nose with distaste. "The old jungle instinct, sergeant. The beast beneath the uniform."

Lawlor looked over at the motley bunch lounging under the conifers, half of them in uniform, half of them not, and felt like laughing, if it wasn't so tragic. The word snagged the flow of his thoughts like a breakwater for, yes, things most definitely seemed to be heading in that direction.

"If you don't mind, sergeant —" Kincaid was holding his hand out for the soiled square of olive-green cloth, and for a moment Lawlor felt reluctant to relinquish it, not because it might be evidence, but because a sudden unsettling image of a sweating black face had swum into focus as though in association with that scrap of army issue, detailed, individual, even though he still was unable to picture the woman, the owner of that face, that handkerchief, had done to death. He felt the "evidence" leave his grasp and waited for the image to go, too, but it stayed as though imprinted. How long would it remain like that, he wondered.

Kincaid held the piece of cloth close to the dog's muzzle and for the first time it became animated. Shaking himself free of lethargy, as though dispelling fleas, Slipper sniffed and slavered. For a moment it looked to Lawlor as though in his throes he might devour the precious remnant. Then, raising his dripping snout — the leash had been slipped from his throat — he belled at the sky on a single hoarse but carrying note. Kincaid and his hired hand exchanged delighted grins. "Go! Go, boy!" they cried and, nose to the ground, the lumbering old hound picked up speed and headed straight for the opening in the mound.

Everyone watched and waited in silence for what seemed like a long time after he disappeared inside. Lawlor's legs began to ache. He envied the Major's shooting-stick, but knew he must stay on his feet for as long as it took. The rest, meanwhile, had either flopped earthwards or leaned against the nearest tree-trunk.

From its snug little fob pocket he slid out his watch. Nine thirty-four. The sun, filtered by foliage, dappled the open spaces, seeking a face, a hand here, a piece of equipment there. The metal of a rifle barrel gleamed momentarily, then dulled as the light passed it by. Nothing could be heard save the thud of a distant axe somewhere a fraction later than the edge bit into bark.

Kincaid lit a fresh cigarette, then passed one to the man in the boiler-suit. Some sort of intimate complicity seemed present there, it came to Lawlor.

Then Slipper emerged and stopped right there as though conscious of all this unaccustomed attention. He sniffed at the air, then at the ground beneath his paws for a moment. Lawlor felt a lift of anticipation despite himself. Kincaid and his man flung their half-smoked cigarettes aside in an almost identical movement and even in that simple gesture Lawlor again scented conspiracy. The rest of them, it occurred to him, were surplus to requirements here. Two men and a dog constituted the only real presence here, the squad of Specials brought along merely to feed their commander's vanity. As for himself – he left the thought unfinished for purely tactical reasons.

The dog began edging forward, slowly at first, then picking up speed as the scent gained strength, Kincaid and the man with the rope keeping their distance as though anxious not to intrude.

Lawlor stayed where he was, unsure whether to follow or not. For a moment, in one of those strange diversionary interludes which seemed to distract him more and more these days, he felt concern about the two cigarette butts buried in the grass. He was on the point of seeking and treading on them when Kincaid hallooed a short sharp huntsman's cry and the Specials began running and jingling through the trees. In a moment Lawlor was all alone in the glade. He could hear Slipper baying steadily, the sound alien and unsettling.

Then it came to him where he had heard the sound before, in the cinema dark, of course, a man running, running, through swamps and fields full of unfamiliar crops, glistening face in enormous close-up, terrified and knowing, like everyone else watching, that he stood no earthly chance, that being the nature and demands of such dramas. That

143

other dark face took its place and Lawlor started to run now, too, as though it might be within his power this once against all the odds to influence the film's outcome.

His boots made no sound on the matted brown needles as he ran, only his breath gusting, testimony to his unfit condition. Ahead of him he could hear the old dog's excited cries coming faster, faster, and he felt panicky that he might arrive too late for the kill. *Kill*, he thought? The word seemed a trifle excessive. Yet he couldn't help himself, continuing to graft on scenes from old black-and-white movies he had seen.

The trees seemed to have closed ranks, he began noticing. No movement could be seen between their thickening trunks. Lungs whistling, he kept pounding on in response to the sounds of the invisible dog. Then that changed in tone to a sudden burst of howling. He thought of the man with the rope and his ill-treatment earlier and for a second time anger took hold and it was still with him, hot and satisfying, when he broke clear of the trees and saw that his prediction had been faulty.

Before him, spread out in a ragged arc, was the hunting party and everyone in it was looking at Slipper who was running back and forth, muzzle down in a frenzy of frustration. The reason for his distress was plain to see there in front of him in the form of a fast-moving stream of clear, clean water. On its opposite bank lay rich pasture. Cows grazed there, Ussher Greer's herd of prize-winning Ayrshires. Heads up, they stared at the animal as if perplexed by such behaviour, a little more than usual perhaps, soft-eyed puzzlement being their natural state.

Lawlor broke his stride, ambling forward almost casually now, recognising stalemate when he saw it. Kincaid ignored him. He looked a little paler than usual. The Free Stater kept glancing from the dog to owner and back again as if impatient for the order to cross the stream.

Someone like that needed to be taught the niceties of criminal trespass, Lawlor told himself, and no better man to do it than himself.

Accordingly, he addressed Kincaid, aiming his message through the master at the man. "End of the line, Major," he said savouring the Americanised expression. It might have come from one of those films he'd been remembering just moments earlier.

At that precise moment a figure materialised in a corner of the distant meadow. A familiar white head rose into view above a five-barred gate and hung there.

One of the B Specials sauntered down to the stream's edge and waved. The man leaning on the gate didn't return the greeting, however, and, embarrassed, the Special – it was young Rolston – dropped quickly to his knees and lapped up a handful of the fast-flowing water.

Lawlor's mouth went dry at the sight and thought of it, but stayed where he was, knowing the time for that would come later as a tiny reward for victory. And he saw it that way now, he and the watcher at the far gate sharing the credit between them.

"Looks as if you've drawn a blank, Major." His voice was pitched a little louder than was necessary for the Specials' benefit but not enough for his distant ally to catch. That seemed a pity somehow. "Maybe your man doubled back. I mean he'd be crazy to leave all that nice thick tree-cover back there. For that." And he pointed towards the flat green sward facing them. "You said it yourself. Animal instincts? Back to the jungle? Or did I get my information wrong."

Kincaid looked up at the sky, soft, fleecy clouds stippling a bird-egg blue expanse. A beautiful day and as far as Lawlor was concerned getting more perfect by the minute.

"I have faith in my dog, sergeant. He knows where the trail leads better than any of us. And it's our duty to follow, trespass or no trespass. The ordinary rules do not apply. This is an emergency."

"Well, I'm not all that convinced it is myself, Major," returned Lawlor, plucking a blade of grass and chewing on it like one of Ussher Greer's sleek milkers. "An emergency. We could easily have some trouble here. Of a different sort."

By now all could see the chill glitter of a shotgun barrel above the far gate like a warning flag.

"Weighing everything up, I think you would be advised to come back another day. Better still, leave the entire matter in the hands of the proper authorities over at the base."

The man in the pale rainproof tapped the side of a boot with his metal shooting-stick. It was retracted by now, which Lawlor took as a further sign of victory on his part. Yet why didn't he feel quite so triumphant as he had been? The stem in his mouth tasted bitter suddenly, harmful, even. He spat out the cud and felt a wet trail linger by the side of his mouth.

"Well, if that's the way you feel about it, sergeant, then, of course we must all bow to your authority. Please remember one thing however. If we happen to have another dreadful murder on our doorstep and, God forbid we do, you may well be seen as the one who might have done something to prevent it."

Lawlor looked at him and his little smiley weasel-face, hating him for implanting that barb, knowing its venom would spread later like an infection, which he would try to treat with the drip of the whiskey bottle.

The Free Stater was grinning again as though at some private joke and, angered, he snapped, "I don't know you, do I? What do they call you?"

"Duffy. Pascal Duffy."

146

He could see the Specials stiffen at the sound of the name, made even more suspect by the accent that delivered it.

"Have you papers? Work-permit?"

That wiped the smirk off his dial all right. Then Kincaid intervened. "Don't worry, sergeant, I'll see they're left in at the barracks next time I'm passing. Will tomorrow afternoon be soon enough for you?"

He was smiling like his hired hand as he said it and Lawlor recognised in that smile that any advantage he might have imagined had been the merest bubble, like one of those he could see floating past him on the stream in front of him.

After that there seemed nothing left to say or do. The one he now knew was called Duffy put the rope back on the dog and set off after his boss who had walked away without word or gesture. Then the others began to shamble off as well, back to the fringe of trees, almost blue-black now as the sun crawled towards its zenith.

Lawlor stayed where he was until the woods had swallowed them up. He could feel the heat penetrate the flat stretched fabric of his policeman's cap. Sweat broke on his brow, trickled out of his armpits. The stream looked inviting, the surface weed drawn taut like bright green hair by the fast-moving current. Getting old − older − had none of the advantages he used to believe would arrive automatically by right with age. Another bubble. He was thinking, of course, of the water and of its cool and almost silken touch and of how when he was younger nothing would have held him back from stripping off and plunging in.

For a moment he looked over at the man leaning on the gate. He would, if anyone would, surely understand the desire to immerse oneself in that purifying rush, allowing all the pain of past and present defeats to wash away. They stared across the flowing divide at one another too rooted in their own stiff codes to betray themselves by word or gesture. Lawlor wondered if the other realised how he had intervened on his behalf. But the brief rush of sentimentality on his part was quickly suppressed. He turned away, feeling those eyes still on his uniformed back.

As he trudged towards the trees across the heathy no-man's-land he was still thinking of that lush pasturage beyond the stream and of how it must, no, might well, have looked to the runaway. Eden. Like something from one of those spirituals they were supposed to be singing all the time. Promised land. Then he thought to himself, *all this heat is turning your head, you're a country policeman, Lawlor, not some sort of brain-doctor.*

But re-entering the church-like gloom of the woods it came to him there might well be a connection between both callings after all. Both entailed getting into the head, if not the skin, of the subject, in his case, the wanted man. Even though he had been relieved of any responsibility in the matter he had still an itch to know, damn it to hell, something even more than that, if he were to be honest with himself.

Because of it he began to retrace his journey back to the Ice-House, keeping the sun high on his left side. Its rays were filtered by the foliage, but there were open patches where it blazed down unimpeded. He caught himself avoiding these, almost as if, already, he really was trying to get under another's skin. For a moment, embarrassed at himself, he glanced around in case someone might see him skulking from tree to tree in this way.

But the woods remained silent, motionless, and Lawlor stumbled on until he reached the mound, halting a safe distance away in the shelter of the trees where he could plan his approach. As he watched a rabbit hopped into the open and began nibbling away, proof, if it were needed, that he had the place to himself. He moved forward and seeing him the creature froze, then shot off.

A few feet from the low dark mouth – the Kincaids must have employed a race of dwarves to draw ice for their banquets, but then Kincaid was low in stature himself, wasn't he, he had barely needed to stoop earlier – Lawlor considered what the runaway must have been feeling when he first saw that grassy construction. How desperate he must have been to crawl into the lair of God knows what horrors, bats, rabid foxes, snakes, for he felt sure no one had bothered to tell him about Saint Patrick driving the serpents out of Ireland that time.

Sharing a little of that same imaginary dread Lawlor crouched low and poked his head forward into the darkness. A smell of damp, something rank, too, assailed his nostrils. He moved forward and a cobweb stuck to his face.

Inside he struck a match and before it went out he could distinguish a domed roof, the stone leaking pale frozen drips like ragged teeth. He lit another, its sulphur reek getting the better of that other rotting one. This time he caught the gleam of water in the deepest recesses and edging forward to get a better look the toe of his boot dislodged something small and round and the sound of it triggered off a soft plop in the distant pool. *Rats*, he thought. He hadn't considered *rats. So obvious, too, for Christ's sake!*

Suddenly sweating and panting he backed out into the blessed light desperately pawing at his cheeks to get rid of those sticky spider's strands.

Fine bloody sleuth he was turning out to be, shaking like a girl, he was, once more swivelling his head in case someone might be witnessing his shame.

And then he realised someone was spying on him after all, for his roving glance caught hold of a face, small, pale, framing a pair of intense eyes meeting his own. He pretended he hadn't seen his young watcher deep in the trees, a child, boy most probably, hoping to catch another and better look at him on the return, but when he swung back the face had disappeared.

Lawlor stood there straining for the sounds of retreat but nothing disturbed the silence save the hum of a swarm of midges rising and falling in a mating dance in a shaft of sunlight.

Kincaid had no children of his own, it came to him, so this must be a trespasser like himself, but smaller and a lot more agile. There was a clutch of young ones in the gate-lodge he recalled, for he had dealings there a year earlier. That poor mongol creature burned to a cinder in the whin fire. It came back to him. Taggart was her name, the mother. A different father for each of her brood, according to Boal and Burnside, who had a relish for such details.

On the way back to where he had left the bicycle he felt certain the same eyes were still watching him like those of some very young, very alert woodland animal. And when finally he found the machine where he'd laid it, carefully and secretly, he thought, but now with two flattened tyres, he cursed the owner of those eyes.

"God damn you!" he called out to the unresponsive trees. "Don't worry, I know who you are, all right!"

He couldn't help himself. It was the sort of thing people in his line of work always used as a threat whenever they had nothing to go on.

But on the long walk home, for he had forgotten to bring his pump yet again, he settled on a different culprit. It was the Free Stater who had done the deed. Who else? And he resolved to make him regret his treachery first chance he could get.

All of these events had taken place two days earlier. Now he was reviewing them high on his slope above the mourners gathered about the opened grave and staring down into it in that ridiculously intense way as if they had never seen one before. It always entertained him, that.

He watched and waited until the last one, sated with whatever morbid longings places like these inspired in such people, had slithered back down the incline to the gates. Kincaid's car had pulled out and away first with what seemed an excessive roar and burst of acceleration. A score of black birds flew up from their rookery high in the trees, rising and falling in the still air like burnt paper. Lawlor studied their antics until, one by one, they settled back cawing on the ramshackle nests. He had never much cared for crows. Sort of seagulls in crape, just as malevolent, just as predatory. Farmers were entitled to an extra cartridge allowance for shooting them but their colony was safe because of its site near the graveyard.

His own ammunition was in a litle leather pouch fastened to his belt. He wondered what it would be like to blaze away at those raucous scavengers high on their platform of sticks. Sometimes he itched to use his gun on something, anything. Hadn't fired it in twenty years. There it hung, buttoned in its holster, as pristine as on its first day of issue, carefully oiled and pulled-through on a weekly basis. And what for? He knew, of course. For the moment when it came without warning, like that night a week ago at closing-time when, instead of being drunk in a sidecar driven by a half-wit, he might easily have been at the scene with it in his hand and able to save someone's life.

Down below he could see the two grave-diggers putting the finishing touches to the fresh mound of earth, patting it with the backs of their spades as if it were a potato clamp and not the grave of someone it had been his bounden duty to protect. And once more he realised that where her face

151

should have been there was a blank as if the covering soil had obliterated the memory of her for good.

He thought of the man instead, he who had put her there. For a moment there he had a vivid picture of a face, yet one he had never seen before. Seconds only it remained, fixed in the flare of a held lighter, dark, sweating, the whites of the eyes the size of marbles, glaring in terror into the hidden recesses of that awful watery cave. Then it was gone and the man in the heavy, sodden greatcoat started off down the slope through the graves.

Duty called. The real duty. There was paperwork, always paperwork, and then he had a truancy order to serve on some poor wretch who had more children than she knew what to do with. And then there were a couple of petrol offences, a compulsory tillage order, and a new promulgation to digest instructing him and the two Bs what to do if a German pilot ever happened to bail out over their area. *"Fire at the parachutist, not the parachute. Kill them on the way down."*

Boal and Burnside would certainly enjoy that part. Perhaps it was the silk that was the real concern. After all, every woman's knickers seemed to be made from the stuff, according to his two constables. Yes, as he was constantly being reminded, there did happen to be a war on.

SEVEN

When he wakes it's still dark outside. Only much later does he come to realise he must have slept right round the clock, one whole day, one night, swallowed up by sleep. But he has no way of being certain, his wristwatch making no distinction between a single sweep of its luminous hour-hand and the next, brightening, then fading, as the light changes along with it.

It becomes something of a terror to him, this missing portion of his life. And he sees it that way, too, nothingness, like a slice cut from a cake. Someone ate it up, some stranger, the pie-eater, when he was out dead to the world.

And at first he also thinks he's back on his army cot, beating reveille to it, once a farm boy always a farm boy, savouring those precious minutes before the groans and the cursing and banging of metal foot-lockers explode all around him. Eyes closed, he waits for the distant squeal of the bugle but it doesn't come. This stillness, too, is different, no moaning, no snoring, no breaking wind. His bed feels hard, lumpy, as though there are rocks in it. And there's a strange smell, definitely animal, not human, not GI.

Opening his eyes he sits up and suddenly it hits him, where he is, everything that has happened this far speeding straight at him, then past in a blurred rush, like a ride on a roller-coaster. Except, of course, for that one stolen piece from the pie which is his life.

Remembering, he weeps, hand covering his mouth. His palm smells as if it's been in contact with that animal he detected earlier. *Goat*, he decides, *yeah, goat,* recalling the old grey-beard and his harem he and Pearl had disturbed that day way back in summer. I'm in his territory, he tells himself, his home ground, how about that, that mean motherfucker, horns pointed like pitchforks.

He'd goaded him, shaking his jacket at him, that Sunday afternoon, *olé, olé,* Pearl half-fearful, half-excited by it all. "Over here, you horny old son of a bitch, over here!" a few minutes in time a black Tyrone Power in *Blood And Sand*.

Afterwards they made love on his greatcoat, his Horniness watching. And it was as if he was putting on a demonstration, one rutting male to another. Thrusting harder, deeper, he aimed for the very heart of something, some place dark, untouched, he'd never been before. No other man before that, before him.

Lying on his spread coat later, lining cold against his skin, her cheek imprinting his dog-tags on his chest, having a smoke, it comes to him she enjoyed it like that, hot and heavy, the way the guys always said women liked it. Cries of pleasure, not pain. While all the time he has his eyes fixed on old Horny up on his grandstand over there scoring him points for rhythm and style.

From now on he will have to match today's efforts, it will be expected of him, and although he knows she will never betray her feelings on that subject, he still knows she will be marking him on a scale from one to ten, not being able to help herself. Like Billy-Goat Gruff over there.

154

Suddenly he felt the entire universe was watching, laughing at him, knowing things he didn't.

His only experience had been with his cousin Lily Mae Avery under a bridge one time. Looking back on it, even then she seemed to know a lot more about the business than she let on. Then there was that skinny redhead when he was drunk that time in Fort Bragg, a whore. Best not to dwell on that, but he had, at least that day on the island he had, and going back in the boat, he and Pearl, they had their first serious row together.

It wasn't so much what he said or what she said in return, it was more them not actually speaking at all and letting a real bad feeling develop. He kept thinking of all the men she'd been with before, and most probably after, and couldn't look at her, even though she faced him pulling on the oars. Instead he trailed his hand in the water, pretending to be fascinated as if he'd never ever done such a thing before. They parted with barely a word, him pounding down hard on the pedals, kicking up gravel, eyes fixed on his front wheel.

Of course he turned up a couple of nights later bearing gifts, a bunch of flowers, box of candy and an old leg of lamb he'd snitched from the camp's cold store. He felt it lying chill against his chest all the way under his tunic like a block of ice. His heart felt roughly the same. But then it started to thaw, and him along with it, once he got to the house and the kids jumped up on him, leading him inside in triumph, pulling off his coat to reveal the strange-shaped parcel underneath. They all laughed when they saw what it contained, even Pearl, and he felt himself swell in the warmth and goodwill of the kitchen.

As the song says, making up is always the best part, nothing held back, and when he made his farewells later outside they kissed like a couple of high-school kids on their first date. That was the good time, a fresh, innocent time of new beginnings, no regrets or recriminations.

He's thinking of all this as he lies on his strange bed of driftwood and dried leaves. He realises he's still wearing his uniform although it smells and feels like someone else's, some down-and-out's, some juice-head, someone who's met with a serious accident. Covering him is an army greatcoat, but not his own, cloth far too coarse, buttons thicker, more oval than Uncle Sam's, and for a moment that old green-eyed monster gets going again just like the day of the picnic. But he puts it out of his head, Pearl doing her bit for the war-effort, entertaining the troops. All of that is incidental now. What concerns him is him, here and now, and he continues to stretch out there under British khaki, hands clasped back of his head, brain racing like an over-wound clock.

At some stage he detects a streak of pink slashing the darkness outside, low at first but gradually seeping, the colour of cherryade, through the cracks in the wall facing him. For the first time he begins to get some indication of where he has landed up, where Pearly has dumped him, as the light quickens and spreads.

He's in a one-roomed ruin of some sort, stone-walled, windowless, as far as he can make out. Half the roof is missing, but not where he is, and the floor is strewn with dead leaves and dirt-droppings, almost knee-high in places. What looks like the dead mouth of some type of fireplace yawns darker than the surrounding shadows. He lies observing all this, eager as a hound in heat, as if he might miss out on something, some element which could turn out to be crucial to his survival.

The doorway facing him has been partially blocked by what appears to be not a loose old door come off its hinges, as he believed in the dark, but a six-by-four slab of shuttering. He placed it there himself. *Raft*, he thinks, anticipating future events, and indeed it appears as if it might easily have been in the water, bleached the way it is, silvery grey. Just like he would be, too, most likely, washed up along the shore, a big fat old wrinkled whale of a thing all swole up and stinking to high heaven. The thought of him beached there, unrecognisable, unclaimed and alone, makes him feel sorry for himself all over again and he falls to bawling like a baby again.

But it's no big deal, for there's no one to see or hear, bar the cockroaches or the mice using the rafters as a race-track. The patter of tiny paws must have woke him up when it did after he had slept through his overdose of shuteye. By his Ingersoll wristwatch it's a little after four, which in turn tells him if he doesn't shift himself right now to get some idea of the lie of the land outside his refuge, any later will be too risky. Someone might spot him from the shore, some farmer, some fisherman, even. So he rises and stretches, muscles aching all over as if he's been on a rack, and goes over to the door.

He's still wearing his shoes and socks from last night, or whenever the hell it was he forded that river, then the boat ride, then scrambling ashore in freezing water a second time. His feet feel like twin lumps of thawed meat, cold and mushy, he's shivering all over, so he goes back and pulls on the greatcoat lying there. Three sizes too small, wouldn't you fucking well know it, his luck, tailored to fit some short-ass limey midget, its cuffs just about reach his elbows. Still, it's all he's got, so he hunches into it and moves towards the tilted slab of wood that blocks the doorway. As he does so he notices writing on one of its cross-ties, that stencilling unmistakable, PROPERTY OF US ARMY, and despite everything, despite his parlous state, he lets out a bellow that freezes the scampering mice overhead dead in their tracks. It's the first

157

real laugh he's had in a very long time. Then he thinks, *enjoy it while you can, sucker, it may never happen again, not the way things look for your chances, anyway.* He lays hold of Uncle Sam's slab of army-issue lumber. Washed up. Like himself. Once primed olive green, now wore down to the bare wood. His fingers trace its dry, scaly surface. A long time out of the water, months, maybe even more, but not too much longer. After all, the GIs only arrived here a little over a year ago.

Then he thinks, *okay, it came ashore all by itself, nothing mysterious in that, is there?* But at the same time just how the hell does it get to end up here propped against the inside wall where he found it when he got here? Deciding not to pursue the matter – he figures there'll be plenty of time, and how, to go into such things later, he's not going anywhere, is he? – he slides the slab a little to one side just far enough so he can peer out.

He's about a hundred yards from the water's edge, which by now has taken on the colour of the insides of a watermelon, rose running through to blood-red. The distant shore, the land, is just a dark ruled line – it looks a million miles away – which cheers him up in one way, then depresses him in another, for how will Pearly make that journey a second time? Already he's expecting her to come rowing out of the sunrise and him not here a day. Or is it two?

At this hour the surface of the great Lough is like Jello. Nothing disturbs its coating as far as he can see. The far shoreline seems utterly lifeless as well, not a solitary climbing thread of smoke anywhere to betray an early riser. *I have it all to myself,* he rejoices, then next minute becomes nervous, checking his wristwatch, shaking it, holding it to his ear, winding it tight which is real dumb, in a sudden shiver of panic lest it stops on him leaving him time-less. More slices

158

stolen from that pie. But then he tells himself, *get a grip, you dumb-assed nigger son of a bitch, you worthless no-good black trash.*

It's this thing he does sometimes when things are going bad for him, abusing himself in this crazy way. He's heard others doing it so often, cursing him out, it doesn't seem to affect him as it should, as if the words mean little or nothing, pouring off of him like water in the shower. And he feels much better for it, too, just the way he does after the morning sluice, washed clean of whatever it is that's bothering him, that's bugging him. Like right now.

Crouched down, peering out at the beautiful rosy Irish dawn, he's reminded of just how bad he needs that soap and hot water, for he smells himself, rank and ripe as his absent friend old goat-face. What he wouldn't give to be in the shower-block right now. Sometimes he would be standing in there in the steam and under the roaring jets as often as four, maybe five times a day, if they let him. And mostly they do, him working in the heat of the cook-house and all as he does. But then all the guys love to do the same for some reason. Seemed to be a thing with them to be even more sweet-smelling than the next joe.

They had this sergeant in Fort Bragg one time, real Klansman material, red hair, freckled face, arms like hams, who used to needle them about it. "You ain't a never goin' to wash that colour off of youse boys no matter how hard you try. It's per-man-ent. Deep-dyed. Ain't none of you boys never come across runnin' hot H_2O afore?"

Rich coming from a cracker asshole brought up in a one-roomed shack with an outhouse out back among the bushes. Course no one'd ever remind him of that to his ugly face, they weren't that intent on suicide. They just laughed and grinned and joked right back at him, showing their pearly whites the way they were brought up to do, old Jim Crow being everywhere, even under Uncle Sam's shower.

★

159

He comes to a decision, now or never, and starts squeezing out through the space between the propped-up door and the rotten jamb. It'll be door from now on, he tells himself. Got that? *Door.*

The air outside is fresh and pure, just a hint of those morning frosts to come. They arrive early in this part of the world, silvering the grass, sealing off ponds and potholes with a thin skin of ice like cellophane. He just loves all that fairy-tale stuff, never having seen much of it before, snow, neither, which comes later.

He crouches there a moment, then takes off his shoes and socks, laying them to dry on the step. The middle of the stone is hollowed out, he notices for the first time, and suddenly he knows just what made it that way. Generations of people sharpening their kitchen knives, year after year, after year. And now him. A runaway nigger from Duck-town, North Carolina, US of A.

Bent over, feet bare, he begins circling around to the back of the house — cottage, cabin, hut, crib — he doesn't know what name to give it anymore. All he does know it's where he must hide up like an old fox or possum, only coming out at night from now on. *This is the first, last and only time you venture out in daylight, boy, just this once, and only to get some idea of the lie of the land. Got that, you miserable, marooned son of a bitch? Let's move it then.*

And he proceeds to do so, holding on tight to the walls as he goes, like some old blind guy, all the way right around to the back where it's knee-deep in stinging nettles, him almost crying out with the pain then as his ankles brush against their sharp-pointed leaves. Shored up against the stone at his back, rubbing first one foot then the other, he looks about him for some of that weed Pearl told him was good at relieving the sting and sure enough he sees some growing close by as though planted there for just such an emergency in case some asshole who knows no better goes blundering about on bare feet. Dock, they call it, or *docken*, and it seems to do the trick, tamping down the fire to a dull, throbbing, but bearable heat.

Shoes on from here on in, sucker, he chastises himself, suddenly seeing this place he's fetched up in as some sort of hellhole jungle, Irish-style, alien territory, hiding God knows what horrors, despite being green and beautiful and sun-kissed by the early morning dawn.

Ahead of him what he sees is a line of low scrubby trees with glimpses of rough ground in between. No sign of open water beyond, so maybe the place is a lot bigger than he imagined it to be the first time he was here with Pearl and their picnic. Remembering all that prize chow he'd carried ashore that day, a whole Virginia baked ham, clove-studded, syrup-coated, pickles, potato salad, tomatoes, sweet rolls, pecan pie to follow, beer, soda pop, wine, too, he recalls, his stomach rebels at the treatment it's been taking lately. He can't recall exactly when it was he ate last and the thought leads him on to the question just when exactly and what will be his next meal, if any.

Hunger is beginning to take its toll so he decides to get moving before he faints where he stands, a big, barefooted man used to his four squares a day but with the prospect of all that being nothing but a beautiful memory. The look on her face next time, or the time after, she sees her butterball of a boyfriend, slim as a toothpick, lean as a razor. The idea entering his head that way helps take his mind off the truly desperate situation he's in right here and now, most likely, future, too, so he starts picking his way across the uneven ground at the back of the house, bumpy as an old ploughed field, infested with all types of weeds he's never seen or heard of, maybe more of those stinging mothers, too. Starting out shoe-less was a big mistake, but somehow a lot better than squishing along in those ruined army lace-ups of his.

161

Ever so delicately, as if walking an invisible rope, he heads for the trees and soon it starts to pay off as his feet get used to their new way of walking. Coming closer, the trees seem to be a lot more regular in height and size, spaced out, even, than he at first thought, maybe planted as a wind-break to shelter the house. Some hermit, maybe, happy to live out here on his lonesome away from the world, nobody but his goats for company.

For a moment, feeling vulnerable, he freezes on cold, damp feet. Not a sign of old Horny anywhere. *Just where the fuck can he be?* Crouching low in his crippling Tommy's greatcoat – it grips like a straitjacket, even though he's never been in one, least not yet, anyway – head swivelling left, right, left again, he sniffs at the air as if playing that old bastard at his own game.

He arrives safely at the first tree. Some kind of crab-apple as it turns out, little hard mothers the size of marbles growing head-high in abundance. He pulls one down, breaking it off, smells it, bites into it, spits out the flesh as it turns dark almost instantly. The taste, vinegar, puckering up the insides of his mouth.

Water, he tells himself, *must have water and soon*, but none of that stuff that surrounds him on all four sides of his new home. Meet Mister Robinson Crusoe. Fucking Friday, more like.

The land, far side of the little orchard gone to seed, slopes off and upwards, gorse and brambles taking over, blocking his progress. But there are beaten tracks winding in and out of the waist-high briar, just wide enough to accommodate a smallish animal, or a man mindful of his feet, so he follows the one that looks the most used. Currant-sized pellets of fresh dung stick to his bare soles, but he's past caring about such things now.

With the smell of goat strong in his nostrils, he presses on,

162

eager to reach the top of the rise and what lies beyond. He imagines something startling, unexpected, but also something which will cheer him up too, changing his fortunes, maybe, like a stream of clean water, or even an alternative place of refuge less run-down than the one he's been landed with. More important, less exposed to the eyes of those who are hunting him. And he knows there are such people, with all the certainty of a condemned man. *Lie low, play dead, and you just might make it, soldier-boy*, he tells himself. *Ex soldier-boy.*

And with that in mind he reaches the summit and sees open water way below, spreading straight ahead, a whole ocean of it. Instantly he hunkers low among the thorn bushes. This is the outer limit as far as he's concerned. He has run out of island. Due west, according to his calculation, stretches the pale, glittering expanse until it hits the farther shore, ten, maybe, twelve miles, he reckons, although who is he to judge such distances?

For the first time he sees smoke ascending, some sort of village, a ribbon of white along the water's edge catching the light. What he takes to be a window suddenly bounces the sun straight back at him and he crouches even lower as if maybe it's a spyglass that's been trained on him and not a reflecting pane.

Fearful suddenly, he goes backtracking down the way he has come, his army coat catching on the thorns as he slips and slides. The weight and tightness of it irks him. In a rage he tears at it, allowing it to swing free save for one brass button fastened at the throat.

Halfway down the zig-zagging trail he decides to follow a branch off to the left. This one loops back inland where he feels safer, hugging the curve of the land in a more natural fashion. And he finds himself slowing in the same way, as if out for a constitutional and not a nervous reconnaissance, and even though the sun behind him is beginning to climb

163

now with what seems alarming speed. His feet slap the trodden earth, slick with droppings. They seem fresher than those on that other path and, sure enough, rounding a bend, he comes upon the little flock in a hollow scooped out of the hillside, five or six of them, maybe, lying in the grass together chewing, half-asleep, or near enough.

He stops where he is, sinking on to his heels. No sign of old Horny anywhere. This dip they're in is all verdant and lush and, straining forward, he sees, then hears, water. Standing stones are scattered about in various stages of elevation, reminding him of some kind of graveyard, but much, much older than anything he could ever be expected to know about, coming from where he hails from. At their centre the grass grows taller, greener, and it's there he detects water bubbling up out of the ground to run away, losing itself beyond the ring of outer stones.

They look so contented there, those little old nanny-goats stretched out like that, jaws gently grinding away, it seems a shame to have to disturb them, but he must, for his throat is dry suddenly, more parched than it's been so far.

Carefully he rises to his feet, the greatcoat falling free. He stands there hoping they'll see him and scatter. To clap his hands would be unthinkable. Instead he begins to hum, quietly at first, then gradually increasing the pitch and volume. "Campdown Races". What a stupid song. *Doo-dah, doo-dah.* But then he must look stupid, too, posing there, serenading a bunch of goats instead of striding down among them like an avenging angel. His head really is full of crap, all fucked up. *Avenging angel! Jesus H. Christ!*

He flaps his arms. Still they don't budge. The hell with it, he thinks, and makes his move and as he does so out from behind one of the leaning pillars appears old Horny himself, chewing, calm as you please, and obviously not caring what he does or does not do, sing, dance, juggle or play the ukelele. They look at one another, the man on the hill and the ancient billy down in the hollow below. *What an old bastard*, thinks the man, *older than time and with everything he wants right to hand, water, grass, as much poontang as he can handle. Why should he move over and let someone else muscle in on his territory, avenging angel or not?*

They continue to outstare one another, but it cannot last, so the man on the hill stoops, taking up a stone, and he lobs it down amongst the huddle of sleeping goats. Bleating in alarm they rise up on rickety legs, the kids staying close to their mothers. Old Horny surges forward, beard jutting, ears flat, and for a minute it looks as if he'll come charging right up the slope at him.

But he doesn't, he stops instead, beside the spring, pawing the ground, turning it to mush. Slow, slowly, he starts to calm down, left hoof gently stroking the ground now like he's trying to put it all back the way it was before this interruption occurred, all green and untouched-looking.

You come on down here to me, he seems to be saying, *you don't scare me one little bit, mister. See, none of us is spooked.* And it is true, for the rest of the flock have all settled down again a little ways off in the shelter of the outer ring of stones, even the little kids, some of whom are tugging hungrily now on full udders. For all they care he may as well be a tree or a bush. Or one of those old stones they keep rubbing themselves against.

And suddenly the man on the hill sees himself in the eyes of the world, not just those of a mangy bunch of wild goats, the world and everyone in it, a joke figure standing there humming, throwing stones, a black-faced scarecrow in an overcoat three sizes too small for him.

But the moment passes and with it his resolve to get to that water he can see running to waste down below. Still, thirst seems to have evaporated along with his nerve, so

165

slowly, sadly, he retraces his route back the way he has come, back to his own part of the island. Borders have been drawn, he now sees that, territories marked out, as sure as if they've been written on a map. Even so he can't help muttering, *I'll be back, old Horny, count on it,* for he still has a little pick of pride left in him, not much, just about the size of a thumbnail.

When he reaches the ruin – least it's *his* ruin – he creeps around to the front, slow and careful in his old greatcoat like a camouflaged turtle. The distant mainland looks just as he left it, this side must be the late risers' side, and the waters in between are still pink and undisturbed. For a moment he looks longingly towards the shoreline. He can hear the soft *splash, splash,* of tiny waves cresting on the stones. Who's to see if he goes crawling down there to drink his fill, for it's still rainwater, spite of being the same shade as his overcoat. But he hasn't the nerve, least not yet, not now, maybe when it's dark, so he squeezes back inside again past his drying shoes through the crack he's left between the old door and the wrecked frame.

The place is even more of a disaster area than at first he realised, shafts of light lancing through the busted roof and showing up the pitiful mess below. Barely fit for a dog, let alone a goat. Half the slates lie in a broken heap under the open sky, the floor, if you can call it that, littered with bits of lumber and broken lath, and there's other nameless rubbish, too, that must have got blown in over the years, building up in the corners in tangled drifts. In the dark, moving by instinct like some animal, he'd pulled out armfuls of the stuff to make a crib for himself. In daylight it looks no different from the rest of the trash, except for Pearl's old worn wool overcoat spread on top.

He goes over and sits down on the lumpy heap. *So this is*

it, he tells himself, *home sweet home for the foreseeable future.* He doesn't dare allow himself think ahead beyond here and now, for he knows if he does he'll really go bananas, even more so than at present.

Leastways you can always say you've got a roof over your head, not like some other poor bastards. In Africa, maybe, asshole? Well, about a tenth of one, anyway. And he laughs at that. *Oh, thank you, Lord, thankee, thankee kindly, for being so good to this poor, dumb-assed, sorry nigger.* This time the laughter is not so pleasant or unforced, but it's still a laugh, he can still laugh, he can still manage a laugh. Then his mood changes and he thinks, *don't be so goddam pleased with yourself, butterhead, you can't live on it,* for the first time forgetting his thirst and concentrating instead on just how ravenous he is.

The sack that Pearl brought ashore with her is hanging on a nail where she put it. In case of vermin. *Rats,* he thinks, *please God, not here as well, please, please.* But he seems to be okay in that department, for the present, anyway, and he hauls it down and empties its contents out on her old maroon-coloured coat. A loaf of bread, two cans of pressed ham from the PX, something wrapped in newspaper, eggs, he discovers, too late, as one of them collapses messily in his hand. There are other items as well, one blackened saucepan, one knife and spoon, a cup missing a handle, but it is the grub he's interested in. And how.

Before he knows it he has devoured the best part of the loaf and both tins of ham, cramming it all into his mouth until his cheeks are bulging like a chipmunk's. And immediately regrets what he's done, for Lord only knows just where his next meal is to come from, and when.

Instead of being content with a full belly he's really depressed now and lies there on his bed of branches as the light outside grows stronger with all the promise of a fine and glorious day ahead. But not for him. For all those people lucky enough to be outside in it, walking free, no cares, no worries, no fear, the way he used to be up until a day or so ago. Already that blessed period in his life, his young life, seems ages away.

Age, ageing, he thinks, *it's what's happened, is happening, to me*, and he has this overpowering urge to check to see if it's really true. But, of course, running across a mirror is like coming on a set of hen's teeth in his present circumstances. Instead he falls to examining the backs of his hands for tell-tale signs. He doesn't know what they are, but he'll know when he sees them, holding them up to what little light there is entering by way of the holes in the roof. They seem much the same as usual, a little grubby, maybe, and he could sure do with a manicure, *ha, ha*, but he still isn't satisfied, nothing will reassure him, he realises that, so to take his mind off such sick notions, and they are just that, he's not that far gone he doesn't recognise it, he takes out his wallet, flapping it open on an old fallen shingle lit by a patch of sunlight.

He begins making his inventory. After all, it's what every shipwrecked asshole does on day one. Money, two red ten-bob notes, a rubber, Trojan brand, in its little squashed packet, both items equally useless to someone in his present situation. Then in the inner compartment, two photographs, one of Pearl and himself astride his old pushbike, another of his folks back in Ducktown on the stoop of the family residence. That one he's never shown Pearl on account of being too ashamed of the old place, a saggy-roofed share-cropper's cabin, his folks, too, the Lord forgive him, even though they were in their Sunday-go-to-meeting clothes at the time, cousin Benjamin having snapped them with his brand new box Brownie. Thanksgiving, 1938. Hard times, poor people, another world away.

Last of all, folded over and over again to the size of a postage stamp, something he's forgotten he's kept in there,

168

from an old *Saturday Evening Post*, an advertisement for his dream car, a cherry-red Chrysler convertible, white-walls, a real sporty-looking guy smoking a pipe with a Lana Turner lookalike in the passenger seat, regular sweater-girl type, tits like a B-17's nose cones, somebody to get all hot and bothered over. Maybe she was the dream, not the car. He can't remember.

Miraculously he is just starting to get a boner on, well, the beginnings of one, anyway, when he hears the distant drone of an engine. At first he thinks it might be an airplane or even a Catalina, one of those big old Air Force flying boats that put down in the Lough on occasions, but the sound is much higher, more frantic in tone than that, and there was no splash as it hit the water, ploughing up waves.

On hands and knees, redskin fashion, he heads for the crack in the door and looks out. He can see nothing but flat water. The engine noise gradually gets louder, then louder still, and he lies there in the dirt waiting for whatever makes it to appear.

They're coming to get me, he whispers to himself, *those bastard MPs, sure as shit, and they're gonna twist my two arms up behind my back, then kick hell out of me for shooting one of their buddies even though I didn't do it. I didn't do it, I tell you*, he suddenly wants to yell out to the approaching craft like a kid in the school-yard accused in the wrong.

Then the thoughts start arriving thick and fast, all bunching up on him, jostling one another like the guys in chow-line. *Never even got a head start, did you, sad fucker, never even got to enjoy one miserable day of freedom either*, for suddenly the dump he's in seems like a palace to him, a goddamned Taj Mahal, roof or no roof.

Then, boy oh boy – just wait for it – he thinks, *how did they manage to find out where I was in the first place*, feeling sick, all that mess of food in his gut turning to pig swill on the

169

instant and threatening to come boiling up and out of him if he doesn't manage to control it, control himself. *Pearl told them, that's who. Pearl. No one else knows, no other soul but her.*

He's lying there, his right eye glued to the crack, when suddenly he sees the boat, some kind of motor launch, and, yes, it's military, all right, camouflage and a pennant flying from the prow. Yet it keeps on coming hard on a course that'll take it way, way past out there in the middle of the channel.

There's a line stretched tight coming from the stern, on the end of which is a big square kind of a thing the size of a fucking billboard on four floats. Suddenly he's dying to see the farther side of it, the one turned away from him, for he feels convinced there has to be some kind of written message there, has to be, something important, involving him. But what in hell can it be?

For one crazy moment he thinks, *the war is over, the Japs have surrendered, the stinking war is over*, and almost, but not quite, he wants to get to his feet, intent on running to the water's edge his hands in the air as if all will be forgiven and everything he's endured up to now dispersed like a rotten dream he's been longing to wake up from.

What stops him is the sight of the tow-rope being cast off and the launch – it's an MTB, he recognises its lines by now – continuing on its way, leaving the billboard like the side of a house bobbing in its wake. *Why doesn't the crazy bastard keel over*, he frets? *What's keeping it up?* Has to be some kind of weight in the base below the water-line like one of those fairground dummies you can never push over no matter how hard you try or how many dimes you shell out.

Then, again, there's no wind, no real current either. *Can you believe it, here he is lying on his belly like an old hog in its wallow and working out equations, for Christ's sake, the square on the fucking hypotenuse*, when he sees a flash and a puff of smoke on the distant shoreline followed by something landing in the water, throwing up a spout as high as a two-storey house. Somewhere in between there's a whistling scream, then a roar, or maybe it's the other way round, he can't tell. And maybe at the same time as the detonation, he can't tell that either, don't care much, the laws of physics being very far from his mind at this point, for by now he's crouched on the floor with his two hands clapped tight over his ears.

And as he lies there, bowels unclenching, which has become a regular habit with him now, it comes to him what's painted on the landward side of the floating billboard bucking up and down now with the after-shock of the shell landing like that. It's a big old bull's eye, that's what. Those gunnery bastards over there are training their thirty-pounders in his direction right this minute. And then the next round comes whistling over and sends up another gout, this time slightly to the right of the target.

Left, right, fore, but never aft, the barrage continues for the best part of an hour. He can smell the cordite in the air from where he lies, not daring to move in case a stray comes in on top of him. But, of course, these gunnery guys know what they're doing. *They do, don't they?*

When they stop he looks at his watch. *Chow-time, lucky bastards.* Then the launch comes back and manoeuvres itself up alongside the floating butt and a GI in oilskins leans out and hooks up the tow-line. He can see him clearly but not close enough to know if he's ever served him franks and beans with apple betty to follow in the mess-hall. The sight of that doughboy, all easy and relaxed about his business that way, maybe a little bored, too, and looking forward to his lunch with all of the other guys makes him want to weep, but he holds it in until the boat and the great floating siding

171

go chugging off together out of sight and the water becomes calm and empty again, returned to the fishes once more.

He rises then and goes to the bed in the corner and lays himself down on Pearl's old coat. *Forgive me,* he whispers to her, by way of the warm wool, *I didn't mean to doubt you, honest, baby.* But deep down something in him about the size of a pinhead still remains not entirely convinced.

EIGHT

The town hall clock was striking seven as Lawlor wheeled out his bicycle into the deserted roadway and pushed off past darkened housefronts. It felt good at this hour to have the streets to himself, a curfew-breaker with no one brave or authoritative enough to challenge him. The notion was a childish one, people weren't really constrained to stay indoors, blackout or no blackout, but he indulged himself anyhow.

Pulling hard on the handlebars like a pair of metal reins he fairly hurled the great old roadster over the gleaming cobbles, the night air bathing his brow and cheeks in a damp, refreshing rush. All day he had dozed off and on in front of the Day Room fire, banked up despite his strictures about conserving coal, until his eyes smarted and his temples pounded.

Boal and Burnside arrived back at tea-time having been out tramping fields since early morn checking ragweed violations and both exclaimed at the heat of the place, also, without saying as much, at the state of his lobster-red face. It was obvious they thought he had been drinking. He saw it as their eyes moved as one in search of the Power's bottle. But not a drop had passed his lips, not a solitary sip.

Lately he had started thinking his hard boozing days might well be over, a miraculous falling away of bad old habits. It wasn't uncommon. Walking examples of freshly acquired temperance were a daily sight proudly wearing their bright new Pioneer pins and boasting about their sudden sainthood. But, God help him, he'd rather go down a roaring drunk any day than end up like one of those whited sepulchres.

Mrs Neeson had left them one of her burnt offerings squashed between plates in the oven and he watched the others chip away at the congealed mass. Her cooking didn't seem to bother them.

"What is it?" he asked, for he genuinely couldn't tell.

"Liver and bacon," mumbled Burnside, jaws working.

"Aye, nice bit of juicy calves' liver kept over specially by McCabe the butcher," amplified Boal.

"How does he ever manage to get his hands on such a thing, what with the rationing and all?" he heard himself enquire as if he were truly interested.

"Ways and means, means and ways," said Boal.

"Black-bloody-market, more like."

"Ach, sarge, live and let live. Sure, we're all human."

"Some more so than others," chipped in Boal with a grin. "As the actress said to the bishop. Eh, Crawford?"

And that's where he'd left it, and them along with it, pulling on his greatcoat and heading out to where the bicycle silently gathered condensation in the evening air.

And so Lawlor set off through the emptied town with the misshapen brown-paper parcel tied to the saddle-stem like something sprouting from his backside. Inside was his second pair of boots, for he was on his way to the mender's. At least that was his excuse. Even sergeants of police need a cover for their enquiries. He told himself that, like some amateur boy detective. And even if they aren't all that certain what in the name of God they're looking for in the first place.

But then anything was better than lying sprawled in front of a furnace for the best part of a night listening to Sandy MacPherson and his BBC theatre organ, interspersed with the two Bs and their sly, twisting insinuations. As the days passed he was becoming even more of a joke to them, a blind man could see that. And getting to be one to himself, what with his abstractions and silences, and all that concentrated staring into the coals, as if the answers to his questions lay there spelled out in red-hot capitals only he could read.

A revelation, he thought, Eureka. But, no, that was what revealed itself to you in the tub, wasn't it? That old Greek cod, wreaths of steam forming the magic equation there in front of you, or in the steam of the mirror. Forget the fire, try a bath next time, Lawlor, if you can be bothered to haul all those kettles of water up two flights to that Arctic bathroom.

He emitted a laugh at that, more a bark than a real laugh, that quickly turned to a cough then a clearing of the throat in case anyone was listening. He rode on.

He was heading for the signal-box on the outskirts of town where Freddy Dunbar held court in his stilted hut high above the gleaming points of the LMS. As well as tending the levers Freddy went in for a spot of cobbling on the side, courtesy of the railway board, of course. Not exactly company policy, but not interfering with his official duties either. At least he *thought* the rail people approved. Good point, that.

And it really was surprising the number of people who brought their shoe-leather all that way, not just for his skills with hammer and last, but because of the gossip that buzzed around inside that glassed-in box, now curtained off against the

175

Luftwaffe bombers, like bees inside a hive. It was as if from his vantage point our Freddy had a grandstand view of every foible and failing that went on behind every window in town and beyond into the surrounding countryside as well.

If ever you needed to find out who was doing what with who, when and where, even why, you ended up at Freddy's *Rancho Notorious*. "Welcome to *Rancho Notorious*," he would call out cheerily to visitors as they climbed the steps to his crow's-nest. It was his joke, his creation, and the name stuck. For Freddie was a character, you see, and you could get away with a lot of things in this town once you were perceived to be one of those.

Pedalling onwards, the skirts of his greatcoat flapping like two sodden wings, Lawlor wondered if he himself might ever have attained such a distinction. Somehow he thought not. When he departed this place for good, which must be soon, the memory of his posting would fade like snow off a ditch. Gone but forgotten. Something to put in the obituary column. Or on a tombstone.

But to hell with them, and while he was about it, those stuck-up bastards at headquarters. One bastard in particular, namely Inspector General Terence Shillington who only last week had written to him personally (*fancy!*) thanking him for his long service record and reminding him, oh, so tactfully, of his approaching birthday, fifty-five, to be exact, which just so happened to be the official retirement age. No mention of an extension until the war was over, say, unlike some others he knew of in the force. The pasture's waiting, old horse, eat grass. Of course, he knew why. Someone, maybe even some persons, plural, had dropped the hint at some regimental do, maybe on the golf-course. "*Not one of us. Outsider. Always has been. More than a bit partial to his grog, too, from what I hear tell.*"

Kincaid. For an instant that mocking grin of his floated up into consciousness like the belly of a dead trout. Other corpses, other faces, waited to follow, a regular shoal of them, enemies he had made in the course of his duty in this tight wee community. It went with the job, all that animosity. He would carry it with him when he left like a piece of luggage, a portmanteau of grudges. More and more as the day of his departure drew near Lawlor had the notion he should lighten the load somewhat, maybe settle a few old scores. Unfinished business. Right now he was intending to do just that or, at least, clear his conscience, which was the next best thing.

Reaching the railway bridge he rode under its dripping limestone arch, the echo of his passage ringing out shockingly for the first time since he had left the barracks. On the far side he swung the bicycle to the left away from the road marching off to Rushy Hill, pedalling instead along a beaten cinder path parallel to the tracks until it grew too narrow for him to continue. Thorns tore at his greatcoat. He dismounted, feeling them claw the serge covering arms and chest. In that instant his bulk enraged him, a bear in uniform instead of the lithe and shadowy sleuth he had in his mind.

Coming on a gap in the hedge he squeezed the bicycle through until it was hidden from sight, trying not to dwell too closely on a possible puncture. On foot he continued along the path. High above on the crest of the embankment were the railway lines, stilled and silent at this hour, for the last passenger train had steamed through at seven. Much later goods wagons would start rumbling past, dark and slow, like tarpaulined ghosts in the small hours.

Lawlor pressed on, parcel outstretched before him like an offering, for it was intended to allow him to appear without too much explanation or elaboration. Then he began to agonise if the pair of boots he carried inside their creased brown wrapping really did need attention after all. *He should at least have changed them for the ones he was wearing, for God's sake.* But it was too late for that now. Just as well he was retiring, he told himself, as this latest panic assailed him. His nerves weren't up to it any longer. Too many whiskey nights followed by the same quota of nervy days.

He thought of the bottle he kept upstairs in the wardrobe for emergencies. A slug of the hard stuff would have taken the edge off his present jitters but, then again, did he really wish to breeze into *Rancho Notorious* reeking of peppermints, fooling nobody, especially Freddy Dunbar?

About thirty yards or so from the signal-box he stopped where he was, for he had heard the sound of singing on the air. At first he thought it must be the wireless. "Apple Blossom Time." A male quartet. Unaccompanied. But then something about the quality of the voices told him, yes, it came from inside the box, okay, but not from a battery set tuned to some light music programme, Carroll Gibbons, say.

Moving as stealthily as his size tens would allow he reached the foot of the stairway leading up to the square outpost overlooking the tracks. A razor-thin sliver of yellow light lay across the threshold of the doorway above him, while the windows on all four sides of the cabin were curtained tight as coffin lids.

Lawlor hung there for a moment adjusting his vision to the darkness. A pale dusting of stars was abroad. He could make out the Plough and several other constellations as well whose names he used to know as a matter of course in the old days when he devoured books until his eyes burned and then he would blow out the lamp beside his sleeping wife and lie there, often until the dawn sometimes, with all those words and pictures still imprinted in his brain and on the back of his retina like images on a negative.

He began the ascent, gripping the damp wooden handrail. It felt slick and greasy to the touch. All those paws reaching out to steady their owners, and now his, now him, climbing up, too, into the cockpit in search of dirt and slander.

On the topmost step he halted and listened. The singing was still going strong inside, pure sweet voices in four-part harmony. *Like choirboys*, he thought. *What would innocents be doing in such a den?* But then Burnside had once said Freddy kept a cache of dirty pictures which he liked to pass around to favoured visitors, not the pin-ups of Lana Turner, Jane Russell and the like that patched the walls, but postcards he had brought home from France and Gay Paree after the Big War.

Burnside seemed to know a lot more than he should about the supposed goings-on in *Rancho Notorious*, but then Burnside was like that, wasn't he? He had also suggested, with a smirk, that contests of a particular nature took place whenever the saucily posed mademoiselles came out. Whether Freddy actively encouraged such competitions among the lads to see who could bring himself off first wasn't clear, but it was rumoured he didn't exactly forbid that sort of carry-on either.

Lawlor took a deep breath and rapped on the door. Instantly the singing died in a ragged fall on the far side of the darkened glass.

He heard one of the boys call out, "Is that you, Dinger?" before he twisted the knob and pushed his way inside.

Freddy was sitting in an old bus-seat, serene as a Buddha, paring the bright new sole on someone's shoe. A woman's, Lawlor noted with shock, for some reason. Four lads in their early teens, the choristers, perched on a bench in the far corner. All were watching him as he filled the doorway.

Then Freddy said, "Has it stopped raining outside?" and Lawlor felt suddenly awkward, for he had been expecting to be welcomed to *Rancho Notorious* like everyone else. *Why not me*, flashed through his mind in an irrationally peevish reaction.

"Are you stayin' a wee while, sergeant?"

But Lawlor was staring at the row of levers. There was something startling and mystifying about that bank of gleaming instruments. All were upright, all except one, that is, which had an oily scrap of towelling draped over its snout. In his head he tried to make some connection between that single canted shaft and a section of movable rail outside in the wet dark, but he lost the thread somewhere beneath the pitted floorboards and the machinery in the engine-room below.

"Shove over and give Sergeant Lawlor a pew, will you," instructed Freddy and dutifully the songbirds shifted to the left, displacing the one on the end who wore glasses with a round of brown paper over one eye. It gave him an oddly knowing air, but perhaps that was in Lawlor's imagination. To his shame he caught himself scanning the floor for tell-tale stains while surreptitiously sniffing the air for the scent of freshly spilt young seed. But the boards were blackened beyond redemption and the only odours in that hot, enclosed space were the smells of new leather, heel-ball and paraffin.

With a grunt Lawlor lowered himself on to the bench, balancing on one buttock, until without being told another boy gave up his place to join his friend crouched on the floor. No one spoke for a while after that. All eyes stayed on Freddy as he slid the shoe he was cradling on to the smallest foot of the three-pronged last. With his mouth full of nails he proceeded to hammer a ring of them around the rim of the upturned sole. When he had completed the circuit he laid both shoes aside and reached for the parcel.

Lawlor didn't know whether he should unwrap it first or not but then the boy – it was young Niblock, wasn't it? – took it gently from his grasp and passed it around the circle until it reached the old man sitting in the bus-seat. Deftly he sliced the string with his curved knife, stripping away the paper. In his hands the boots looked enormous, giant-league,

180

the light from the overhead oil lamp striking glints off their burnished leather.

Hefting them, Freddy said, "Them boys have seen some mileage in their day, eh, sergeant? Not like the rubbish they turn out these days. Utility!" He spat the word out venomously and a bead of spit followed, fizzing furiously around the hot stove-lid until evaporating. It left a sour smell in the air.

"Do you know what I'm goin' to tell you, I had a pair o' new men's brogues in here only the other day. Damn near ninety-nine per cent cardboard. Made in Morocco. Now wouldn't you think they'd have decent shoe leather in Morocco?"

"It all goes to the Germans," piped up a voice after a pause. It was the specky one with the blacked-out lens.

"Meet the Professor," said Freddy and the others tittered.

Lawlor relaxed with them at this point, unbuttoning his greatcoat. Then he took off his cap and the songbirds stared as though mesmerised by the sight of this ruddy-faced policeman with his bottle-brush crop like snow on a pillar box.

"You're certainly very snug in here," he ventured, offering his outstretched palms to the heat even though the stove glowed a dozen paces away.

"Aye," said Freddy, "no shortage of coal here thanks to the management." He motioned to one of the youths beside Lawlor. "Scoot away down, will you, young Brian, there's a good chap, and bring us up another bucket of slack," and the boy rose and headed for the door.

Freddy's eager little helpers, thought Lawlor, as the bench yielded up another place. *Freddy's little nest of linnets singing for their supper, or whatever else it is that excites their downy young wands.* But there was nothing in the way of disapproval there, nothing censorious. Live and let live, as Boal had put it, and as the cosy intimacy of the place reached out and softened

181

the edges of his mood he began steering the conversation towards the real object of his visit.

And the task was made easier for him when Freddy set aside his boots in a basket on the floor, lit a pipe and settled back against the soiled moquette and leather of his bus-seat. Lawlor noticed it had even got one of those little ashtrays that open out like a drawer still embedded in the armrest, as well as a dimpled strip of brass to strike your matches on. Freddy used his nail. His hands were as darkly impacted as the leather he worked upon.

"They say Jelley's pub's been put on the market. Did you hear that? She left it to some nephew in the city but he wanted no part of it. Can't say I blame him."

"Aye, I heard something along those lines. Never did much trade anyway, mind you," countered Lawlor, lying about any knowledge on his part of such a sale, but warming up to the game of cat and mouse none the less.

He loosened the top button of his tunic, something he rarely did in company, but suddenly he felt emboldened as though the heat had relaxed his personal habits along with all the rest of him.

Freddy clapped a horny thumb over the bowl of his pipe, sucking hard to get it to draw. Then he took it out of his mouth and examined it as if he didn't quite know how it had managed to get there, an alien object of some kind.

Still studying the briar intently he said, "Well, them three darkies got what they deserved, anyway. Prison for the rest of their natural lives, eh?"

Lawlor knew he was quoting what had been reported in the papers. It sounded strange, somehow, "*natural lives*", as though there could ever be anything *natural* about such an existence, locked away behind bars like that until they rotted.

"They say one o' them took a fit of the head-staggers in the courtroom. Had to be handcuffed to a table leg."

That wasn't in the newspapers, for it wasn't true. Lawlor had been there. But he let it pass. The more lurid the stories circulating the better it suited him, he told himself, for then he felt he would be able to sift through the debris of fiction and speculation and maybe, with luck, hit upon one of those tiny nuggets of truth that would send him heading in the right direction. So far he had no inkling of where that might be, even what might be waiting for him there. All he did know was he had to lay a ghost to rest, this faceless spectre of a murdered old woman whose grave was already grown over and would soon be indistinguishable from all those other grassy plots in that ancient Covenanters' cemetery on the hill.

"The nigger that's on the run, I don't mean to be nosey or anything, but are them Yanks any closer to catching him?"

"Not as far as I've been told. It's out of our hands. But I'm sure you know that already."

"Aye, so I've heard," said Freddy removing the pipe from his jaws and firing another gob of spittle at the stove. Unerringly it found its target as before, sizzling away on the hot lid like a demented bee. "Sure, what would them cowboys know about these parts anyway?"

"You think he might still be in the locality, then?" suggested Lawlor, prodding a little. It had been a good week since the killings, so, hardly likely, was what he left unsaid.

"I'll tell you what I think, sergeant," confided the old signalman leaning forward. "I'd bet he's in Dublin right this minute walking up O'Connell Street as free as a bird, happy as Larry. Sure, isn't it a fact it's full of deserters, goose-steppin' Nazis, all sorts of fifth columnists."

The notion was a popular one and openly expressed at that, the Southern capital holding a position in peoples' imaginations halfway between Sodom and Dodge City, despite the considerable traffic, more to the point, *trafficking* for contraband tea, sugar, nylons and the like across the Border with the Republic.

"Are you saying he made it all that way on his own? Without help?"

There was a pause and, too late, Lawlor realised he'd sounded like the policeman he was. The boys were staring at him and then over towards the old man on his scrapyard throne. Maybe they knew something no one else did. Maybe . . .

But then a bell chimed in the confines of that hot, stifling cabin and Freddy and his little apprentice band looked up at the clockface on the wall in the same movement as if the signal was one they all recognised and shared a common interest in.

"The seven forty-three," Freddy announced. "Down track. Randalstown Junction."

Instantly a babble broke out.

"Can I do it?"

"You did it last."

"It's my turn, I tell you."

"It is not!"

"Let me, Freddy."

"*Freddy!*"

The old man grinned at them benevolently, then took a coin from his waistcoat pocket. On the instant the squabbling ceased, all eyeing the bright half-crown twirling between his fingers.

Then, changing his mind, he said, "I tell you what. Maybe the sergeant would like to try his hand," and for a moment Lawlor was indeed tempted to work the lever, sending the oncoming train the merest fraction sideways on to the down track.

"No," he said, "no, you require an expert. Let the Professor do the job," surprising himself by his own boldness and everyone laughed except the boy with the glasses who reddened then stood up in readiness.

184

"Now," commanded Freddy and the boy gripped the middle lever without being told. He braced his puny legs – he was wearing short trousers, unlike the others – and on a second louder, "Now!" he hauled backwards with all his strength, his face showing a mixture of exertion and terror. The lever slid smoothly into its greased socket and a burst of ironic applause broke out as the boy dropped, grinning now, back into his nest in the corner.

A second bell rang, followed by the sound of the approaching goods train. The signal-box shook as it rumbled past, wagon after wagon, an invisible jointed snake beyond the blacked-out windows. No one could speak until it passed, a good minute and a half, by Lawlor's calculation, then Freddy said, "Tea?" almost primly, and Lawlor realised the invitation was addressed to him. At this point he loosened a second collar button on his tunic.

"A special," volunteered Freddy explaining the phantom train. He tapped the side of his nose with a blackened forefinger. "Hush-hush. Careless talk costs lives. Is that not right, boys?" and there was a patriotic chorus of assent.

Lawlor sipped his mug of strong-brewed tea. Plenty of sugar, too, he noted. But then why should there be ever any shortages here while the trains ran past, with the odd package dropping off conveniently at the foot of the steps from time to time? Freddy's network of information, suddenly it struck him, wasn't only confined to the town but stretched across the wider area of the county as well.

Deciding to impart some information of his own – this was a two-way transaction, after all – he said quietly, "Came into town on quite a few occasions, it seems, our man the runaway. According to McCambridge the chemist. The other three had only just arrived that very day as it turned out."

"Well, Ownie McCambridge would certainly know if

185

anyone would. Never away from the shop window, the same gent."

Lawlor permitted himself a smile and one of the boys tittered. Malice starts early in these wee places, the sergeant noted.

"Maybe he had a sweetheart."

"Wouldn't surprise me. Money to burn and no shortage of volunteers to help spend it, black or not. The lower class of female, mainly."

Catholics was what he meant, although Lawlor had it for a fact Father Driscoll of St Comgall's denounced such "foreign entanglements" from the pulpit regularly. But romance, or what passed for it, knew no boundaries, as regards religion or class, even, when it came to entertaining the Yanks and taking their money. Lawlor had seen it with his own eyes. Still, he let it pass.

The old devil sunk in his broken down love-seat had by this time brought his tools out again, the cobbler's knife, the last, the hammer and pliers. They all watched fascinated – people do in such circumstances – as he tore the heels off a pair of men's shoes, ox-blood, expensive looking.

Lawlor wondered who their owner might be and once again he had the feeling that all his years in this place had been spent looking in the wrong places. His enquiries should have started here. For an instant he had this image of Boal and Burnside, the two Bs, sprawled on this same bench, laughing, tea-drinking, tunics unbuttoned to their belt buckles, dissecting the secret vices of half the county, his own included, it wouldn't surprise him. *Dishing the dirt*. A yankee expression.

"Certain of the ladies are partial to *dark meat*, if you follow me. Saw it in France myself." He winked across at Lawlor, for the boys were open-mouthed by this stage.

"You young shavers are far too green to know what the sergeant and me is talking about. Isn't that so now, sergeant?

Dark meat, is it? Sure none of youse has ever had a taste of turkey, never in your puff."

But Lawlor's mood had altered. Suddenly he felt soiled by such talk. He had lowered himself, he saw that now, coming here, colluding with this foul creature reclining in his greasy easy-chair, in carpet slippers, of all things, as if in the domesticity of his own parlour. He had a wife and grown-up daughters, three lipsticked beauties who only went out with officers, according to Boal and Burnside. One was reputed to have earned herself a Persian lamb. *Fur coat and no knickers.* Again in Boal's words. Roberta, with the big diddies. And all of them doting on dear daddy who they always informed their dates was a "railway official" by profession.

The boy at Lawlor's side, fresh-faced, blond, fourteen at the most, blurted out suddenly, "I know somebody who goes with a black soldier. I saw them once together down near the Lough shore one time."

One of his companions remarked quietly, "Sure it wasn't your big sister?" and a scrimmage broke out, the two of them wrestling in the middle of the floor in an oddly controlled manner as if this happened quite frequently and had a ritual attached to it as well as rules.

Freddy continued to sip from his enamel mug, gazing blissfully off into space as if the contest was taking place a million miles away and not at his feet. Finally Lawlor stood up, he felt he had to, and the sweating combatants broke apart, falling back into their old places.

"If you two young buggers don't watch yourselves the sergeant here'll give you a free night's bed and board in the barracks." Again he winked at Lawlor who had begun buttoning his tunic, for he felt suddenly selfconscious, an interloper, in all his red-faced bulk. The others were staring at him, he thought, eager for him to leave and let them get back to their private pursuits.

187

Still on his feet, he said, "I'll call in next week for the boots," adding, "I'm in no great a hurry," which was a mistake, he could tell by the old man's knowing grin.

As he was about to move in the direction of the door the boy on the bench burst out, "*But I tell you I know –*" before stopping short, his eyes fastened on old Freddy whose look had hardened. The boy dropped his head to stare at his hands.

Lawlor gazed down too at his lowered crown, cropped like a convict's, before asking softly, "What do they call you, son?"

Raising his eyes, he looked frightened, but not at Lawlor, he murmured, "Niblock, sir. Brian Niblock," and Lawlor said, "Ah," as if he knew all about him, family, school, where he lived, the very food he ate.

It was a mean trick, he recognised that as such, but one that had become second nature, the nature of the beast. And the beast, clad in his heavy serge uniform, leather of belt, pouch and holster creaking like harness, walked out into the night, closing the door behind him on whatever diversions they had been enjoying before he appeared on the scene.

That was the other thing about his calling, you always arrived *after* something had taken place, never *during*, never *just before*. That was what happened to other people, normal people, who lived through events, were there, when they, *it*, occurred. *It* was like a smell hanging in the air. He sensed it every time he came through a door, nostrils a-quiver like a bull mastiff for the trailing scent of delinquency. Why couldn't he be there just for once when events happened, instead of always having to reconstruct what took place afterwards. It was a foolish, not to say unreal concept, but he kept thinking about it all the same. Why delude himself, it was that single occasion, that one time out of all the rest, for it always seemed to come back to it these days, that one time when he could have been there but wasn't.

At the foot of the steps he stopped to listen, greedy for any last morsel. The wind overhead hummed in the telephone wires connecting the distant stations on either side, the tracks below reflecting their course in the moonlight. Head to one side to pick up what he could glean, Lawlor hung there, still gripping the wooden handrail.

Give it to a count of ten, he told himself, but on eight he heard the sound of sobbing coming from above, one of the boys, he felt certain he knew which one, followed by an angry bark from Freddy. The crying ceased, there was silence, at which point Lawlor moved quickly away into the shadows, for he had a sudden vision of the banished, tearful youth appearing at the top of the steps and catching sight of him frozen guiltily below by the light of the moon.

But the door didn't open and a little later a solitary voice began to croon, "Don't sit under the apple tree with anyone else but me." Another voice joined in, then another, until the little harmony group was back in business as if nothing untoward had happened. But Lawlor felt certain that it had, and once more burned with the unfairness of not being part of things.

He began crunching back along the cinder path, no wider than a rat-run in places. Halfway to where the bicycle was stowed safely away in the hedge he heard a curious metallic ringing noise. It seemed to come from the rails on the embankment above. He stopped to listen. The telephone wires whined, too, on a high shrill note, as if in concert, then suddenly there came a roar and a darkened engine rushed past out of the night with just the glow coming from the fire-box to light its progress.

The wind of its passing and the shock of it sent him reeling into the briars. He hung there as if impaled until it disappeared down the track in the direction of Randalstown, one tiny red unblinking tail-light vanishing into the blackness. In the silence that followed he felt convinced he heard a burst of laughter coming from the signal-box as if there had been a conspiracy not to warn him. Then the song resumed again and he walked on.

The back of his hand stung for it had been torn by a thorn. He sucked the salty blood, feeling his anger feed on it. *His uniform*, he told himself bitterly, *this damned throttling uniform was his problem*, marking him out, making him a target for mockery.

And it was for that very reason, in a fit of frustration, he had laid it aside two days earlier, pulling out his civvies from their mothballs at the back of the wardrobe and putting on his old moss-green Donegal tweed suit which he hadn't worn in an age. It still fitted, *just*, and he had buttoned himself into it – a dozen or more on the waistcoat alone, like polished oak galls – before going down for Boal's and Burnside's once-over in a haze of napthalene.

They eyed him in silence from behind their newspapers, still brimming with details of the trial, enough roughage for the pair of them to chew on for a twelvemonth.

"If anyone wants to know to know where you are, what do you want us to tell them, sarge?" enquired Boal sweetly, meaning Quigg, who else, who had been on the rampage ever since the night of their "bar-room massacre", as one English newspaper described it. For, oh, yes, a reporter from the *News of the World* had been across asking questions and generally making a damn nuisance of himself.

"Tell them, tell them I'm off to see a man about a dog," he said heading out into the permanently chill passageway.

Not so very far from the truth either, he reflected, sliding on his bicycle clips. A tan mongrel. Or a darker breed, even.

And he kept thinking along those lines all the way out of town, creating this picture in his head of something rabid, slavering, belly close to the ground, and him stalking it, keeping on and on and on until finally they confronted one another, him and his quarry. After that everything was unclear, insubstantial, like the debris from a bad dream. He shook his head trying to disperse the mist in his head and nearly fell off his bicycle out there in the middle of a perfectly empty bone-dry country road. He really didn't know what was wrong with him these days, really he didn't.

On the ruler-straight stretch leading to the army base – Lassiter Lodge, after the big old house that lay at the heart of all that recently concreted-over farming land – Lawlor slowed, then coasted the remaining yards, one foot on the pedal, the other trailing alongside. The red and white painted pole barring the entrance stayed firmly in place until a uniformed soldier emerged from the guard hut, a rifle held diagonally across his chest.

"Kindly state your name and business, sir," he commanded crisply and Lawlor handed over his identity card with its RUC crest.

"I made an appointment to come and see Captain Harper," he told him.

"The Captain is expecting you?"

"That's correct."

"Just one moment, sir."

Lawlor stood in the hot sun, his paw clasping the saddle of his mount like some great boiled crab. The rest of him felt much the same under its heavy Donegal weave. The afternoon was still and cloudless and as he felt the sweat course slowly down the gulley of his spine he realised it had to be a colossal blunder coming out dressed in this fashion. Better the uniform by far, and not because it was in any way cooler, but because he looked exactly like some fat perspiring cattle-jobber, all dignity as well as authority stripped away and hanging in the back of the wardrobe where he'd left it.

He stood there outside the lowered barrier as casually as he could listening to the soldier making a phone call from inside the hut. It seemed to take a very long time but then the pole slowly began to rise to the upright position and without being told Lawlor wheeled his bicycle under it.

The soldier reappeared, without the rifle this time, and said, "You can leave the boneshaker here, sir. Don't worry, it'll be perfectly safe." He was grinning as well as chewing gum and looked about nineteen, barely fit to use a razor, let alone a gun.

Lawlor stared away from his pitted young face up the straight roadway that led to the heart of the camp. There were huts on either side, laid out like the teeth in a comb and all painted the same colour as the soldier's uniform. Everything seemed to have been washed in that particular shade of pond slime, even the grass, as if a deluge of regulation US olive-green had fallen from the skies over-night, drenching this particular corner of his own country.

And then a jeep appeared in the distance, khaki-coloured also, speeding towards them.

"Here comes your ride, sergeant," said the sentry and Lawlor waited obediently until the vehicle skidded to a halt, its long radio antenna bowing languidly in the windless air. He clambered aboard beside the driver, older, more taciturn, hips like a woman's. Lawlor felt squeezed as if he might pop like a pip from the narrow seat at any moment.

They sped past the Quonset huts, row after row of them, doors wide to the world. He could see beds laid out like more teeth in a comb with symmetrical mounds of belongings piled on top of each one as if in readiness for some sudden dramatic exodus. *Where is everybody*, he felt like asking the slab of squeezed khaki sausage by his side, for the eerie absence of life was beginning to worry him. Everyone knew they could up and leave for the war-zones of Europe literally at any moment, but surely he would have heard something.

As if sensing his disquiet the driver grunted, "Manoeuvres. The whole goddamned outfit is out on field manoeuvres. Big gung-ho operation with the limeys up-country some-wheres. Don't ask me where, buddy, I'm only a driver. Nobody tells me nuthin'."

Which makes two of us, Lawlor was thinking, as the jeep slowed then took a right turn away from the sleeping-quarters into another section of the camp where the buildings were larger, more spaced out. Signs of life appeared, soldiers in work-clothes listlessly engaged in what looked like desultory tasks, digging, painting, washing down vehicles, loading, unloading. They passed four squatting men stripped to their vests peeling a mountain of spuds. And all of them, without exception, black.

"Welcome to Harlem," said the driver, easing off on the accelerator as though intent on giving his passenger a guided tour whether he liked to or not. Lawlor wasn't sure if he wanted to. "Ever been to New York?"

Lawlor shook his head, gazing out at those sweating dark faces. For the most part they ignored the jeep and its occupants but some, one or two, stared directly at them as they idled past. That look, concentrated, but strangely lacking in curiosity, somehow, came as a shock to Lawlor who had become used to the white-toothed grins of the town's Friday-night visitors. Suddenly he wanted this man by his side to speed them off out of here away from this unsettling community, as suddenly alien and unimaginable as the place the other had just mentioned.

"Don't. Take my word for it. Visit the real Harlem, I

mean." Lawlor looked at him. "Yeah, Lagos on Lenox Avenue?"

Then he laughed. "God help us all if the Krauts ever landed. Probably try to croon 'em to death."

He swung the jeep down another roadway and now they were passing rows of parked lorries, armoured cars, and what looked like tanks under camouflaged tarpaulins.

"Not too much singin' goin' on, that's for sure. Not right now, it ain't. 'Cause they're all confined to base, is why. Until further notice. After that little episode in town. Brought it down on their own heads, brought it on themselves, sure as black's black and white's white. Hey, you happen to know an old bird lives in town, Fonsey Magee? Real hoot, old Fonsey. Regular Gabby Hayes."

Lawlor did know the character in question, a sponging low-lifer of the first order, but let it pass, pretending ignorance.

Moments later they were tearing up what used to be the driveway to the old Lassiter mansion, only now it had been sheathed over in knobbly new concrete that hummed under their tyres. The Stars and Stripes was flying from the tower above the big gaping front doors. Two MPs in white helmets and gaiters, flanking the steps, watched them disinterestedly.

"At ease, men!" the driver called out cheerily, spraying a fan of gravel with his back wheels almost to their polished toecaps.

"And screw you too, Birkmeyer," retorted one of the MPs in matter-of-fact tones.

Lawlor climbed stiffly out, feeling a sudden rush of heat to his face and neck. His suit was throttling him. Either he had expanded, or it had tightened. He felt like a mummy in its clammy, heathery embrace.

The driver announced, "A visitor for Lieutenant Apple-yard. Expected. Papers all in order."

"Don't be an asshole, Birkmeyer. Get lost."

And the crew-cutted private with the German-sounding name sped off, hoisting a fat middle finger in the air.

"Straight along the hallway. Just knock on the door at the end with the lieutenant's name on it."

Lawlor mounted the steps past these two impeccably turned out sentries. They looked like toy-soldiers who might be put back to lie side by side in a tissue-lined box at Lights Out. And then he thought of those other dark, closed faces in their drab fatigues he had driven past a little earlier.

The separation between white and black, or *colour*, as they preferred to call it, was something that hadn't engaged him too much previously. Or, if it had, he had allowed it to wash over him, or past, a glimpse of something caught, just, out of the corner of one eye. After all they might well be gone tomorrow, a midnight flit on the grandest scale possible, and everything they had brought along with them. Here behind its perimeter fencing lay a world with a code and customs all its own. Not his code, not even his language, it would appear. Yet here he was seeking entry to this world, prepared to ask questions, too, in an attempt to understand. He wanted to *understand*, that was it, what it was about, what one man in particular was about, one man who once had been a part of this other shadow army he had just glimpsed of poorly dressed labourers and kitchen hands kept hidden away in a corner of their own little policed territory.

Lawlor took a deep breath readying himself for further surprises, although there was nothing alien or unsettling about the place save a mingled reek of strong cigars and boiled coffee in the air.

He proceeded up the corridor unable to keep from noting how run-down the place was, bare, dented walls, abused woodwork, the doors he passed all liberally scarred by penknives.

The last one on the left had a square of paper tacked to it with the single word "Appleyard" on it, reassuring in its familiarity, unlike some of the other unpronounceable surnames these people seemed to possess. "Come in," a voice called out at his knock. He twisted the chill brass knob and pushed.

The room was something of a shock, big and bare like a ballroom, with two enormous windows overlooking a park, and stripped of everything, carpets, curtains, furniture, save one desk, one chair and a set of khaki metal filing cabinets. At the desk, face on, was someone young enough to be Lawlor's son — if he'd had one.

"Pull up a seat," commanded this uniformed stripling and Lawlor looked around in panic until he realised there was indeed another chair pressed against the wall behind him.

"How may I help you, sir?" He was smiling now, which was something of a relief, pale, freckled hands steepled in front of his face. Blond, with rimless spectacles, and definitely pigeon-chested, this was someone who would almost certainly spend the duration behind a desk, a succession of desks.

Lawlor began to feel more self-assured. Freeing a button he attempted to make himself appear more at ease on the hard wooden chair while indulging the fantasy it was he who was conducting the interview and not this boy-soldier in the bookish glasses.

"I actually requested a meeting with Captain Harper," he began. *Not you, sonny jim. Not you.* "On a matter regarding —"

And here he stalled. It was the first real hurdle, for he was still not all that certain in his mind what he was doing here.

The young pen-pusher looked embarrassed. "Sergeant Lawlor, the Captain has been called away on urgent military business. He has asked me to apologise to you personally and, in his absence, stand in for him. If there's anything I can help

196

you with, anything, anything at all, sir, I'm at your service. Can I offer you a little hospitality, some coffee, perhaps?"

Lawlor shook his head and, astonished at his own effrontery, not to mention new-found cunning, said, "The Captain promised to keep me up to date on any fresh developments regarding the Jelley pub shooting. The soldier – what's his name – Washington, wasn't it? The one who fled the scene? Has there been any word of his whereabouts, even capture?"

The lieutenant took his glasses off and began rapidly polishing them with a clean khaki handkerchief. His eyes looked suddenly very vulnerable, even more youthful than the rest of him. There was a fresh indentation across the bridge of his nose. "That's CID jurisdiction, sir. They have exclusive handling of the case."

Lawlor stretched his tweed-clad legs out in front of him. This was beginning to be more like the real thing. He stared up at the ceiling at a wrecked chandelier missing most of its crystals.

Softening his voice, he said, "Lieutenant, I feel certain you must be aware of the terrible effect this business has had on our local community. Everyone's still in deep shock. People don't feel safe in their beds at night. There's a fair bit of anger, too, that a killer seems to be still on the loose. Now, while I feel confident that your own people are doing everything in their power to apprehend this man before he slaughters another innocent civilian, it wouldn't be unreasonable to suggest we work in harmony, would it, now? The Captain, if he were with us, would back me up, I feel certain, for he told me so the last time I saw and spoke to him." The half-truth slipped out of him as easily as a plum stone.

The young lieutenant swallowed and put the glasses back

197

on again. "I'm afraid I haven't any authority in this specific area," he said firmly.

Time to turn on the charm, decided Lawlor, smiling directly at this nervous toy soldier. "Look," he said, "all I need is a little background information for my report. The barest of details."

"What sort of details?"

"Well, the man himself, for a start. I mean I saw the other three at the trial but our friend the runaway is a complete mystery. You might find this hard to believe, lieutenant, but the wildest tales are circulating. Over six feet, heavily scarred, the strength of three, a convicted felon in his own country . . ." Now he was really indulging himself. Boal and Burnside would be proud of him.

The lieutenant stood up and walked across to the great French windows. They were criss-crossed with brown tape against bomb blast. He stood looking out at the overgrown jungle that used to be the pride and joy of at least a dozen under-gardeners.

"Sergeant," he said, addressing the latticed panes, "let me assure you there are no personnel in the US army, white, or colored, for that matter, with a jail record."

Lawlor said, "I'm glad to hear it. Pardon me, but maybe a wee cup of your excellent American coffee wouldn't come amiss after all. Now that I'm here."

The lieutenant looked relieved – after all, hospitality was one of their big things, Lawlor had noticed – and punched a bell on the desk. A corporal appeared and was ordered to go fetch both coffee and cookies.

"Your accent," said Lawlor, growing bolder by the minute. "Southern, isn't it?"

"You know our country, then, sir?"

"Just from what I've read. And the cinema, of course."

The other laughed. "We watch British movies, too, you know."

The coffee arrived and was duly poured. Cream *and* sugar.

"We're all of us good old Dixie boys. All the officers, I mean."

Lawlor looked at him.

"Allow me to explain something to you, sir. Our Services of Supply units are predominately colored. Like this one right here at Lassiter Lodge. We're proud of what our men do, but the simple fact of the matter is the *nigra* doesn't make a good fighting man. Does not. What he does do best is what he's used to doing back home, and back home he's used to working with people who know his ways. People like myself and Captain Harper, sir. We've grown up with the dark aspect all our lives, we speak their language. And that is why we have been given this command. The men under our command feel more comfortable taking orders from someone who understands them, not someone who comes from New York or Chicago, say.

"Now I'm going to be blunt at this point and I hope you don't take it the wrong way. The fact is, Sergeant Lawlor, you people just didn't know how to handle our colored troops when they arrived here. Not to put too fine a point on it, you spoiled them, sir, with wine, women and song, sir, and that in turn makes our job ten times harder when it comes to trying to turn them into a disciplined and responsible service corps.

"Now I'm not blaming anyone, there's been a lot of misunderstanding on both sides, but, Sergeant, what took place in that public house in your town three weeks ago was in my opinion a direct consequence of treating the *nigra* the same as if he is white, which he is not, cannot be, and never ever will be."

The speech was a long one and towards the end of it

Lawlor noticed the lieutenant's coffee mug was shaking in his hand. Powerful feelings were at work here, strongly held beliefs which had travelled nearly four thousand miles to flower intact among the fields and hills of Lawlor's country. He had opinions of his own, but in that moment, listening to this passionate manifesto with its curious mixture of resentment and guilt, he decided not to allow them to enter into contest with each other. He would keep his ideas to himself, reserve his counsel as well as his judgement, and so he sat there with his thick white mug on his knee feeling the hot base imprint itself on the tweed of his left trouser leg. Hadn't these people ever come across *saucers*?

Then the lieutenant was on his feet. The interview was at an end. He said, "I'm sorry I haven't been able to be of more assistance. But to be honest with you, Sergeant, I can't really see how we can help you further in this matter. Believe me, you'll be informed the instant this man gives himself up, which I expect to happen literally any day now."

So, thought Lawlor, *I was right all along, they haven't done a damn thing after all. Just sat on their well-upholstered American arses and let nature take its course.* The nature of the beast on the run. It made him even more determined in his uncertain quest and he continued to sit there nursing his coffee mug.

"Records," he began. "Surely there must be a service record somewhere for this Washington."

His listener sighed. Patience was beginning to wear thin, even that much-vaunted old-world politeness of the Deep South had its limits. Taking out his army-issue handkerchief he began rubbing his spectacles again.

"Every recruit and draftee is thoroughly processed from the moment he enters the services until the day he leaves, so the answer to your question is, yes, we do have service documentation, but such information is strictly classified, as I think I've indicated."

200

"Have you seen it?"

"No, sir."

"Do you know the man? Have you ever met him?"

This time he rang the bell on the desk in front of him before replying wearily, "We have over six hundred and fifty men in Fifth Quartermaster. Does that answer your question?"

Lawlor rose. "No, it does not," he said, "but never mind, I can see I've taken up far too much of your valuable time as it is."

The door opened and the young corporal who had brought the coffee earlier reappeared.

"Take this stuff away, Cunningham, and while you're at it, would you kindly see that Sergeant Lawlor collects his ride out front."

The corporal saluted and Lawlor stood there still reluctant to admit defeat. *One last try*, he persuaded himself, *why not, for I'll never be seeing this scrawny little organ-grinder's monkey ever again.*

"Tell me something. No one supplied a photograph of the wanted man to the papers. Why? Did no one consider it important enough? *Him?* Or was it classified as well?"

"Goodbye, sergeant."

But then he relented, sighing on a deeply exhausted note. "On his way out, Cunningham, make sure Sergeant Lawlor sees some of those group shots that were taken by that photographer from *Stars And Stripes*. On the rec-room wall."

"Yes, sir!" barked the eager young corporal and held the door open so that Lawlor had enough room to squeeze past.

He went in front of him, rubber-soled shoes sucking thirstily on the parquet of the long hallway, until they reached a door that looked even more brutalised than the rest. Music pounded inside, loud, throbbing music, one of those swing orchestras, either on a record or the radio. His

201

guide proceeded to push open the door and Lawlor saw a big barely furnished room blue with cigarette smoke. Perhaps twenty or so young men in unbuttoned tunics or undershirts played cards or sprawled in armchairs while all the time the music flowed over them in waves from a big glass-fronted music-machine the size of a sideboard that rippled with coloured lights up against a far wall.

"Ask your friend if he'd like a beer, corp!" one of the card players called out, raising a foam-filled bottle in a lazy fist, but Lawlor shook his head even though his throat was tight with thirst. Once again he felt conspicuous, even gaudy, in his green-flecked suit in the midst of all these lounging soldier boys.

Cunningham shouted, "Turn that juke-box down a notch or two, fellas!" but there were no takers, just a unanimous and good-tempered lack of respect for the other's rank.

But Lawlor was intent instead on what covered the entire wall away from the pounding music-machine. It was a collection of mounted photographs, faces, hundreds of them, staring out of their frames at the photographer and, then, beyond that in time and space, at him, Lawlor himself. Faces, curious, posed, suspicious, and nearly all black as if they had been captured for the camera in Africa and not here in mid-Antrim.

Moving closer he gazed at those grouped figures, some in uniform, many not. He began to focus on the ones dressed for labouring duties, not the parade ground.

Then the corporal was by his side. "This one here, I guess, sir, is the one you want to see," he said, up close and breathing chewing-gum fumes. He placed a forefinger against the glass. "Right here, see? D Company. Canteen detail."

Lawlor leant in, searching the faces as if one might leap out at him, startling in its ferocity, but they all remained impassive, uniform, betraying nothing, frozen in time by the photographer's thumb.

"He's here, you say, this Washington?" he said to the corporal.

"I guess."

"Can you point him out?"

"Never had the pleasure of meeting the worthless son of a bitch."

Lawlor sighed deeply and the corporal responded with a laugh. "You're absolutely right. They do look all the same, don't they just? We gotta go. The jeep's outside, sir."

But Lawlor hung on still, face close to the glass, stubbornly searching. The dance-band music roared and pounded like surf as he concentrated on this specific record of a sunny day somewhere. There was grass and clear sky and about twenty men arranged in formation for posterity. Most wore white cooks' garb, aprons and striped trousers, while one or two were stripped to the waist like Hottentots. They looked as though they had just left whatever it was they were doing and the instant the shutter winked would slouch back to the heat and noise of the kitchen again. Lawlor felt a bit like a photographer himself trying to imprint each dark face on the frame of his memory before they were taken away from him for good. He knew he would never be back in this room again.

The corporal saluted. It was time to go.

As they were heading back down the long ravaged corridor the soldier said, "Do something for all of us, sir. Plug that no-account black son of a whore on sight."

Lawlor looked at him in surprise but the man by his side remained silent, staring straight ahead until they reached the open front door.

There he saluted, but Lawlor was reluctant to let what

he'd said pass. "Is there no one who knows or has met this man? No one?"

The other gave a sharp laugh. "Mebbe around about forty to fifty other wet heads, but you ain't gonna get a peep outa any one of them. Take my word for it. I guess it looks as if you're on your own, Sergeant."

Saluting a second time he walked away and Lawlor saw the jeep waiting for him parked outside on the damaged gravel.

Now, two days on, cycling back in the dark from the signal-box, the two events seemed to be coalescing in his head in some strange way. On each occasion those he'd questioned appeared to know something he did not and were intent on keeping it from him. It was like a game of blind man's bluff. Voices kept whispering to him, *hot, cold, oh, now, you're hot again*, as he blundered about, head held high, sniffing for clues. He had a sudden searing image of himself, this blinkered clown surrounded by grinning tormentors.

And then his mood began to change as if suddenly drawing sustenance from all that malice. He remembered the corporal's closing words about being on his own. *Why not*, he thought, *was that so bad?* And then he had another image, this time of someone younger, agile in body as well as brain, reaching out to his faceless quarry. Only now he was seeing that face for the first time, for it was in his head, an amalgam of all those other faces in that photograph, and it was fearful, sweating, knowing that he, Lawlor, was closing in on him by sheer persistence and cunning.

The feeling was a good one while it lasted and it stayed like that, a warm covering against the damp, dark night all the way back to the barracks.

NINE

Tom, Eric, Wilma, the three young ones, had just been fed, boiled egg mashed in a cup followed by *panada* — bread, warm milk, sugar — easy stuff, when the boy looked up and saw Wesley McQuillan grinning in at him through their open doorway. Despite the gravel he had come up like a ghost. The boy's mother didn't approve of Wesley, the family, neither, and Wesley was aware of that. Silently they stared at one another. The boy still had a saucepan in one hand, a damp dish-clout draped over his shoulder like a sash. The children were happily guzzling away at the kitchen table.

It was four o'clock on a warm Thursday afternoon and he hadn't been to school for a week. Upstairs, a vinegar-soaked pad lapping her temples, his mother lay resting. Lately she hadn't been well, some female complaint which hung in the air, unspoken, unexplained, like a rank smell, keeping him at home to look after the place and all the stupid things that went with it. He had now become the *woman* of the house, he told himself, and seeing Wesley McQuillan waving in at him with a stupid smirk on his ugly face merely compounded his shame.

Wesley kept signalling for him to come outside and join him and eventually the boy gave in, simply because he was more afraid of his class-mate than of his mother lying listless and unmoving overhead.

Making certain the fireguard was in place and the children preoccupied, he laid the saucepan down, moving into the sunlight. As he did so Wesley produced a packet of Willie Woodbines, sliding one into his mouth. He made a striking gesture and Raymond, the boy, dutifully went back inside again to fetch a couple of matches, no more, in case they might be missed from their big box on the mantelpiece. The three little piggies hadn't looked up from their trough, not once.

"I've something to show you, Taggart," confided Wesley hoarsely – his voice was just breaking – taking him by the arm and pulling him into the shade of the trees.

The farmer's son was a good year older than he was, bigger, more grown-up by at least another five because of the life he led, a man's life on the home farm. He had orange-coloured hair razored to the contours of his scalp because of ringworm and his freckled hands were peppered with warts. The smell, too, of the milking-parlour clung so stubbornly that no one would sit next to him in class except the boy who only did so because he knew he must.

For it was his destiny to be the other's after-school companion in crime. *Why me*, he kept wondering, each time the summons came and together they would set off on yet another expedition of destruction, robbing nests or peoples' fruit trees, stoning the white china insulators on telegraph poles, firing whins, drowning Tommy Cathcart's cat Fluff for the umpteenth time. They kept on immersing the old half-blind tabby just to see how far they – it – could go, a scientific experiment, Wesley holding him under in the water-butt until the ascending bubbles started coming faster and faster like the ones in a soda-siphon. He didn't seem to mind about getting scratched either, just laughed as it streaked away from them, a sodden bundle of fur.

"Only four more lives to go," he would cry, and then they would slope off to plunder somebody's orchard. "Your turn, Taggart, I'm always the one who baptises the cat," as if it were some sort of terrific treat, even honour, and then the boy would find himself creeping under some hedge or other, hating it almost as much as he did his grinning red-headed champion. For, yes, he did protect him in the playground, that had to be said, mashing anyone foolhardy enough to say a word about his mother or the fathers he had never known.

"Here, have a drag, it'll grow hairs on your charley."

Cravenly he put the wet tip to his lips.

Wesley watched with close interest. "Draw deep, no bluffin', now."

They stood together under a spreading beech, its olive-grey trunk scarred with initials, hearts and arrows, some almost as ancient as the tree itself. *1836*, he could just make out. Wesley saw him looking, a bad mistake on his part, and took out his clasp-knife. It was one of those black, criss-cross handled army surplus jobs saved up and sent away for, with a curving spike like a walrus tooth. For taking stones out of horses' hooves, Wesley said. To the boy's horror he unfolded the spike and jabbed it savagely straight into the bark. The knife just hung there.

"Now hand over the fag."

Obediently he passed the lit Woodbine across, trying not to inhale. His mouth was full of smoke. With closed eyes and a look of rapture on his face Wesley sucked hard. The boy breathed out. Already his head was swimming, he felt sick, but not half as sick as at the sight of that knife sticking out of the Major's beloved tree. Seven in all, The Seven Sisters, they were called, planted and given names when the house was first built.

This one, Wilhelmina, bore a record of every single generation of Kincaids.

"What was it you wanted to show me?" he heard himself enquire in a high voice, still unable to take his eyes off the outrage embedded a foot away in the growing wood.

"What's your rush? Hey, you missed the school inspector. Old Joe Malone nearly shit himself. Should have seen his face when nobody knew the capital of Turkey."

"Istanbul."

"Constantinople." The boy let it pass.

A pigeon suddenly rocketed out of the upper reaches of one of the remaining six Sisters and he jumped nervously. Wesley only laughed.

"You're like an oul' woman, you are. I saw you in your apron."

"You did not!"

"Don't contradict me. I fuckin' well did, I tell you."

And he put his great red hands about the boy's throat, not squeezing, just holding him calmly, captive there, and grinning good-naturedly all the while as if they were the greatest buddies imaginable. And the terrible thing was maybe he, Wesley, felt it to be true. That was what bothered the boy most. What if he were to ever find out he didn't feel the same way? So he stood there, docile, unmoving, breathing in the mingled reek of tobacco, sour milk, damp hay, and maybe something else better not imagined.

Tiring of the game − for if the victim makes no attempt to struggle or fight back, where's the sport in that? − Wesley turned his attention back to his precious army knife once more. The boy watched him tug it from its resting-place then wipe the spike a couple of times on his jersey. He kept his eyes fixed on the wound, desperately willing it to close as if by some miracle.

"What did you want to show me?" he asked trying to keep the nervousness out of his voice.

The other glanced at him. "No big hurry. Sure, it's lovely here."

He looked around approvingly, patting the fat trunk he had stabbed just moments earlier. Then he looked upwards. "Ever climb this?"

"No, the Major wouldn't like it."

God curse him but he opened up the knife once more, only this time it was the big blade he selected, and started carving something in the bark.

"No! No!" the boy cried. "Don't! You mustn't!"

But the other only laughed at him covering up what it was he was cutting into the dappled outer covering, soft as cheese rind.

"The Major'll go mad, I tell you. He's very particular about his trees."

"Sure, it's only an oul' copper beech. We'd chop it down for firewood if it was on our place. Beech is great for the fire, you know. There," he concluded triumphantly, standing back and wiping the knife for the last time. "We can go now if it makes you any happier. I can put the date on another time."

But the boy stood where he was staring at the other's handiwork, the taste of bile, bitter in his mouth, prelude to him throwing up, for his life was now over, ruined, in ashes. *RT* he read, *his* initials, not Wesley's. *No, damn him, not his.* He craned forward. Perhaps the wound was only superficial, not as deep or as damaging as he first thought, but then he felt his arm being gripped roughly yet again.

"Why are you so worried about that oul' cunt Kincaid, anyway? And that skinny dame he's married to. Sure, she's only an oul' huer, everyone knows that. Now stay close to me and see what I came across on my travels."

And Wesley McQuillan led him away off through the plantation like someone going to meet his end. Anyhow, that's what it felt like.

Taking care not to create undue noise or disturb the pheasants they travelled by a covert, looping route, bringing them out at the rear of Glebe House. Both dropped on to their bellies in the grass without a word having to be spoken.

"Well?" whispered Wesley close to his ear. "Now do you see it — *them*?"

"See what?" As far as he was concerned the vista was much the same as usual, two greenhouses flanking an expanse, half untended lawn, half paving. There was also a selection of washing strung between two posts, but that was always present because of the constant laundering that went on.

"Look close," breathed Wesley. He seemed to be getting excited in some unexplainable way. "There, on the line. Your woman's stays and bloomers. Peach."

The boy looked at him. "Peach?"

"Aye, that's what they call them. Peach." He laughed. "I'd give my entire sweetie ration just to see her oul' face when she finds them gone."

The full horror of what was about to take place gripped the boy in a clammy embrace, for this was infinitely worse than having his initials carved into the Kincaid family tree. He tried to rise but the other held him close. He smelt tobacco on his breath.

"You grab the stays, I'll go for the knickers. Okay?"

"No, no, I can't, I won't, they'll see me. Mrs Cupples the cook is in and out all the time." This last was a lie, for she spent most of her day sitting hunched in a Windsor chair

210

giving orders. "I'm not doing it, I tell you. I don't care what you do."

"Oh, yes, you fucking well are." And taking his bare forearm he twisted with both hands in opposite directions until the pain of the Chinese burn forced tears to his eyes.

"There's tons more where that comes from. Now go and grab them corsets, for I won't tell you a second time. And if you're a good boy I might let you have a sniff at the drawers when it's my turn."

Slowly, dutifully, the boy rose to his feet. Something beyond the pain had changed his mind for him. Maybe he was too frightened of things, of other people, for his own good. Maybe he should be a wee bit more like his evil friend, taking delight in pilfering and pillage. A whole regiment of people who richly deserved to be harried suddenly poured through his head like a photograph being pulled past, all suspicious, all distrustful.

And somewhere in amongst them was the face of his mother. She was no different from the rest for, deep down, he knew she distrusted him too. She'd lied to him, hadn't she, telling him Willie had gone for good without saying goodbye while all the time rowing out to him at night in secret while they were supposed to be tucked up fast asleep, innocent little heads on their pillows.

For he had followed her again after that time at the Ice-House, spying on her as she dragged out the old rowboat to set off over the water to be with the only one she truly cared for. Not him, not her family. But someone who'd turned out to be a murderer. The whole countryside was talking about what he had done by now. And only he and his mother knew where he was hidden. It made him frightened whenever he thought about it, carrying all that burden of knowledge and guilt for her sake. "Okay," he said and started off across the expanse of flattened grass towards that

211

distant white wall of washing. He was doing this to spite her, all of them, and if he got caught, well, too bad.

Half in love with martyrdom already he arrived at the clothesline without a single, solitary angry or questioning voice to greet him. Partly relieved, partly disappointed, in some odd way too, he buried his face amongst the freshly laundered sheets, the big house staying still as the grave. *Where the hell is everybody*, he asked himself, then caught himself thinking – *just when you're needed*.

He could smell the rich, fresh fragrance of drying linen and for a moment closed eyes and mind to everything but that marvellous scent. Imagine having spotlessly clean bedclothes every night of your entire life, ironed, too. But then he heard a whistle and an angry Wesley was waving to him, his reddish fuzz a match for his complexion.

"*Fuck! Fuck!*" he distinctly heard him cry out, the only person his age he knew who dared use the word or its variants. Everyone else at school was afraid to, as if their tongue might swell in their mouths the moment it slipped out.

Then he heard his own name being called which was much more shocking by far, identifying him for anyone who might be listening and watching at the big windows. Reaching up and scattering pegs to the wind he grabbed two garments that vaguely looked and felt like the ones he was meant to seize, pale pinkish in colour – *peach*, he supposed – with complicated fastenings and trailing ribbons, just as sweet-smelling as the sheets, maybe more so, but still he refrained from burying his nose in them as he ran, because of where they might have come from.

With a face on him like thunder Wesley was waiting for him. "Hand them here, fuck you, Taggart!" he growled, snatching the bundle out of his hand.

For some reason he had upset him, but how and why the

boy couldn't quite work out. Not only had he done as he'd been ordered, he'd also returned with both prizes, not one.

"I've got to get back home right now," he told him, but the other only gripped him hard, marching him deeper into the shadowy plantation until they reached a corner of it even he had never been before. Somewhere not far from the old Ice-House, he suspected. And because it came to him there had to be some looming connection between that earlier guilty secret and this latest one, there in the soft, damp leaf-mould under one of the Major's overgrown Christmas trees, he dug his heels in. To his surprise Wesley relaxed his hold and began to laugh.

"Take it easy, young Taggart, the job's a good 'un. See?" Holding up and shaking out the booty for his approval.

Uncertain of what to do next the boy stood there longing desperately to get back to the house and his three young charges. "Look," he began, but before he could finish Wesley had thrust a handful of flesh-coloured silk in his face. Recoiling, he heard him burst out laughing again.

"Scared you'll catch something? I'm not," burying his own raw red cheeks in the lacy froth. "Lovely," he sighed, "just lovely."

Next he proceeded to drape one of the Major's wife's undergarments over a low-hanging branch for closer inspection. He seemed excited by its intricacies, exclaiming over every delicate ribbon, hook and stiffener. "This is made out of the bones of a real whale, did you know that?" flexing the invisible stays in their seamed sockets. "Unbreakable, too," he said. "I saw one of these same yokes in the Littlewood's catalogue, only not as snazzy. Great big lumps of women wearing next to nothing. Jasus, enough to give you a hardener for a week. This is a French corset, and this one here is what they call a two-way stretch. See?" and he tugged the second garment to demonstrate.

The boy was thinking *so this is what passes through his head when he's alone, milking, say, or out in the fields rounding up their old piebald mare Bessy. Women with no clothes on, or as little as makes no difference.* He himself had once been shown a tattered copy of *Lilliput* that somebody had found behind a hedge, not Wesley, one of his other class-mates, and together they had pored over the photos in its middle section, blondes shading their eyes and staring out to sea. Yet none of them, not one, seemed to have any semblance of hair *down there* for some odd reason. Like his own mother, for instance. That particular memory had burned a permanent image, staying hard-edged as a medal, no matter how much he tried to erase its image.

Now when he heard Wesley ask, "Have you ever seen her buck naked?" he experienced a sudden blur of outrage.

"What the hell do you mean, McQuillan?" he cried advancing on him.

But Wesley only laughed. "Sure, I'm not going to let on, am I? And don't fret, you can have her oul' things all to yourself after I've finished with them. Look," he said, his turn now to move closer until they were toe to toe, "you can just make out the mark of her fanny." Sure enough there was a faint yellowish blemish that appeared to have resisted all Mrs Cupples' Rinso and boiling water.

"Jasus, you're the lucky man, Taggart, watching her in her pelt whenever you feel like it. I bet the same blade never draws the curtains. Tell me, what's she like? What's *it* like? What colour is it?"

The boy watched him exciting himself, one hand spasmodically bunching in his pocket, the other still clutching the two-way stretch, as he now knew it was called. His face was growing redder by the minute and presently without shame he unbuttoned his trousers and aired his standing flute.

"Come on," he panted, urging him to join in, "just

214

imagine you're on top and her dyin' for it. She talked to me once, did I ever tell you that? 'Young man, please be good enough to inform your father that Major Kincaid has a heifer that requires servicing.' Christ, I'd love to service her, I can tell you. Wouldn't charge her a wing. That voice, and, oh, oh, the gorgeous smell of her!" he groaned, stroking ferociously now.

It was hard for the boy to comprehend quite why he should find her so alluring, this skinny, half-mad creature with a Gold Flake dangling out of the side of her mouth most of the time, and always in wellingtons and men's trousers, too. Back against a tree, he continued to look on as if all this was happening at some distant remove, in the cinema, say, for disturbing as witnessing it was, still he knew he wasn't really part of it, could remove himself whenever he cared to. Well, no, not now, not right away. As in the pictures he would just have to sit it out until the performance was over.

So Wesley kept on pumping away and although the boy recognised what he was doing, for he had done it himself on the odd occasion, watching someone else wasn't the same thing. Was this how he looked, he asked himself, face red and sweating, jaw clenched, mouth set, dribbling? "She's crazy for it, I tell you. And that oul' hopalong husband of hers with the game leg doesn't mind a bit who she does it with either. Officers, airmen, soldiers, particularly the black ones. They all relish a taste of the liquorice stick, that's what Freddy Dunbar says anyway."

His stroke began to accelerate, faster, faster. "*Oh, Esmée, darling, sweetheart,*" he moaned, "*kiss me, oh, kiss, kiss me!*" and then it was over.

The boy stared at the sudden milky shower dappling the leaves. The wounded flesh of the Major's tree had seemed to run with the same pale juice. And just as they were connected in that strange way, so it seemed to him they were connected with him also, even though his hand had not been involved. But that didn't matter, no one would believe him, his signature already there, plain to see. The white stuff glistening on the leaves might well be obliterated with a rub of the toe, but to him it would always be there, indelible, in this hidden corner of the woods.

As if nothing out of the ordinary had just taken place he heard himself say, "I have to get back now, Wesley, for my mammy's not well. I'll see you at school on Monday."

Hunkered on the grass, his breath returning to normal, Wesley glanced up at him. "What's the matter with her now?" he enquired, grinning evilly. "Up the pole again, is she?"

"Watch your filthy mouth, McQuillan."

Laughing at him, the other got to his feet. He stretched lazily, then using the Major's wife's underthings the way you would a rag, he wiped his thing and when he had finished he took the crumpled ball of silk and flung it away from him to land in the bushes. The boy stared at the pale patch of intimacy hanging on the thorns.

"You're a pig," he told him, his voice quivering, "a dirty, rotten pig, McQuillan."

After that Wesley just had to hit him, he had no option. The boy took the first blow full in the face, feeling the blood spurt as something seemed to loosen inside his nose. The pain came later.

At the time he remembered looking, not at his attacker's face or fists, but at his still-protruding prick. It seemed extraordinary to him in that moment that someone should be in the middle of attacking him with his thing hanging out. Still it didn't seem to deter Wesley from hitting him a few more times, more like cuffs for luck than full solid punches like that first one. He seemed to have lost interest and, anyway, the boy had subsided to the grass by this time shielding his weeping nose. He wondered if it were broken like photographs of boxers he had seen. Part of him fervently hoped it to be true, the combination of hero and martyr appealing strongly.

Wesley told him, "You asked for that, young Taggart, for you've been getting far too big for your boots lately. You and that oul' mother of yours. Who does she think she is, anyway, telling me to keep away from your place? Sick, is she? I bet it's some disease she's got goin' with all them soldiers. Maybe you have it too. And don't go tellin' people about what happened here today, for if you do I'll only say it was you who picked her ladyship's best bloomers off her line. Which is true, isn't it? *Isn't it?*" And for the first time he looked down and buttoned himself. "So, cheery-bye, young Taggart, and if you're wise bring a note on Monday. Joe Malone's on the warpath. Says he's goin' to report the next truant to the polis, no kiddin'. That inspector, when he looked at the roll-book, scared three colours of shite out of him."

And he walked off back home through the woods, leaving the boy huddled on the grass alone with his shame in the shape of a pulpy nose, but much worse, those two abused scraps hanging on the bushes like a tinker's washing-day.

What could he do with them? Nothing, seemed to be the answer. For he couldn't just put them back on the line in their present state, torn, most likely, and still damp, certainly, with Wesley McQuillan's spunk. Neither could he leave them where they lay, hoping for some miracle worked by the weather and birds building their nests. That would take a lifetime and long before then the Major, or Duffy, his man, would be bound to have come this way. So what if he simply buried the evidence? But that wouldn't do either. For he was thinking now of old Slipper the Major's dog who could scent a bead of mouse-shit through sheet steel.

Still in a frenzy of indecision he plucked the evidence of his crime from off the bushes and balled both together to make a single handful. As he did so a drop of bright blood from his nose fell and was absorbed instantly by the pale silk. He stared fascinated at the scarlet blot for several minutes until another joined it, then another. *No going back now*, he told himself, and pushing the doubly soiled bundle under his jersey and pressing it flat so it wouldn't look too conspicuous, he set off back the way he and Wesley had come.

He didn't stop until he got near his own house, to the famous beeches, in fact, closing his eyes for a moment, for this crazy notion had come to him, the way it would in bed sometimes when he was having a bad dream about dead babies again, that when he opened them the tree might be there the same as before. But, of course, how could it?

Going up close to the largest and thickest, Wilhelmina — Wesley had chosen well, knowing what would hurt him most — he covered his initials with his outstretched hand, holding it there like a protective shield until he felt the sap stick to his palm. Then he gathered up a handful of earth, plastering it over the seeping wound. But the mark that was his name, no one else's, was still there, darkened only slightly. He took up more soil, rubbing it in, using the Major's wife's things this time, but he still could make out his mark.

At least part of the evidence had been destroyed, he told himself, looking down at the useless rags he held in his hand. But despite that he still stuffed them back up his jersey again. They made his skin shiver and contract.

The house was as he'd left it, door wide to the world, smoke rising straight and true from the chimney. He edged around to the window at the side in case his mother was up and

218

about, pressing his eye to one of the little diamond panes that were the same as the ones in church.

There was no sign of her, but the three little pigs were still at the table where he'd left them, not eating any longer, however, but playing intently among the dirty dishes some imaginary game with toy soldiers, battling it out for supremacy among the cups and saucers. They belonged to him, a regiment of Scots Fusiliers hand-painted from the bare metal out, from pictures in a book that came with the set. A present. Willie had got them for him Christmas past along with all the little jars of paint and a camel's-hair brush. The paint smelled like chloroform. At least he liked to think it did, even though he had never been next or near a hospital. But that's what he imagined anyway, as he sniffed the fresh enamel and felt his head swim so pleasurably.

Coming into the kitchen silently, and them engrossed like that, he took them by surprise and they looked up, three guilty little animals caught in the act, which they were, but he only put a hand to his lips urging them to silence while managing to convey a reprieve at the same time. Normally he wouldn't have been so big-hearted in this regard for he really loved his squad of miniature fighting men in their kilts and bonnets complete with thistles, and jealously at that, but he had much more pressing concerns on his mind right now.

It had come to him on the way through the woods what he must do, mapping out in his head each consecutive and crucial stage of the procedure. First of all he had to find the key to the old boathouse, next, pull out the hatchet embedded in the block outside, then go back into the woods with it, then ... And he was going through the list in this fashion, like a set of tables, say, or the principal capitals of the world, which he was good at, when his plans hit an obstacle right before they could even get going.

Overhead his mother moaned loudly and he froze halfway across to the geranium in its pot on the windowsill where he knew she kept the key. The children at the table played on regardless, for nothing would distract them now that he had given them his blessing, not even their own mother crying out like that. Picturing her lying up there half-asleep, but not far now from wakefulness either, he looked at the ceiling. You could see through the cracks in the boards from up above if you had a mind to and suddenly convincing himself the entire universe was aware of his guilty plans he moved swiftly over to the flowerpot and lifted the dry saucer underneath. *The key was gone, missing.* She had taken it and hidden it somewhere else. Even more treacherous, had it about her in a pocket, or on a string around her neck.

There could only be one good reason for her moving it, at least in his mind, anyway. She didn't trust him, had in fact anticipated this very occurrence all along. But why so, he asked himself. She hadn't spotted him spying on her, couldn't have, he had been far too careful for that.

Standing there as if all the time in creation was at his command, he pondered these matters. He could smell the sharp lemony tang of the geranium plant, its flowers bright as the bloodstains on the bundle under his jersey. This was what being man of the house really meant, no one to help or turn to when something really drastic needed to be done. He looked at the three little *generalissimos* at the table marshalling their toy troops. By right he should be there alongside them sharing their battles, Badajoz, Solferino, Jena, Marengo, all those funny-sounding names commemorated in cut stone beneath that old Sir William Nicholson leaning so nonchalantly on his sabre in the town square.

Then his mother groaned a second time and the ceiling shook ever so slightly as if she had put a naked foot to the floor. Silently and swiftly he left as he had come, barely pausing to jerk the angled hatchet from its socket in the block.

At the colonnade of beeches he brought the first part of his already flawed great plan into play, taking their old hatchet and cutting a patch where his initials had been. The bark now bore a single pale badge, square in shape, perhaps too regular, for he was thinking of shifting the blame on to some wild thing, a squirrel, say, even a rabbit or a hare, although it would have to be crazed or unduly acrobatic to leap up all that way.

He hacked at the trunk some more just to make it appear not so man-made, but finally he moved away as satisfied as he could be back into the trees again. Already the sun was laying broken stripes across the grass, so he began to race himself, one hand clutching the hatchet, the other holding the bundle close to him under his jersey.

At Ussher Greer's rapid mill-stream the water rose to sting the tops of his thighs, drawing a line on the flesh like a cold knifeblade. There was no sign of the old man, Rex, his dog, either, but he continued crouching low, hugging the far bank until he had left his land far behind.

Soon he came to arid, pebbly terrain where scraggy scrub alders grew. No one knew who owned this section, but then maybe no one did for it was merely part of the shoreline of the Lough, useless and dry as desert. Tortured fragments of driftwood, old tin cans, bottles and cork floats littered its dreary expanse. He could see the water, silver-grey, flat, heavy as oil, stretching far away to another land on the horizon where people might possibly speak a different language, even though Geography and maps told him it was only Tyrone.

For a moment a shiver of fear passed through him, for now he could make out the darker bump of the island

221

breaking the level stretch of water like the head of some emerging sea-monster. For some equally crazy reason also his imagination became seized with the notion that the man out there, all alone and invisible, was watching him. Deliberately he kept his gaze averted so their glances wouldn't meet.

What he did next was in keeping with that craziness, for he went scuttling sideways, crunching over the storm-drift, until he had the boathouse squarely between himself and the island. Panting, he dropped to the ground, laying hatchet and bundle on the shingle by his side. His grandfather's old shed lay feet away. He was in its shadow, its padlocked door on the far, hidden side, directly facing the water.

His intention had been to hammer at the hasp until it snapped, but he no longer could go through with that course of action now that Willie with his famous negro X-ray eyes would be able to see him.

It was all completely daft, of course, but the idea wouldn't go away and he crouched there on the washed gravel knowing he would never be able to bring himself to make his way around there in the open, hatchet in hand.

Probably he couldn't have busted that old lock anyway, too strong, too old, too rusty, he told himself that, but he knew he was only deluding himself. He was a coward, was the simple truth of the matter. Willie, Wesley, his own mother – he felt convinced there were countless others he could add to the list if he had the time – they all could see through him, despising him as someone insignificant and worthless. Look at how they treated him, lying to him, laughing at him, belittling him and bending him to their will. Well, if they scorned him so much he would just hate them back. He did hate them. He didn't care any longer about any of them. The whole world, for that matter.

And as he sat there he began attacking the ground with the hatchet as if it was them he was chopping and not the dry stones rolled up by the storms, for everyone knew the Lough was a tideless sea. Soon he had a hole dug as deep as the length of the handle, for the ground hadn't felt rain for weeks. He was in the middle of a desert, he told himself, digging a well, and as the pebbles flew and fell in a hail of his rage, suddenly it came to him. No, he hadn't struck water, but something far more satisfying, a way of not only getting into the shed, but of getting back at them as well. Which of course was why he had come all this way in the first place. He had forgotten that.

He sat there beside his gravel castle shivering slightly, for a little wind had risen as it usually did at this time of day, the land cooling and air moving in to fill the empty space, something he had also learned about in Geography. The surface of the water had gone all rough like fish scales or a bird's feathers blown the wrong way.

Taking up the hatchet once more he crunched across to the back wall of the hut and began digging down into the soft soil at its base. At first he used the axe blade as a pick but soon he was able to scrape like a dog, using hands instead of paws, scooting back loose grit in a steady stream. When this new hole of his was deep and wide enough he crept in and under the rotting timbers.

Head first, he emerged in darkness. Narrow stripes of light from the cracks in the boards criss-crossed the blackness. On the floor something humped and expansive took up most of the space. It lay within touching distance but he had no need to reach out to know what it was.

Hauling himself upright he smelt the dead air of the place, undisturbed and tomb-like until his mother had come along on those two occasions. It was his turn now to stand in the half-light and consider the boat. Yet it was not the boat that concerned him, it was the oars. The outcome of his mighty plan had been to take them and hide them, for if they were gone, he reasoned, how could she row across to the island and Willie?

Then like a blow it hit him. Even if he did find them – they were there in the shadows somewhere – *how would he be able to get them away?* They would need to be made of rubber to go back out through that hole he had just dug. Something different, something more drastic was called for, so he scrabbled back out the way he had come. It was much harder this time and his heart quailed at the thought of having to do it again and then again, for he would have to, he knew that.

Pushing the hatchet before him into the mouldy darkness like it was a weapon – but, then, it was, wasn't it? – he crawled after it. This time he nearly stuck, half of him buried under the old rotting lintel, the rear half of him kicking wildly in air. His hair and face were coated with dirt, his hands felt raw, but he struggled on. He felt the hatchet rise before him into open space and he followed behind pulling himself up and out like a cork from a bottle.

Then he lay down panting for a time until his sweat started to dry. His skin felt caked and parched, he could smell the stink of the grave on him. After a while he thought he heard something move in one of the far corners, followed by a rustling, a tiny squeak, it sounded like, and he rose up in a panic, grabbing the hatchet in both hands and bringing it down on the side of the boat. Then he calmed down directing his aim at one spot below the water-line where it would do the greatest and most lasting damage. Inside he was not calm, however. Inside he was filled with spite and hate and revenge.

Damn you both, he cursed as the wood started splintering, *for making me do this, smashing up my grandfather's good boat so it won't be able to make the crossing out to the island any more.* Damn his mother and damn Willie Washington, most of all, for putting his great black thing into her. It was all his fault

224

with his presents of candy and peanut butter and his uniform like a field marshal's instead of a corporal in anybody's else's army, and his hair smelling like coconut.

Then the hatchet bit through the curving boards of the boat and he ceased striking his dark enemy. Let him starve out there. Why should he care? He had made his mother sick, putting his thing into her in that way. She cried all the time because of it and the only way she would get better was by staying at home with them and not seeing him any more. One last blow he delivered just to be on the safe side – the opening was now big enough to put his hand through – then he squeezed back out through to daylight again and began filling in the hole.

The sun was starting to set like a fat red ball over the water, over in far Tyrone on the distant shore of the Lough beyond the island. For a moment he thought of his enemy out there, crouching, hidden, watching and waiting for the boat which would never now arrive. He had seen to that with his trusty axe.

When the soil was patted down to his satisfaction, flat just as he'd left it, he wrapped the Major's wife's things around a stone, tying them tight and secure, so they wouldn't go adrift.

Last thing he did before leaving was carry the weighty little parcel down to the water's edge and hurl it out as far as it would go. It made a gulping sound like the biggest pike in the Lough taking on a bite. Then he ran back home the way he'd come, believing that everything in their lives would now be changed back to the way it had been before the Candyman had arrived on the scene.

At Ussher Greer's mill-race he washed his face and hands in the chill, speeding water. Then he washed his hands a second time, thinking of Wesley McQuillan and his warts, for warts were supposed to be catching.

225

TEN

In the beginning, belly-down on the bare floor, he just lies looking out through the space between the propped-up slab and the door frame – what's left of it – out at the flat expanse of water, scanning it for signs of life. But after a morning of this he moves his makeshift bed up to the opening itself. This, after all, is where he will spend his daylight hours from now on, stretched out studying the view like it was some page of a book he's been made to memorise for his own survival. Mighty hefty book. Mighty big page. Size of a goddamned county nearabouts.

And never the same. Which is surprising and very unexpected from his perception of things.

Early on his eyes start to get tired just trying to keep up with all those variations. From silver through gunmetal gray to ink black, the colours run in and out and through one another. Next minute it's blues and greens and all the various wintry shades between. Then there's the surface itself, streaked, striped, zig-zaggy, sometimes, like the back of an old cotton-mouth. All of this he's recording in the finest detail because it's all there is to see and do.

Nothing living moves out there. Not up top anyway. On one occasion he detects a little run, then a flurry, which turns into a wedge of rapidly moving water. Hungrily he follows the restless head of the arrow, imagining that silvery shoal close to the surface, for that's what it is, he just knows it, going to waste, just begging to be caught. *Where the fuck are all you famous fishermen, then*, he catches himself shouting out in sudden rage in spite of the fear of being heard.

All he can think of is food, grub, chow, vittles, eats. Pearly's little stash has run out by now. It happened yesterday when he bolted down the last of that stale loaf she'd brought, mopping out the insides of the Armour bully-beef can until it shone like a new dollar. So he lies there on his steadily contracting stomach dreaming of every meal he's ever had. Lists. He makes lists. Chitlins, ribs, sowbelly, ham hocks, crawfish, cornbread, sweet potato, grits, collard greens, pound cake.

Then he travels out and away from home right up to the present, two, three days ago, in fact, and the last meal he's ever cooked. Take twenty pounds of hamburger meat, brown, add ten cans of evaporated milk, season, simmer, keep stirring, dish up on toast. Result. Creamed beef. Serves fifty. Never would he have thought he'd live to see the day when he'd give everything just to lick out an old empty skillet of SOS. *Shit on a shingle, to you.*

And that's the other thing, he's started having these long, involved conversations – arguments, mostly – with this other person, this *you*. *Don't you give me that bunch of horse manure*, he'd hear the echo of his own thoughts, as he lay watching the distant shoreline and the watery nothingness in between. *What do you mean, give yourself up, argue your case! What fucking case? Never had one from word go, right from when I ran into them three niggers in field uniform. And running away when I did only served to sign and seal my death warrant. You saying I shouldn't have run? Well, just mebbe you're right about that, Mister Fucking Einstein, but you ain't me and I certainly ain't you.*

Even though his know-it-all companion is only a voice in his head, and faceless, at that, one thing for sure, he just has to be *white*. Has to be. *Did I really say death warrant? Oh, sweet, sweet Jesus.* And he starts shaking, for this is the first time since that night in town he's allowed his imagination to spill over into forbidden territory, him hanging at the end of a rope. For once you spell it out in words, even inside your own head, the bad stuff takes over, the deep-down ugly stuff, the stuff that does for you. He's seen it happen to a lot more besides himself. Back home.

Leastways he has that going for him, not like some pale-face peckerwood who never had the Kluckers breathing down his neck. White folks never really get that, do they, how you can keep it bottled up inside, all that pain and grief and shit, and you smiling back at them at the same time. That's the hardest part for them to understand, till one fine day you get loaded and it all comes boiling out in a rage and you start shooting people. Like them three bozos who got him into all of this. *All this*, he thinks. *My own little desert isle, all mine*, as the sun inches up in the east, a big fat old pink balloon near fit to burst.

But then mebbe that's what they're so feared of, just waiting and watching for that bad nigger blood to show itself. Like it's do or die every time some colored stiff looks as if he's getting too friendly or familiar.

It was funny but for a minute lying there in the dirt like that he almost felt a little sorry for all those asshole noncoms who'd ever bawled him out or made him do his kit all over again. It was as if he was seeing things he'd been blind to up to now, brain clean and shiny new like a lovingly tended piece of kitchen equipment, that big old Häfner slicing machine, say, he used to cut up ham with.

228

Then other times he just dozes off, what with his eyes getting weary with all that vigilance, face down and buried in Pearly's old coat. It feels warm and comforting. Smell, too, for he fools himself into believing there's a lingering trace of her scent there, that sweet-smelling stuff she puts on just for him. "Evening In Paris." Some joke, the two of them strolling hand in hand beside a famous river in an even more famous city both of them have only ever read about or seen in a fucking travelogue.

He has this sudden angry ache at what has happened to them both, the lowdown shitty unfairness of it all, while some fat businessman type who sells cheap perfume for a living kills himself laughing every time he thinks of that title he's dreamt up, knowing only poor assholes like them are going to spend their money on the crap just for those words on the label.

Yes, you, you rich Frog bastard, I'm talking about you. Not in a thousand years would you ever find yourself in my shoes, or a million others just like us. And suddenly he has this terrible image of pile upon pile of broken, beat up old shoe-leather, all torn, patched and flapping, and he weeps bitter tears into the dry wool because it seems to him he can't think of anything sadder or more desolating than poor peoples' shoes.

And just to remind him he sees his own pair of army Oxfords lying side by side curled up at the toes and bleaching already with all they've been through. Beyond redemption. Unless he can lay his hands on about a gallon of tan shoe wax somewhere. *Lord*, he prays in bitter jest, *send this poor nigger castaway down a drum of Esquire, and while you're at it how about a supply of Rinso, an electric iron and some button polish, too.*

Even though he's lying like a hog in his own wallow he still feels like he's in uniform. Which he is, if you can call it that, after everything that's happened to it, the thing being he

229

really loved that set of army duds, right down to that last little-bitty bone stiffener in each shirt collar. Truly he did.

When they doled out this pile of brand new folded khaki at the induction center it came right up to the bridge of his nose, which was a miracle in itself, but when he had a chance to examine and sniff all of that beautiful wrapper-clean cotton, wool and gaberdine up close – yeah, *gaberdine*, just like those movie stars' suits – he felt he really had gone to heaven. And the boots and shoes, best of all. Christ, he even got his own proper size for the first time in his entire life. Forty-six, wide-fitting. *Wide-fitting!* Nobody had ever told him that before.

'Course a lot of the other guys at Fort Bragg liked to gripe about how ugly and itchy all their stuff was compared to what they were used to back home. But he knew that to be a load of prize horse-shit. Most, if not all of them, were just barefoot share-croppin' niggers same as he was. It was only a little game they played to cover up how shamed they felt deep down about where and what they'd come from.

Which was another thing whitey would never really understand either. Just because he felt that way himself some of the time, for, let's face it, white trash made up most, if not all, the non-colored intake in those Southern outfits, how could some nigger ever come close to feeling the same way? The army did that to you, white or black, it taught you another world was out there where clean underwear, hot water and four squares a day were considered normal and once you got used to them it was going to be awful hard going back to Ducktown, Peabody County, or any of those other jerkwater places they hailed from. As old Stovepipe Davis used to say, "*Shit, man, we were so poor we didn't even know there was a Depression.*"

Stretched out and smelling as high as month-old Limburger, he has this sudden yearning to spruce himself up, get back into

230

shape again, at least half-way to how he used to be. If he really puts his mind to it he might be able to clean up his tunic jacket and his slacks, then shirt, tie, underwear, and finally, socks. But he don't have no socks. For the life of him he can't remember what could have happened to them.

Somewhere he's read first thing happens in an auto wreck is that people's shoes get sucked off like they've been hoovered clean away, but he still has those and he ain't been in no car crash. Might feel that way but, no, he ain't. It makes no sense to him. So, forget socks. He'll manage to survive on bare feet. Nobody looked at them a lot anyway, ankles being sort of invisible, even in the army. Shoes, yes.

The way he would prepare himself for that Saturday early-morning drill and kit inspection when he first joined up, *Jesus*! It was as if he had to be that little bit better than everyone else, and that included the one or two real hard-chaw veterans who were drafted into every hut to try to bring the rookies there like himself up to snuff. Some hope. You could tell from their attitude that was never going to happen, barring some kind of miracle.

One corporal showed his particular contempt more than all the others put together, a big, almost blue-black buck called McLennan from Georgia who made life a hell, getting them to do their kit over and over and over again till some of the younger guys were near to tears. Not him, though, not William Purdy Washington Junior, no, sir. He just kept his head down, refusing to give in, a-folding, polishing, brushing and pressing until it was just right, that perfect, soft, layered pyramid on top of the stretched bed blanket you were supposed to be able to bounce a dime off, like it was some fucking beautiful work of art, not a speck of lint, not a crease, not an inch out anywhere. He even started sacking out on the floor alongside his crib Friday nights so as not to upset all that marvellous symmetry. In some of the huts he'd heard of

231

guys so keen they even stashed away a duplicate set so as not to disturb their number one kit.

He might well have gotten to that stage himself until one day McLennan told him with a great big grin on his ugly black kisser he was being assigned to mess-hall duties forthwith.

"No more kit inspection for you, sonny jim. Seems like Uncle Sam wants you for a cook. Mind you don't go slippin' none of that ole bromide into my stew now."

It was one of those army notions, like in prisons they put stuff in your coffee or your chow to keep you from jerking off too much. There was even a song about it. "My cock is limp, I cannot fuck, the nitrate it has changed my luck, the nitrate it has changed my luck. One, two, three, four. One, two, three, four . . ." calling out the words in march time on manoeuvres. He hears himself humming it softly to himself now.

Sure enough there's not been a lot of sensation down below in his own three-piece set for some considerable time. Not since Pearl rowed ashore last and he came over all hot and horny. Least, he thought he was. Too eager, too hasty, too rough. He'd made a grab for her thinking that was what he had to do. Nothing like laying some pipe to take your mind off of things, get the two of them back to where they'd left off, for it had always been such a sweet thing between them. He'd learned to hold back until her time came and then they'd hit the wire together yelling like a couple of savages.

Then later he'd light up a Camel and she'd smoke it along with him just like in the movies, the two of them lying out there under the stars listening to the wind in the trees and often they might get round to a repeat performance, only this time slower, not so furious, teasing out the business like it was some real high-class meal he'd just prepared specially for the pair of them. A beautiful filet, say, or a lobster thermidor or chicken à la king, for he'd gotten himself a proper recipe book he'd struggle through sometimes in his bunk while the rest of the guys were deep in *Life With Father, Joe Palooka*, or the ones who could read, a Clarence F. Mulford, promising himself one day, one day, he'd cook some of that.

This was the closest he'd ever got to his goal, feeling his rod move up inside her soft, wet pussy making sweet, silent conversation one to the other, clenching and unclenching in their own special Morse code.

But not this time, this time it died on him before he could get started, his cock going from standing to limp in a minute flat, something that had never happened to him before, even with that redhead whore in Fort Bragg that time. She'd even complimented him on how hard it had stayed, so big, as well. "*I guess, this has to be my lucky night, honey,*" the sort of thing a guy tends to remember even if it is a bunch of flapdoodle.

"I have to go," Pearl had said as he lay on top losing sensation fast in the place he needed it most. She must have felt it too, but if she did she didn't say nothing, just, "I gotta go." He wanted to bawl like a baby for he hadn't planned on something like this happening. Who would? So he rolled off then and they got up together, standing there on the foreshore like two strangers staring out across the water to civilisation.

He watched her row off back the way she'd come, oars dripping silver in the moonlight, *clop, clop, clop,* and thinking, not only had his dick lost the war, just maybe he had as well.

That was a real bad time for him right about then for he started into hating her a little, being so dependent and all. Not so long ago he'd been the big cheese and he had gotten used to it with his presents from the PX and his dry-cleaned uniform and John Thomas always eager and ready for action. Now she was running the show from her end, the landward end. Over there. What if she didn't show next time? What if there happened to be no next time? What if she went to the MPs instead? What was stopping her? Why did he even trust her not to?

He puts his hand up over his mouth to keep himself from crying out there in that desolate place, shivering a little as the air cools and a breeze comes up. Because he has to, that's why, for if he don't he's a goner. He just has to believe, *has to*.

The scent of her is still on his fingers, her pussy, and he sucks on them, her, as well, in his head, and, lordy, if that old yardarm don't start coming up stiff as a boy scout's pole; only about twenty minutes too late. Next best thing, he proceeds to give himself a hand job standing out there and jerking off under the moon by the lakeside, shooting his load when the time comes into the darkening water to mingle with the waves. Fish food. *See what you're missing, honey, grade-A jissom, pure and pearly white. Don't pay no heed to Mr Charlie, honey, no matter what he tells you. Some things are all the same, spite of what your outside color just happens to be.*

Then he goes back up the slope again to his bad bed on the floor of the shack and another night with the Irish wildlife, for he can hear them out there stalking and killing one another, filling their bellies while his grows ever flatter by the minute. Maybe he'll just fade away to skin and bone, then nothing, do everybody a great big favour. Pearl included. By now he's starting to build up a real mean feeling towards her spite of all she's done for him. He can't help himself. And that wiseass character *you* is shoving his oar in again.

Okay, okay, so maybe you are right, maybe she has it just as tough on her having to keep on lying and pretending all the time when people start into asking questions. For bet your life on it, they will. Then, again, just how many ever knew about us, anyway? Nobody, according to her. Sometimes it was real

234

hard for him not to get the notion she was somehow ashamed of being seen with him, pulling him into bushes and behind walls and hedges and all, like he was some kind of leper, when people happened by. Then other times he kidded himself maybe she was the jealous type wanting to keep him all to herself.

Right now, though, he's glad she did what she did at the time, keeping him under wraps and away from everybody. Everybody, except her kids. He'd forgotten about the damned kids in all of this. Now they come crowding up into his head, four little pale-faced ghosts blaming him for getting their mamma into this mess. But it is the older one who looks by far the most serious – the rest are only little chickabiddies – fixing him with that reproachful look of his.

It was there right from the start, as if he recognised trouble when he saw it in the shape of this chubby black guy advancing on them with a stupid grin on his face and holding a bunch of candy and comic books in both hands. He used to sit real still, all hunched up in that funny little fireside chair of his, watching him do his Santa Claus number, never once taking his eyes off him as if this stranger might be after the family silver. Or his ma, who was a lot more precious, far as he was concerned. Every time she laughed, which she did a lot of then, he looked as if he wanted to kill her stone dead, and whenever the two of them chimed in at the same joke, then the three small fry followed suit, not understanding, just going along for the ride like kids do, boy, did it really piss him off.

"Raymond," Pearly would say, "come over here and see what Willie has brought you."

Once it was a toy railroad engine, the rest of the cars and track and stuff to follow on the instalment plan, when he lightened up his act, sort of blackmail, you could say, and not something he was overly proud of, but he felt he had to get

235

through to him no matter what it took, short of strangling the little prick. Every time he came back to the house on one of his visits he'd find himself glancing across at their old sideboard just to see if it had moved, that black and red Hornby choo-choo still in its box. *It was the Flying Scot, for Christ's sake!* But all it only ever seemed to do was gather dust. Then, again, he tried fooling himself maybe the kid took it down and played with it when he wasn't around. Maybe he just didn't want to give him the satisfaction of catching him with it in his hands. But whatever the truth of it was, it sure as shit kept right on bugging him.

Things got so bad he started imagining himself swelling up the instant he got there, filling that pokey little house with his dark-skinned, sweaty presence. Everything seemed so scaled down in this damned country. Always it was as if he might end up breaking something and the boy kept on watching him as if he couldn't wait for it to happen. But it never did, never, and he could tell he was disappointed.

At the time he wondered if he'd always been such a sourpuss, giving grief to all those other gentleman callers before him, but he hadn't the nerve to pursue it. Anyway, that happened to be a real delicate area far as he was concerned. He didn't care to hear too much about who had preceded him, especially some guy in a uniform three sizes smaller than his who might have fathered one of those poor little bastards. *Why couldn't she have waited for him?* It was real stupid of him, he knew, but he couldn't help thinking it.

With Pearl he always felt on borrowed time anyway, and not only because he might be shipped overseas any day to help feed an army that everybody kept telling him marched on its stomach. That part was something neither one of them cared to dwell on too much. Like a couple of high-school sweethearts, they pretended, instead, they were going to live happily ever after, back in the States, most probably, when

236

this crazy old war was over, like one of those nice all-American families on some *Saturday Evening Post* cover. How could he bear to tell her no mixed-race couple was ever likely to figure in one of Mr Norman Rockwell's nice pictures? Pigs would fly first. Bacon on the wing. Pork chops in the sky.

And a groan escapes him, for there he has strayed into forbidden territory again. Mouth filling up with spit like some old dog dreaming of a bone – prime barbecued ribs in his case – he concentrates on the blank sheet of darkening water to help take his mind off his stomach. Sunset. Somehow he has managed to get through an entire day just lying and thinking, his life passing before him like something up on a movie screen. Past. Not present. As for the future, that's like looking down some godawful black old well, knowing if he gets too close he's gonna tumble in and be lost forever.

And sure enough, as if it's happening for real, he hears his own despairing cry in his head like a locomotive's wail, dying, falling like a stone. It goes on for a long time.

When he opens his eyes he's covered in sweat, shaking, mouth parched. *That old well-hole may well be dry after all*, he tells himself. *No splash at the end of it, just one terrible great old thump.*

He starts into thinking about the boy again. Raymond. Maybe it wasn't all his fault, maybe he should have tried a little harder to get to know him better. It had to work both ways, not just him grandstanding all the time about his terrific life on the far side of that chain-link fence. Land of the free and ice-cold Dr Peppers, five varieties of cream soda, Popeye cartoons, Hershey bars, hot dogs, funny papers an inch thick. All that shit that appeals to little kids as well as hick assholes like himself and his buddies.

He'd listen to himself sounding off like the worst kind of hot-air artist, biggest this, fattest that, longest the other, and

237

wonder why was he trying so hard to impress. It certainly wasn't working with young Raymond, that's for sure, sitting there in that little old judgement seat of his next the fireplace like some kind of old man, eyes like stone. What he should have done was take him aside, just the two of them, out in the woods somewhere, for he liked being there, all kids his age do, he did himself once upon a time, and set him down on an old tree stump. *No, not beat the crap out of him, Mister Wise Ass.* But tell him instead all about his *real* life back in Ducktown. No fancy automobiles, no electricity, no running water, no WCs, no books, no shoes, no toys, no hot dogs.

Seven of us in one little old three-roomed shack and that came down to two, just a kitchen and a sleeping place, when the cotton got picked and baled around about Christmas time. One room cleaned clear out and piled to the rafters with new cotton. *Can you imagine that?* A mouse could not have squeezed in there. Open up the door and there it was, solid, facing you, a new wall, only all bulgy to the touch, and the taste and smell of it everywhere, in your clothes, your hair, your food, not sweet but oily, *oily.* Cotton looks nice and soft and pretty, only it ain't, kid, it's nasty and mean and gets in your lungs and kills you if you don't move into some other line of employment before it's too late.

This sport had other plans. You see this sport had this cousin Alonzo who was a conductor on one of them big old trains running all the way clear to Chicago, even New York sometimes. He used to visit us driving the biggest, most expensive, shiniest car any of us had ever seen. Fancy clothes, gold watch, diamond stick-pin, smelling like a flower shop, hair brilliantined down, shiny as hell. A real hotshot. I wanted to be just like him, I tell you, riding the rails from state to state. Like being a sailor, was how he used to describe it, sailing from port to port, seeing new places and faces and holding down a real important job too.

238

"Nobody gives Alonzo Burgess no shit, not when they're on that great ole train of his, they don't. All aboard! All aboard now!" he'd yell out in our twelve-by-ten kitchen, then blow on his silver whistle till we'd cover up our ears and him laughing fit to bust.

He told me one time he might be able to get me a job as cook on the good ole CCR soon as I reached sixteen so I could work my way up in the world like he did.

"Who knows," he'd say, lighting up one of them big, fat cigars rich passengers would give him, band still on it, "who knows, sport, but some day they might even make you a rail conductor just like your cousin Alonzo. Wouldn't that be somethin' now? Wouldn't it?"

I tell you I couldn't wait to grow up and get out of that place. That's all I ever dreamed of. But don't get me wrong, kid, it weren't all bad in that spot we called Ducktown. Believe me we had some fun times as well, just like you and your brothers and sister, for I know you do. One time . . . And suddenly in the middle of his silent sermon, lying there on his flat belly like that, three thousand miles from that place he's trying to describe, he hears himself laugh out loud remembering the day in Primus Wilson's cane patch.

Like any other ordinary day it all started off innocent enough, just him and a bunch of the other kids chewing on a stalk apiece, all sneaky-like in a ditch out of sight. Nothing no one would notice or miss, especially old half-blind Primus. Boy, was that cane sweet and juicy! Early on in the season it was, way before chopping time and then the carting off of the crop over to Kennedy's molasses mill. Real hot, too, sultry, and him and his young companions just lying there munching on that sugar stick.

Some more school-kids happened by and they snapped off a piece as well, all of us down in the bottom of that old dry drainage trench with those baby green feathery fronds up above and all around, still as still, and not saying a word to one another, just sucking, happy as a bunch of young heifer cows. Pretty soon we helped ourself to another piece, then another and another, the sap running down our faces and our bare chests, turning everything sticky, even our hair.

Soon we couldn't stop. It was like we couldn't get enough, and soon big holes started opening up in that old cane patch, but we didn't care no more, we were too far gone, just like wild things crazy-craving for the taste of syrup. By the time it got dark none of us could hardly eat no more, some of us were sick as well and old Primus's entire crop was ruined, a whole season's worth wiped out in an afternoon.

'Course we were all caught and soundly whipped. You could hear the yells clear into the next county going on for half a day near, but that was one wicked, wicked day, I tell you. You got anything to beat that, boy? Then there was one other time . . .

And more memories bubble forth, memories from those early days in the bottoms where he was raised.

He recalls being high in the peanut gallery of the local white movie-house and looking down on a palpitating sea of pink faces, bare necks and arms, fans fluttering like wings, while on the screen, cowboys in pale pointed hats fired back over their shoulders at one another or dropped down out of trees in ambush. People got themselves hung from those same trees, too, sometimes, but always white, which was hardly the way it was in his part of the country. The movies looked real, but weren't, but on those steamy Saturday nights up in nigger heaven no one ever paid too much heed to that. In the end the good guy always shot the bad guy wearing the black hat with the silver band – usually he looked a little off-white, Mexican, mostly – and then finally got the girl, who sang. They always covered their ears and rolled up their eyes around about that part or when kissing came up.

Sundays, no face-chewing, just loads and loads of singing. Evergreen Baptist Church was where they all congregated over by Five Road Corners, morning and evening services as well as scripture class. And about as hot inside as Litman's old movie theatre, what with all that corrugated iron some of the wilder kids used for target practice. Stones falling like heavenly hail, but nobody taking a blind bit of notice on account of that gospel racket. Awful loud voices those old folks had.

In the early days, so he heard tell, practically slave times, they used to worship out in the woods in something they called a *brush arbor*. Just branches bent over and twisted into a shelter big as a house. The idea of that appealed to him. Old Tunis Campbell who was old enough to remember Number One War told him his grandaddy told him about it. He could understand why they needed to get far out into the wilderness like that.

Also deep in those very same woods an old prostitute had her crib. No motels then. No "love accommodation" for negroes. So the men would sneak out at night to Priscilla to be serviced. If he'd stayed on in Ducktown he'd probably have ended up in that old brass bed of hers himself, banging on the springs just like everybody else. Got a dose as well most like. But, hey, hey, that ain't the kind of stuff a kid should be listening to, especially a nice, innocent lily-white kid. So, here endeth the lesson. To be continued at a later date . . .

That night, emboldened by all those recollections of colored folks having a real rough time of it, near to death almost, he creeps out and goes foraging in the almost-dark. Almost, but not quite. So he takes all his clothes off to make himself more invisible, only the pale rounds of his eyes to give himself away, just like one of those night-fighters the guys used to kid women about. *That old injection wears off soon as I hit stateside, then I'm white again, just like you, honey. Now, spread those sweet legs of yourn . . .*

Crouching low, he goes down to the water's edge, sucking on a Life Saver he's discovered deep in one of his pockets, real slow, for he wants it to last, for it's probably the only sweet thing he may have in his mouth. But recalling that crazy, crazy day in Primus Wilson's cane patch has set up a deep craving in him about as bad as on that afternoon fifteen years earlier.

That little night breeze has sneaked up again and he's well and truly shivering in no time. Cupping a double handful of water, he drinks deep and keeps on drinking 'til his stomach swells tight as a drumskin. It tastes just the way it looks, that old Irish lake-water, sort of stale and brackish, like it's been standing, letting everything settle down in it, only not quite. But to him it's nectar of heaven, those first few gulps, for he's started worrying he might end up drinking his own piss if he doesn't manage to prise himself loose from his prison shack.

This is the best he's felt in a very long time. Maybe it's to do with the dark and him blending in so well. He just doesn't know. *Enjoy while you can*, he tells himself, then he wades out into the chilly depths to his knees – it's real pebbly underfoot – and starts splashing himself all over, but quiet as quiet, paying particular attention to armpits and everything south of the Mason Dixon line. He has this notion in his head – it's been growing there for some time – he should make himself presentable for Pearl when she next comes, even straighten out that old uniform and wrecked shoes of his, but it's much too dark to consider any sort of laundry work right now.

She won't be coming anyway, not tonight, she won't. He

just knows it. Yet he feels almost relieved in spite of his hunger. Give him more time to get back into shape. Suddenly he's full of plans. What he'll do is he'll fill that old pan she left him then sponge down his uniform in the morning, daylight falling straight down from the hole high in the roof.

So he heads back up the rise again, the water cooling then itching like bug bites on his bare skin. Inside he rubs himself all over with Pearl's coat and pretty soon he's ready to go down that hill a second trip clutching the empty pan this time. And he tells himself it will be a comfort to have something at hand to drink beside him for the first time, even if it's intended for something else.

That night he sleeps soundly. The liquid heaviness in his stomach eases him into a deep slumber and holds him there, fast, like that, unmoving under that other weight above of old coats for several hours. How many he can't truly determine for the dial of his watch seems to have dimmed in some mysterious way as if it, too, has been losing its strength as well. But he does know it's still deep in the small hours by the dusting of stars he can see through the hole in his roof, tiny throbbing points of light like fireflies piercing the velvety blackness.

He lies there listening to the thud of his own heart, for something has wakened him, he can tell, the sound different from the usual night noises of the place. Straining high on the points of his elbows, he swivels his head like it was the needle on a compass towards the source, waiting for it to announce itself a second time.

And it's out there all right, he knows, somewhere beyond the doorway, alive, breathing like himself, man or beast, and so, rigid as a rock, he listens, still jay naked beneath his pile of old coats. For the first time he realises to his great surprise

243

they've gotten to be a comfort to him, that dusty smell blending with his own. No one, no thing, has the right to make him forsake his nest, now that it's taken him this long to get used to it. More and more he's beginning to act and think like an animal, so, rising up from his bed, he prepares to do battle for his territory if he has to.

At the triangular slice of open doorway, black, black night beyond, and the water invisible beyond that again, he grips the rotten wood of the door-post and listens like he's never listened before. And soon his patience is rewarded for a bleating sound is heard, a welcome surprise because of its unexpected ordinariness. One of old Horny's young family lost and strayed from the tribe, most like, for the cry is far too thin, high and nervous to come out of that old whiskery throat.

But then he realises it isn't a goat he's hearing after all, seeing, as well, now, for a pale, squat outline emerges from the darkness coming closer with slow, clumsy steps towards him, a white, woolly ghost still crying as if it's lost its mom. *Jesus H. Christ*, he thinks, *a sheep*, a goddamned, genuine live piece of mutton on the hoof out here of all places and at this godless hour, too. It keeps on coming as if by scent now and he could have swore the sound it made was as close to *ma-ma, ma-ma*, as an animal can make. He goes cold, then hot, then cold again, losing his nerve, for this is far too crazy to be happening to him.

The sheep, a young ewe he can tell by the shape of the head, comes right up to the slab across the door. He's hiding behind it, naked as the day he's born, and would you believe it, shaking, too, because of a dumb sheep that has him confused with its mamma.

He can smell it real strong now, a kinda damp, musty old smell that tells him it must have swum ashore all by itself. It's *baaing* louder and louder by now and pushing up against the slab trying to get in.

244

He has two thoughts then. One, somebody will hear it if he doesn't do something real fast. And, secondly, that somebody just might be its owner, happening to be looking for it across on dry land, if not right now, certainly tomorrow in daylight, when it will show up like a piece of washing.

Fuck, he moans, *fuck you, sheep*, and he pulls back that old slab of six-by-four ply keeping out the world and now this four-legged fleecy visitor. As if it's home, it goes straight in, and after bumping around a time — one of its legs is hurt, he notices — it settles down peaceably enough, breathing hard with a sort of accordion wheeze that he just knows will eventually drive him nuts.

"Well, Mary," he says to it, for that'll be its new name from now on, *"what's it to be? It's either fuck you or have you as tomorrow's lamb chops. Or, maybe, both in that order."*

And then it takes a dump over in the far corner away from his bedding, otherwise it would be instant fricassee. *Don't tempt me, Lord, don't tempt a poor sinner now.*

First it farts and then he hears that swift patter on the floor like peas falling on a drum, but he can live with them little black pellets, the same way he can with mouse-droppings. This far he has held back from soiling his own nest spite of his fear of the outdoors and his natural needs, but right now, as if on cue, he feels an overpowering urge to follow young Mary's example but manages to stave off the feeling, and a little while after he settles down again, pulling the coats up over his head. He can hear his new companion munching on something she has found over there on her side of the house and soon he drifts off.

While he's asleep she also finishes off all the precious water in the saucepan he's placed by his side.

ELEVEN

As September ran its course and the days started drawing in
Lawlor noticed a change in his own tempo. Oddly enough it
appeared to quicken instead of easing off, in anticipation of
all those hibernating hours ahead in front of the Day Room
fire. More and more his time and energies were taken up
raking the roads as if intent on committing to memory every
solitary stretch of countryside before leaving it behind for
good. Retirement loomed somewhere out there not too far
ahead. Only he knew the exact date, while convincing
himself Boal and Burnside were marking off a mental
calendar all their own.

At first they watched his comings and goings with sly
amusement. Then that began to change to a sort of impatient
irritation. *Just what was the old bugger up to*, he could hear
them wondering, *out there from crack of dawn wearing out
precious rubber.*

To tell the truth he wasn't exactly sure himself. His brain
whirred nearly as fast as the spokes, as he pushed uphill, then
sailed down dale. *Loose ends*, he kept repeating to himself,

loose ends, over and over, the words reverberating until they lost any sense they might have had.

Airily they floated in front of him just beyond reach, those mysterious disconnections, elusive as thistle-down. Or the swarms of plaguing mayfly peculiar to the Lough shore which rose and fell before his progress like drifts of smoke. That one-day dance of death of theirs arrived much earlier in the year, of course, as their name implied, but just occasionally an Indian summer such as this would draw them out unseasonably. Instead of choking the eyes and mouth as one bicycled through, now they melted off a little way in front, thinning and feebly re-grouping, or rolling sideways to carpet the water with their dying bodies.

Preoccupied, Lawlor pedalled along those little by-roads that hugged the shore barely noticing how the glutted trout made lazy dents in the surface. This sudden new appetite to be out all day, every day, on his own, thinking without thinking, seemed to burgeon with each fresh mile covered.

He would roll back home tired, pleasantly drained in brain as well as limbs, well after the other two had eaten, to his own waiting burnt offering which seemed to be growing ever smaller on the plate by the day, a rasher less here, one egg instead of two there, fewer and fewer slices of dipped soda or potato bread. Mrs Neeson relied heavily on the frying-pan.

The two Bs would be stretched out, toes practically touching the grate, noses buried deep in the day's newspapers, yet he could still sense an animal alertness, that eagerness for reaction on his part. But even if they were secretly plundering his plate, he said nothing, betrayed nothing, just kept on munching the stiffening mess glued to the dish in front of him.

He wasn't all that hungry as a matter of fact anyway, for the first time in an age actually shedding weight and not

247

suffering any pangs because of it, as if all that leg-work was burning off surplus poundage. He felt much, much better for not taking a drink. All in all it added up to a sense of getting himself ready for something, tuned up, like an athlete anticipating some form of contest, yet not having any proper inkling as yet of what it might be.

Meanwhile, tunics loosened and top trouser buttons undone, the other two would start to talk among themselves as if he wasn't there, yet trying to draw him in the way it used to be before he started acting like an oddity. Tonight, in suitably hushed tones, Boal began by recounting the latest atrocity to come from the rumour mill, swearing he had heard it from someone trustworthy, who'd heard it in turn from someone equally reliable, and so forth, the chain of credulity straining back like stretched elastic as far as the unsung genius who had made it up in the first place.

It went as follows. A mother whose son was a prisoner of war received a letter from his Stalag with a PS asking her to steam off the German stamp to give to a younger brother for his collection. She did so, only to discover, written under the stamp the words, *They have cut out my tongue.*

This led to a scalding tirade of anti-Jerry abuse with Boal jumping to his feet pummelling the air in a pose that might have come straight from one of his many boxing periodicals.

"Bloody Nazi filth! Slitty-eyed Jap savages!"

Lawlor was tempted to add, "*And greasy Eytie ice-cream vendors,*" but fought the urge, head studiously bowed as he mopped up the remaining smears of HP sauce while the two fireside fusiliers ranted and raged.

The target of their wrath next shifted from the enemy abroad to those at home, secret or not all that secret German sympathisers right here, by Christ, who, by their calculations, included every solitary RC north and south of the Border.

Lawlor continued polishing his plate until it shone in the

glare from the Tilley lamp on the dresser. Any minute now he might have to start in on the cutlery, for he was damned if he'd give these two armchair patriots the satisfaction of driving him upstairs early to his bed. Not this particular night anyway.

Then Burnside, always the more vindictive, spat, "When all this is over bar the shouting there'll come a day of reckoning, let me tell you. People'll not forget or forgive the boys who sat back and did bugger all for the war-effort. Took all they could from the Crown while down on their knees praying every night Adolf would win the day."

He just happened to glance towards the upstairs as he said it and incredulously Lawlor thought, *is that what these two really think I get up to before crawling in under the sheets of a night?* It was hard not to laugh but he managed it out of long practice. How many years had it been now, listening to such rabid bullshit? *My God*, it came to him, *almost twenty!* He shook his head, appalled in spite of himself, and the pair of them, Mutt and Jeff in a long line of constabulary comic turns, locked their gaze on him.

He heard himself ask sweetly, "Is there any more tea in that pot, Victor?" and at the mention of his name like that softie Boal dived for the big enamel pot basking on the hob.

Burnside hissed through closed teeth, shaking out his *Belfast Newsletter* as if to dislodge yet another quisling he'd discovered lurking there like a crumb among its pages. Had something he'd read sparked off all this rage? Often it did. Last week it had been a report detailing the trail of damage left by a platoon of American soldiers on manoeuvres upcountry somewhere. A farmer's bridge had been blown up, trees chopped down and a small wood devoured by flame-throwers. No warnings had been given, or apologies offered afterwards.

Nearer home, and this gave Lawlor the greatest pleasure,

Kincaid himself had suffered similar depredations, game shot, eggs and chickens stolen, slit-trenches dug in his precious plantation. The honeymoon with Uncle Sam's boys was well and truly over, it would appear. That old rumour had resurfaced once again about the GIs being paroled convicts on account of the short haircuts they sported.

All this left Lawlor untouched. The war and its consequences was still only distant thunder as far as he was concerned, and more and more he didn't even bother to disguise his apathy even though he could tell it enraged Burnside and to a lesser extent Boal, now filling his mug with tea.

"These truancy orders, sarge," he ventured, tilting the fat-bellied pot. "Five lined up so far. Should I make a start on them in the morning?" Lawlor said, "That's lovely, Victor," and Burnside snorted sarcastically behind his newsprint.

There hadn't been a proper inspection of the report book for weeks, the paper mountain on the table in the Day Room was one unsteady, slithery mess and not a single summons for petrol, blackout, tillage or any other violation had been processed or served since the night of the shooting in town. That also had been let slide into limbo, almost faded away and out of mind like the dried bloodstains on the floorboards of the dead woman's pub, which was shuttered now, doors and windows blinded, just like its owner. Yet why was it every time he cycled past, Lawlor still couldn't refrain from imagining the scene and the cruel manner of the slaying as if he had been present, a witness, head and heart reverberating to the sound of those shots and the ensuing cries of the victims.

Correction, *victim*. Let the Americans mourn their own. He could only grieve for one at a time, even though she had been almost, but not quite, a stranger to him. It was that imponderable that stayed with him, preyed on him on his travels all day and every day, gnawing away like some bothersome ache. *Loose ends.*

Boal said, "I hear another load of townies has just moved into Teddy Gault's oul' place out on the Barnish road."

"Oh?" said Lawlor, still in never-never land.

"Burnin' the banisters for firewood already, I expect." This from Burnside, emerging from his newspaper and homing in on yet another of his pet hates. "Bloody evacuees. Belfast vermin. And not a single husband or father among the lot of them."

"He could always be away fighting for his country," said Lawlor, acting the innocent, but delivering a dig all the same, for there was no reason in the wide world why the two Bs themselves shouldn't have joined up, except for a preference to do their soldiering from the recumbent armchair position like now.

"Those poor, poor craturs, bombed out of house and home. Have you seen the state of them? Barely a stitch on their backs."

They looked at him and he returned the look. Burnside's face had gone dark with blood. "Maybe we should take a few of them in ourselves," he suggested sarcastically.

Boal gave a nervous snicker. "Ach, now have a bit of sense."

"No, no," said Lawlor enjoying himself now, "Crawford's got a point. We have the room. For a start we could always let them have the old jail wing. That hasn't been used for twenty years. So they tell me, anyway. I'll put it up to headquarters, will I? I'm sure they'll approve. Chesney's red-hot when it comes to anything to do with the war effort. Feather in our caps as well." As opposed to the white variety he himself had frequently been threatened with.

He smiled at them invitingly but they sat there slumped in a sullen fog, pondering on what he'd just said yet trying not to look as if it mattered. The clock ticked and the wireless burbled low, tuned to the Home Service, its dial a glowing, faint yellowish brown. A talk about how you could do almost anything with the homely spud in the war-time kitchen except maybe make it taste more interesting. The set worked on two batteries, wet and dry. Boal was the one delegated to see they were charged regularly.

"Well, I'll be off to my warm bed now, lads. Don't stay up too late if I were you. We'll take a gander at what's behind that oul' bridewell door tomorrow first thing."

And he headed upstairs merrier than he had been in an age, knowing he'd sailed pretty close to the wind back there, oh, sure, with his fantasy about giving shelter to a bunch of whey-faced slum dwellers, but enjoying cranking up the pair of them far too much to care. Anyway, it made a change. Normally it was they who put their minds to tormenting him any chance they got.

Three grown men behaving like playground sneaks, he tut-tutted silently, peeling off his uniform. And over a period of how many years? Ten, at least. There had been others before them. Cut from the same cloth, as he recalled, resenting the foreign blow-in with his down-country accent. Worst of all that Romish religion which, even though he didn't appear to practise any more, still must imbue him with its deluded beliefs.

For a moment standing there beside the big brass bed he tried to pinpoint when last he'd got down on his knees to say his prayers. Once upon a time he and Nuala would recite the rosary together side by side on the chill linoleum of that old barracks bedroom in Granard, his first married posting, she in her white nightdress that crackled with starch, he in pyjamas with a cord that kept pulling out on him, a giant safety pin the only yoke to thread it back through again. He sat down on the edge of the bed remembering. Small intimate and precise details of that sort could always set him off.

And at first the memories are like that, events and places bathed in soft warm tints, pinks, yellows and golds, sunrise, sunset colours, the two of them together in that first year of marriage. Being a policeman and the wife of one constituted a sweet coalition that kept the world outside the barrack walls at bay, a world increasingly turning against them and their kind with every day that passed.

And now he's remembering other things from the cold, darker end of the spectrum, monotones and greys shot through with searing flashes. He clasps hands to his head to ward off the demons, but they're already in there, ready and waiting as always to torment him. Mention of the old jail and the terrible twenties when it housed the Shinners was what had got them going, rattling the bars just like those other fanatics screaming out to one another.

In Granard town they had a single lock-up for the station and that was only ever occupied by the town drunk on a Saturday night. He was in there sleeping it off when the telephone wires were cut and that terrible silence descended on them. At the time what seemed to be happening to them, one old sergeant and his three rookies, was almost laughably predictable, like a re-run of the last Western they'd seen. A buckskinned Spencer Tracy in a loghouse holding out with his band of brave chums against a painted raiding-party.

But he learned one lesson that night. Every act of evil is very nearly a replica of one that's gone before, yet familiarity is no consolation. First time, second time, even third, fresh undiluted terror takes hold the moment the progression starts to unfold.

They came on bicycles shortly after the wires went dead, soft and silent as shadows. Then the first commands rang out in Irish, as foreign-sounding to those inside as Comanche, even though they had all learned it at school. The siege lasted until just before dawn while the rest of the town buried its head under the blankets. They were the servants of a hated, foreign Crown, after all, only getting what they deserved.

That night re-played itself in Lawlor's head, the gunfire, the shattering glass, the *crump* of home-made grenades going off against the outer gate, the smell of burning paraffin as flaming brands came sailing up and over the wall. Inside the Day Room they stood, crouched or lay full-length on the tiled floor, stripped to their vests and drawers. The heat was intense, fiery August, the fields in the countryside beyond the edges of town bursting with a bumper harvest. They all kept gulping down great draughts of water from the jugs and basins they had laid out in readiness in case one of the torches caught hold.

Their limbs felt leaden, their brains jellied with terror. One of the constables, young Jack Riordan, had soiled himself. They could all smell it over and beyond the reek of cordite and burning lamp-oil. He held on to a table leg as if he was in a sinking ship instead of a battered drum, an upended bucket, or a sealed coffin, more like, at the height of the horror. And then it was over and their attackers melted off as silently as they'd come back to the hills and woods just like those same painted redskins in *North-West Passage*.

He fell down panting on the floor like a tired old dog, tongue lolling. They all did, clutching at the cool flags, and then for the first time he remembered Nuala upstairs in their bedroom. It was in the back extension for their newly-married privacy. He'd decided that would be the safest place for her to be when the telephone was disabled and contact with the outside world severed like a cut nerve.

Racked with his sin of omission he flew upstairs,

hammering on the door. *"It's over, all over, darling! Open up, it's me! It's only me!"*

But she refused to let him in to her despite his pleas. Down on one knee like a desperate suitor he pressed his lips then an eye to the keyhole, but it was blocked by the butt-end of the key twisted in the lock.

So then he had to go downstairs and lie about her being fast asleep. *Women,* he told them, summoning up a laugh, God forgive him, *imagine snoring through all of that like it was Hallowe'en and a load of fireworks going off.* The others nodded shakily, still getting their nerves back together.

As the only female in the barracks she was treated like some hothouse bloom, delicate as an orchid. She had that effect on them, making them afraid lest their rough mannish ways might bruise those soft outer and inner sensibilities. The notion of her being indisposed once a month in that certain way was enough to unhinge them. To his shame, he felt much the same way.

She took to her bed for almost a week after the night of the Shinners' attack and he shuttled trays up and down, back and forth, in between barracks duties, but even when she did show herself downstairs eventually, wan and drooping like a dying lily, she wouldn't venture outside. But then, neither did they, if they could help it. Their nerves had been stretched too far, maybe even sundered, like the telephone wires. At sunset the bolts would be shot home, then double-checked, and nothing would prevail on them to emerge until morning.

This was to become the new pattern of their lives, and each day brought news of fresh atrocities to make them even more convinced they were a garrison under siege. A magistrate in Clare was buried to his neck in the sand as the tide came in and his body thrown on a dung heap. Peoples' drives were "trenched" so that they could neither get in nor

255

out of their estates. Dogs were tied to railway lines, cattle maimed, crops torched, Protestants burned out of homesteads they'd worked for centuries.

And all the while Nuala wilted like a cut flower, growing thinner by the day. The rosary beads rarely left her pale, entwining fingers now, lips silently moving through the decade over and over again. Each night he tried to join her on the linoleum alongside their bed in an attempt to bring them together even though any religious beliefs he once harboured had long since faded away.

But it was hopeless, as hopeless as any desire on his part to reach out and touch her through the stiff cambric of her nightdress. It was like lying beside a shrouded corpse and in the dead of night he would watch and listen for her breathing to see if his worst fears had maybe come true.

When things became truly unbearable for all of them, for her condition could no longer be explained away as simply some woman's trouble better not gone into, he sent her off to her mother's place for a rest, a holiday, call it what you will, hoping that the change would deliver her back to him the way she used to be. Her family home was in Waterford at the other end of the island, and a week passed then two, then three.

When the letter finally arrived he took it upstairs and read it carefully sitting by the open window overlooking the livestock mart at the back of the barracks. He could hear the bullocks milling and bellowing in their pens. She'd hated that sound, she'd once told him. It reminded her of the terrible end in store for them, for everyone knew what took place in the awful slaughterhouse where the men in spattered white coats paddled all day in fresh blood the same colour as their faces. She said she could smell it, too, keeping the bedroom window fastened tight even on the most torrid of summer nights.

The letter was neat and small like herself and folded in four. Lilac paper inside a matching lilac envelope. He kept on examining it, holding it up to the light, the watermark said Basildon Bond, smelling it, too, anything to shield him from the shock of the words in her perfect hand. She'd worked in a solicitor's office in Dungarvan when first they'd met, his initial sight of her bent over a ledger, copper-gold hair clenched in a bun as perfect as a burnished bedknob. He loved to weigh it in his hand as if it was alive just before she unpinned it at night in front of the dressing-table and it flowed down over her shoulders.

In the days, then weeks that followed, that lavender-pale square of notepaper telling him she would, could never return, that it had all been a mistake, him, her, any life they might have had together while he was in the force, and that she would always think of him with affection, the document, the bulletin – a bullet, more like, to the heart – became frayed and almost worn away in the handling. At times he would crumple it up in a rage, then next minute, weeping, retrieve it, smoothing it out.

Soon it started to tear along the creases, so now he had four separate reminders of what had ruined his life. He would fit the separate sections together on their salmon-pink eiderdown, a wedding present from the station, poring over the words, searching for a word or expression of hope that might have eluded him first time round. But the more he studied the handwriting the more it became in his mind like one of those same legal affidavits she once copied out for her firm, precise, unambiguous, and as final as any death certificate.

He carried it about with him in his breast pocket between the back pages of his police notebook along with all those reports of other crimes. Then, somehow, he lost one of the leaves, then another, and another, until finally he was left with a solitary quarter, the one with the address on it, *37 Market Street, Waterford*, and *Dear Denis, I hope you are well and keeping* . . .

Not that he needed to be reminded of what the missing sequences contained. Their message continued to burn as if branded on his brain.

Two months after Nuala left him the old RIC disbanded and he transferred North along with about a thousand others, half of them Catholics like himself, and the initials on his cap-badge changed. When first he arrived here he told people he was a widower. If anyone pressed him further he would hint at something dark and terrible he didn't care to talk about concerning an attack on his last barracks in Longford. That usually shut them up.

In the drawer by his bedside was scattered a tiny cache of mementoes. A Claddagh ring, a crucifix on a chain, a powder-puff as dry as a mushroom, a pearl-handled brush, with what he liked to believe was a thread or two of her golden hair still clinging to its bristles, a little tin of Zam Buk salve, a bluey-green flask of lavender water. When the old sores reopened, as now, he would wet the tip of his little finger delicately, for all the world like some old sissy, and sniff the almost sapped scent to punish himself.

Part of him longed to banish the memory of her for good, but another destructive side needed to keep the past alive and freshly nourished every so often on his trips to Mrs McKeever's back-room, where he would sit with his whiskey and wait for certain scenes and sounds to float back like ghosts.

That night he dreams he is under siege once more, only it is inside the murdered woman's pub this time, glasses and bottles behind the bar exploding, then spurting out their precious fluids. He laps from a puddle on the counter like a dog, desperate not to let any of it go to waste while bullets whine and burst above his head. In a lull he hears the attackers call out to one another, only this time he can understand what they are saying. *"Kill the white fuckers!"* he distinctly hears one say, and then from another source, *"Don't leave one of them alive in there!"*

That one, suddenly it comes to him, is him. Not another soul living or dead in the place that he can see, and at this point his despair knows no bounds for how can he withstand all this while managing to keep the bar licked dry? It is one of those impossibly hopeless tasks that only beset one in the very worst of bad dreams, holding back a car from sliding over a precipice, singlehandedly damping down a forest blaze, trying to catch a speeding train, saving a loved one from drowning, all variations on that single theme. More and more bottles are bursting, his throat feels on fire, eyes baked in their sockets, he hears someone using a sledgehammer on the door.

And then the ultimate nightmare, the crescendo of horror, for there always is one, always, he sees Nuala sitting in the shadows, composed and smiling to herself as if enjoying the performance, a play, *Charley's Aunt*, maybe, or *Arsenic and Old Lace*, in the town's Assembly Rooms with him as principal comic turn.

He tries to call out to her to warn her of her peril, but his mouth is filled with some some sweet, foreign-tasting liqueur. She continues to smile happily all the while, combing back her loosened hair with the brush she always uses, the one with its grip of mother-of-pearl. Then suddenly she starts falling backwards, but not as in real life, more like slow-motion as when the projector in Barney Costello's old fleapit runs down and the figures up on the screen freeze jerkily, mouths opening and shutting like gasping goldfish.

He watches it happening, unable to move, even when

259

she's lying on the floor, nightdress spread around her like a tent. She has blood on her breast, yet keeps on smiling, ever smiling. His anguish has reached an unbearable pitch by now, the door panels are splintering, the counter even more awash than before with every spirituous liquor known to man, the darkening purple blotch spreading across Nuala's front getting bigger and bigger.

Nuala, it comes to him suddenly, *Nuala, my God, that's her name,* for he couldn't remember it up to now, and it seems to unlock something, for he drops down off the flooded counter and crawls over to her across the floor bringing his face close to hers. Her eyes are shut but the smile is still there, the smile of a child having a beautiful dream, nowhere like his own, and he opens his mouth to whisper her name, *Nuala, Nuala,* when instead a stream of alcohol issues out drenching her in its foul bath and as he pulls back horrified at what he's done her eyes spring open and the beloved face in front of him changes into that of a stranger, an old woman, ageing before his eyes like in one of those horror films that have Barney Costello's patrons cowering behind their hands.

"*Who are you?*" he whispers, even though part of him already knows the answer.

"*Don't you recognise me? It's only me, Denis,*" she whispers back. "*Abigail. Abigail. Come, come to me, for you haven't always been such a shy boy, now have you?*" and baring her withered dugs she spreads her arms in invitation and just as he's about to surrender himself up to the most frightful part of all and, surely something he'll never be able to explain or expiate, he wakes up.

The rest of the night he just lay there with the debris of the dream fading and gradually drifting away like scraps of burnt confetti. Every so often he would give a moan and a jerk as if it might be starting up over again, the film he had in his head ready to resume rolling anew. Bad enough to be haunted by past events in that bar-room by day, he told himself, but to start having nightmares about them now as well was getting to be too much, even for him.

Something has to be done, he muttered to the bedclothes, *something has to be done*, in the same way he'd been rhyming *loose ends* to himself, *loose ends*, over and over like one of Nuala's hail-marys. Now the tune had changed to, *something must be done. But what? In the name of God, what? Tell me.*

Despite the dream some sleep must have crept his way for the light awoke him next morning coming through the split in the curtains to lie like a bright rod on the eiderdown. He watched it thicken and intensify across the pink satin. And his mood began to brighten along with it, all the darker shadows of the night melting off into the far corners of the room until his mood was sufficiently alert for him to climb out of bed and stand shivering in front of the washstand and its flowery china basin and ewer.

He splashed his face and neck in its flat-smelling water, ridding himself of any lingering vestiges of bogeymen, or women, for that matter, then he went downstairs careful not to rouse the other sleepers. Sounds of steady snoring issued from Burnside's room, whereas across the way Boal slept like someone crucified, face down, arms outstretched, the barest trickle of breath coming from his mouth.

Once he had gone in there, curious and a little alarmed, too, at the absence of sound, but remembered feeling guilty afterwards, for it was like breaking some unwritten rule between them to do with privacy, even though they all poked and pried into one another's affairs, at least *they* certainly did, the two Bs.

He carried the steaming kettle upstairs and shaved, cleansing the coated razor in the hot water in the basin. It was a scrupulous ritual, more so than usual, for some reason, and when his cheeks tingled and shone apple-red he drew on his uniform just as carefully as if he was heading off on official business instead of aimlessly trailing country roads with nothing on his mind save putting in the day.

It was early still and not wanting to wake his two slumbering gendarmes he refrained from cooking a proper fried breakfast. Instead he cut himself two thick doorsteps, pressing them together like buttered bricks, then wrapped them in yesterday's *Newsletter*.

Before leaving he took a last guilty look over at the pile of paper swamping the Day Room table and, not knowing why he did it, he lifted up the latest sheaf of official bumph crowning their own little Mount Neglect. Four truancy orders, three in town, one out in the country. The names were the usual ones, the same families kept offending, except for the last, Taggart, which rang no bells. He thought for a moment. It belonged to the one solitary rural address, he might do worse than pass by that route. *Why not*, he had no other plans, and folding the summons in four he buttoned it into his top tunic pocket alongside the notebook bound with a rubber round cut from an old bicycle tube.

Travelling on silent wheels through the deserted streets Lawlor wondered if his early-morning jaunts had been noticed by anyone else besides Johnny Malone the milkman coming back from the creamery with twin churns weighing down the slope of his jingling trap like a couple of gleaming fifty-pounders. They passed one another by with barely a sideways glance, two men buried in their own private concerns with no room in their lives for idle greeting or banter. But Lawlor knew, just as old Johnny knew, what he was doing was beyond the bounds of normal duty. He had become an eccentric, a source of speculation, even though he had started to feel almost invisible on his late and early flittings to and fro. The notion nagged at him. Perhaps he had gone too far with this business, letting it take him over the way the drink had done, one addiction supplanting another.

With the clean, crisp morning air bathing his temples, for a moment he had this powerful yearning to be like everybody else in this sleeping town, with lives, a life, that ran on regulated, orderly lines just like those blacked-out trains that passed below Freddy Dunbar's signal-box.

By the time he had left the outskirts of town behind and was out among the fields and hedgerows proper, the sun was climbing straight and true into a cloudless blue sky. He loosened the top button of his tunic with one hand while holding the bike on course with the other. The thickly wrapped sandwich made a bulge on the left side of his chest. It had started to irk him, the weight of it, the ugly way it broke the line of his uniform. He dithered on whether to stow it under the saddle, then decided to eat it instead. The simplicity of the solution pleased him no end, and coming on a convenient bank and laying down the machine on the springy moss he sat down and opened up his crude parcel of baker's bread and creamery butter.

The sounds of the countryside began to separate, then assert themselves. Birds, bees, a distant dog, a whinnying horse closer to hand, water running in a thin, tinkling stream close by the soles of his boots. He munched steadily away, stopping every so often to moisten the dry mouthfuls with a draught from the crystal rill at his feet. Then he lay back in the sun and unbuttoning his tunic all the way re-read the day-old *Belfast Newsletter* that had wrapped his breakfast. From headlines to back-page exhortations to Dig For Victory and save waste paper, regulations about warble-fly and ragwort, then all over again, studying the sections he'd skimmed through first time round. A long and passionate article on besieged Stalingrad and how the Russians there were eating dogs and cats. Gallant little Malta getting her George Cross. Heavy US losses in the Solomons. British nation still in mourning for the Duke of Kent killed in an air crash over Scotland. SS men deporting Channel Islanders to Germany.

Again he had the feeling he was living some sort of charmed life, untouched and impervious to events he could only read about, but couldn't properly imagine or feel angry about. Like most of his fellow countrymen South of the Border, in fact. Good old Dev furiously waving his green, white and gold wand to keep the ugly world from contaminating holy Catholic, neutral, little Ireland. The very place he'd probably end up in once his retirement papers came through. Then a slow rotting down like compost in some turf-smoked Midlands hole.

In spite of himself he had the grace to laugh at his own excessive morbidity. *Ridiculous bloody man. No wonder your wife upped and left you. No wonder she gave you up as a bad job, seeing you depressed her as much as you're doing to yourself right now, sprawled on a ditch like some class of a hobo instead of the responsible servant of the law which you still happen to be.* At least for the next month or so, anyway.

It was nearly nine o'clock by now. Time to make his morning call on the woman in Kincaid's gate-lodge with the truant brat, without seeming too eager or heavy-handed about the business.

He reached the entrance to Glebe House about ten minutes later, wheeling the bicycle the final fifty yards or so, then leaning it up against one of the Major's ancient pillars with their carved gryphons guarding the approach. The tied house he was seeking, barely bigger than a salt-box, as the locals liked to term such places, could be seen half-way up the drive, off to the side a little, and with a tiny swept apron of ground front and rear.

Lawlor began crunching towards it, his metal-shod boots squirting out gravel as he went, but then he stopped, not because the sound grated — it did — but because suddenly he was remembering when he had been here before, and not that time recently when he'd run across Kincaid and his brave band of human trackers. No, long before that, five years at least. He felt shocked by his lapse of memory, for an occasion like that didn't usually end up consigned to some corner of consciousness like something falling down the back of a sofa.

Moving into the shade of a beech tree — its bark bore a recent blaze, he noticed — he allowed his mind to reach back to that afternoon when he had to bring such terrible news. The child's body had been taken to the Cottage Hospital where it squatted on a slab, blackened and unrecognisable. No one knew what was worse, that awful graven posture — there must have been no attempt at struggle, no movement whatsoever as the fire engulfed it — or the fact that it looked like a human cinder.

He and Burnside had the task of driving her into town to see the body, to identify what was unidentifiable. But there was a sandal buckle, two doll's eyes, and a cheap child's ring of the sort sold in a Lucky Bag. It was these items that triggered off her desperate grief, far more than the rapid glimpse she was given of that charred homunculus under its sheet.

As they drove her home slumped in the back of the old police Riley he and Burnside convinced themselves there was a smell of burning in the car even with the windows down. Lawlor watched her in the mirror. She pressed a handful of the dead child's clothing to her lips, for she had insisted on taking them with her from the house, praying perhaps that some dreadful mistake had been made. Above the pathetic clutch of baby's things that gagged her grief, her eyes held his, not unseeing, but probing, questioning, as if it was his fault that little infants were allowed to play with matches.

"Fire is the commonest killer of young children, followed by water," he had announced at one stage, regretting it instantly. *Useless, useless man.* Even Burnside seemed to be able to squeeze out more compassion.

On their way back to the barracks, however, his pity had evaporated as he talked about her and her fondness for entertaining His Majesty's armed forces. Once she even had the gall to complain about strange men, locals, civilians, hammering on her door at midnight as if the house was some class of a kipshop – *imagine it!* – and her inside quaking, with four equally terrified little ones. Five, then.

"An official report, you say? I didn't hear of it."

"Ach, we didn't want to bother you. I talked to her about it, sure enough, and put the word out to a few of the boyos involved, but what can someone like that expect, droppin' her drawers for every tommy and jack tar that happens along."

Lawlor remained silent for the rest of the journey, his mind filling up like a cesspool with inappropriate images and desires. Certainly she was a fine-looking piece of goods all right, ripe-breasted, a sturdy set of hips on her that would transport any man lucky enough to be granted her favours. For some time afterwards, even though his uniform was hardly the right shade, he allowed himself to imagine he himself might have somehow been conscripted into that band, select or otherwise, for Burnside had a habit of malicious exaggeration at the best of times.

On a couple of occasions, to his shame, he had even

cycled along slowly past the mouth of the driveway hoping to see her again, maybe engage her in some form of light conversation that might lead to . . . Well, you never could tell, could you? Such were the sorry dreamings of someone whose wife had left him and whose only release came by his own hand in the dead of night alone in a bed the size of a battleship.

And then there was one other occasion, the last. Winter. The ground covered in white. He tried to concentrate his memory. Out in the fields with someone, a man in uniform, laughing (*how dare she?*) the pair of them snowballing like children. And then they were gone into the woods, vanishing before his eyes as if he'd imagined it, him pedalling past like some silent torso above the hedge. Maybe it was all in his imagination, he couldn't be sure, and not just that particular episode either, a lot of others as well just recently.

Okay, back to the present and the job in hand, sergeant, he told himself and continued walking, only this time on the soft, deadening ribbon of grass that flanked the gravel. A thin curl of smoke was rising from the doll's-house chimney. Better still, *gingerbread,* he decided. Diamond-paned windows, sills a foot from the ground, pierced white bargeboards lining the eaves. The fairy-tale door, pointed at the top, chapel-fashion, was wide open. No signs of life, though. He could hear a pheasant go *krrk, krrk,* in the undergrowth, overlaid by his own heavy breathing.

He dabbed at his brow and as he did so a fat old setter dog waddled out through the open door to stand panting in the open, its rib-cage working like a bellows. Something enclosed its head and muzzle as if it suffered from some odd affliction, a malignant extension to its anatomy. But then Lawlor recognised what it was. Someone, someone had strapped a gas-mask on it for sport and next minute the very culprits, two giggling boys and an even younger girl, who seemed to be on the dog's side, judging by her expression, burst into view. The instant they saw him standing there like some dark avenger come to mete out retribution they ran back inside leaving old Spot blinkered and still breathing rubber. The dog saw him, too, and wagged his tail resignedly, it seemed to Lawlor, eyes regarding him through a haze of celluloid.

"Here, boy," murmured Lawlor, but the dog stayed where it was, head cocked and waiting as if for the all-clear to sound. Ill at ease suddenly, Lawlor took his notebook out, peeling back the elastic band in readiness. But for what? Misuse of civil defence property? *Christ!*

A face appeared in the doorway and the man and the boy regarded one another in silence. It was the eldest, the truant, and he had an enamel basin in his hands, dish cloth draped over one shoulder.

"What's his name?" asked Lawlor genially.

"Bunny," said the boy. He looked frightened.

"Funny name for a dog. Ever chase rabbits, does he?" Lawlor smiled invitingly, but his joke died in the air.

"Bunny here got a licence – sonny?" *My God, he was turning into a regular Tommy Trinder.*

"Oh, he's not ours. He's the Major's. He only comes around here to play."

"So I see. Do you think he enjoys wearing that contraption on his head?"

The boy looked at the dog as if he hadn't noticed anything out of the ordinary about it before. All the while the basin kept tilting in his grasp, a soapy trickle leaking from its rim.

"What's your name, son?"

"Raymond. Raymond Taggart."

"Well, Raymond Taggart, run in and tell your mammy, like a good lad, there's someone here who would like a wee word with her."

The boy's face had gone deathly pale. He was staring at the notebook. *Probably knows fine well why I'm here*, thought Lawlor, *but why such alarm?* It wasn't as if he'd stayed away from school only the once. Far from it.

"She's not well," he stammered. "She's sick in bed. She can't, she can't —"

"Who is it, Raymond?" interrupted a woman's weak voice. It came from the dark interior.

"RUC, missus. Just a routine matter."

There was a pause and then she appeared in the doorway, an old coat pulled over her nightdress. Lawlor looked at her and as if to deflect the force of his gaze she put a hand up to her throat, gathering the collar of the coat closer to her. As she did so the coat swung open, nightdress tightening across the mound of her belly. She saw Lawlor staring and quickly covered herself.

"Mrs Taggart —" he began.

"*Miss*," she corrected and instantly it was he who was on the receiving end, nervy as a swain who hasn't rehearsed his advances properly, although any intimate notions he might have entertained had evaporated. His imagination had tricked him. Her hair looked unwashed and neglected, her complexion blotchy and pale in equal proportions, and he thought he could detect something rank and stale-smelling carried with her from the house like milk turned sour.

"I just happened to be passing —" he began a second time then, realising he was holding the open notebook in his hand like a threat, he stowed it away in his breast pocket where it belonged.

"There's been a whole lot of stuff going missing from the American base lately, blankets, rations, items of furniture, even. Maybe you've heard? Anything that hasn't been nailed down, you might say." He ventured a smile but that face remained blank, a washed-out mask.

269

"We've nothing to do with the base."

"Oh, I know, I know that. I just thought you might have come across some of it, that's all. There's a fair bit floating around, you know. Army property."

Again she said, "We've nothing to do with the base," in flat tones, laying a hand on her stomach as if on oath.

"Fine, fine," he said, already beginning to back away. "Sure, I understand. I'll not be troubling you any further. Well, good day, ma'am," and he turned on his heel to walk away.

"We just want to be left in peace," he heard her softly murmur, and without turning he raised a hand in affirmation.

He made his departure the way he'd come, feeling awkward and foolish, the lot of them hardly able to wait to see the back of him, even the dog, he convinced himself, behind its goggles and mask. *What an idiot*, he berated himself, *what a sad excuse for a Sherlock Holmes*, but when he saw her standing there like that cradling the curve of her belly he hadn't the heart to bring up the truancy order. Instead of which he had hit on the business of lifted army property. Probably not far off the mark, either, with the house at their back an Aladdin's cave of the stuff. Why should theirs be any different? Everyone else was at it.

But let that pass, like so many other things he had put off recently. And, anyway, this one had turned out to be a little more personal than intended, for he was recalling that little charred corpse again and how useless he had been at the time to help or offer consolation. One more piece of unfinished business wouldn't matter.

At the pillars he looked back. She had gone inside, they all had, old setter dog included. On a sudden whim, now that he was no longer under observation, he decided to slip sideways in among the Major's trees instead of mounting up and pedalling off on yet another aimless tour of the countryside. *The Ice-House*, he thought. *Why not?* He'd have one last look at the Ice-House for old time's sake. *Unfinished business. Loose ends . . .*

He began walking through the trees in what he took to be the direction of the mound and the deeper he went the more hushed it all became. Yet it felt different from the last time he'd come this way, aware, attentive, even. High above the same light breeze feathered the tree-tops but down below in the shade there was barely a breath. His feet made no sound on the carpet of pine needles, which somehow intensified the feeling of being observed. Soon he began to sweat and every so often would stop and listen whilst wiping his face. It was as if any life out there, for there had to be, was holding its collective breath and listening to him.

The idea began to take hold, all that invisible force ranged against him, so then he found himself halting at intervals, head to one side, just to catch them, *it*, out, so he would be proved right in spite of all their skills at camouflage.

At one point he even slid behind a tree, staying doggo, back pressed against bark for a good half minute. And as he strained, yes, he did detect something, like a twig breaking, dry, brittle, like snapping bone, then a pause as if whatever had made the noise had frozen in its tracks, one foot, or was it paw, raised in case it made the same mistake a second time.

At that point Lawlor came bursting out from his hiding-place surprisingly quick for someone his size – certainly it surprised him – and sure enough he caught a glimpse of movement behind some bushes, no more than a flicker out of the corner of his eye, but enough to prove his point.

Advancing on his tormentor, he cried, "*I know who you are and what you're up to, Mr Snake-in-the-Grass, Mr Sneak-to-the-Boss!*" for by this time he felt convinced it had to be Kincaid's hired man, the one he'd had a run-in with before

271

and who he also suspected had let his tyres down. *"Show yourself, you Fenian blackguard!"*

His anger was close to boiling point and he unsheathed his baton, sliding it out of its oiled holster and, bearing down on the clump of low-growing elder, he struck out at the vegetation on either side of him, thrash, thrash, like one of the Major's own beaters.

"I'll crack your sleekit head for you!" he bawled, lashing the branches. *"I know what dirty tricks you've been up to, never fear. I've had my eye on you all along! All along, you hear me?"*

And as he raised the hickory truncheon for one final, devastating blow someone cried out in a puny voice and rolled from under the bushes clutching his head as if wood and bone had already connected. Lawlor froze. It was the boy, damn it, the one from the gate-lodge. He was yelling, *"I didn't mean to do it, I didn't mean it!"*

Lawlor grabbed him by a skinny arm pulling him to his feet where he still shook and whimpered, his eyes never leaving the bared baton. With his free hand Lawlor slid it back into its leather tube.

"Now, you little gobshite, just what's your game? You'd better tell me smartish if you don't want to spend some time in the cooler. I'm not kiddin', mind."

And he wasn't either. All his pent-up frustrations had finally come to the surface like a pot boiling over, fuelled by the lies and deceit he'd been fed, as he saw it, by the likes of Kincaid, Boal and Burnside, those Yanks, Freddy Dunbar, even, and his band of bum-boys – yes, yes, he wouldn't put it past him – and now this snivelling runt in his cut-down men's trousers and shirt. WAAF blue, he noticed. *A woman's blouse, for the love of Christ!*

"Right, out with it, and, remember, I'll know if you're telling me lies." He patted his breast pocket. "It's all in here in black and white, remember. Every last detail, every one of your rotten little secrets in this notebook here."

He could tell that frightened him most, the notebook. He had seen it in his eyes back at the house.

"It's my job, you see, what I do, so you'd better tell me before I get round to telling *you*."

The boy looked up at him, pale girly face, mouth soft and trembling, big eyes awash. Any other time Lawlor would have taken pity on him and his little family tribe back there but right now no one was exempt from his wrath. He felt cold, cruel, more in command than he had been in a very long time. So what if it was a kid he was terrorising? He didn't care any more.

"I'm not a Fenian, mister. Honest, I'm not. We're Protestant."

"And you think that makes it all right, do you? *Do you?*" He gave him an extra shake just for good measure.

The boy stared up at him, confused for a moment, then he blurted out, "I only did it to keep her from going across to him. She wouldn't listen, she thought more of him than us, so she did. That's why I had to do it. I just had to!"

He was really crying in earnest now and Lawlor began to soften slightly. Also he was curious, in spite of what he took to be a parcel of childish secrets about to be divulged. Then between sobs he heard the boy say something about a boat.

"The boat across the water? To England?"

"No, no, Granda Taggart's boat. On the Lough shore. At Gawley's Point. I smashed it up."

"You did, did you?" He felt tempted to take the dreaded notebook out again but stopped himself. No need to, any more. "When did you do all this?"

"A week ago."

"When you were supposed to be in school, I take it?"

The boy looked at him. *Careful*, thought Lawlor, *don't*

confuse the issue. "Now, look here, my lad," he said in his best official voice, "you're in pretty bad trouble here. Destroying other people's property is a serious offence. Even if it is your granda's." Then, as an afterthought, he added, "Who else knows about this?"

"About what?"

"The boat."

"Nobody. Just you."

For an instant Lawlor felt his resolve start to unravel. He didn't know if he could keep this going or not, interrogating a child out in the middle of a wild wood like this. But then the same child, with a burst of venom, said, "I don't care if he does die, he shouldn't have made my mammy sick. We were all okay till he came along. I never wanted his candy or his oul' toy train anyway!"

Lawlor breathed deep, the short hairs on the back of his neck bristling. Soft, softly, like someone about to snare a bird, he said, "Who's *he*, Raymond?"

And then after a sob or two the boy gave him the name, the magical, elusive name and, gentle still, Lawlor told him to take him to see this old boat, just the two of them, and that if he did so, maybe, well, just maybe, they would say no more about it, letting it rest that way, *their* secret, nobody else's.

TWELVE

The weather breaks. The storm, thunder like a drum roll, arriving out of the west in the middle of the night. Which one, don't ask, for time has started to go badly adrift for him, hours, then days, even, running into one another like dye in water. He doesn't even bother to cross them off on the back of his old planking door any longer, as he knows he should, as he's supposed to do. Someone in his position. Then, again, he's not really shipwrecked. Not like one of those characters in the story-books, not washed up by tempest or accident. More like left to rot, left to waste away, so as not to upset or inconvenience certain people.

You can tell he's going off Pearl. He can feel it building up inside of him just like that old storm out there.

After the first thunderclaps comes the lightning, turning everything bright as day. In a flash, then another, and another, in rapid succession, he sees the inside of his shelter, the piles of trash, holes in the roof and one wall, and over in the furthest corner, the old ewe sheep, head still facing away from him, sides heaving like a bellows. Its fleece is a dull strawish colour. It wheezes. It has the runs. No more the pitter, patter of little liquorish drops, now its hindquarters oooze yellow. He can smell it, too, ammonia catching him in the eyes and by the throat.

Then the rain arrives, falling like stair-rods, and that stupid mutton-brain just stands there, letting itself get soaked through under the biggest goddamn hole in the roof.

He can't bear just watching it take a bath that way so after a time he gets up from his own dry corner and goes over to its side of the house. He starts into pushing and shoving it, but it's like trying to shift a woolly old Sherman tank. It just stays there solid, like on four table legs, head turned off into the wall letting the rain drum down on it. His hands feel wet and oily all at the same time and the smell is worse up close, so he goes back and lies down in his own spot again listening in the dark to the rain break its fall on that dumb carcase. *Go on, catch pneumonia, see if I give a damn. Anyway, your days is numbered, mutton chops, even if nobody's counting no more. Chops, cutlets, breast, saddle, leg, rack, that's all I see when I look at you. Just meals on legs.*

And he slides off into another of his mouth-watering daydreams, even if it is the middle of the night, where he's cooking up a storm in this great big shiny kitchen all by himself, all for himself, more importantly, one terrific recipe after another, all variations on, *yeah, you guessed it.*

Anyway, why didn't they send him a pig ashore when they were at it? Three times as many fine dishes. More. Nothing wasted, not even that curly little tail. But, swim? He's never seen one swim. Wallow, sure, swim, no. For now he's remembering them old hogs everyone kept in a pen back home fattening them up on turnip greens and kitchen scraps for that big day. Hog-killing day.

Sometimes they'd start into squealing and hollering as their time got near just as if they could tell what was in store for them when Moses Stokes came by with his knives and hammer and his long leather apron stiff with blood. Soon as they caught a whiff of that they'd go loco, running at the fence, tearing up the sod, foaming, squealing, crapping, all at the same time, until three or four of the men got a hold on it and threw it to the ground. Moses would then take up his special sledge hammer with that little squared-off head no bigger than a postage stamp and stun it. *Bang.* Or, more like, *thud.* One strike, that's all it ever took, for Moses Stokes was an expert hog despatcher never known to miss or take a day off work except Sundays, travelling all year up, down the length and breadth of the Southern nation. He just loved what he did for a living, that old black man, lean as a whip, hardly ever spoke or smiled, just did his job, got paid, and was on his way off to his next hog killing. It was the highlight of their calendar year just to watch him in action.

After the pig was out cold it was strung up by the back feet still jerking and its throat cut and the blood caught in a pail, maybe two, sometimes even three buckets-full, for there's a heap of life-juice in an old hog. Blood sausage was what it was kept for. Then Moses would pour kettles of scalding water all over and down its back and sides and shave it clean as a whistle with a special barber knife he carried in his belt.

Next step a real deep cut was made from gullet to cornhole in that baby-pink carcase and then he'd plunge an arm in up as far as the elbow and start hauling out all those steaming intestines, white and yellow and some navy blue. Sometimes he would let one of us do it, too, just for the fun of it, feeling all that mushy heat, which was something, a little scary, too, like old man Hog was still alive and quivering, only pretending to be dead.

People would come up with bowls and pans and suchlike and Moses would dole out heart and kidneys, brains and sweetbreads, liver, as well as the gut to make chitlins out of. Young 'uns would get the bladder to blow up with a reed, then play kick-ball with it while Moses got right down to the real serious side of the operation, namely slicing old Mr Hog up in pieces and parcels, enough to keep a family of nine or ten in smoked and salted vittles for half a year almost. Good old fatback, good old gammon, sow belly, spare ribs, Virginia ham . . .

And he curls up under his mess of old coats waiting for daylight to come, while the heavens continue to rain down outside, inside, as well, in more than a few places.

All the while the sheep in the far corner stays still, like she's tethered there. He can make out that pale shape in the dark like it's a patch of whitewash on the wall, comforting in some crazy way, and so he gets off to sleep knowing it's there and not likely to cause him any grief or trouble. Maybe he'll just put off the moment of truth another little while. Save it for another rainy day when the taste on his tongue and in his head of lamb chops sizzling gets just too damn strong for him to resist any longer.

By morning the rain has passed right overhead and way off to the east somewhere else where other folks are getting their share of it now. But he finds it hard to even think of other people, let alone imagine them going through the same sort of things he's going through. It's something new this feeling, like being the last man alive with hardly any memories of what has happened to him or gone before. Maybe that's okay, for already he's started blanking out the bits he doesn't care to recall or think about too much. Like what got him here in the first place, and then Pearl not showing up for days on end when all the time she said she would.

That's probably the worst part of all, for he knows if he lets it get to him he'll end up wanting to kill something, anything, for want of that somebody he's really mad at, namely the white bitch who has betrayed him. But then he weeps. *No, no, she ain't like that, not his sweet Pearly, she'd never turn him in, or leave him to rot here.*

Something must have happened to her, to one of the kids, maybe, that's what it is, sick or something, he just knows it. Just be a matter of time, any time now, before he sees her come rowing towards him out of the far blue yonder, that old boat loaded right down with all kinds of goodies to eat and drink.

That sort of calms him down and so he rises and looks out through the crack in the door at the new day. The water has changed color with the rain, kind of a regulation army olive-green shade now, like it's been taken over by Uncle Sam in the middle of the night. Goddamn huge paint-job. Shore-to-shore.

But, then, why not, for old Eagle Puss can do damn near anything to anybody he damn well pleases. Leastways, that's what they kept on telling him ever since he joined up. *Might have been a poor barefoot nigger back home, boy, but now you're part of the biggest, smartest, best-fed, best-equipped man's army in the whole goddamn world, and don't you forget it, you hear?*

Sure, sure, sarge, anything you say, boss. And for quite a time he went along with it too just like all them other poor saps. Shit, after what they'd been used to, this was pure paradise, spending as well as saving money, great food, three changes of uniform, free smokes, free rubbers, hot showers, clean beds. What else could a young buck ever ask for?

But tell me, if I may be so bold, mister boss man, why was it they were still doing all the cruddy jobs their white buddies didn't care to do, same as stateside, like digging out latrines, dropping in fenceposts, mopping floors, laying cement, painting doors, shifting loads, washing dishes? Services Of Supply. That was their official army designation. Any roads they'd got the initials right. SOS Save Our Souls.

Old Stovepipe Davis who was in the War One said it was just the same then, no difference, so get used to it, suckers,

279

and they never got around to fighting neither, which was promised them, all those home-town nigger boys just itching to stick it to some Kraut.

This is the sort of thoughts he has running around in his head most of the time when he's not asleep. Like an angry argument he's anxious to put across to somebody, somebody invisible who's laughing at him all the time. Push him too far, though, and he'll do something he might regret, something real bad. He just knows it. But for now, at least, the shouting match inside his head has died down to a low rumble.

Barefoot, for the shoes are too far gone, he knows that now, near crippling him when he did try them on, he shimmies out through his crack in the door and, crouching low in his old trailing coat, he scuttles around to the safe side of the shack. He does it easy and smooth for it's become sort of a daily ritual by now, out and about foraging before the rest of the world on the farthest shore has had a chance to stretch and yawn and open a bleary eye.

The grass is all shiny and wet from the night's rain and feels real cool between his toes, easing them and washing them at the same time. *Surely some sort of a plus*, he thinks to himself, and feels his spirits start to climb accordingly, the din in his head already a forgotten memory.

The path he takes is the one he always goes. First of all a little short bare stretch out in the open which quickens his breath like that War One no-man's-land old Stovepipe was always on about. No bullets, though, not yet, anyhow, but that's what it feels like, some sniper's beady eye on the back of his neck until he's safe and sound and out of sight in among the brambly bushes. He slows down, feeling his heart pump then slip back to its normal slow and regular beat.

This place is coming down with blackberries and he feeds on them a while for lack of something better in the way of nourishment. At least they seem to fill him up, sometimes carrying back a handful or two in his pockets just to tide him over the rest of the day. He can tell he's lost a heap of weight even without the aid of a mirror by the way his pants are starting to flap about the waist. Also he can push two, no, *three* fingers now, between his shirt collar and his neck with ease, something he could never manage before. That big old lardy guy with the beer gut is turning into a leaner, younger version of himself, for he usen't always to be this way. No, once upon a time he was a skinny kid just like every other young buck running around chasing his own tail and all the time hoping he might get some as well.

The fruit starts off nice and sweet in the mouth then gradually turns tart which is the signal he's had enough. Early on he got a run of the shits when he gorged himself unwisely but now he takes it easy. Liquid, it seems, is more important when it comes to keeping the hunger pangs at bay. He hears his morning intake sloshing around inside like it's one of those skins people hump in the desert. Every desert movie he ever did see carried the same message, water first, and grub, well, that can wait. Mind you, he's not sure whether it applies to any place as green and juicy as this.

Anyway, he moves on at this point to the next part of his dawn routine like he's some old guy putting in his day, one step, one tiny distraction, at a time. So, what'll it be today, granpa? *Well, let's see now, son. Guess I could take in a movie or place a bet, maybe have a nice vanilla soda or a popsicle, get a shoeshine, smoke a cigar, shoot the breeze with some old army buddies, even maybe pay a visit to some sweet and kindly lady friend, get myself laid . . .*

Instead, of course, he continues on along the narrow track that's overhung with blackberry bushes, the ripe fruit all wet and glistening in the sun, same deep colour as that garnet pinky ring Stovepipe Davis wears. For an instant his eyes fill up as he wonders if anyone ever misses him back at the base, if they really believe he helped shoot up that bar, maybe kill somebody in the process, for he still doesn't know, and Pearl won't talk about it. Or had he vanished from memory like spit off a stove-lid?

Stovepipe was about the only true friend he ever did have. The younger guys were always a mite too jive-talking for his liking, everyone trying to be Mr Kingfish. Hotshots. Long as he can remember he always felt more at ease round older folks anyway, liked listening to their stories about root doctors and obi women and mojo charms made out of grave-dust and black cats' bones. He loved their music too, bottle-neck blues, jug and harmonica numbers. The cool cats in the detail, leastways, they pretended to be that way, dug swing bands, Dorsey, Goodman, Glenn Miller. White boys' jazz, Stovepipe called it.

In his head he hears him sing, *"Early this mornin', when you knocked upon my door, And I said: Hello, Satan, I believe it's time to go."*

And an all-time favourite of his, *"Why do they call me black when I'm so blue?"* over and over and over again till some of the guys in the hut would hurl a boot or chunk of kindling at him.

He would just laugh at them, showing off that gold front tooth of his. "My twenty-two carat 'surance policy. For when times get *really* rough." Just thinking of Stovepipe cheers him up, he always has that effect on people, even if they are living on berries like some kind of old hermit. Standing there, mouth all stained with their juice — if you could see it on his kind of skin, that is — he looks straight up into the clear autumn sky and forgets for a time where he is and how slim his chances are of getting off this Devil's Island. Another movie. *Pearl will be here soon*, he comforts himself, *mebbe even as soon as tonight.* Yeah, he has a real strong feeling tonight'll be the night.

He has about one hour to kill before the rest of the world wakes up and still in a good mood, he knows he shouldn't be, but he dithers about whether to go visit the goats over on their side of the island. They haven't been too much on his mind lately, for obvious reasons. He's in his territory and they're in theirs and he's more than happy to leave it that way.

Instead he heads off along the track away from the brambles and his own private fruit patch to this place he's been before. On the way he notices fresh droppings and regular runs in and out of the thorn bushes. If he could just lay his hands on a piece of wire somewhere, not too long, about a foot or so would do the trick, old bedspring, maybe, he can straighten out, he could set a nice little snare for himself, have a bunny rabbit put its head in the noose and, bingo, be laying there in the morning ready for the pot. He does have a pot, remember, although he hasn't been able to get up the nerve to light anything under it yet, not even at night when the smoke won't show. At least he doesn't think it will.

Then he thinks, *but Pearl will be arriving any time now with proper food, cooked already, so forget about living off the land, Mr Crusoe, except for the berries he's been cramming away.*

He's also come across some mushrooms on his travels which aren't so bad raw, least not as bad as he thought they'd be. One of his main problems is a lot of the things growing here are different to what he's used to. Like the mushrooms, for instance. Back home they grew out of old tree-stumps or under leaves. This native variety just seems to pop up in the open, clumps of round little button heads like pale peckers in the grass. Kinda along the lines of that manna stuff they taught him about in bible class, appearing overnight, too, like in the Good Book. Pearl told him they were great to eat. She had the kids gather loads of them for breakfast all the time.

But he's feeling okay for the time being, his stomach full of that old blackberry mess. He can hear it bubbling and acting away like there's some kind of moonshine-still working in his guts, sort of comforting in a way, the sound travelling with him everywhere he goes, his own personal juke-box.

But there's a spot he's found, sheltered and something of a sun-trap, and he's heading for it now, mind made up on how to pass his precious morning hour of freedom in the open. Two old rocks rise straight up out of a mess of gorse bushes and in between this little bare flat sort of place carpeted with short turf grass about the size of somebody's kitchen table. No one could ever find him here, never, his back up against one of the warm, bare rocks.

The sun is strong on his face as he stretches himself out and each time he's been here like this he feels safe and content and thinks to himself mebbe being marooned on some old desert isle mightn't be so awful after all, long as he's allowed to stay here all by himself unbothered in his own little out-of-the-way hideyhole.

So he sits there like he's a thousand miles away deep in a cane-break somewhere and the strong sun up there is that same old sun beating down on Peabody County and him a young whippersnapper skipping Sunday School and he's got a book with him. He closes his eyes, letting his mind fill like a basin till it's ready to flow over with remembered sights and sounds. Then he takes the book out of his coat pocket for, yes, it's a real one Pearl brought him, this old paperback novelette, the last time she rowed over. He found it at the bottom of the sack below the bread and bully beef and eggs, most of which he busted, incidentally, in his haste to get at the grub.

It's an old Western-type yarn about a bunch of Mormon ranchers and rustlers having a range war, pretty complicated up to now, but he's beginning to get the hang of it. There's this outcast guy called Venters who's tracking down the bad guys. He has a horse called Wrangler and an old faithful dog named Whitey and at one point he wounds this Masked Rider character at a spot called Deception Pass who turns out to be a girl, Bess, or Elizabeth Erne, to give her her real name. 'Course you guessed it, she's innocent really and he starts going soft on her, tending her wounds and suchlike. Meanwhile, the baddies are after them both hot-foot by now and the pair of them hole up in this canyon Venters calls Surprise Valley.

This is the part he likes best, particularly the description of their hideout which is guarded by this huge, finely balanced, hanging rock put there thousands of years earlier by the Indians to keep their enemies out.

Although he's read past the place, it's page 86 in the book, he likes coming back to it every so often.

"There's water here – and this is the place for me," said Venters. "Only birds can peep over these walls."

Wow, he just loved the idea of that and once more he is Venters hiding out and living on game in his mysterious valley with the bonus of some beautiful female waiting for him to come back to the cave at night with a freshly killed buck slung across his saddle.

But his dreaming time is nearly at an end, so he puts the book back in his pocket and prepares to head back to his prison shack on the shore. He stands there rubbing his face and chin, wire-wool rough with stubble, and wonders if Venters ever grew a beard. Probably not, the girl wouldn't appreciate it. And he was a shave-a-day sort of guy anyway, using cold water if he had to.

Pearl had put in a little piece of soap barely enough to work up a lather but no razor. Mebbe when she'd time to think about it she might bring him one. Then his mind starts going off sideways, at tangents, one thought leading into another. First of all, she wouldn't have such a thing about the house, would she? 'Less of course one of his predecessors had left it there. Second, mebbe she didn't think a black man needed to shave, on account of him being all smooth and shiny like a pool ball, 'cause he'd made damn certain she never got a glimpse of him looking rough, always buffed up and smelling like a true Southern gentleman caller should. But now she had, yeah, seen him hairy as an old cow, messed in his pants and everything, so mebbe she wouldn't be so anxious to get to see him in that state ever again.

Dear good Lord, please don't let her turn her back on me. I'll do anything you say. Anything.

And he starts shaking all over, his day gone all sour on him, afraid suddenly he's outstayed his time in the open and that something bad will be waiting for him when he gets back to his hutch by the waterside.

On the backwards trip, a lot faster than the one out, what does he see but a little outbreak of mushrooms stippling the short grass, something he must have missed before, being so full of himself and his newfound bounce, and he stoops and tears up a handful of the little round mothers, this being an opportunity far too good to pass up, even if he is in a hurry. He's also feeling hungry again and he cleans out the entire colony, stuffing them into his pockets, including the one with the dime novel in it. Rubbing one down the front of his coat, he bites the head off, munching as he goes, back along the narrow, beaten rabbit track.

And, sure enough, doesn't he see one, coming on it suddenly, crouched plumb in the middle of its run, grooming its whiskers like some old lady in front of her bedroom mirror, and it looks straight at him a second, cool as hell, before slowly hopping off into the bushes. His heart is beating like a drum like it's a lion he's disturbed, not some young cottontail who's mebbe never ever seen a man up close before, and he tells himself he should have threw a stick at it, something, anything, instead of freezing solid like an asshole.

Well, fuck it, boy, he thinks, *seems like you're just not cut out to be hunter material, after all,* continuing on down along the path between the blackberry hedges until he sees the back of the ruin blocking off his view of the water.

Down low he goes, as near the ground as he can manage, reminded of some old bent beggar woman he used to see back home hustling about the place for handouts. *Same as you, nigger,* he thinks, *same as you, no different,* and his anger at Pearl comes back again like a dose of heartburn and stays with him all the way to the safety of the walls.

But from this point on it will not leave him day or night, driving him deeper and deeper into the dark hole that has been dug for him, no matter how hard or long he struggles to drag himself out of it.

He crawls the last few yards around to the front, coat tails dragging with their light-as-air weight of mushrooms. Squeezing through the space in the door – he could have made it wider for comfort's sake, but he prefers it this way – his eyes take time to adjust to the semi-darkness. Then he sees the sheep isn't standing up no more, but lying down on its side, legs sticking straight out like she's a replica made out of wood or something. This terrible wheezing noise is coming from its throat but far, far deeper than that, chest, belly, lungs, all involved. He stands there just beginning to realise he has a real bad situation on his hands, mebbe even that very same one he anticipated out in the open earlier.

"*Come on, Mary,*" he says, his brain not catching up with his mouth yet, "*pull yourself together. No need to act up on me this way. For Christ's sake, it's only an old cold you got swimming all that way over here. We two stormbirds gotta stick together. I*

287

*never meant all that stuff 'bout turning you into lamb chops,
anyways. Just kidding, you hear? You hear me?"*

But Mary is too far gone to listen, even if someone was
cracked enough to try to talk to a old fucking sheep in the
first place.

All this time the noise is getting louder. Mixed in with it is
a kind of gurgling sound which is far worse somehow, as if
all that lake water she swallowed is still in there. What it
needs is to be let out, he tells himself, remembering some old
farm guy who once told him you had to cut a hole in the
windpipe if an animal ever took something he called *the
strangles*. Sure as shit, this had to be it, has to be, the word,
the sound, making a perfect match, like the heaves or the
whooping cough.

He goes across to the rafter he's set up on two bricks in the
corner where he's laid all his stuff out like on a shelf. The old
table knife is there, the one Pearl brought him, with the
yellow bone handle, totally useless, until he started sharpening it on the hollowed front step just like all those other folks
before him. He's gotten a real keen edge on it by this time
except he's never used it on anything, not even the loaf of
bread which he just tore apart with his bare hands, being too
hungry to act polite.

He takes up the knife and goes across to the heaving,
choking mass of fleece in the corner and stands there looking
down on it. Some sort of white stuff is bubbling from its jaws
and the stink is real bad, up close, just about as bad as he can
bear without puking. He wonders if he can manage the job
one-handed while holding the other over his mouth. Then it
occurs to him the knife hasn't got a proper point on it, just a
flat old table-knife, that's all, and he really needs it to be
sharp like a skewer if he's to jab deep into the throat with it.

Fuck, oh, fuck, he thinks, for if he just carries out a sideways
cut, which is about all that rotten old knife is fit for, lots of

blood, end of story, forget it. *Why couldn't old Moses Stokes be here to help out,* he moans to himself, which is real stupid. But then he wouldn't even attempt a dumb move like this in the first place. No one would. No one except him, for he can't just let this terrible noise continue. All the while it's growing louder and louder by the minute, filling the space, worst of all seeping out maybe into the open and crossing the water to where someone will hear it. He pictures it like that spreading like a slow wave in the stillness to give him away. Turning his head into a corner he covers up his ears with his hands but the sound somehow still penetrates like it's mixed in with the beat of his heart and his own breathing. All three seem to be keeping perfect time and this really sends him over the edge.

In sudden desperation he throws away Pearly's old knife and grabs up a lump of wood instead and before he knows it he's standing over the dying animal, for she is, isn't she, just look at her, for Christ's sake, just look at her, and down he brings his squared-off club, once, twice, then a third time, putting her out of her misery.

The breath sucks out of it like the air leaving a balloon, only slower, and with a lot more noise. Finally it kicks for a bit, one leg extending, then stiffening, while the other three just crumple and collapse and then it's over.

For the first time he can hear the birds sing outside. He stands there with the bloodstained four-by-four in his hand and listens intently, gulping in every sound like it's precious and won't last, even some old wood beetle chewing away in the rotten rafters overhead.

A little while after that he lies down, but away from his usual position close to the door. He feels drained like he's run a race and some time later on he falls into a deep sleep, face buried in the musty, still faintly tobacco-smelling wool of Pearl's old boyfriend's army coat.

About two, three, maybe even four hours, who can tell – he can't, for his watch has given up on him by now – he comes out of this dream sweating, still thinking it's real and he's back on his army cot where he started out, clean sheets, over and under, and a brand new itchy Gl blanket atop that again as icing on the cake. He keeps his eyes closed tight shut, head buried, not wanting for it to end. His pecker, meanwhile, is in his right hand where it belongs, hot and hard, and he rubs it a few more times for luck, for the sort of dream it was involved a lot of heavy humping with some person, maybe, even, *persons*, unknown.

No one in particular immediately springs to mind, no one he can put a face or pussy to, so he figures it has to be Pearl. But it's a different kind of screwing this, rough, hard, nasty, no quarter given. The only other time he rammed it home in that manner was the first time she brought him here with old Billy Goat Gruff watching.

Why he wanted to punish her he didn't know, just needed to, that's all, like it would clear out all that bad stuff inside of him soon as he shot his load. And sure enough he comes right now like it's a wet dream all along. The charge of jissom he cups in his palm until it turns cold, then he rubs it on the coat.

Outside it's still light, some time in the afternoon, he reckons, and he stares up at the patches of sky changing colour and speed through the holes in the roof. He tries not to think any more for he's been doing too much of that, overloaded brain circling back and forward over the same ground like a dog chasing its own hind legs. What he craves is emptiness, deadness, he sees it like that, so he can find some new direction, surprising him suddenly like a spark in the dark.

So he's lying there like one of those old Egyptian

mummies in the movies waiting to be surprised when *Jesus H. Christ* he is, but not in the way he's expecting, or cares to be, for what does he hear but a blowing out of breath coming from the mound in the far corner. *Sweet Jesus.*

And rising up jay-naked from his nest, joint hanging down, small, cold and still damp, he stares at the sheep supposed to be a goner, only it ain't. He strains listening and there it comes again, a sighing like wind in the trees. *Shit.* His skin is rough with goose bumps, and he needs to take a leak real bad. Dropping his head low, he stares hard as if he's got X-ray eyes, too scared to get any closer, scanning for signs of movement in that old woolly carcase.

He knows what he has to do, but can't. The four-by-four is lying way over beside the sheep where he dropped it but the idea of it splattering warm blood all over his bare skin makes him want to die himself. Instead he takes up the knife, trying to remember how old Moses Stokes slit the pig's throat. He knows he'll have to hold its head back to do it right but the feel of that greasy wool on his hands is still with him, far, far worse than his own love-juice.

He moves closer, the smell hitting him like a bang on the nose, and he waits a moment still hoping the noises he heard were only in his dream. But then there's movement, he sees it distinctly, no mistaking it, and next minute his worst nightmare comes true, even his imagination couldn't make this one up, for with a heave and a strangled grunt the sheep rolls sideways and as he watches with his dick down to about the size of a toothpick it gets to its feet and stands there rasping and drooling and shaking all over.

It's looking directly at him as if it knows what he did to it earlier and wants him to finish the job off proper this time. He never knew an old sheep could look at anyone that way — a dog, maybe, but not a sheep.

They continue to outstare one another, a naked black guy

291

with somebody's table-knife in his hand and a sheep. *Jesus Christ*, he thinks, *how did my stupid life happen to get so screwed up, just tell me that*. And there and then it comes to him just how, and he puts the blame on one person, all of it on one person, as if all the time the notion has been growing inside of him like something getting ready to burst or hatch out.

Better still, explode, for rage takes him over for the first time and he turns that old ewe sheep over on to its back like it's a sack of grain and stabs down over and over again, blunt as the knife is, until he feels the blade breaking through and going into that soft swollen belly. A wave of gas hits him like something out of a cesspit but he keeps on stabbing, *stabbing*, even when he feels his skin wet and speckled and then starting to run, trickles of something he doesn't even care about no more.

When it's over he throws the knife into a corner and staggers across to his bed. Cold and shaking, like he's got a fever, he buries himself in the coats, curling up until his body starts to feel warm again.

Some time later he feels hungry like he hasn't eaten for his entire life and he crams his mouth full of damp, woody-smelling mushrooms, gulping them down, stalks and all, half-chewed in raw lumps until his store is all gone.

And then he sleeps and sleeps and sleeps like an animal, like the animal he's become because of a certain person who has turned away from him, leaving him to die in this place a thousand miles from home.

But maybe it's far more distant than that, a place he only travelled to in his dreams before and the memories of old, old people with the sound of drums still in their heads. As he sleeps that same beat seems to keep time with his heart beneath his bare, black and bloodied chest.

THIRTEEN

"Delicious, Mrs Neeson, that was truly delicious. You've excelled yourself, so you have." He said the words one dinner-time as they were sitting down to another burnt offering, a brown baked rime ringing every plate. Irish stew. Across the board from him the other two stared while the housekeeper nearly dropped her saucepan in shock. Giving a gulp and gasp she darted for the scullery, reappearing moments later in hat and coat.

"What you can do with a bit of rump steak, some Bisto and an onion is nobody's business!" he called after her as she scuttled off without a word.

They listened as the heavy oiled weight of the front door swung behind her with a sound like a distant bomb going off. In the silence that followed the wireless announcer's soft tones could be heard introducing "Workers' Playtime" and Lawlor began to laugh. How could he help himself? First, her vinegary old puss, then this, his sportive fellow-toilers waiting for the radio fun to commence, faces on them like two Lurgan spades.

Earlier they'd had a cruel shock with the first post, a letter arriving from HQ with the name of his replacement, a name, no more than that, but one which sent splinters of ice through their true-blue souls. Sergeant Owen P. O'Donovan.

Lawlor read it aloud, then said, "I'm sure he's a decent enough stick. But then you never can tell, can you?"

He got up from the table smartish then, heading for the bathroom to muffle his laughter in the towel hanging from the roller on the back of the door. Thank God all the doors in this place were an inch and a half of varnished Irish oak built to withstand assault from within or without. Stuffing his mouth he howled inwardly. Jesus, the tremendous, side-splitting, bellyaching joke of it, them thinking they'd got rid of one mickey for good and another turning up as his successor. Of course he might, could be, one of their own sort, but it was scarcely possible, a handle like that as Catholic as Pius XII himself. And what did P. stand for, if not Patrick?

After he'd had his moment of hilarity Lawlor splashed his face liberally with cold water then raked back his helmet of stiff white thatch until it shone like the metal back of the hairbrush. He looked more closely at himself in the mirror and what did he see but a happy man, a relaxed man, a man with only nine days left to go of his jail sentence. And afterwards? He had nothing in mind, yet everything in mind, could go anywhere, see, do anything. Could this be that same man who squandered his days cycling forgotten by-roads, thoughts drumming like hail? Before that, drinking his nights away, pondering the eddies in a glass?

Something had finally gone click in his life like a shoulder-bone snapping back into joint. He was sleeping soundly and eating well, bar Mrs Neeson's foul messes, and was getting through the backlog of paperwork in the Day Room like someone possesssed. The loose ends which had been tormenting him so were finally being sewn up, one in particular, the biggest, deadliest of all just waiting for that final stitch. When the time arrived, *his* time, no one else's, he would tie a ribbon on it, his leaving present to the lot of them, Boal, Burnside, Quigg, Kincaid, Freddy Dunbar. The list was in danger of getting out of hand, taking in the very urchins in the street. But now he had drawn a line under his tally, content to wait and watch their faces when he unveiled his prize.

So he brushed away any lingering flecks of dandruff from the shoulders of his tunic and went downstairs humming.

The two Bs were still sitting there, soulful eyes fastened on the wireless set on its high shelf. Someone was entertaining those factory-hands in far-away West Bromwich with bird imitations. He supposed it must be Percy Edwards. Lawlor stood in the doorway for a moment listening to the fruity pipings of a blackbird filling their kitchen, thinking to himself how could anybody possibly get paid good money for making such noises in public.

Boal had an ear cocked as though desperate not to miss a solitary trill. Now the melancholy cry of a curlew entered the room. *Had a single one of those soot-grimed Brummies ever set foot on a moor, for Christ's sake?*

"Right, lads," Lawlor announced briskly, breaking the spell, "I want a single volunteer to ride out to Darragh Cross. Ned McKeown has been using his official farmer's petrol ration to take all and sundry on jaunts to the seaside. Very commendable of him I'm sure, but, after all –" he paused just like one of those same radio comedians waiting for the audience to join in "– there is a war on."

"I'll go," offered Boal getting to his feet.

Burnside stayed put, daintily buttering a slice of bread like it was something precious, adept as always at being a pain in the arse.

Lawlor looked at him. "Now what'll we find for young

Crawford here? Sure, I know the very thing. That old doll in Irish Street has been breaking peoples' windows again. Time to drop a wee summons on her."

Boal giggled for Nelly was notorious, to be avoided at all times, especially when drunk and on the tear.

Burnside asked, "Do you want me to bring her in? This isn't the first time, you know." He was taking it a lot better than he should.

"Nor won't be the last. Summons her this time, then we'll see."

Boal said, "I'd bring my gas-mask, if I were you," and they all laughed at that, even Burnside, who was the one who had to brave her den.

After they'd gone their separate ways he had the place to himself and he settled down to his steadily diminishing pyramid of official paperwork weighted down with a bullet clip. On the wall in front of him was a calendar from the Northern Bank, a coloured view of the Giant's Causeway at sunset, picture of the month, the glistening stones moulded to perfection like a child's set of building-blocks. Underneath, the dates and days were laid out on a grid, and it had been hard for him to resist crossing each one off on the run up to his release. Last Tuesday of the month. The magic day. Pay-day. His last.

Idly he wondered if there would be a presentation. And the shock of it entering his head unannounced like that, for it had honestly never occurred to him before, never, froze his pen in the middle of its run across the lined paper. For the first time in days his mood took a dip, for he did not want that, no, a hundred times no, for it would only mess up his plan of campaign, dilute the sweet taste of vindication. He began to sweat a little wondering how he might be able to circumvent such a situation even if it was already in train.

Jesus, what if they'd planned some sort of a surprise for him! An inscribed watch, or a framed picture, maybe, something hand-painted and scenic along the lines of the one facing him. To remind him of how happy his stay here had been.

He stared at the famed hexagonal stones, one of the seven wonders of the world, so they said, and here in dear wee Ulster, too, of all places, and at that point the phone began to ring.

"DI Quigg here," barked the voice on the other end of the line as if the hard-edged tones weren't sufficiently recognisable enough, and Lawlor put his pen down, holding the heavy black receiver away from his ear as if it might be infected, waiting for the bad news to engulf, then sweep away all his carefully laid schemes.

Some two hours later he was sitting in the passenger seat of his superior's Wolseley now racing out of town, followed by a second police car carrying four constables from HQ. His own gallant little platoon sat behind Quigg and himself, for by some miracle of mind over matter Boal and Burnside just happened to show up at the barracks earlier than expected. The state he was in, Lawlor suspected they were already privy to the great secret which Quigg had only told him about minutes earlier, not wishing to divulge it over the phone, in case, as he put it, somebody with big ears might be listening in.

"Operation Cherokee was supposed to take place a week from now but has been brought forward on orders from Washington, no less, so I'm told. But then these people have always been a law unto themselves. No consideration for anyone but number one. The only good thing about it is we'll be shot of them sooner rather than later. Don't misunderstand me, they are our allies, but you would hardly think it by the carry-on of them."

It was the first time Lawlor had ever heard him speak so openly like that about the Yanks. At his back he could sense the two Bs fidgeting with excitement.

"I dread to think what we're likely to find. According to the intelligence I've been able to gather, half the prostitute population of Belfast and round about have already moved in."

Directly behind, Boal shifted and whimpered softly while Burnside's reflected face in the driving-mirror remained a picture of serene elation. "So much for military secrecy, ha ha. By the look of things the telegraph lines between Dublin and Berlin must already be red-hot by now with the news."

The little convoy sped onwards. Beyond the rolled-up windows the day was overcast with a moist wind from the west that promised rain. The settled spell had run its course. It was stifling in the car, four grown men sweating freely in tight, heavy uniforms. Quigg had on a brand new rubberised raincoat over his finer barathea issue. It gave off a vaguely fishy smell.

They passed the old dead linen mill on the Randocks Road with its cluster of red-brick factory houses radiating from the giant windowless hulk like a shoal of sucker fish living off a whale. Not any more, though. Lawlor knew that Burnside had been reared in one of those same mean little dwellings but he noticed he looked neither to left nor right as they went racing past.

Soon after they saw the smoke climbing high above the beech trees that ringed the base, dark sideways-drifting oily plumes which seemed to have been started in different places. Quigg pressed his boot to the boards but was forced to release it around the next bend for ahead of them there appeared the tail end of a ragged convoy of people heading towards the smoke. They were scattered across the roadway, men, women and children, many pushing empty prams or carrying sacks and baskets, even tin baths. Far ahead, high above the heads, rode one man on a flat cart.

Burnside said, "Bobby Beck," for it was, indeed, the rag-and-bone man of the town.

Other faces started becoming recognisable, from the back streets, mainly, but here and there some respectable people, too, keeping their heads down as Quigg wove in and out, back and forth, sounding his horn to drive them into the ditch.

At his side Lawlor sat staring straight ahead as if already he had packed his case and belongings and was here merely as an observer. Which he was, and the more he saw the more his estrangement deepened, for now it came to him where he had witnessed scenes like this before. On the Pathé newsreels in Barney Costello's old cinema, refugees fleeing from fires along straight foreign roads, only here they were heading in the other direction, *towards* the destruction.

"Looks as if we're going to have our work cut out for us," said Quigg swerving around an elderly woman pushing a wheelbarrow on the very brow of the road at startling speed.

Burnside twisted to look back at her through the rear window. "Oul' Nelly Doole," he told them. "That summons I tried to serve her will just have to keep."

"Hit the oul' bitch with it when she catches up," said Boal. "She'll only –" then broke off sensing Quigg's displeasure.

Lawlor betrayed nothing, feeling nothing, allowing himself to be driven into the heart of something he no longer had any control over. Numbed by the speed of it all, it was as if he was back in the Macushla once more, distanced from the scenes taking place in front of him, as foreign as anything on celluloid.

Then Burnside let out a cry. "Holy shit!" he exclaimed, despite their driver's presence, and then Lawlor, too, saw the mob milling about the entrance gate to the base, fifty strong, maybe more, the vanguard who had arrived early to be first in line. Only there was no line, no queue, merely a rabble, quite a few spreadeagled and clinging to the perimeter fencing like human starfish.

Quigg rolled his window down and they all heard the cries of the crowd for the first time, nothing specific or intelligible, just a general baying that spelled trouble.

"What do they want? What ails them?" Boal sounded perplexed, genuinely so, frightened, too, which was to be expected.

Grimly Quigg told him, "We're about to find that out, constable."

The second car drew alongside. Up until then Lawlor had forgotten they had reinforcements, five hefty, red-necked strangers in uniforms like their own, who hauled themselves out stiffly as though they had been crammed into a tank and not a police car. Two of them already had naked batons in their hands and all looked nervous, even more so than Boal did.

Burnside, however, appeared to be in his element, chest thrust out, thumbs hooked in his armpits in that intimidating stance he liked to affect on duty.

Why didn't I come down hard on this preening bastard when I had the authority, thought Lawlor, *the energy*. Then, remembering the name of his successor, he had this sudden pleasing image of someone infinitely more ruthless than he could ever be yet, at the same time, a younger version of himself, making the other's life a misery, hell on wheels. Two, to be precise, for he saw him out sweating in all weathers on the Humber pushbike, the one he would bequeath to him with relish on his last day. He would even lower the saddle to accommodate the gobshite as a parting bonus.

Quigg barked, "You come along with me, sergeant. The

rest of you stay here. And keep your distance, stay with the cars. Take no action unless you have to. Kelso, you're in command."

Burnside didn't like that part, oh, no, obvious by the way he dropped his fists from his oxters, glaring at the crowd in the distance as if it might be they who were responsible for this humiliation.

For a moment the sergeant and his superior stood eyeing one another, and not for the first time did it strike Lawlor that there was really no one in this northern country he had inherited with his job that he liked or even cared about. After Nuala had gone there was nobody left. Perhaps he had invested too much of his life and himself in her so that when she left everything else went too.

Quigg said, "Let's go and see what's going on, will we?" and they went forward together in that steady slow strolling motion that men in their line of work employ in such circumstances.

As they came closer a man darted to meet them halfway. He dragged what appeared to be an old golfing bag, of all things, held in place with strips of khaki webbing. Lawlor recognised him as Teddy Banville, perpetually jobless, with a consumptive wife and a brood of young ones.

"They're burning everything, the bastards!" he was shouting. "Lock, stock and barrel. Tables, chairs, beds, blankets, the very oilcloth on the floors. Look!" He pointed at the smoke rising up in fat black swirls. They could smell the reek of burning rubber. *Tyres*, thought Lawlor. *Precious Firestone.*

"Worst of all, they're destroying perfectly good grub. Chickens, sides of bacon, cheese, loaves of bread. Or else dumping it in Greer's burn."

"How do you know this?" questioned Quigg as if the

evidence of his eyes wasn't there before him. "I mean, about the food."

"Because they paid off all the civilians from the PX, that's why. They saw it with their own eyes. Wouldn't let them take away a single orange. Not even a pound of fucking sugar."

Lawlor watched Quigg flinch. Obscenities always made him react in that way, that rarity, a good-living, born-again policeman, baton in one hand, bible in the other.

"Now you listen here to me, mister," he laid into the unfortunate, and Lawlor saw the would-be looter buckle like his flaccid old golfbag. "Your friends and yourself are causing a serious breach of the peace here. You'll disperse if you know what's good for you. In the meantime the sergeant and I are going in to have a look for ourselves to see just what's going on. If you take my advice you'll be gone from this place by the time we come out again. I'm sure you have a wife and family waiting for you. They don't want to be visiting the Crumlin Road jail for the next six months or so. You follow me?"

And the man melted before their forward passage like snow in front of a shovel.

The crowd, too, appeared to grow docile and silent at their approach. *God help them if that's their spokesman*, thought Lawlor. Again, many of the faces were familiar, like those he had passed earlier on the road.

Then a woman cried out from among the mass, aiming her plea directly at him, not Quigg, "For pity's sake, sergeant, use your authority. People are starving and in there right now they're destroying perfectly good rations. They're worse than the ones they're going off to fight, so they are. Is this Ireland or are we in Nazi Germany?"

Lawlor tried hard to place who she was, name, address, that sort of thing, but drew a blank. What recall he retained

302

of these people was fading fast, like his recollection of the slain widow, the one he had planned to avenge, while at the same time absolving himself with his inspired feat of detection. But his final triumphant throw of the dice had come unstuck, the wheel of chance moving too fast for him.

He needed to stop and think, adjust to these new conditions, but knew that was impossible now. He tried telling himself his secret would keep, but for how long, and why, now that the great evacuation had begun. By all the signs this place would only be inhabited by vermin and ghosts in a matter of days, maybe even hours, an acrid smoking wasteland, and just what would he do with his prize then? Who would he tell? Who would even want to listen?

"When do you think they'll make the big move out?" he heard himself ask and Quigg looked at him as if doubting his usefulness in this situation.

"A law unto themselves," he told him. It sounded like one of those ever ready, snappy bible quotes of his, and maybe it was.

The crowd opened up a path for them right to the striped pole in the down position, and at their approach those clinging to the fence like apes, young men and boys, began dropping to the ground as if a sudden electrical charge had gone coursing through the netting. Quigg told all of them to disperse just as he had addressed the man earlier, only in louder, angrier tones, and a proportion did fall back only to re-group a short distance away to observe and await developments.

All those hungry eyes. Lawlor wondered what it would take for them to get up the fire to rush the gate, what sort of anger to make the worm in their bellies turn.

Some of the smoke from the fires started drifting towards them, a shift in the wind off the Lough, and people began to cough and splutter. Quigg strode forward, one gloved hand held over his mouth, laying the other on top of the metal barrier, and immediately four helmeted soldiers appeared out of nowhere. One of them, with three upside-down chevrons on his sleeve, cocked his weapon audibly but Quigg stared him down, just that length of red and white pipe separating them.

"Sergeant," he said opening his raincoat to let him see the flash of his insignia. "Sergeant, under international law we have the right to enter this compound to investigate any possible disturbance that may affect our civilian population. If you have any doubts or queries on the matter I suggest you contact Colonel Hoffmann to verify the situation."

"Hell, no need for that, Captain Harper'll do just as well. Talk to him yourself. You'll find him up at the Lodge yonder," gestured the sergeant, a big man, far bigger even than Lawlor, with a face like raw beef. He winked conspiratorially at Lawlor, one non-com to another.

"Bend yourselves down, gentlemen, if you wouldn't mind. Raising up this here old pole might just give 'the civilian population' the wrong idea."

So they ducked under the barrier, and as they did so a roar issued from the throats of the watching crowd, a mixture of betrayal and derision, it sounded like to Lawlor standing there trying to get his puff back. *No transport*, he was thinking, then saw the grins on the guards' faces and got the picture. *No jeep.*

Quigg got it too. "Come on, sergeant," he ordered, "let's show these people we haven't lost the use of our legs, unlike themselves, the US armchair infantry."

They started marching towards the fires, at least five now, by Lawlor's calculation. Glancing back he saw the soldiers passing a square whiskey bottle between them while the crowd looked murderously on.

In silence he and Quigg strode up the ruler-straight road. The Americans when they came had laid down a network of such roads in a grid pattern like the ones back home, obliterating whole townlands as well as their ancient names. They had been poured in concrete sections, these instant avenues, every twenty feet or so a tarred joint causing a rhythmic disturbance in the noise of tyres passing over them. That sound, a staccato heartbeat varying in frequency according to the vehicle's speed, had become almost as familiar as the cry of the corncrake had been in these meadow bottoms before they arrived.

Lawlor wondered how long it would take for all of this to revert to the original flatlands once the occupying army had gone. In his mind's eye already he saw weeds shooting up, penetrating the hardcore, fracturing concrete, Nature taking back her old territory. He even tried remembering what it had all looked like once upon a time before the yellow bulldozers arrived, but drew a blank, yet one more black hole in his memory.

They passed a double fingerpost, one of its arms reading, *Berlin − 678 miles*, the other pointing in the opposite direction, *New York − 4438 miles*. They followed the latter, for it led straight to the fires and the Lodge itself, which they could now make out in the distance, a pale stuccoed cube outlined against the lowering sky.

Presently they reached the first of the huts where the troops were billeted and a wave of dance-music poured out to meet them mingled with shouts and drunken singing. A woman, half-dressed, lurched from one of the open door-ways. She had a soldier's cap jammed down over her blonde perm and carried her shoes in her hand, red high heels, Lawlor noted, her mouth a smudged gash of the same hot, devilish shade. When she saw them she drew up short and began frantically pulling her shoes on for flight.

305

He and Quigg halted, staring. Then as they watched she fell over in a tangle of silk petticoats, nothing underneath, it would appear, and as they continued to gape, a man, a soldier, hard to tell for he was naked save for a pair of khaki undershorts, came out after her.

"Sure I'll marry you, honey!" he was shouting as though they'd been interrupted. "Didn't I say I would? All I want is a little souvenir, that's all. Is that so bad?" Then he tripped as well, the pair of them sprawling in the dirt together, bare limbs meshing in slow motion.

Quigg's face had gone from purple to putty and back again. "Sodom," he muttered. "We've entered Sodom," marching on, head held high.

They travelled past more dormitories, doors wide open, men half in, half out of uniform, the blare of radios and gramophones at full blast. By now couples were copulating openly against the curved outer walls of the huts or on groundsheets spread on the grass. Lawlor recognised one of the women, old enough to be the mother of her partner, well known in town for this sort of paid activity. She saw him but only threw her head back laughing as the boy soldier pushed between her legs, his trousers about his ankles, snowy backside startling against the green of the corrugated tin.

Despite himself Lawlor felt his own rod tighten and stir. It was like one of those Roman orgies he'd read about, better still, *seen* in the picture-house, suitably doctored, of course, only here he could smell, even touch, if he'd had the courage or the inclination to join in. For the first time in a long time the taste of a drink on his lips would have been a blessing.

They came to the first great fire, the heat striking them like a blow. Higher than a house the flames roared and all about men stripped to the waist were feeding the blaze with chairs, tables, cupboards, bookcases, anything that would burn that came to hand. Every one of these stokers was black. Their naked torsos shone with sweat, eyes and teeth gleaming in the hellish red light. *A scene from the pit*, thought Lawlor, who had stopped once more, unable to draw himself away. Already he had forgotten about Quigg.

Three soldiers came staggering out of a nearby hut under an immense load of bedding, mattresses, blankets, sheets, pillow-cases, and proceeded to hurl the lot on to the pyre. They danced around their handiwork laughing extravagantly. They might have been drinking like the rest of the soldiers but for some reason Lawlor thought not.

At all the other fires similar scenes were being enacted, save for what was being fed to the flames. Paper, official-looking, crates of it, entire filing-cabinets-full, overturned on the ground, as well as books, fuelled one. Then, on another, foodstuffs, the very produce the people outside were clamouring for, was going up in smoke. He saw gallon drums of tomatoes pierced with bayonets, jars of pickles, jam and ketchup smashed, men pelting each other with eggs, apples, oranges, as if they were snowballs, syrup being poured on the blaze like golden paraffin. He began to feel sick at the stench, the waste, the wholesale, whooping destruction, then angry, too.

He heard Quigg cry, "Come on, come on!" and turned a look on him that made the other draw back.

Evidently Quigg must have thought he might be tempted to respond in some way and his voice sounded more reasonable when next he spoke. "Sergeant, it's out of our hands. All we can do is talk to Captain Harper. Maybe prevail on him to do something. We have no jurisdiction here. None."

"What about the women?"

"We can only wait until they come back out to our side of the perimeter fence." He looked embarrassed, the first time Lawlor had ever seen him so put out.

"You might have a long wait on your hands," he told him. "They seem to be dug in for the duration. Their boyfriends, too, by the look of things."

He couldn't resist the coarse riposte and watched the other look away, wondering if this cold fish wasn't in the slightest bit aroused by all the unashamed riding going on. He knew he was. Some of these tarts weren't as ancient or raddled as that old huer Bella Badger from Irish Street. Diseased, too, he wouldn't be surprised. An entire ward for VD cases had been set up in Lurgan Hospital, so he'd heard tell. At the thought his own tackle discreetly contracted to its normal modest dimensions and he fell in alongside his DI.

The last leg of their journey together took them past no more bonfires, no more half-naked, leaping savages either, but away off to their right they did see a driver in his truck driving back and forth, foward, then reverse, over a heap of crushed bicycles with as much care as a farmer ploughing a field.

The screech of rending metal followed them right the way up to the original gravel sweep in front of the commandeered mansion. Already someone had hauled down the Stars and Stripes from its pole over the pillared entrance. Knots of soldiers stood or lounged about the front steps. At least they were in uniform, which was something, but a procession of other men in overalls were carrying crates and boxes through their midst and loading them on to a convoy of parked lorries around by the side of the house. As expected all these GIs were black, but not laughing or enjoying themselves like those he had seen earlier laying waste to army property. More sullen and resigned, it occurred to Lawlor.

Returned by now to his old domineering self, Quigg strode straight to the steps. Dutifully Lawlor followed. He felt depressed, inward-looking. Most of his anger had ebbed away for there was just far too much to be incensed about, like spitting into the heart of one of those raging fires.

They climbed up the chipped marble steps and the men talking and smoking there ignored them. The mood seemed different here, closer to the hub of things, more aware of what lay ahead, for it was clear they were going off to fight a real war instead of the dummy variety they had been engaged in over the past months, churning up the countryside with their tanks and lorries and riddling the fields and woods with foxholes.

Two civilians, they made their way up a long stripped corridor, brushing past the negro bearers, and no one spoke or paid them heed. Despite their strangeness they had become invisible.

Quigg knocked on a door it was obvious he had entered before, more times than Lawlor had realised, pushing on the dented wood after a voice from within ordered them to "*Come!*"

A man was sitting facing them behind a desk swamped with papers. The rest of the room was stripped bare, not even a chair for them to sit on. Captain Harper, for it was the officer Lawlor had seen at Jelley's pub the night of the shooting and later on at the trial, stared at them without speaking. His tunic was undone, paler, buff shirt and tie loose. Dropping down almost from view, he opened a drawer and came up with a bottle and three glasses. Bourbon whiskey. Aiming the bottle at them neck first and getting no immediate response he poured himself a hefty shot of the syrupy brown liquor, too sweet for Lawlor's taste, although only Quigg's presence stopped him from joining the man.

In silence they watched him, Lawlor wondering who would be the first to give in, like one of those games children play, first one to speak is a sissy. He knew damn well it wasn't going to be him even though he had a lot he wanted to ask this man, once travelling to see him but getting no satisfaction, not even a face-to-face meeting. It still rankled.

Quigg coughed and Lawlor decided he was the one about to capitulate, but, no, he was wrong, for the American with the bars on his sleeve said, "Ain't it the damnedest thing, gentlemen. You spend best part of a year of your life training to go into battle and then the big day arrives and you're all fired up and what happens? I'll tell you what happens. You're left in charge of a sorry bunch of non-combatants, ditch-diggers, motor-pool mechanics, dishwashers and laundry hands, and so far back from the action you might as well have stayed home in Georgia sunning yourself. Now, I don't know what it is you've come to see me about, but whatever it is, sure as hell, your timing is about as bad as it can be." And he helped himself to another snort from a bottle that looked already half-killed.

"Captain Harper —" Quigg began.

"To hell with protocol, call me Bob."

Lawlor noticed a silver-framed photograph amongst all the paper flotsam piled on the desk, a smiling woman and child dressed for sunny weather, white-painted house in the background. The man drinking intercepted his glance.

"My boy Bob Junior," he told him. "One little rascal. I miss him a lot, but what am I gonna say to him when he asks what his dear daddy did during the war? Commanded a latrine detail?"

"Captain, your men are out of control," Quigg burst out. "Burning army property, drinking to excess, fornicating publicly."

"Not my own dear colored boys, surely?"

"No, the other — troops."

"You mean the boys going off to close with the savage foe? Understandable, I'd say."

310

Quigg glared at him. "Surely it's your bounden duty to control your men — all of them."

Another drink. Lawlor could smell the liquor taint the air. His mouth felt dry. The captain put down the bottle. Jack Daniel's.

"Mr Quigg, I suggest you look after your side of the fence while kindly allowing me to attend to mine. Please do not come here trying to dictate to me what to do or what not to do. Believe me, as soon as we can get out of your country and your hair, we will, but from what I've seen an awful lot of folks will be mighty sorry to see us go. That old gravy-train has just about made its last run. Aw, for Christ's sakes, Quigg, loosen up, have a drink. A lot of those young kids out there letting off steam right now will be dead in a month, can't you see that?"

Quigg stepped back. A cruel red rim encircled his scalp where his cap had bitten into the flesh. "Sergeant," he said to Lawlor, "we'll be on our way. We'll take this higher up."

The man behind the desk laughed. "Be my guest, and while you're at it kiss my sun-tanned Southern ass. Higher up?" he echoed. "Go right to the top for all I care. But somehow I don't think you're gonna find much joy. Patton himself may well be plastered on this auspicious occasion."

Quigg was at the door by now and a second time ordered his sergeant to come along but Lawlor had an urge not to budge. He felt it rise inside like an undigested ball of something.

"What about Washington?" he heard himself ask and the man behind the desk blinked at him as though puzzled.

"Washington's four thousand miles away, sergeant," wearily he told him. "Nobody gives a hoot in hell what *they* think. Not tonight, anyhow. It ain't their show no more."

Lawlor moved a step closer. He could feel his face redden. "I'm talking about a person, not a place. One of your men who killed a defenceless old woman and escaped scot-free. Over on our side of the fence, captain."

There was silence in the room. Outside a truck started up and the glasses on the desk shivered.

"I command you to come away this instant!" Quigg was shouting at him, "It's not our affair!" and Lawlor turned to him and said, "Neither is this, so just what the fuck are we doing here?"

"What did you say?"

"You heard me."

He paused, then as though to a fretful child, he continued quietly, "I'll be out in just one wee minute. I have some private business with the captain here. Something just between the two of us."

Quigg put on his cap, buttoned his raincoat, adjusted his belt. Cold as ice now, he told him, "You may have only a week left to go, Lawlor, but I must remind you you're still bound by your oath to the crown and to the orders of a superior officer. You have a pension to consider. I may be forced to suggest a review of that particular arrangement. Have a care."

When the door closed after him the American replenished his own glass, then filled up another for Lawlor. "Let's drink to both our joint departures. Cheers, as your people say."

"*Sláinte*," Lawlor corrected him, wrapping his fist around the tumbler of russet-coloured bourbon. Both drank, one man sprawled half-drunk behind the desk and the other standing in the dead centre of the room.

"Major Kincaid mentioned something about you taking early retirement."

"Did he now?"

"Health reasons."

"*This*, you mean?" moving the glass slightly in his hand as he said it.

312

"Something like that."

"He's a liar."

The captain sighed, rising from his chair so that they were both now on level terms. Much the same height, too, which surprised Lawlor, recalling someone slighter in build in the hissing glow of the Tilley lamp lighting up that scene of carnage in the bar.

"Where will you go?"

"No idea. First things first."

"And that first thing is?"

"What I tried to see you about the time I came here."

"Yeah, I'm real sorry about that. Something came up."

Suddenly it was very peaceful in that room with its bare, battered walls and solitary desk, olive-green, metal, abused. It may well have been the whiskey, damping down any urgency he might have brought with him, for when he spoke his voice sounded slow and ruminative as if he were thinking aloud. "I just wanted to find out something about the man, that's all. What he was like. Maybe even what made him do what he did. He was only a blank, you see, not even a picture in the paper. Not like those other three. Do you understand? I needed to – needed to set my mind to rest."

The young captain sat on the edge of the desk cradling the glass and looking down at it like it was the photograph of his family, the only two things important to him in that room right now.

"Sergeant," he said, eyes still lowered, "I have a kinda confession to make to you. Rather, the men you saw in the dock that day last month have. It might go some way to easing your mind. Then, again, it might not, I don't know. One of them, Private Clyde Price, broke down a couple of days after the trial when we separated him from his buddies. Oh, coupla real hard cases. He told us that Washington was an innocent bystander, had nothing to do with the shooting, just happened to be in the wrong place at the wrong time."

"Then why did he run?"

The colonel smiled as if to an innocent child.

"If your skin color was the same as his, sergeant, and a white woman got killed, believe me you would run too."

"But if he's innocent he's got nothing to fear."

"Not exactly, my friend. The punishment for being AWOL, is dishonourable discharge with an added ten years to life hard labor."

Lawlor stood there, a mixture of emotions churning inside. A second time the captain proffered the bottle, but Lawlor covered the mouth of his tumbler with his hand.

"Anyway, he's no longer a priority," the other went on. "By the time he's found or gives himself up we'll be long gone. Another world away. Corporal William Purdy Washington will be forgotten."

Without thinking Lawlor said, "He won't give himself up," and the man facing him looked at him.

"I hope you're right. For his sake. He'd be better off dead."

He paused, then said, "I kinda wish you and me had met up a lot earlier, sergeant. We have something in common, seems to me. We're both of us in the wrong job. Just like that poor runaway son of a bitch somewhere out there."

Lawlor put the glass down, then offered his hand. "Good luck," he said. "Maybe you are right about being in the wrong job, but remember you have a family. You'll be going back to them some day."

At the door he turned and saluted and the other replied in kind.

Then he said a curious thing, the American officer. "I hope, sergeant, you get your man. To set your mind to rest."

Lawlor closed the door behind him and found himself in

the bustle of the corridor once more, the stream of men in khaki work-clothes unremitting as ever. He drew himself back against the wall as one of the negro soldiers bearing a cardboard box marked "Libby's Peaches", nearly the width of the corridor itself, came abreast. Silent and intent he padded by and looking down into the carton Lawlor saw it was filled to the brim with stacked, framed photographs, the very same ones he convinced himself he had seen on the Recreation Room wall the last time he was here, a thousand anonymous coloured faces fixed for eternity in time and space in a foreign country. Deep down in the pile somewhere was the face of the man who had haunted him for well-nigh a month now, face of a monster, killer of innocent women – only now he'd learned he was neither of those two things.

Lawlor put the idea out of his head. This wasn't the time nor place to digest such a revelation. Later. He would deal with it later, the way someone might ponder an extra piece that had turned up in a puzzle he had thought he had mastered.

But by the time he'd got to the end of that thronged corridor his mood had changed. Like the men streaming past he'd started to sweat, realising suddenly he had no time. It had almost run out on him, events, and then this new development, coming together to wreck all his prized plans. He looked down at his watch on its fob chain as if he might only have hours left to do what he had to do when he heard the distant shots, three in rapid succession, like fire-crackers going off, then Quigg's voice shouting for him to *hurry, hurry*.

Together they began running back the way they'd come, two middle-aged men suddenly made ridiculous in their metal-shod boots and bulky overcoats. Quigg seemed almost as unfit as himself, it occurred to Lawlor.

Past the raging bonfires they pounded, then the huts with their wide-open doors, the racket from within even louder now. They saw two men, stripped to the waist, flailing wildly at one another, then some way further on a couple of women hard at it also. The last thing Lawlor noticed before reaching the gate was a sign he must have missed before. "Please Drive Carefully," it read, "That Child May Be Yours." But if Quigg had also seen it he gave no sign.

Drawn up on their own side of the lowered barrier stood the guards, rigid, stern-faced, rifle barrels still tilted upwards. There was a smell of spent powder in the damp air. They faced the crowd which had dispersed as soon as the shots had been fired, for it was clear what had taken place, the outraged mob surging forward, then scattering like quail as the soldiers let off a volley over their heads.

Ducking down under the pole, Quigg made directly for the constabulary still huddled close to the two cars.

Lawlor stood for a moment on the other side of the barrier catching his breath. The American soldiers ignored him. Grim-faced, they looked ready to loose off another round, even into the crowd this time if need be. Then Lawlor lowered himself under the striped pole, blood-red and white like a barber's sign, and joined Quigg and the rest of the squad by the cars. "Reinforcements," he heard him say, "to control this rabble," even though it was obvious any notions of future rebellion had been obliterated for good. Several of the people already were trudging wearily back down the road in the direction of home.

"Kelso, take the second car and when you get to a phone contact Major Kincaid and tell him to order out his Specials. And tell him to bring a tender. Arrests are on the cards. I smell definite IRA involvement here. Sabotage of the war effort."

316

He looked directly at Lawlor as he spoke, daring him to contradict him, but the sergeant felt too tired in body and spirit to point out the patent absurdity of the other's claim. He stood there feeling as if only his uniform was keeping him erect, like someone encased in armour. His bed called but he knew it would lie empty, maybe until dawn, judging by the way things were heading.

And so it turned out.

About half an hour later Kincaid arrived, fresh-faced and alert, with a squad of B Specials in his train. Like some sort of occupying general he surveyed the area and started deploying his troops, many of them bleary eyed and unshaven unlike himself. Under his macintosh could be seen a snowy white shirt-front and dicky bow.

Lawlor noticed how he ignored the Americans, not once looking in their direction, or even at the glow of the fires reddening the night sky beyond their post. At one point they heard the distant crash of breaking glass celebrated by loud cheers and the few remaining men and boys in the crowd stirred at the sound. Instantly Kincaid ordered the Bs to go in amongst them demanding identity cards.

It was raining by now. Lawlor buttoned up his collar and watched the coat of wet varnishing the cars. Their headlights illumined the scene pooling out directly into the gathering dark. The soldiers' helmets bobbed in the drizzly gloom like round floats. Cigarettes glowed, there was muted laughter. Relaxation had returned once more. He saw that the tips of their rifle barrels had somehow become sheathed in pink rubber. Maybe it was a joke meant to affront, maybe not, for Lawlor had heard of how the Yanks would sometimes roll French letters over the muzzles of their equipment to keep out the damp.

He was smiling to himself at the thought of it, prophylactics warding off leaks from the outside as well as in, when Boal came across as if keen to share in the joke.

"Bit of a shambles, eh, sergeant?" he said gesturing around him.

"You can say that again, Victor."

The other brightened as he always did at the unexpected use of his first name and Lawlor felt a sudden warmth towards this essentially decent soul. He wouldn't exactly miss him when he left but he would most certainly wish him well, unlike his sparring partner over there.

"You and Burnside happened to be right on the spot when you were needed," he said, for he was still curious as to how quickly and conveniently the pair of them had arrived back from their rounds.

"Aye, Crawford sure has the knack of knowing about things even before they happen sometimes. He could nearly tell you where you shit last." He said it with pride as if some of his partner's impressive powers of premonition rubbed off on him.

Feeling reckless, Lawlor angled, "People say he knows the country hereabouts better than most. Every square inch of it, leaf, branch and hollow. Including most of the Lough, I dare say."

"Aye, he likes to go duck shooting. Him and the Major over there and some of his swanky friends. Crawford knows all the best hides."

Knowing he was treading dangerously Lawlor probed even deeper. "As a matter of interest, that old island out there. I've often wondered about it. No one lives there, I take it?"

"Goat Island, you mean?"

"Is that what they call it?"

"After the wild goats. Every so often they have to be

318

culled. Again the Major and some of his shooting pals take care of it. Matter of fact, they should be going out there any of these fine days before it gets too rough to cross over. Crawford goes along as well. Says it's great sport. Better than the Wild West. And the Major supplies all the ammunition out of his own pocket."

He paused, looking at Lawlor who had put a hand up to his throat. "Why don't you ask Crawford to mention it to the Major if you'd care for a day's shooting yourself. You might get it in before you go. Do you want me to ask Crawford myself?"

"No, no, that won't be necessary. Not my kind of sport."

They stood there on the wet road together, awkward suddenly, as if something had come between them, but only Lawlor knew what it was as his brain reeled under yet another cruel and unexpected burden of knowledge. He wanted to laugh out loud at the sheer unforgiving swiftness of it all, like a blade coming down. He felt boxed in, savagely curtailed, and he fumbled at his collar to physically loosen it, whatever *it* was.

Then Boal shifted awkwardly and mumbled, "I'd best be getting back to the cars over there. I expect the DI will be handing out more orders in a minute. Looks like we'll be having a wild long night of it, eh, sergeant?"

Lawlor stared at him and began, "Victor" — then thought better of it. "Run along," he told him. "I'll be across myself in a minute," and Boal sloped off back to where the others hung about the still hot bonnet of the glistening car. In that moment watching him go Lawlor felt the loneliest being alive. It was why he had started to reach out to the other in that way then stopped himself.

He heard Quigg shouting something about the blackout and the headlamps went out leaving them in raw darkness. Inside the guard hut almost at the same time the Americans' own light came on, honey-coloured, infinitely richer than anything they could ever run to on their side of the barrier. The fires, too, continued to glow extravagantly, lighting up the night sky, a tempting target for any twin-engined marauder, and Lawlor sent his thoughts out across the black fields, beyond the base itself, then across the flat reaches of the water to where his tormentor studied the same glow in the sky as he did. It gave him a strange feeling to think of that thing they both shared.

Closing in, he thought. *You and me, mister, are coming closer every minute, only you don't know it yet. And only I know just how little time I've left to get to you first.*

FOURTEEN

He dreams. But the dreams no longer die on waking like the ones he's used to, they arc across, bridging night and day, so that clock and calendar time retreat even further.

He lies watching a fiery tongue of sunlight creep across the floor, searing a track in the dust. It measures time for him, *his* time, for in his dream he's back in a place where people spell out the span of days and nights by looking at the sky. Light, then dark, then light again. On a raft of hallucination he drifts. At times he shivers under the old army blanket-coat as the sights and sounds in his head edge him towards terror.

Bare-torsoed, a man holds up a cockerel dripping blood, then whirls it about his head spattering the circle of upturned faces with bright drops. And even though he's been dreaming he feels the hot whiplash stipple his own cheeks long after he scrubs them with the rough, stinking wool.

He sees old Daddy Grace who used to chew up peoples' likenesses and swallow them, photographs they'd bring him to cure what ailed them. Other root-doctors too. Pipe Ellen grinding up potions of toe and fingernail clippings, mixing them with whiskey. Stick Daddy carving his animal head sticks. Doctor Buzzard whispering a black-cat-bone charm can make you invisible. Madam Truth the fortune-teller.

He dreams of graveyard dust, owl droppings, the hairs plucked from a cheating woman's armpit while she sleeps. Mojos. Hoodoo. His chest feels heavy like he's been rid by a witch in the night. Ghosts are all about, he tells himself, the island infested with them, and so when he wakes properly it's with a start, coming bolt upright like a corpse out of his coffin. Jack-in-the box. He listens fearfully, every sinew stretched. There are sounds, definite sounds, moans and groans, then a sudden cry, high and fearful, someone tapping wood on wood.

By now the snaking tongue of light like a lit fuse on the floor is barely a foot away from the end of his bed. He starts rocking to and fro clasping his knees, singing to himself to head it off.

Up on the mountain my Lord spoke, out of his mouth came fire and smoke . . . M is for Mary, P is for Paul, C for Christ, who died for all . . . What you gonna do when your lamp burns down . . . Pray tell me where you're travellin' to, Likewise from whence you came . . . Down in hell, down in hell, always midnight, down in hell . . . One of these mornings bright and fair, gonna put on my wings and seize the air . . .

All jumbled up and tripping through his head in a muddled stream.

Then another very different catch comes to mind.

One of these mornings, gonna wake up crazy, kill my baby, nobody's bizness but my own, ain't nobody's bizness but my own . . .

It's what he should have done all along when he had the chance, for then he wouldn't be where he is now, no better than some old animal waiting, just waiting. But for what? Certainly not for her, for he knows now she won't ever

322

come, not now, not ever. He wonders how long it will take for it to finish. Him. The thought eases through his head like a waxed thread passing through a needle's eye leaving no trace.

Up he rises then, shifting his bed of boughs and old khaki wool sideways towards the wall, a foot is all it takes, so that the creeping arrow of light will miss its target. Crouched in this new position, he charts its progress slow as slow, barely moving, brightening, then fading, then gathering strength again, according to the day outside.

Off in the distant corner the carcase of the old ewe sheep gives off a growing stink of putrefaction, clusters of flies already gorging on its rotting flesh. Its jaws move as if it's alive still, chewing cud, but it's only the bluebottles crawling there. He wonders how did they fetch up here out of nowhere, maybe getting ready to die the way flies do. But, then, how do you pass up such a fine feast, even if it is going to be your last? For an instant he inhabits the short intense lifespan of a blowfly, even becoming one in his head, the way those old African root-doctors were supposed to be able to.

And further now even than that he travels back to a time and place he's only been transported to in dreams before. The sound of drums speaking in tongues, heat, great humidity, and the taste of strange herbs in his mouth. Eyes closed the better to smell, feel, savour, the dream-scene explodes on his senses like a sunburst, myriad colours, scents and sounds swamping his brain. He sees water, a boundless blue ocean of it, and a great ship with sails rocking gently on the swell. Smaller boats pull away from the mother craft carrying white men bearing gifts, bolts of cotton and flannel, knives and mirrors, trinkets, nails, tinware. The people on the shore hide even when the mirrors flash the sun back at them.

Then one of the slavers holds up a square of scarlet cloth, fluttering it like a banner of blood, and the dark-skinned ones crouching in the brush come creeping out one by one drawn by the crimson lure. It works every time, a scrap of old red petticoat drugging them until, *eeny, miney, mo*, wrists and ankles shackled, laid out like matches in a box, they're in a stinking hold bound for Pharaoh's Land.

But at this point the picture in his head starts to fade just like in a movie and he waits for the screen to come alive again, but it just stays that way, dark grey with little speckles of twinkling static, so he opens his eyes again and he's back in his own rotten prison smelling his own stink.

Lying there, brain imprinted still with scary images, he asks himself if he really dreamt it at all, or was it something someone told him once upon a time, passing on their own dreams down a long line like a bucket chain, all of those people receding into the mist and steam of a forgotten continent.

His slender sundial on the floor tells him it must be getting into late afternoon by now and his stomach reminds him too he hasn't eaten for maybe a day, maybe more than that, so gathering himself together on hands and knees he starts crawling for the door. He's growing shakier by the hour, but the urge to fill his complaining stomach is enough to make him brave the air. He pulls the door far enough to the side so he can squeeze through.

Then his head starts swimming and he holds on to the bleached wood a while, panting, until it clears, but still it continues to feel like it might float off like a fairground balloon leaving the rest of him tethered, same as those captive people in the dream, nowhere to run, nowhere to hide. And thinking it he breathes in a poisonous whiff from the butchered sheep and fleeing before it pushes out into the light blinking, on all fours like the animal that he's become.

In his head he sings silently. All manner of wild and wacky verses bubbling up which won't be denied no matter how hard he tries to head them off. It's like he has this old Victrola machine wound up inside his brain and hell-bent on playing right to the end of the record. Here comes one now.

A peanut sat on the railway track, His heart was all a-flutter, Along came a train – the 9.15 – Toot, toot, peanut butter . . .

He used to sing that a lot of the time to Pearly's little ones even though they never did take to those big jars of Sunkist he brought from the PX under his coat. Too much like number-two, the youngest one told him in all innocence one time. She looked disgusted when he dipped his finger in, then licked it, teasing. What they really coveted was the glass jars, not what was in them, fishing for small fry down at the creek under that old weeping willow tree. He used to go there with them sometimes on those long lazy summer evenings, Pearl by his side, a few bottles of Falstaff beer tethered and cooling in the wash, the swifts making low jerky passes over the surface of the water.

The memory of it flits through his head just like those same old swallows, but stirring no emotion, just as if it happened to somebody else, someone he'd maybe heard about, a stranger.

Then another tune cranks up.

Delilah was a woman fine and fair, Her pleasant looks, her coal-black hair, Delilah gained ole Samson's mind, When he first seen the woman that looked so fine . . .

The words carry him clear around to the back of the cabin, still bent over like some sideshow chimp in a human's overcoat. But still it doesn't feel all that forced or false to him, somehow, this new gait he's taken up out of caution, and deciding to stay with it for a bit he continues hopping along, four-legged instead of two, over the rough scrub land on the blind side of the shack till he reaches the safety of the bramble bushes and trodden rabbit-runs. He never did get round to making that snare. To be honest he didn't exactly apply his mind much to it at all, just letting things drift.

And still drifting but in a bouncy kind of way he goes hopping on, sometimes varying the action, favouring his legs for a time, then switching the weight over on to his arms and wrists. Soon his palms are raw and bleeding but he doesn't care, convincing himself they're bound to toughen up with time and usage.

And just about then too he starts into this laughing fit, for he's found out something about himself he'd never have hit upon, not if he hadn't been scared of being spotted and started going around this way. Ever since he can remember some son of a bitch or other has been calling him ape, baboon, some type monkey, and now here he is hunkered down and feeding off trees just like those bad-mouthing rednecks always told him he was.

He's still laughing fit to bust, tears rolling down his cheeks, first wash they've had since God knows, when he stops dead, for everything has gone quiet. Birds, creeping things, the very wind itself, holding breath and listening to this crazy braying idiot. Crouched there, the blackberries turning to bile in his mouth, for he's down to the hard and half-ripe by now, he listens as well.

And then he hears it too, that other sound behind the noise of his laughter, a distant drone like a bee lost in the ether. He searches the sky. So immense is it, all that water below making it stretch and spread, he doesn't know where to direct his gaze. A bunch of seagulls drawn inland by someone ploughing somewhere is about all he can pick out against that misty grey dome. He listens more intently, head cocked in the direction the high hum seems to be coming from.

A cottontail appears on the track near where he's

crouching, both of them on equal footing. They study one another for a moment, its pale muzzle twitching then, cool as get out, it continues about its business.

And then finally he gets to see that dot in the sky, expanding in keeping with the noise of its single engine, a plane, itsy-bitsy, fragile, almost as if it shouldn't be airborne at all, but to him in his state as doom-laden as a great old B–17. The profile puzzles him, definitely not one of Uncle Sam's, he decides, remembering the outlines in that little aircraft-recognition book he used to bone up on, even if he was to end up in a kitchen. Pointed wings and tail, stogey-shaped fuselage, in place of the cigar-band, a bullseye.

He sinks down beneath the thorny boughs. Closer, closer it comes, until now he can make out the colours on its wings. A Spitfire. It passes low overhead and through the network of branches he can even make out the pilot in his perspex bubble, close-fitting helmet and all.

Badly shocked he lies there. It's the closest he's come to another human being since he got here except for that old MTB boat. He continues to stay where he is until the tiny insect aircraft fades from sight and sound before leaving his hidey-hole. He listens some more, but, yes, it's gone. He grazes on the fruit a while longer then decides he's had a bellyful of the great outdoors. The songs inside his head have all dried up by now. In their place a gathering dread he can't put a name to. The shadow of the plane has left its mark on him. Satan's wings.

He feels afflicted, spell-bound, just like those folk he remembers seeing back home wasting away and aiming to die before too long. Not unless the conjure was lifted from them. Not unless the spell was turned around. He cries out in terror then and with coat tails flying scuttles back to the shelter of his ruin where he crawls inside curling up under the weight of old khaki, knees to chin, fingers in mouth.

★

Some time later through the crack in the door he makes out the red glow lighting up the sky, way across the water. But in the east, not the west, where it should have been at this hour.

Out of the east, he repeats to himself, *out of the east,* faster and faster, rocking in his foul nest. *When the world ends the fires of hell will start up in the east.*

FIFTEEN

Sunk in the back of the boat, Lawlor put the chill, slightly concave quarter-bottle of Redbreast to his lips and drank deeply, the neat ten-year-old going down like mother's milk. He didn't even shudder. Not a spasm. So much for abstinence and the grand new regime.

But then all of that had taken a toss the night of the fires and the evacuation out at the American base. Panic at seeing his plans turn to tinder as everything combustible went up in smoke, then being told that others might get to his quarry before he did, had left him in despair.

Still, on a morning like this and at such an hour, a man might be forgiven a sup of liquid warmth. For one brief moment he swithered on whether to offer his sweating oarsman some as well, but decided against it. Once and once only had he seen Francey McKeever the worse for wear and that after just one measure someone had tipped into his orangeade when his mother's back was turned.

All seemed perfectly normal until they were on the road together, then the fun started. It was the closest to perdition Lawlor had ever come on those twisting night journeys back from the remote waterside public house. The combination flew like Jehu's chariot, while high above him Francey howled and sang rebel songs, twist-grip throttled back to the hilt. The wind screeched, Lawlor cowered, and that thin membrane of rusted metal beneath his weight rang like an anvil under the fusillade of loose road-chippings.

As the sun came up and he limped upstairs to his cold bed inside the sleeping barracks, *never again*, he vowed, *no siree*, he would do his drinking closer to home from now on. But then they slipped back into their old ways like two reprobates. Sometimes it struck him poor old not-all-there Francey really looked forward to his nocturnal jaunts as a jarvey on three wheels. Of course they barely communicated on those dark neglected byways – that was part of their unspoken arrangement – but of the two, the man riding erect and proud in his goggles and leathers was by far the more elated.

Not this time though, not with brown lake water sliding under him instead of a speeding backroad, not with his hands gripping wet wood instead of black, pimpled rubber.

It had been obvious from the start Francey wasn't all that keen on his proposal, but by dint of bullying and some hinted-at threats of a police nature, somehow he had managed to get him down to the water's edge where the family scull lay drawn up on rollers. The way he played it he made it appear like a tipsy whim on his part, this craving for a midnight row, something he'd never done before and, of course, this would be the last opportunity now that he was days away from leaving these parts for good.

Only he didn't really want to go boating in the dark, for it wouldn't fit in with his plan – *yes, he had a new one* – so he had to spin out his stay in the widow's back-kitchen for as long as possible into the small hours and that meant a steady intake of her private store of John Jameson. Consequently he was well oiled by the time he felt the stern of the boat sink under him near to the water-line itself.

He was still feeling the effects right now, his stomach clenched against the jerk, then racing roll of the boat, his head muzzy, and the moment he spoke the discovery his tongue was several sizes too big for his mouth. "Bring her around this way," he commanded, slurring the words, while waving a hand off to the left and north of the slipway.

A light still burned in the upstairs storey of the pub, the widow-woman lying awake and worrying no doubt about her wandering boy. Lawlor should have felt some remorse but didn't, for he was too far down this road now to care. He kept his mind set on his course of action as if an invisible line was drawn in the peaty waters ahead of them and inside his head he was following it.

"No, no, more to the right now, damn it! I'll do the navigating."

Away on the farther side of the Lough a knife-edge of rosy brightness like lamplight under a door stretched then began to thicken. The air around them and the water beneath remained dark, but gradually a separation became apparent. In spite of the whiskey Lawlor kept shivering. The metal buttons on his greatcoat felt icy to the touch. They shone as if luminous. Facing him, Francey laboured inside his own uniform, a long, leather, vaguely military affair that creaked in harmony with the drag and suck of the oars. He was wearing his airman's helmet, but mercifully had left the goggles at home.

Off to their left the land drew closer as the inward curve of their route deepened, but Francey pulled on regardless now, his mind set on his immediate task. Lawlor watched him, sharing his concentration for a moment, all that unthinking energy focused on the twin grips of the oars. The water hissed past falling in flakes, lustrous like the buttons on his

331

greatcoat. Above and beyond the creak of the thole-pins stretched a silence as dense as milk. It was as if they were enclosed by it, two tiny labouring insects under an immense invisible dome.

For the first time Lawlor wondered if the one he was seeking was awake and listening to the rhythmic beat of their approach. The island was far off out there somewhere over to their right and invisible, but all was so still at this hour that sounds would travel as clear as a voice down a wire. *Don't worry, I'm coming, I'm coming, Mister Runaway. But not from the direction you're expecting.*

At some point they pulled in very close to the shadowy rim of the lake itself and a great storm of screaming wildfowl erupted suddenly from the flatlands where they'd been feeding, boiling up in the air like a paper storm. In terror Lawlor cried out, rocking the boat as the beating mass swept over their heads. He imagined he could feel the feathery wind of their passing. Widgeon. Hunters waited patiently for them hidden in the reedbeds. Ever since the gun and ammunition restrictions the flocks had grown to immense proportions, something Lawlor had forgotten.

They sat there motionless on the water as if deprived of will, for Francey, too, seemed petrified, staring white face framed by the tight-fitting oval of his aviator's helmet. Schoolchildren wore something along the same lines, fur-lined and fastened under the chin. How pathetic he, Lawlor, had become, out here like this with a simpleton as conspirator and an unwilling one at that.

"Row," he ordered. Then in a burst of cruelty added, "You better do as I tell you if you know what's good for you. The army's looking for motorbikes with sidecars. You'll never see that old Velocette of yours again. I just have to say the word."

And a defeated Francey resumed dragging on the oars once more.

After a time, looming up behind the other's head, Lawlor made out a darker mass rising from the water. "Slacken off," he told him, "just let her sit a wee while," and his slave obeyed.

From under his coat Lawlor brought out the whiskey warmed by the heat of his body. His legs felt numb because of the cramped position he had taken up, low in the well of the boat, his boots steeped in an inch of bilgewater. Gradually the dinghy drifted about until it was stern-on to the island, and as it did so Lawlor saw a change sweep over Francey's face. Dropping his hands from the oars he hugged them close to his sides, rocking to and fro faster and faster until the boat itself began to roll as well.

"For Christ's sake, take it easy," hissed Lawlor, gripping the wooden sides, not daring to raise his voice this close to his goal. "Listen, listen, it's all right, it'll be all right about the old bike. I'll take care of it. No one'll lay a hand on it. I promise, I promise."

But Francey wouldn't be persuaded or consoled, so in desperation, Lawlor opened wide his coat and palmed his Webley revolver, laying it on the cross-plank between them like a played ace. There it lay at the end of its whipcord lanyard gleaming faintly and in appearance not all that intimidating, curiously enough, just a piece of oddly formed metal. Francey looked down at it then at Lawlor. Slowly he put both hands back on the handles of the oars again.

"Francey," said Lawlor in a gentler tone of voice, "I want to get on to the island. I want you to take me there."

"No, no," the other told him, shaking his head violently. "Bad place. Bad man get Francey. Old-Ride-The-Goat."

Lawlor's breath forsook him. His face felt clammy.

333

"Francey," he said, leaning closer, "have you seen someone there?"

"Ride-the-goat, ride-the-goat, ride-the-goat," the words coming out in a rushed singsong.

"I'll tell you what I'll do, Francey, I'll give you my police cap here if you land me on the island. You've always liked my sergeant's cap, now, haven't you?" He took it off as he said the words, baring his cropped white head to the raw air.

"To keep?"

"To keep."

"Badge and all?"

He nodded solemnly in reply, dangling the cap like some precious trophy.

"You'll only want it back."

"No, I won't. I promise."

"Promise?"

It was about the longest conversation they'd ever had together and in a moment of remorse Lawlor felt glad no one else was privy to it. "Have we got a bargain?"

Francey nodded, never once taking his eyes off the cap in Lawlor's hand, as if it might fly away under its own volition to skim the waters of the Lough like some soft, flat, magical black stone. He resumed rowing and, still ashamed, Lawlor reached out and retrieved the police revolver, putting it back in its holster.

For the first time some inkling of what he was about came to him, the heft and feel of the gun in his hand hitting home. Raw energy had buoyed him up this far, for he knew he daren't anticipate what might take place once he felt his boots sink down on to that island shore. In his head and heart he was deeply confused, still not knowing precisely what he was doing here or why. Only the force of his conscience drove him, like the downward-pulling weight of an old clock. What would happen once that weight reached the end of its drop he couldn't imagine, or how much time and energy he had left in him before it did.

By now the bumpy contours of the island ahead were standing out clear against the surrounding misty grey. Low trees and some form of rocky outcrop broke that outline. This, the western side, was different in character to the one nearest the town, where he knew his quarry had been set down. Lawlor had spent time with the big Ordnance Survey map back in the barracks noting the terrain as well as pattern of the foreshore. The idea was not just to arrive under cover of dark but on the side least expected.

All this time the light was getting stronger, air and water by now clearly separated. Francey's face, too, had broken free of its backdrop and Lawlor studied it closely as if to forestall any sudden change of heart on his part. Most of his adult life he had relied heavily upon the force of his uniform and position to dominate and cut a swathe before him, but out here like this, just the two of them in a frail craft, man to man, he strained hard to hold on to his supremacy. Soon, terribly soon, it would again be man to man, but under far crueller and demanding circumstances.

And then Francey stopped rowing. About a dozen feet or so out from the pale fringe of shingle that would be landfall he let the oars trail in the water like two lifeless, wooden limbs. They sat there facing one another and Lawlor knew he was going to have to wade ashore, there would be no easy leaping from bark to dry land the way he'd imagined it.

"Take me in closer," he demanded even though he recognised defeat when he saw it.

"Give me the cap."

"I'll give it to you when I get back."

Francey gathered up the oars again, his face hardening into a sullen mask.

335

"You promised, so you did," he muttered and Lawlor held the cap out to him.

The other's face barely altered even when the prize was safely in his hands. Would he put it on, Lawlor wondered. As had happened so often in his life here was one more occasion when an outsider seeing it for himself would be hard put to believe his eyes. Crazy. He felt like laughing out loud at the grotesque parody of it all, two loonies in a boat like this, preparing to switch identities. He wasn't all that sure who was getting the best of the bargain.

"Okay, it's yours," he said, "take it. Only move in a wee bit nearer, the water's too deep."

"No, it's not."

Lawlor trailed a hand overboard as if to check, but there was nothing to console him there but watery blackness.

"Francey," he said, "this is just between the two of us, you hear what I'm telling you. Not a word to anyone, just you and me. No matter what happens."

Then as if catching some terrible finality in his own words, some presentiment better not thought of, let alone articulated, he added, "I won't be all that long. Just sit tight and wait for me. You'll do that, won't you?" Francey kept his eyes lowered to the police cap in his hands, its insides tidemarked with another man's sweat, maybe measuring it mentally already. He continued to say nothing so, with a sigh, which changed to a grunt as the boat shifted under him, Lawlor hoisted himself up and sideways so that, delicately for someone his size, he lowered himself down into the depths inch by blood-chilling inch.

First he felt his trousers grow heavy, then his under-drawers, finally his socks, as lake water seeped through the lace-holes of his boots. Then their soles struck bottom. Francey was right, it wasn't deep, but for a moment it was like balancing on a bed of marbles. He let go the gunwale and began the slow careful sleepwalking trudge ashore.

On reaching dry land the first thing he did was pull off his boots and drain them, then squeeze the surplus from the rest of him. By the time he was shod and on his feet once more he was shivering, legs like twin icicles. He looked and he listened, sniffed the air, too, as if somehow, mysteriously, he had fetched up on some tropic isle instead of a square mile of unclaimed, Godforsaken, untamed, water-girt Irish wilderness.

In the misty half-light he could make out the boat and its solitary occupant sitting unmoving on the still surface. Francey was watching him and, embarrassed at being observed, Lawlor started off up the facing slope towards a cluster of trees, dragging his sodden limbs as if they belonged to somebody else. When he was deep among the alders he sat down on a stump and buried his head in his hands.

For a long time he stayed like that, unable to summon up sufficient resolve to push on with his quest. He realised he had started using highflown words like that in his head a lot of late, *quest, quarry, runaway*, showy cotton-wool words that insulated him from the reality of what he was about. The ugly truth was he hadn't thought things through the way he should have done, the way he was supposed to, the way he was trained to do.

There and then on that mossy old stump of a tree he started sifting through the situation trying to salvage some sense from the mess he had got himself into. Of course he could always go back and wet both legs a second time a lot earlier than planned, allowing himself to be rowed back to the mainland and sanity, putting all of this behind him, just like the island itself receding into the mist. Was that an option? No, it was not.

337

So, he would go on then, would he, patiently quartering this rump of desolation rising from the water like a boil on a backside until eventually he would run across its only other inhabitant. Then what? Arrest him? Arrest Man Friday? Take him handcuffed back to where Francey crouched in the boat wearing his cap? Francey would certainly love that, him with a black-faced ghost in tow. You wouldn't see him for stink. So now we have two castaways instead of one, for, remember, he had sworn him to secrecy.

He stood up. He had decided on what he would do. Well, near enough.

The light was pearly now, a fine vapoury haze obscuring everything like seeing it through gauze. Maybe the sun had broken through on the far side of the island but not here.

The Ordnance map with its slew of unpronounceable townland names, many probably antiques by now like those scoured away by American bulldozer blades, had at its core an empty uncharted space, a hole where a heart should have been, for lands under water have no names. It was the great Lough and Lawlor studied its magnification with the aid of a domed glass, the island swimming up out of the paper to meet him. Dotted lines of fathomage encircled its shore, fine as fusewire, but the rest, the land, was mere empty paper, nothing, a true desert, save for a tiny broken square barely bigger than a fly-speck close to the shore, the one on the far side from where he had landed. It could have been anything, there was no clue to be found in the legend, a ruin, a sheep-pen, a monument, a well, even, but it was where he would find his man somehow, he felt certain of that.

Keeping an image of that creased old map in his head he looked up at the sky. If he headed for that growing crown of light directly east he must reach his objective in little over half an hour, maybe less, even if the terrain turned out to be difficult.

So he left the cover of the wind-sculpted trees and came to a place where the land climbed up to about the height of a house.

Lawlor began to sweat. He allowed his greatcoat to swing open to let the air about himself and soon the state of his trouser-legs was almost forgotten. At the summit he looked back. The boat had barely moved and Francey looked about as big as an insect. From this distance he couldn't make out whether he was capless or not.

Ahead and down in a hollow place he saw a ragged ring of lichened standing-stones. So it was true that people must have lived and worshipped here at some bygone period. Careful not to betray too much interest, he had found out that at a time much more recent than that fever victims had been brought out here and left to die.

Up to this point he hadn't heard the cry of a solitary bird nor seen anything on four legs either, and in a morbid moment he wondered if there might not be some connection between that history and the air of desolation hanging over the place. He remembered Francey's terror at the notion of getting too close to the shore, but before his imagination started to take off with him a straggly column of wild goats appeared below, emerging from between two of the largest dolmens.

Like a hunter Lawlor dropped to one knee. An ancient billy, streaked and grey as an old rug, trotted out last of all, beard on him like a hay wisp. He raised his head, jabbing the air with his horns, sniffing the breeze. Lawlor crouched closer to the damp earth watching the little family browsing below while the patriarch stood sentinel on a rise. He wondered if he would be spared when the real hunters did come, for he must have led a charmed life up to now, all those years on him.

In his head Lawlor heard shouting, shots, the barking of

dogs, bleating, he saw blood, the future scene playing itself out for him. He promised himself he would not anticipate any of that by actions of his own, not if he could help it.

The goats were still grazing away as if to a plan and purpose. In the stillness their teeth made a crisp cropping noise on the lush grass. So he edged back down the way he had come seeking some other route that would bring him to the far side of the island without disturbing the ruminants or their territory.

He began to feel relaxed, the strangest thing, as if out for a day's adventure in the countryside the way he used to do as a boy, with a stick and a dog, head bursting with derring-do. Filling his lungs he glanced about him. The air was fresh and pure, unsullied with the stink of house-fires, early dew hung in droplets on every leaf, he saw ripe berries glinting like jewellery. For the first time, too, he detected birdsong as if Nature had finally relaxed its vigilance. A track of sorts with fresh currant-shaped animal droppings curved off and upward, circling the hill where he had looked down on the goats. He decided to follow it.

Still he was easy and at peace in himself, almost as if he had forgotten why he was here in the first place when, brutally, that feeling was changed utterly. Rounding a bend in the track, squeezing between walls of briar, he saw ahead of him what looked like a heap of cast-off clothing in the middle of the path. He stopped short, for something – it could hardly be called an arm, it didn't look animate or human enough – emerged from this ragged nest reaching out to the ripe pickings on the lowest branch of a blackberry bush.

Lawlor watched, his whole frightened body in his gaze, as the bundle of old clothes fed on the purple fruit. He could see no head, no mouth, nothing but a dark arm plucking down the bounty and disappearing with it under the rags, once khaki, but now so soiled as to be like the trodden earth itself.

As he continued to stare the sergeant caught a glimpse of a pair of legs, bare and black like the arm, but the soles a dusky pink, which somehow added an even more unsettling dimension to the nightmare. The arm stopped moving, the whole bundle as well, and Lawlor waited to be discovered. His breath caught in his chest. He saw a head, the hair dense and matted with leaves and debris, eyes that stared at him, wild and fiery, then the tatterdemalion leaped up and he heard himself shout, "*Easy! Easy!*" as if to an animal.

Even after the figure had disappeared in a flurry of flying coat-tails he continued calling out, "*Here! Here!*" short barks of command that were the entire opposite of what he intended to convey.

For a time he stood there, shaken, his proud plan of action in ruins. He tried to work out in his head what could have brought this creature to such a pass. They were the same flesh and blood and humanity, reason told him so, but fear of something alien and incomprehensible started to grow at the back of his mind like a root in a cellar.

Without intending to his hand went out to the buttoned butt of his revolver, then in the next move towards the bullet pouch on the opposite side of his Sam Brown belt. He had left his baton behind at the barracks hung up by its thong thinking it would merely be an embarrassment, an encumbrance on the boat journey. Also he believed at the time he wouldn't need it, not against someone he intended to treat with some reasonableness now, even civility, for his original feelings had undergone something of a reversal regarding his quarry. Again the word seemed even more inappropriate, especially after what the American officer had told him, remembering also something he had seen but had put out of his head the day of the court-martial when the corporal had been sentenced in his absence.

During that wearisome two-day trial in the big mess-hall at the base he had sat at the back with the other civilian observers. Quigg was there, and Doctor Delargy, various people from the Press and, of course, Kincaid. The accused had been placed at a table facing the military court, the defence and the prosecution on either side. Little defence was offered, however, the prisoners looked as though they knew the verdicts in advance, but one of them, he who the army psychiatrist had testified to be of the lowest mental category, a skinny beanpole of a creature, wrung his hands throughout. His sobs could be heard long before the President of the court laid down his ruling. Dishonourable discharge from the service with hard labour for the term of natural life.

Just prior to that, however, they were asked if they had anything to say on behalf of their missing accomplice. The other two sat staring down at their folded hands but the young thin one with the IQ score of 42 seemed as though he might speak out. His mouth opened and shut a few times while everyone waited but then Lawlor saw his fellow-prisoners send him a look that silenced him as effectively as a knife-thrust.

At the time he put it down to rancour pure and simple on their part. It seemed to say, *keep your yap closed, we're already done for*, but knowing what he knew now, he felt enmity there, some grudge against the missing man, crueller and deeper than mere malice. At the back of his mind somewhere Lawlor must have entertained some notion of telling the man all this, even, God help us, offering to listen to his story out here, man to man, just the two of them alone. Now that was no longer possible. Perhaps it never had been. Maybe the whole thing had hatched itself inside his

342

own head, spawned by guilt and a bad conscience. Without thinking he crossed himself.

Once more he laid his hand on the weapon strapped to his waist. In all his years he'd never been afraid to confront anyone face to face in the course of his duty – those yelling Shinners in '22 had been different – but now he felt apprehensive, something impending, it seemed to him, waiting to do for him on this Godforsaken isle. He told himself, *go back, reverse the fatal flow while you have time*, but knew he could not, it was too late for that now, maybe, for him, as well.

Crouching slightly, but not as bent to the ground as that scuttling bundle of rags he was pursuing, he moved forward cautiously along the path. Briars tore at his clothes, clawing the wool. At one point, to give himself an extra charge of valour, he uncorked his bottle. It was almost done for, so he drained it, then hurled it far up into the dense swathes of thorn bushes, watching it land without a sound to hang suspended neck-down among the brambles. He wondered how many seasons it would take before disappearing downward into the earth for ever.

Eventually he came to more open terrain, slowing his pace accordingly, creeping from bush to bush like some great black clumsy bear. The sun was up and clearly visible now, facing him, its pale amber light striking directly into his eyes. He stopped under the last alder before the expanse ahead left him no cover. The whiskey was starting to do its job, he felt a pleasant muzziness in his head, not so conscience-bound or jittery. Leaning up against the mottled trunk he closed his eyes, trusting in the hard stuff to get him through the task ahead.

He unbuttoned himself and pissed, then in a dramatic reversal of intent he brought out the Webley on the end of its lanyard and loaded it, spinning the chamber and pressing home six bright new slugs which had lain greased and untouched in their pouch these ten long years – more, maybe. For an instant he felt a bit like Randolph Scott, then one of the frightened townsfolk the lanky hero nearly always shamed into backing him. He put the primed gun back in its holster, noting the difference the ammunition made to its weight.

Ahead lay an expanse of weedy shingle all bumps and hollows like an overgrown graveyard but there, close to the shore, was the object he had seen on the map the size of a freckle, but here, close up, in reality, a rickle of old fieldstone walls partially roofed with a crazy crow's nest of broken timbers.

Lawlor stared at the ruin. He had no logical reason to suppose his man was inside but then if he wasn't he might as well give up, for to comb this entire island looking for him after this would be as hard as finding the right bubble in a soda-siphon. But in his heart of hearts he knew he was here, had to be, as if over all these past weeks, troubled by his obsession, he had managed to get into the other's head, under the very hide of the man, thinking as he might think, reacting as he would react.

So he moved forward putting his trust in instinct and the detective process, which in Lawlor's book would always be one and the same. He could see the tideless Lough ahead of him level as milk in a pan. Its sheer expanse looked so much more tremendous on this side. On the far, facing, landward rim he could make out a smudge of smoke still hovering over what he took to be the American base. Nothing moved between, not a boat, nor a bird, no fish rising, no sign of life whatsoever on that enamelled flatness. No witnesses, either, to what might be about to unfold.

About a dozen yards from the rear of the ruin he stopped,

sniffing the air. A foul stench drifted towards him, something rotten, truly horrible. He went closer, placing his feet with ridiculous care on the gravel, even though his approach must have been noted. The stones had broken and fallen away in a score of places, there were dark gaping holes, any one of which could harbour a pair of savage eyes.

Lawlor kept his own fastened on one such opening, convincing himself that was where his watcher lay, their glances locked. In the middle of it all this crazy notion took hold that he should be waving a handkerchief, signalling his intentions. But then, just what were they?

He got up to the nearest wall and put his hand out to touch and hold on like a blind man and then, trying to avoid those awful staring embrasures, he groped his way all the way around until he reached the front of the partially-roofed shell facing out on to the water. And, sure enough, as he'd anticipated, there was an opening there and blocking it, a door of sorts, bleached to blazes by the weather.

Lawlor stood for a moment gathering himself. The stench was much worse now and seemed to be leaking out through the cracks between the wood and frame, something dead or dying. He took a grip on himself and rapped on the door, three hard businesslike knocks, the sound startling in the stillness. A second time he hammered on the barricade, rough and dry to the touch like pumice.

"*Washington!*" he called out. "*Corporal Washington!*"

He stopped, not knowing how to proceed, what to say, the situation way beyond the use of mere words for either of them. He brought his ear up close to the bare wood but could hear nothing inside so, sweating cold drops of dread, he grasped the edge of the barrier – it looked to be made of heavy plywood curled and frayed at the edges – and hauled hard on it so that it slid sideways. On the instant the stink smote him with new vigour and he covered up his mouth and nose.

For a moment he could see nothing specific in the gloom. Broken shafts of light from the ruined roof picked out areas of the floor knee-deep in driftwood. Off in darkened corners lurked shadowy mounds, any one of which might be human. There was a steady dedicated buzzing of insects. He tracked their rise and fall to one of the mounds, paler than the rest, something unspeakable rotting there under its pelt and beneath its halo of greedy flies.

He slid the door back further and more daylight flooded in and he saw a row of opened food tins, each with their own little bluebottle colony, a saucepan, a mug and a candle stub laid out on a board. Close by he made out what looked like the tattered remains of an old book lying in the rubbish face-down, half its pages missing. Lawlor stood there stunned for an instant staring at this collection of objects so unexpected in their domesticity.

"Washington," he repeated yet again, but not so warlike as before. Nothing answered save the hum of the flies so, biting on the bullet, he stooped under the lintel and stepped inside.

Good God, how colossal the stink was! He felt himself gag thinking he might throw up over his boots.

"Show yourself, God damn you!" he cried throwing glances into every dark corner.

Never did it occur to him to look up and the business might have ended there and then like that, unfinished and trailing regret in its wake for him for the rest of his days, when something small, light and round fell from the rafters to roll at his feet. Lawlor stared down at it with incredulity, then there followed a steady patter as more of the same followed, blackberries, of all things, *blackberries*, a rain of tiny glistening fruit as if shaken from a bough high in the roof.

And he looked up then and saw what appeared to be a

346

gigantic swollen nest wedged close to the slates. The fall of fruit was leaking from it, from a pocket, or maybe even a clenched fist, to be precise, for he recognised that mass now for what it was, marvelling at how anything human could have stowed itself away bat-like, up high like that, compact and curled up.

Something truly terrible had occurred here, something he would never understand, had no desire to understand, and he laid his hand on his revolver and the moment he did so the thing nesting in the rafters dropped soundlessly to the floor in front of him in a rush of billowing khaki.

Under its covering of old army coats the creature was completely naked. It squatted in the dirt facing him, not looking directly at him, yet alert, somehow, to his every move. Carefully with his left hand Lawlor kept working at his holster – the brass stud that kept it fastened was stiff in its socket – not for a moment shifting his gaze. The other's eyes rolled in his head, the whites startling, hair matted stiff with debris like an old yard-brush. He had a beard, which was a great surprise. Strung on a chain about his neck were two metal tabs, dog tags, the Americans called them. The rest of him was in shadow, but his stalk hung down, dark and thin like the handle of a whip.

"Washington." Once more Lawlor came out with the word as if to an animal ordering it to heel. And it seemed hideously appropriate for he and the woman and that boy of hers between them, they'd left this creature to rot the way one might abandon an unwanted dog. Or, in his own case, turning a blind eye because he wanted to parade him as a trophy in his own time and at his own convenience.

Only that was impossible now, it wasn't going to happen the way he'd planned it, and Lawlor knew it in that instant with a truly terrible finality. All of it, the whole filthy business, would finish right here in this pigsty of a place just between the two of them and so he stood there, his fingers on the butt of his gun, waiting for the end to begin.

And the one they called Washington, *it*, for Lawlor had purged himself of all feeling or pity, gave a hop like a frog and Lawlor called out a warning, "*Stay where you are! Come no closer!*" finally drawing his weapon clear of its holster.

The crouching one looked up at it as if it was a toy meant for his diversion. He was smiling to himself or, maybe, it was at Lawlor, and he gave off a rich stink, distinct and separate from whatever it was that rotted away in the corner. Lawlor felt his disgust deepen. Somewhere inside he knew it to be cruel and wrong but he couldn't help himself, stoking the emotion the way you would a fire.

"*Say something, damn you!*" he heard himself bark as if it was some other person and not him who was whipping himself into a rage.

"Can't you speak?" And then giving in to the insanity of it he yelled, "Why don't you admit it, you were part of it all the time! An old woman who never harmed anyone and you and your darkie pals gunned her down in cold blood. For the fun of it. Not even for money. Look at you. An animal, that's what you are, that's all you are, a bloody animal. Own up, damn you. *Own up, I say!*"

The poison spewed out of him like filth from a drain but he couldn't stem it, not now, for he needed to punish, not because of what the other might have done, but what had been done to him, Lawlor. And mixed in with the desire for retribution was fear as well, that same fear he had felt all those years ago when he'd cowered in the dark in his own shit, listening to the taunts of those Fenian irregulars outside the walls of the burning barracks and his new bride upstairs holding on to the the bars of their bed not knowing if he would be able to protect her or not and, worst of all, him not

348

knowing whether he had the backbone or resolve to act if and when that final moment arrived.

"*Hell roast you for one murdering nigger bastard!*" the words coming out of him like scalding spittle and the gun in his hand pointing directly at the naked savage squatting before him in the filth of his own leavings, "*Keep your distance!*"

But he would keep on coming closer and closer – *why wouldn't he heed him, why wouldn't he, damn him?* – a hop at a time, cupping his knees, and Lawlor pressing back and back until he was up against the wood of the door with nowhere to go and all the time the other smiling up at him, damn that sweet, forgiving smile of his, far, far worse than spitting anger or fear could ever be.

Then he lifted his hands from off his black burnished kneecaps, stretching his arms out wide in a parody of brotherly love that made Lawlor's blood run cold. His lips moved, too, as if the power of speech was returning at last and right then at that precise point the gun in Lawlor's hand went off.

Of its own volition. That fact hammered itself into his brain. *It went off in my hand, it went off in my hand,* as if he was already preparing his own self-defence even while his victim still squatted there in front of him like something carved in stone, a ragged, seeping hole torn in his chest.

And questions continued to seethe in his head. Did it go off before his hand touched me or after? Did the impact of his outstretched hand on my boot jar the firing pin? But mercifully he stopped there, thank God, letting the reality of what had taken place in that foul place sweep over him. He was half-deaf from the detonation, the air thick and reeking, and he had just shot another human being for reasons he would never be able to explain, maybe in a courtroom, yes, but never, ever to himself. *No.*

The pistol hung down from the knot at the end of its

lanyard and when he sank to one knee, weak, almost senseless, it too fell to the ground with him, a dead, still-smoking weight, pulling him to the side, threatening to topple him over in the rubbish alongside the man dying there. A bloody froth bubbled from his mouth and his eyes already were beginning to glaze over.

Lawlor edged closer but only so far. In death, as in life, the being before him repelled him, but there was nothing he could do for him, even if he wanted to. He told himself that. He wanted to say, *I didn't mean it*, but it would have been a lie. For a moment it seemed as if the man expiring there before him would speak or try to and in spite of his abhorrence Lawlor moved a fraction nearer to catch his last words.

He brought his head down beside the other's cheek and felt his weakening breath on his face. Something was forming on those rapidly paling lips and as he strained to make sense of the soft plosives a word that sounded like *"pearly"* emerged, but before another could follow there came a terrible gargling deep in his throat and blood gouted from his mouth and finally it was over.

Lawlor looked down at the still-squatting corpse. The round woolly head had fallen forward on to his chest where the bullet had done for him, lodging in the lungs and thorax. *Less than a minute*, Lawlor found himself noting almost calmly as if already making his report, except that there would be no report.

He drew back then, for the dead man's bowels had loosened, and stumbling out into the air, where he was unmercifully sick, he staggered down to the water's edge to drink long and deep to wash away the foul taste of his own vomit.

He sat down there for a long time looking across to the land on the far side of the great Lough. It was still early and the first house-fires of the day had yet to be lit. The smoke from the base had long since dispersed, the sky an almost perfect azure streaked with white cirrus. He had this great desire to sit here like this forever, legs outstretched with his hands buried up to the wrists in moist soft sand. The air was cool and pure and when he closed his eyes he could have been a boy again or transported back to any other age rather than this one.

As he sat there, the water lapping close about the soles of his great boots, he detected a faint *put-putting* noise, very distant, and he searched the expanse in front of him for its source. It sounded like a boat with an engine, rare enough in these parts, and presently he saw a slowly moving speck close in to the facing land trailing a thin silver disturbance in its wake. Idly he wondered who could it be out at this hour, not fishermen, surely, for their boats were always of the oared variety like Francey's. And then it came to him with a cruel shock, as if he hadn't endured enough already, that it might be Kincaid and his hunter cronies setting their sights on this very spot.

On the instant he felt as conspicuous as a bullseye and he began scrambling back up the shingle slope on hands and knees towards the safety of the ruins.

When he reached the half-open doorway he hesitated, not ready yet, if ever, to confront the horror of what lay within. But the distant boat, its engine popping away, still kept on course, but bearing a shade further out, little by little now, away from the mainland and, choking back his nausea, Lawlor stumbled inside.

For some reason he half expected to see all exactly as he'd left it, but in his absence the dead man had somehow toppled sideways as if turning away from the light and into the dark where he belonged, now crouching, knees to chin, in a foetal position. His bare soles had turned as pale as Lawlor's as the blood ebbed from his body and for a moment the man who'd done for him stood staring down immeasurably shocked by the sight of a dead white man's feet.

He turned to the doorway then and, lying down, trained his gaze on the motorised dot on the horizon waiting to see if it would head his way. It would be his punishment, he had deserved it, but lo and behold, the little craft kept travelling on and out of sight. He poked his head out further and further into daylight and followed it as long as he could, but eventually it disappeared and he decided judgement had been postponed to some other time and by some other route.

He went back inside after that and stood staring about him as if intent on committing every detail to memory, methodically going over the scene of the crime as if it had been committed by someone else, turning over and examining what might have been overlooked among the dirt and disorder.

His mind felt anaesthetised, a machine doing what it had always done in such circumstances. With a stick he prodded and re-arranged the pathetic array of belongings laid out on its makeshift shelf, a few dented utensils, a candle-end, an old table knife. Over in a corner in a soiled heap lay what looked like the remains of a uniform, along with a pair of large-sized ruined shoes missing their laces. He picked up the book, too, he'd noticed earlier, most of its pages ripped out, probably for firing, although there didn't seem to be any sign of ashes anywhere.

Lawlor wondered whether the other had laboured through it up to page eighty-six before using what he'd read to wipe himself. The title was across the top. *Riders Of The Purple Sage* by Zane Grey.

"*As he strode down the sloping terrace, rabbits scampered before him and the beautiful valley quail, as purple in colour as the sage on the uplands, ran fleetingly along the ground into the forest."*

As he read the words he had this sudden image of a black hand holding the page up close to that inch of guttering candle as the desolate night hours slowly passed. But he quickly put it from him, needing to keep his imagination in check as long as he could.

So, still the good detective, he studied the little hoard of edibles the other had been living on like an animal, blackberries, some shrivelled hazel-nuts, crab apples, God help him, a few maggoty mushrooms. Christ Almighty, those old toadstools would surely have finished him off, anyway, after making him lose his mind first, for he recognised the variety with the sulphur markings, one of the half-deadly *amanitas*, from the chart they had pinned up on the Day Room wall, every autumn sending some poor kid to the hospital.

But finally he had to come back to the corpse again, for it was as if he'd been putting off the moment until then. Right now he would have given anything for a drink from that bottle of Jameson he'd tossed away in the bramble bushes. Down on his hunkers he sank among the litter of driftwood and dry bracken and he examined that lifeless form, barely clothed by its old English army coat. It lay there, its back turned as if sleeping, and it seemed to him a great pity to have to disturb such a peaceful arrangement, but he knew he had to, he had to, for there was only one course open to him now, only one forward route possible, drastic as it seemed.

And so he took hold of him by those ashen heels of his and began dragging that dead, dead weight over the thickly strewn floor towards one far wall. It was the one most affected by weather and neglect. Half its stones lay tumbled, out as well as in, and those remaining trembled loose to the touch. Panting with the effort of it, Lawlor carefully

353

positioned his burden close to the lower course so that it lay face turned to the wall. And it seemed somehow fitting for him to be laid out in that fashion and he looked at ease lying there, hands clasped across his bare black chest like some swarthy Crusader turned sideways in his tomb. The face too was at peace as if smoothed out above the stubble and before covering him up for good Lawlor looked down one last time.

What had gone through that mind right at the very end, he asked himself. That word he'd uttered before he'd been able to say "*gates*". Right at that moment he must have seen something, some place beyond all of this and now he was where he belonged, at rest, finally.

And here came the interesting part. Wasn't it he, Lawlor, or, rather, the gun in his hand, who had helped him there? For a moment it all sounded so plausible, my God, so comforting, too, him performing the ultimate favour for him like that, putting him out of his misery, for he was remembering too with an added rush of justification what the American captain had said about him being better off dead.

It all seemed so perfect he almost started believing in it, him in the role of benefactor, a public one at that, for didn't everyone want to forget this man, putting a lid on him as if he never existed, even, he suspected, the woman who'd once been so close to him. But he stopped himself in time, sickened by his own pretence, bad enough to even maybe put a gun to his own head.

Instead he turned his attention back to the task he'd already set himself when he started dragging the body across to lie in state close to the wall where he'd decided to bury it. But first of all he collected up every trace of him ever being here, the empty Spam tins, the paperback book, the candle, the knife and utensils, and arranged them alongside like a little collection of funerary objects. Then he took up the old shoes and filthy uniform and placed them carefully on top. He covered the corpse as best he could before laying the first stone in place, which was the hardest part of all, like shovelling soil into an open coffin on to an upturned face. Dead and all as he was, it was hard to keep from flinching as the cold, raw fieldstone touched that yielding frame.

It took him a long time for he would stop every so often, shaking and sweating, not knowing if he could continue or not, entombing what seemed to be something still warm and responsive. Once he even dismantled the cairn sufficiently to feel for a pulse, but there was nothing there, just a stiffening of the flesh as if it had already turned to leather.

Finally, the thing, the construction, was complete. It even looked as though the wall had simply collapsed in a long untidy barrow for, deliberately, he had made it seem not too perfect. In the far corner the unknown animal carcase still exuded a fearsome stink but he decided to leave it there where it lay as if it had just strayed in to die out of the open. And maybe it had, for all he knew.

He took one last lingering look about the place as if some of the tricks of the criminal trade had rubbed off on him, meticulous to the last. It was an odd feeling, but with no trace of the crime any longer visible, his conscience seemed to have become clear and untroubled again.

He went outside. By now the morning was well advanced. Across the calm, dimpled water he could make out the first smoke from invisible chimneys ascending into the air. Slowly he circled the ruins, once, twice, then a third time, like a surveyor. Nothing missed his attention. He seemed to float outside himself, observing and, at the same time, impressed by his own actions, so calm, so contained, so capable. He began to shiver then, not because the sensation might soon

355

pass, but because he might continue to feel this way from now on like a deadened limb with its circulation cut off.

On the way back he came upon the old goat again. It was grazing on a low-hanging elder bush and it stopped chewing as he came wandering up the track towards it. He halted as well and the two regarded one another for a moment, yet at the same time there was something off-hand and disinterested in their appraisal this time. Lawlor felt no fear, nothing, and the other soon resumed his browsing as though he, too, recognised his business here was over and done with for good.

As Lawlor went past he could have stretched out a hand to touch that ancient matted hide. His smell lingered long after he was out of sight.

Ambling along as if still on a morning stroll Lawlor, the sergeant – a day away from dropping that title for good – made out finally the western sheet of water gleaming through the scrub trees. Strangely enough he didn't really expect to see a boat out there close in to shore and when he did so he took it as mere chance, an accident. That his loyal boatman should have waited so long and patiently for his return was of no consequence to him. The truth of the matter was he could just as easily have been content to sit down and watch the water change colour, alone and forgotten, like the one he'd just buried, till darkness set in and maybe even beyond that as well.

He had no plans any more and the moment the expression registered with him it seemed as simple and uncomplicated as an elementary equation or the four times table.

And even when he was back on board that small craft once more with the man at the oars facing him still wearing his policeman's cap, the same mood of indifference stayed with

356

him. The prow sliced the heavy flatness and the displaced water gurgled at Lawlor's back. He trailed a hand in the wake until it felt numb, as dead to sensation as he himself was still, and shortly after that, when the other boat came heading across their path, its engine put-putting away and blue smoke issuing from a little covered cabin affair, Lawlor stared straight ahead as if blind to its presence. It was the motor vessel he had seen earlier on the far side of the island and soon he could make out faces he recognised, Kincaid's and Burnside's among them.

The two boats passed and no one called out, not a word of greeting or question even, Francey as unseeing and seemingly oblivious as his passenger, capless in the stern.

Long after they had drawn apart the men in the bigger boat stared after the smaller one in silence, but Lawlor only looked ahead through his companion as if he could see something ahead of him that no one else could. He was waiting for the feeling to return like a man waking up from an operation and for the ether to wear off, yet with the terrible intimation that somehow maybe it never would. Loose ends forever unravelling. For an eternity.

★　　★　　★

Ussher Greer was in his hayloft looking out through the airholes high in the eaves when he saw the dog again. There it was, in the same spot, at the same time, moving through his young willow grove. A year, maybe two from now, there would be withies, pale, pliable sally rods bursting forth as though fired from a gun. Water and willow, he loved the congruity, so when he sighted that hated tan and white shape rooting among his precious saplings he put aside his pitchfork and backed down the ladder to the barn floor below.

Rex was waiting as he crossed the yard but he got him by

the collar, dragging him over to the potato-house where he closed and barred the door on him. Then he went inside and taking down his gun from the pegs above the dresser he broke it open, thumbing home two bright brass-capped orange cartridges.

Outside it was a beautiful, still afternoon, Hallowe'en just days away, the fields yielding up their harvest painlessly, not a storm, scarcely a shower, even, to spoil the gathering in. Only one thing marred the pleasing prospect. But before he got to the little plot close by the water's edge the old hound saw him and its muzzle came up. It studied his approach across the pasture but only for a moment before returning to its depredation among the tender young shoots once more.

Ussher Greer cocked back the hammers on his gun. At the same time he couldn't help but be curious about why his old enemy should be so boldly unconcerned about being discovered. Up, down, went the muddied muzzle while the back paws kept shooting out a powerful spray of earth. Then the head rose high with something in its jaws, something white and trailing. Ussher Greer picked up speed and as he did so the dog started off, its pale fluttering burden still clenched in his mouth.

It was heading for the river and the man with the gun changed course to get there first. Of the two he was the faster by far for it was a fat old thing, its hunting days almost, if not completely, over. As he trotted through the lush green of his own meadow the man was thinking to himself that their ages might be a match, dog years being five times that of a human's. But his breath was beginning to catch him so he concentrated instead on that distant gleam of fast running water.

At the river bank he bent over gasping. Blood-motes jigged in front of his eyes and the gun felt strangely cumbersome in his hand. Then he saw that the dog had moved further downstream.

The pace by now was telling on both of them and he trailed the slowly moving animal until he made out that other glint of flat water ahead, away from the river, through a clump of low trees. Moving into, then through the little grove to where it thinned away and the soil was bone dry and littered with drift he caught a clearer sighting of the dog. It was digging yet again but as he peered closer he saw that a hole had already been dug there and old Slipper was busy burying whatever it was he had so carefully transported to the place.

Ussher Greer edged forward until only a dozen paces separated them. Still it ignored him, the dog, scrabbling away in its shallow pit. Nearer moved the man with the gun. Then finally the old dog stopped. It looked up and towards him and he saw that its muzzle was wet with something, not its own slaver, but something bright and reddish, staining hair and paws the colour of fresh jam. He stamped his foot snapping a dead piece of wood and it retreated cringing to lie on its belly, doleful, runny eyes never leaving him for a second.

Ussher Greer walked over and looked down into the hole. He saw a torn and ragged scrap of cloth, it looked like a piece of bed-linen, lying on the top of something, and he reached in to pull it away and the moment he did so the old hound threw back its head and howled loud and long seeing it in his hand like that.

Stumbling back the man let the gun drop. It made no noise on the soft sand. Spittle ran from his mouth as he felt his breakfast shift inside. When he came upright his eyes were wet and there was a bitter taste in his mouth. The dog howled and howled and continued to howl, a terrible hoarse and broken-hearted wail until finally Ussher Greer lifted up his shotgun emptying both barrels to end that eerie cry with a double detonation that seemed to freeze the entire Lough and everything on its near shore into shocked stillness.

Some little time later he took up the little ravaged corpse and gently wrapped it in the pillowcase. That tiny clenched face, those naked doll-sized feet and hands, they smote him cruelly, so perfect, despite the dog's mauling, the skin tawny, the hair tight and curled into a helmet of dark fuzz. Looking down on it, *poor mite*, he thought, *maybe you're just as well off not growing up in this heartless place after all, forever different and destined to be apart. Even more apart than the rest of us.*

Going over to the dog he hauled it to the sandy grave, laying its still-warm carcase alongside that other chill little bundle in its bloodied linen wrapper, hardly bigger than a loaf of bread. He covered both with soil until the spot looked as it had been, desolate, unfrequented as a desert, only the feeble breaking of the waves disturbing the stillness.

As for himself he felt drained, yet somehow strangely complete, as if he'd brought something to a conclusion, a tying up of threads, the end of a chapter. This whole countryside was manured with corpses, he told himself, as he stood there listening to the silence. What difference would two more make?

And so he returned by the way he had come, back to his beloved waterland where nothing from that ugly warring world beyond its liquid boundaries could punish or affect him. But then why should it, he asked himself? Why should it?